MACBETH THE KING

'MacBeth the King!' they shouted. 'Hail the King! Hail the King! Long live MacBeth!' and drank deep, each to empty his cup to the dregs. MacBeth alone remained seated.

When at length the hubbub subsided, he rose slowly. 'My friends, I thank you all,' he said husky-voiced. 'You do me too much honour. I accept your naming. I shall seek to be a true and good King, honest, just, a protector of the weak, and as strong as God in His wisdom allows. But—I am not the King until I am crowned at Scone. Then will be time enough to hail me. . .'

Macbeth the King

Nigel Tranter

CORONET BOOKS
Hodder and Stoughton

Copyright © 1978 by Nigel
Tranter

First published in Great Britain
1978 by Hodder and Stoughton
Limited

Coronet edition 1981
Fifth impression 1990

Printed and bound in Great Britain
for Hodder and Stoughton
Paperbacks, a division of Hodder
and Stoughton Ltd., Mill Road,
Dunton Green, Sevenoaks, Kent
TN13 2YA (Editorial Office: 47
Bedford Square, London WC1B
3DP) by Richard Clay Ltd,
Bungay, Suffolk.

British Library C.I.P.

Tranter, Nigel
  Macbeth the King.
  I. Title
  823'.914[F]   PR6070.R34
  ISBN 0-340-26544-2

AUTHOR'S NOTE

To WRITE ANY historical novel about actual personages, against the background of their deeds and times, with any integrity, demands not only much research but considerable deduction, assumption and sheer informed invention, since so much is never recorded. To write a novel on the life of MacBeth, set in the mists of eleventh-century Celtic Scotland, demands much more than the normal. Especially when so much has to be "unlearned" on account of Shakespeare's tremendous play, brilliant drama but a travesty of history and of MacBeth's and his wife's characters and careers. Few historical royal couples, surely, have been so grievously traduced.

Much that follows has to be personal interpretation and guesswork, for in the main only the major features and details have survived the nine centuries and the deliberate destruction of records, by the Romish churchmen, Edward the Hammer of the Scots, the Reformation upheavals, and so on. Nevertheless, enough remains to reveal a strange and exciting story of strong characters in a period of drastic change, and a notable man-and-wife partnership. Where our own chroniclers fail us, or have been silenced, those of Ireland and the makers of the Norse, Orkney and Icelandic sagas, sometimes come to the rescue.

There remain strange lacunae and questions, to which no certain answer can be given. For instance, was Thorfinn, Earl of Orkney, MacBeth's half-brother (as I have made him) or only his cousin? If Malcolm the Second had only two daughters, as is generally accepted, then these two men *must* have been half-brothers. Again, when did Gruoch, Queen of Scots, die? No amount of research has uncovered this date. Yet, despite Shakespeare's "Lady MacBeth", she was a figure of great importance and refining influence in Scotland for seventeen years.

It all makes the unravelling of the story the more intriguing, to myself at least.

N.T.
Aberlady, 1977

PRINCIPAL CHARACTERS

In Order of Appearance

MACBETH MAC FINLAY: Mormaor of Ross, son of Finlay, Mormaor of Moray.

NEIL (NATHRACH) MAC FINLAY: Illegitimate half-brother.

THORFINN SIGURDSON, EARL OF ORKNEY: Son of the Princess Donada, MacBeth's mother, by an earlier husband.

THORKELL FOSTERER: Viking foster-father of Thorfinn, and warrior.

GRUOCH NIC BODHE: Princess. Widow of Gillacomgain, Mormaor of Moray, grand-daughter of Kenneth the Third.

LULACH MAC GILLACOMGAIN: Son of above, truest heir to the Scots throne.

BETHOC NIC MALCOLM: Princess. Wife of Crinan, Mormaor of Atholl and Abbot of Dunkeld.

MALCOLM THE SECOND: High King of Scots, by-named Foiranach, or the Destroyer.

ECHMARCACH, KING OF DUBLIN AND MAN: A vassal prince of Malcolm's.

DUNCAN MAC CRINAN: Prince of Strathclyde and Cumbria. Favourite grandson of the King. Later King Duncan the First.

DUNCAN MACDUFF, MORMAOR OF FIFE: Premier Scottish noble, Chief of Clan Duff.

CORMAC, THANE OF GLAMIS: Important noble and veteran soldier.

MALDUIN, BISHOP OF ST. ANDREWS: Ard Episcop, or senior bishop of the Celtic Church. Chancellor of the realm.

KING CANUTE, or KNUT: Self-styled Emperor of the Anglo-Saxons and Scandinavians, King of England and Denmark.

MALCOLM MAC DUNCAN: Illegitimate son of the Prince of Strathclyde by the miller's daughter of Forteviot. Later Malcolm the Third (Canmore).

GUNNAR HOUND TOOTH: Viking captain.
INGEBIORG FINNSDOTTER: Wife of Earl Thorfinn.
MALMORE, ABBOT OF IONA: Co-Arb. Head of the Celtic Church.
MACDOWALL, LORD OF GALLOWAY:
CATHAIL, ABBOT OF SCONE: Keeper of the Stone of Destiny.
FARQUHAR O'BEOLAIN: Hereditary Abbot of Applecross and progenitor of Clan Ross.
LACHLAN, THANE OF BUCHAN:
MARTACUS, MORMAOR OF MAR:
HARALD CLEFT CHIN: Viking captain.
ROBARTACH, ABBOT OF IONA: Malmore's successor.
EWAN, ABBOT OF ABERNETHY: High Judex or Justiciar.
CRINAN, MORMAOR OF ATHOLL: Father of King Duncan.
PAUL THORFINNSON: Later Earl of Orkney.
EDMOND, BISHOP OF DURHAM: Saxon prelate of the Church of Rome.
SVEN ESTRIDSON, KING OF DENMARK: Canute's nephew.
ESTRID SVENSDOTTER: Mother of above and sister of Canute.
POPE LEO THE NINTH:
DONALD MAC DUNCAN: Elder legitimate son of King Duncan. Later King Donald Ban.

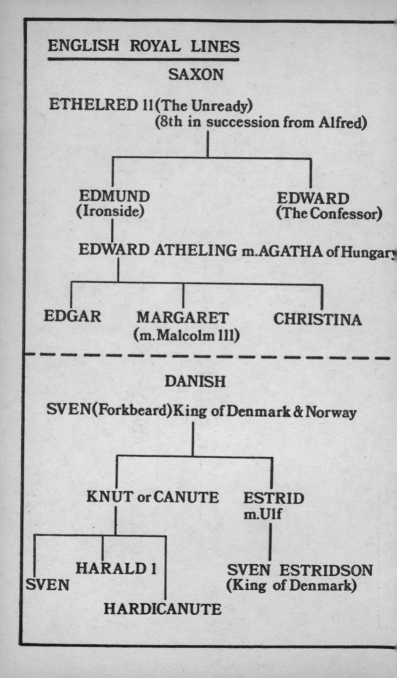

ENGLISH ROYAL LINES

SAXON

ETHELRED II (The Unready)
(8th in succession from Alfred)

EDMUND (Ironside)   EDWARD (The Confessor)

EDWARD ATHELING m. AGATHA of Hungary

EDGAR   MARGARET (m. Malcolm III)   CHRISTINA

- - - - - - - -

DANISH

SVEN (Forkbeard) King of Denmark & Norway

KNUT or CANUTE   ESTRID m. Ulf

SVEN   HARALD 1   SVEN ESTRIDSON (King of Denmark)

HARDICANUTE

SCOTS ROYAL LINE

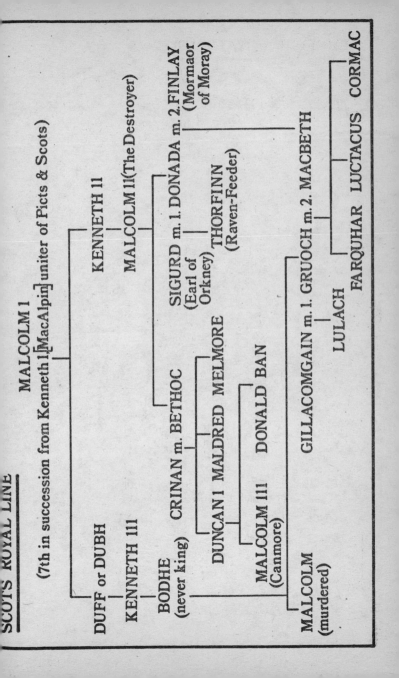

MALCOLM I

(7th in succession from Kenneth I MacAlpin uniter of Picts & Scots)

DUFF or DUBH

KENNETH III

BODHE (never king)

CRINAN m. BETHOC

DUNCAN I   MALDRED   MELMORE

DONALD BAN

MALCOLM III (Canmore)

MALCOLM (murdered)

KENNETH II

MALCOLM II (The Destroyer)

SIGURD m.1. DONADA m. 2. FINLAY
(Earl of Orkney)   (Mormaor of Moray)

THORFINN (Raven-Feeder)

GILLACOMGAIN m. 1. GRUOCH m. 2. MACBETH

LULACH

FARQUHAR   LUCTACUS   CORMAC

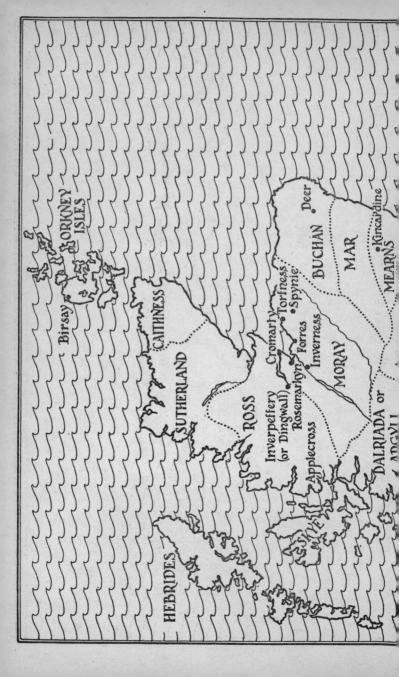

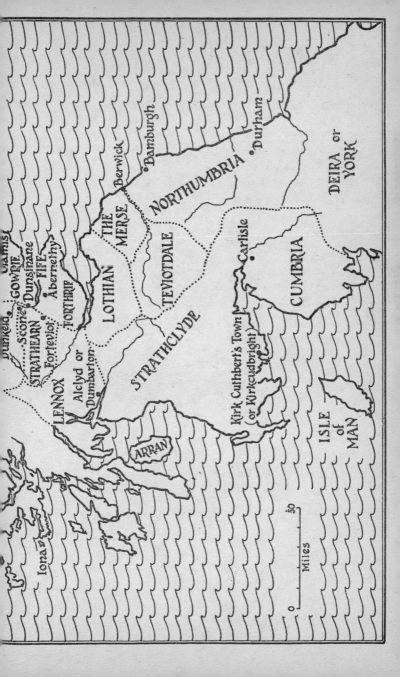

Iona

Dunkeld

Scone

GOWRIE

STRATHEARN

Forteviot

Dunsinane

FIFE

Aberrethy

FORTHRIF

LENNOX

Alclyd or
Dumbarton

ARRAN

STRATHCLYDE

THE
MERSE

Berwick

Bamburgh

LOTHIAN

TEVIOTDALE

NORTHUMBRIA

Durham

Carlisle

Kirk Cuthbert's Town
(or Kirkcudbright)

CUMBRIA

DEIRA or
YORK

ISLE
of
MAN

0   50
Miles

Part One

1

THE TALL, FAIR-HAIRED man stood on the high cliff-top amongst the wheeling gulls, grey eyes narrowed against the glitter of the sun on the wrinkled sea as he gazed south-eastwards.

"I count twenty-eight sail," he said, in the soft, lilting Gaelic, which might have seemed to come oddly from so strong-featured a young man, so deep of voice and of such strange, quiet but withheld inner force. "His full strength, I think. Which must mean . . . retiral."

"Retiral, yes. Retiral, to be sure!" his companion agreed, without agreement. "With lesser men it might be called flight. But the Raven Feeder never flees. He but retires to Cromarty to rest himself!"

"You have an over-sharp tongue, Neil Nathrach. Hold it."

"Yes, my lord Mormaor." The speaker, holding the two shaggy Highland garrons, grinned wickedly. He was an extra-ordinarily different-seeming man to be so closely related to the other, slight, dark, wiry, quick and flashing-eyed, the dark Celt indeed, as against the fair. *Nathrach* meant serpent. Yet they had had the same father.

His half-brother stared out to sea wordless, assessing, deducing. He had a great gift for silence. But at length he spoke again.

"I see no pursuit. So the King bides at Inverness. Meantime. We need not sound the call-to-arms yet, I think. How say you?"

Neil Nathrach made no answer.

"You think otherwise?"

"I am holding my tongue, MacBeth mac Finlay."

"Watch, then — or one day I shall cut it out." That was said as softly as the rest, but flatly also. And the dark man's mobile features tensed suddenly. He knew that the other was capable of doing it.

He swallowed, and found the horses in need of attention.

They stood on the summit of the South Sutor of Cromarty, the taller of the two towering rock bastions which guarded the narrow entrance to the Cromarty Firth, lofty, windswept,

15

spectacular. Southwards, across the wide Moray Firth, the great land of Moray stretched from green plain to blue mountains, a noble prospect; eastward only the Norwegian Sea. And behind them their own firth opened to what was really a vast landlocked bay, at the head of which stood Inverpeffery, that the Vikings called Dingwall, capital of the mormaorship and province of Ross, one of the seven lesser kingdoms of Alba, or Scotland.

MacBeth — more properly *Mac Beatha*, Son of Life — was calculating again. He reckoned, at the pace Thorfinn was apt to drive his longships' oarsmen, that they would make their landfall in well under the hour.

"Back to Rosemarkyn, Neil," he said. "Tell Malduin mac Nechtan to stand down his companies, meantime. And to send word to Inverpeffery. A guard of five score at the boat-strand. To greet our guests. Take both horses. I shall not need mine."

"Yes, lord."

MacBeth looked after the other as he mounted and rode off, and a faint smile played about his firm mouth.

Soon he set off downhill, long-strided, the two miles to the small haven of Cromarty, or Sikkersand as the Norse had it, in the jaws of the firth-mouth.

He had not long to wait before the first of the fleet of long-ships, the dreaded Viking host, appeared round the headland, driven fiercely by all but naked oarsmen, four to an oar, twenty-benched, the great single square sails above painted with the black raven symbol of Orkney, the high-beaked prows open-mouthed in savage menace. The first and largest vessel turned landwards, more a galley than a simple longship, with forty double-banked oars. It flew at its single, central masthead a great white banner bearing the spread-winged raven of the Earl Thorfinn Sigurdson, the Raven Feeder, of Orkney and Caithness, the most dreaded emblem but one in a score of kingdoms.

Only this one long, low vicious-looking craft turned into Cromarty's haven, where MacBeth stood alone on the strand, backed at a respectful distance by a cluster of watchful and none too happy fishermen, whose every instinct was to flee from that raven symbol, rather than trust their lord.

The galley's snarling-dragon prow had barely made contact with the shingle when an enormous man leapt down from between the ranked, colourful shields, into the shallows, and came striding ashore. The quiet waiting man was tall and well-built, but this newcomer made him seem of very modest size, the great golden helmet with the flaring black wings adding to

16

the impression. Whereas MacBeth was dressed simply in a belted tunic of saffron linen, its lower half forming a knee-length kilt above bare legs and sandals, his only sign of rank a dirk-belt of solid gold, this other was in the full panoply of war, in the Norse fashion, black leather long tunic studded with metal scales as armour, breeches bound to the knee with leather strapping, golden earl's shoulder-belt supporting a huge wide-bladed sword, bare hairy arms hung with bracelets of gold and bronze, the medals of his kind, white bearskin cloak hanging from one shoulder by a great jewelled clasp. This man, unlike most of his race, was dark-haired, black as one of his own ravens, with forked beard, down-turning moustaches and the hottest of pale-blue eyes.

"The Son of Life himself — looking still as death! As ever!" this apparition cried, in a voice to match his appearance, mighty, harsh, yet in as good Gaelic as MacBeth's own. "Smile, man — laugh, at sight of me!"

"May any man smile at sight of Thorfinn Raven Feeder?"

"Not any man, no. But *you* might, now and again. God's Body — do I not fight your battles for you?"

"Do you, then? I thought that you fought only Earl Thor-finn's."

The giant came stalking up, and clasped a great hand on each of the other's shoulders, to shake him bodily. "You got my messenger?"

"Yes. Inverness has fallen. And Gillacomgain is dead."

"Dead, to be sure. Burned alive in his own hall. With half-a-hundred of his people. Barred in. And by his own High King."

"And yours. And mine."

"Yours, perhaps — not mine. I have none such."

"You hold your earldom of Caithness of him. And Orkney of King Knut."

"I hold both by my own sword-hand! That alone. As I hold the Hebrides."

MacBeth shrugged. "So Gillacomgain is dead. I cannot weep for him. He and his brother slew my father and took Moray. But . . . burned to death! That was ill done."

"Does Malcolm Foiranach do other than ill?" Even the Earl Thorfinn's voice held a hint of something like dread at the naming of Malcolm the Second, the Destroyer, High King of Scots.

The other did not answer that. "So he has taken Inverness. Slain Gillacomgain of Moray. As he has slain all others who might heir his throne. Save three. Four, if you count a woman. So, he will come for me! And you. But your messenger said he is not marching on Ross? And he has not followed your long-ships. You did not fight with him?"

"Was I to fight Gillacomgain's battles for him also? I, Thorfinn? I held to my borg and port at Torfness. Sent out watchers to Inverness, all over Moray. When I fight Malcolm mac Kenneth it will not be in any other man's quarrel."

"Not mine, then? The mighty Thorfinn folds his hands, and watches!"

"Yours and mine, brother, could be the same, in this. Is he not grandsire to us both?"

They eyed each other for a long moment, eyes level grey and hot blue, considering, so different yet with something akin, some basic character — for these too were half-brothers, unlikely as it seemed. Malcolm the Destroyer was old now, but none the less terrible — more so indeed, since he saw his end approaching and would leave the way made straight, before he went, for the grandson Duncan mac Crinan, on whom he doted. All others of the two royal lines must die, as so many had already died, that Duncan should reign undisputed. The High King had had only two daughters — Bethoc, who produced Duncan; and Donada, who married first the Viking Earl Sigurd the Stout, of Orkney and produced Thorfinn, then on Sigurd's death wedded the Celt, Finlay mac Ruari, Mormaor of Moray, and produced MacBeth. Three grandsons of the High King — and the finger of death on two of them.

MacBeth nodded. "You have come here, for whatever reasons. And are welcome. What is your intention?"

"I shall stay with you a little time, Brother, here at Cromarty. To discourage our royal grandsire. He is the less likely to move into Ross, against you, if our united forces are here, waiting, than if I had remained on the Moray coast, at Torfness. He will learn of it quickly. He will not attack my Torfness, I think. It is too strong. We are ready for him. So, he will not long remain at Inverness. If he does not advance on you, he will retire, south-wards. An old man, his own fireside will call him. And, when he retires, through the Mounth passes by God's Blood, we shall have him! We go by sea, you and I, across to Torfness again. A forced march inland to the hills which he must cross. Surprise attack — and an end to Malcolm Foiranach! Who has lived too long already. And to Duncan his lap-dog, who is with him."

"No." That was quiet, but flat, final.

18

The earl frowned — and when he did so, he made a frightening sight. "I say yes! It is he, or us. Or *you* — for he will never take Thorfinn! This could be our great opportunity, man. As he struggles home to Fortrenn, through the passes. He would not look for it . . ."

"No. He is still High King of Scots. And I am Mormaor of Ross, and no rebel nor regicide."

"Fool! He would crack you like a louse between his fingernails, mormaor, grandson or none! If he could lay hands on you."

"He is still High King. Sits on the Stone of Destiny. And I am one of his lesser kings, as are you, for Caithness. We have sworn a great oath, brother. On that Stone. To cherish and support him. He may betray *his* oath. But I shall not. Not before I take it back, before a Council of the Kings, at the same Stone."

Exasperatedly the big man glared at him. "You were ever an obstinate dolt!" he declared. "Why I waste my time and patience on you . . .?"

"Because you need me, hot-head! As, God knows, I need you, yes. But not to slay our mother's father . . ."

Impatiently the other turned to look back at his ships, marshalled, sails down, oars holding gently against the tide-run, waiting there in the narrow mouth of the firth, the most feared and effective naval force in all the northern seas.

"You do not deserve my protection!" he all but snarled.

"Perhaps not. Will you sail away again, then? Back to Torfness, in Moray? Up to Caithness? To Orkney? Or the Hebrides? Or even to Ireland itself? The seas are wide — and none may stop Thorfinn Raven Feeder."

"Fiend seize you . . .!"

"To be sure. But you came here for more than my protection, I think? Glad as I am to have it. How many men have you there? Which host you wish hidden in my firth of Cromarty."

"Twelve hundred. Thirteen hundred. Heroes all."

"No doubt. But too many for Rosemarkyn. I am presently at my summer hall there. Your hundreds must needs go up the firth to Inverpeffery. But, lacking your presence, can I let your sea-wolves loose on my town? Or must we leave Rosemarkyn and accompany them? To protect my people."

"Devil roast you — you have an ill tongue in your head, Scot, Cruithne, Pict! Any other speaking so would never speak again!"

"I take advantage of your fond brotherly love, yes! But see you, I have my poor helpless folk to consider. Like lambs before your . . . protectors!"

"Thorkell Fosterer will go with them. To Dingwall. Or whatever you call it now."

"Very well. Let us be on our way."

"Praise be! I feared that we would take root here!"

The half-brothers turned and strode down to the tide-line. The dragon-ship was now closer inshore, indeed with its ferocious prow driven up actually on the shingle — the longships were built for this — and a gangplank reached down steeply to the beach. Thorfinn ran straight up, without pause, extraordinarily light on his feet for one so large; he was still a youngish man, of course, only in his thirtieth year, three years older than MacBeth, who climbed up less dramatically but ignored the other's mocking hand held out to aid him on to the high prow platform.

Amongst the fierce, shaggy Norse throng who awaited them thereon, all bulls'-horned helmets, hide jerkins, steel plating, silver jewellery and bracelets, one squat, immensely broad man, with the longest arms and ugliest face in Christendom, stepped forward, grinning hugely.

"Greetings, lord," he said. "You grow more like a man each time I set eyes on you!"

"And you like an ape, Thorkell!" But MacBeth grasped the other's hand nevertheless. Thorkell Fosterer, Amundi's son, was Thorfinn's foster-father and chief lieutenant, no blood relation but one of the greatest fighters and most successful ladies' men in all the North.

The earl eyed them both. "Which the greater fool I know not!" he barked. "My lord mormaor or this swineherd's get from behind an Orkney peat-stack!"

There was a roar of laughter from the other Vikings.

"The Raven Feeder is always right," Thorkell observed. "His size ensures it. But whose is the greater folly — the fool's or he who relies on him?"

Thorfinn grasped MacBeth's arm, and started to push through the throng. "Come and see another sort of fool." He turned his head. "And you, Ape — get yourself to another ship, with most of these house-carls I must use for fighting-men. Take them, and the rest, to Dingwall. I go to Rosemarkyn with this sober brother of mine, for a little. He fears for his innocents at Dingwall. So, I charge you — do not burn all down. And rape only the women.

20

Who will esteem you, I swear, for the attentions of real men! Come, Son of Life."

He led the way down from the fighting-platform and along the boarded walk-way between the tiered rowing-benches, where the brawny oarsmen, many stark naked, sprawled at ease after their exertions, amidst a powerful smell of sweat and rampant masculinity. Their quips and ruderies, as the earl and mormaor passed, were lusty and uninhibited — for the Norsemen were not great respecters of persons — Thorfinn at least giving back as good as he got. Then, at the decked-in cavity beneath the high stern-platform, the big man paused, stooped to peer in, and shouted, "Come out, woman. We have company."

A faint stirring, after a moment, in the dark, cavernlike interior, and two persons came slowly to the entrance, a young woman holding by the hand a curly-haired child of perhaps two years. The little boy looked frightened and hid behind his mother's skirts. But the woman certainly revealed no signs of fear, concern, or even interest. Holding her head high and proudly, she ignored Earl Thorfinn, glanced briefly at MacBeth and then looked away along the lines of leering, unclothed rowers, calm, expressionless. But she held the child close to her side.

MacBeth drew a long quivering breath. She was the most beautiful creature he had ever set eyes on, dark of hair and eyes, of lovely chiselled features, alabaster skin and with a superb figure. Tall, holding herself like any queen, she was clad richly, but her clothing torn and peat-stained.

"The Lady Gruoch — it can be none other!" he exclaimed. "Princess, I, I greet you. I . . . am sorry."

She inclined her dark head, unspeaking.

"What does she here, on your ship?" he demanded of his brother.

"Ask *her*. She asked to be brought to you. The saints know why! She escaped Malcolm's grasp, with Gillacomgain's brat — how I have not learned. Some of my people found her, and brought her to me at Torfness borg. I offered her comfort, refuge, even my bed! Oh, yes — it may be almost time for me to think of taking a wife, even, and raise sons! But she would have none of me. A fool-woman! I do not wonder that she refused Duncan the Palsied, who seems to have sought her. But Thorfinn is another story!" The giant shrugged. "But, no — she must be brought to MacBeth mac Finlay. God knows why women so lack judgment!"

21

That man raised an open hand to the woman. "I am honoured," he said. "We met but once, lady. When we were both but children. You may not recollect. But I have heard much of you. And, I swear, you are more beautiful even than they told me!"

Gillacomgain's widow eyed him levelly. "I remember you. And have heard you reputed as honest," she told him quietly, in a voice softly Highland as his own, melodious after the harsh and jerky Norse enunciation. "I had to go to someone. For the child's sake."

"Yes. Welcome, then, to Ross, Princess. You will be safe with me."

Thorfinn snorted.

"Yet . . . my husband slew your father. And took Moray, which should have been yours. And this is his son." That was said in the same even, almost impersonal tone.

"Even so. We are cousins of a sort. And that was a dozen years back. *You* were not concerned."

"I am, was, Gillacomgain's wife."

"Yes. But . . ."

"More important, she is Bodhe's daughter, King Kenneth, of blessed memory, his grand-daughter," Thorfinn interrupted cynically. "Sole heir of that royal line, since Malcolm Foiranach murdered her brother. Let none forget it. Malcolm and Duncan do not, it is clear. That is why Gillacomgain was burned in Inverness. And, hopefully, this woman and child with him! We shall not hide what that means by polite words and small talk."

There was silence at that, for a little. It was stark truth which had to be faced. Gillacomgain, Mormaor of Moray, had died, not because of his many sins but because he was married to this Gruoch nic Bodhe mac Kenneth, with better claim to the high throne of Scotland than had Malcolm himself, or any of his grandsons. She had escaped him, but nothing was surer than that he would try again. For this child at her knee should be King of Scots, whether she ever was queen or no. And if MacBeth, of Malcolm's own line, was endangered before in the road of Duncan's succession, he would be infinitely the more so if he sheltered the Princess Gruoch.

This knowledge in all their minds, they looked away. The fleet was on the move again, this dragon-ship also, heading westwards now into the calm waters of the great landlocked basin of the firth.

MacBeth sank down on one bare knee before the shrinking

child, holding out a hand. "This small one is a fine fellow. He will be a stout support for his lady-mother one day. How is he called?"

"Lulach."

"Lulach mac Gillacomgain mac Maelbride mac Ruari! As I am MacBeth mac Finlay mac Ruari. So we are kin, you and I, young one. I greet you!"

"Where are you taking us?" the mother asked. "To Inverpeffery?"

"No. To Udale Bay only. Then we ride over the ridge of this Black Isle to my summer house of Rosemarkyn. There is no safe anchorage for ships there, on that southern coast. All save this craft will go on to Inverpeffery."

"And . . . the King?"

"We keep close watch. All along my Ross border. Never fear — we shall not let him lay hands on you."

"Is he not the kind one!" Thorfinn mocked. "The gentle MacBeth. Watch him, woman!"

It was only a few miles to Udale, a sheltered bay on the south shore of the firth, where the dragon-ship disembarked its important passengers. Save for one other vessel, the main fleet rowed on for a further ten miles, to where Strathpeffer opened off the firth to probe into the hills, and the province of Ross had its seat. At the township of Balblair, above the Udale anchorage, MacBeth borrowed sturdy Highland garrons to carry his party across the high spine of the great peninsula of Cromarty, known as the Black Isle, seven miles to Rosemarkyn.

*   *   *

The hall-house of the mormaor at Rosemarkyn stood on a terrace above the shore, at the foot of a steep lofty bank, part cliff, part sand hill, pockmarked with holes in which darting martins had their nests and over which jackdaws swooped and squawked. It was a long, low building of timber covered with clay, inside and out, to seal the draughts and prevent the danger of fire, reed-thatched, two storeys in height save in the centre where the great hall itself rose right to the smoke-blackened roof-trees. The wings flanking the hall contained many chambers, a small private hall, armoury, sleeping accommodation and storerooms. The kitchens, bakehouse, brewhouse and servants' quarters, with the stables and byres, lay across a cobbled yard at the back, dug into the side of the bank, a deep draw-well in the yard's centre. Orchards lay right and left. The house was commodious, unassuming but pleasant. It was no dun, no rath, or fortified dwelling, and Thorfinn jeered at it as totally undefendable. But MacBeth pointed out mildly that he looked to his people for defence, not to walls, ramparts and palisades. Certainly, all around were the cothouses and cabins of his clansfolk; if they could not protect him, walls would avail little. Besides, it was only a summer residence, for the sea breezes, the boating and fishing, the swimming and hawking. Although it looked directly across the Moray Firth, near where it narrowed at Chanonry Ness, to the Inverness plain, Strathnairn and the Laigh, as no other of his houses did — which was why he was here now — it was no place for warfare. The churchmen, who knew a pleasant spot when they saw one, had been long established here, the old Irish saints under Moluag making this their base in Ross nearly five centuries before. Indeed, the name meant the Monastery of Ross.

The good bishop thereof sat, well-placed, at MacBeth's table now, comfortably liquored, amiable.

Unlike the new southern and English fashion of dais-table on a platform at the head of the hall, with the other tables running at right angles to it below, MacBeth maintained the old Highland custom of all eating at the same lengthy board, with himself, his kin and guests, in the centre and facing each other. They all sat relaxed now, the woman having retired early, to be with her fretful child.

Thorfinn, sprawling on MacBeth's right, the bishop on his left, yawned cavernously. "You must show some sign of life in the matter, Son of Life," he declared, slurring a little. "Hopeful inactivity . . ." He had some difficulty with that phrase. "Hopeful inactivity will avail nothing. You have her in your house. All Scotland will know it by tomorrow. Malcolm the Destroyer will know it before he sleeps tonight."

"What of it? And *you* brought her to me."

"Only because she asked it."

"I shall do as I told her. Give her refuge, for so long as she requires it. I can do no less."

"You can do a deal more. And will be expected to do so. By herself, who knows? She is a notable card in your hand. To play."

"And If I do not seek to play the cards? Leaving that to you!"

"You *must*, man. You cannot help yourself. That Gruoch and her son are the keys to Scotland. Hands will be outstretched to

24

grasp them. Not only Malcolm's and Duncan's. So long as you hold them, you must fight for them." He drank deeply. "Either that or cast them from you."

"Where should I cast them?"

"*I* will take them again, if you wish. I am a Mormaor of Scotland and a grandson of the King, God damn him, equally with you! I could play this card, likewise."

"She rejected your offer."

"Women have been known to change their minds. Or have them changed for them!"

There was a pause.

"More important than the Lady Gruoch, there is Moray." That was Neil Nathrach from across the table. "Has it escaped your lordly notices that there is now no Mormaor of Moray?" As a son, albeit illegitimate, of the former Mormaor Finlay, he was entitled to make the point.

"Until Malcolm Foiranach appoints one, Serpent!" the earl said.

"Aye. But Moray, lord, will not just tamely accept any camp-follower of the King. As a Morayman, I know. We are not the easiest folk to manage. And it is the greatest mormaordom in Alba."

"So?"

"The High King will not find it easy to find a man. Too many who might have suited he has already slain. And until he does, Moray is wide open to MacBeth mac Finlay!"

"You have the glimmerings of sense, now and again, in that black snake's head of yours, Bastard! Is it not what I am saying? In part."

"Wed the Lady Gruoch, claim Moray in her name, her son's and our father's — and march in. And perchance this Viking might support you — at a price!" Neil Nathrach was no kin to Thorfinn.

"Careful, Ill-Begotten!" the big man rumbled.

MacBeth eyed the amber contents of his goblet. "You are generous with your advice, both of you," he observed. "So concerned for my future. And hers."

"You need the advising. Sitting there when you should be up and doing."

"Doing what, Orkneyman? Where?"

"Go you up to her, man. Take her. Here and now. She will scarce be surprised, since she has thrown herself upon you. Take her. Wed her after, if you so wish. But show her, and all men,

25

who holds Gruoch nic Bodhe now. And the brat. That is what matters. And there is more than Moray at stake."

"God be good — she was but widowed yesterday! Do you take me for a brute-beast?"

"Better now than later. I say that she must expect it. Had she not asked for you, *I* would have had her, myself. Every day will make it more difficult for one so lily-livered as the Mormaor of Ross! Women need firm handling, like horses or hounds. They take advantage, else."

"Hear Thorfinn Raven Feeder, the great woman-handler! Save us — she is a princess of the line of Alpin! And the finest woman in Scotland!"

"The more reason . . ."

"No. She sought my protection, not my arms and loins! She shall have it, while she needs it. Say what men will. You hear, Malduin?" He turned to his seneschal, sitting next to Neil. "The Lady Gruoch will receive every courtesy of my house. And the child. At all times. Until I tell you otherwise. Neil, you will behave towards her better than your usual! Keep your tongue between your teeth! You hear me? Now — enough of this. Have the fiddlers to play, Malduin . . ."

*   *   *

For the present, the threat to the North was past. King Malcolm's army started out on its long march south. Crinan of the Hounds, Mormaor of Atholl, Hereditary Abbot of Dunkeld and Primate of All Scotland in the Celtic Church, Malcolm's son-in-law and father of Duncan, was left in charge of Moray, and was unlikely to seek any major trial of strength with MacBeth and Thorfinn.

There were still two months of the hosting season, and the Vikings' feet, or rather their sword-hands, were itching for more exciting and profitable voyaging. Thorfinn was for off, north-abouts. He would leave a stand-by force at Duncansby, his Caithness base, which could be with his half-brother in a day, at need. The longships sailed from Inverpeffery, much to the relief of the inhabitants, dropped MacBeth and Neil Nathrach at Udale, and headed for the open sea, a headache for others.

At Rosemarkyn, the Lady Gruoch had spent most of the warm summer days out of the hall-house, up in the deep wooded ravine behind, where the Rosemarkyn Burn came rushing, in a series of cascades and shady pools, from the upland. MacBeth went seeking her, presently, alone.

He found her in a green glade beneath the soaring crags and scaurs, sitting with her feet dabbling in the swirling frothy pool of a waterfall, her skirt kilted above her knees, while her son splashed naked as a trout in the shallows. Because of the noise of the fall she did not hear him coming, and he stood for a few moments watching as fair and peaceful a scene as could delight the eye of any man. She was quite breathtakingly lovely.

Not wishing to alarm her, he waited until the child Lulach looked up, when he waved a hand reassuringly. Eyes suddenly wide, the boy ran to his mother, stumbling on the stones. She looked round.

"It is only myself, MacBeth," he called. "Come to pay my respects, Princess."

She did not take fright, hastily draw down her skirts or otherwise rearrange herself — that was not the style of this woman. She considered him almost thoughtfully, unsmiling.

"Why do you call me princess?" she asked. "It is long since anyone did that."

"Because you *are* a princess and you *look* a princess," he answered, moving to her side. "Lulach — is he well? More content?"

"He is better, yes. More himself. I thank you."

"It must have been a grievous thing, for a child. Did he . . . did he see anything?"

"He saw more than sufficient, yes. Fire. Blood. Dying. Enough to remember."

"I am sorry. Sorry indeed. And for yourself, lady. It was an evil deed. And you . . . bereft."

"Bereft? Scarce that. But it was evilly done, yes. No man should be locked into his own house and burned alive. Even Gillacomgain!"

He was silent at that. Stooping, he picked up a pebble to toss into the peat-dark pool.

"You think me hard to speak so?" she asked, but quietly still, in the same almost meditative voice. "Perhaps I am. But I cannot mourn my husband. I never loved him. I never knew him, save as master. Nor he me, save after the flesh. I did not choose him. He *bought* me, six years ago. When I was fifteen years and he fifty-two."

"I am sorry," he said again, spreading his hands helplessly.

"You have no need to be. Such is frequently the lot of women. In especial, princesses! I tell you, only that you do not expect me to act the widow too sorely. I have lost something, yes —

27

houses, servants, position, all worldly goods. But I am scarcely
... bereft. I have my child — even if he is his father's also. Do
you think me so strange?"

"I think you a woman of great spirit. Brave. To be so young."

"Young? I was never young, I think. I have lived all my life
with the shadow over me. The shadow of Malcolm the High
King. That one day he would come for me. Either to spill my
blood, or to marry me to Duncan mac Crinan. After he had
murdered my grandfather the King, my uncles and my brother.
It had to come."

He nodded. "A great man, a warrior, a great King, gone
wrong. Strength turned sour, to evil. He would have Duncan
wade through blood to his throne. But — he is gone now. Gone
south again with his host. You are safe, meantime."

"But only meantime," she said. "So long as he lives, and
Duncan lives, I shall never be safe. Unless to wed Duncan —
and I would sooner die."

"Fear nothing — I shall protect you," he promised.

She turned to look at him, directly. "Why?"

He cleared his throat. "It is ... what I must do. What any
honest man must do."

"And you are honest?"

"You said so, your own self. The day you came to me. You
said that you had heard me to be honest. So you came."

"Honest as to the generality, yes. But this matter is scarcely
that, is it? To challenge the King. To put yourself and your
people at risk. By protecting, holding, one whom the Destroyer
wants. To do so much, even a passing honest man must have a
reason. Moray? Or ... more than Moray?"

Frowning, he took a turn away along the bank, and back.
"You speak ... most directly, Princess. To answer you in like
fashion is not easy. Moray, yes, one day, perhaps. The other —
who knows?"

"And I am a stepping-stone to both."

"To be sure. But — I am not seeking to protect you for that.
Or ..."

"*Or*, MacBeth mac Finlay? Let us hear how honest you are,
in truth!"

"Or, not *only* that, I thought to say."

"Yes. So there we have it. You wish to be Mormaor of
Moray, as well as of Ross. As indeed could be no less than your
right, as your father's son. And one day you might even be
King of Scots. I prefer when men are honest. So Gruoch nic

28

Bodhe, despite her dangers, has her uses. Weighed well, considered, she is worth the hazard?"

"Have it so if you must," he told her flatly. "But I say to you, that is not all of it. I would aid you without all that. I could do no less. We are kin, distant but of the same blood of Alpin. I am more Cruithne, Pictish, you more Scot. But we are sib. And you are a woman, alone. In need of help. And very beautiful."

"And if I had been ill-favoured? It would have been different?"

He brushed that aside with an impatient gesture of his hand —he who was a determinedly patient man.

"No — let us remain honest, my lord mormaor," she went on. "Better that way. If I had been ill-favoured, you would not be considering wedding me?"

His quick-drawn breath betrayed him. He looked away, and it was moments before he found words. "I did not say that," he got out.

"No — for that would have committed you. And you are not fully decided, I think. You hesitate — as well you might. Yet you fear that if you do not, another might. And gain what you seek."

He shook his head, unspeaking.

She gave a small and humourless laugh. "But do not so fear, my friend. The grievous choice need not be made. For I do not intend to marry again. You, or any man. I have had a sufficiency of marriage. So spare yourself the agonising, my lord mormaor."

MacBeth swallowed audibly. "This is . . . foolish talk," he said.

"Perhaps. But at least you know where you stand, where all men stand. Not wed to Gruoch nic Bodhe!"

"But — what then is to become of you? A woman alone. Young as you are."

"I have Lulach. I shall seek some quiet far place. Where none shall know me or mine. Live there, a simple woman with a child. Until Gruoch, grand-daughter of King Kenneth is forgotten. Aye, and after that."

He shook his head again. "I understand your feelings. You have been sore hurt. But — it is not possible. Not for *you*. You are a princess, one near to the throne. The most near, many would say. Your son the true heir. Think you that you can hide yourself away, like some cottar-woman, and not be sought? Many would come looking for you. Yourself, you say that other men will seek to wed you. For who you are and what you can give. You must needs have a protector, *some* protector. It is not possible, I say."

"You are telling me that there is no place in all the wide North, in your own Ross even, where I could dwell hidden, secure? Some lonely glen, some far shieling, an island even, Mormaor of Ross?"

"Would you turn eremite? Recluse? *You!* Live in a cave or a cabin?"

"If need be, yes. Rather than, than . . ."

"Than marriage to such as myself!"

"Yes."

"You mislike men, Princess?"

"Have I cause to like them?"

"Perhaps not. But all men are not brutes, monsters."

"No doubt. But how, and when, does a woman find that out? Before marriage, or after?" She turned directly to him. "See you, my friend — if so you would indeed be — I will make a compact with you. I have naught against you — indeed, did I not come to you of my own will? Find me some place, quiet, secure, within your protection — and I will yield you all my rights to Moray. I cannot *give* you it, for it is not mine to give. You must needs take it for yourself, if you want it. As others have done in the past. But I can give you my support. And yield you Lulach's claim to it, in his father's name."

"You would do that? So much?"

"Yes. For peace, safety, quiet. Besides, I would rather you held Moray than others I could name."

"And the child? What of his future?"

"I would expect him to be . . . considered. His rights. One day. God knows what will be best for him — *I* do not. He has a right to the throne. Better perhaps that he had not — or never knew of it. An accursed heritage. But — that is for the future. A future which may never dawn. Meantime he and I require sanctuary. Will you find it for us, MacBeth mac Finlay? In exchange for Moray?"

"I will find you sanctuary, yes," he promised. "As for Moray, we shall see."

Presently he left them there, and returned to his house.

2

THE SANCTUARY MACBETH provided for the Lady Gruoch and her son, for the next few months, was in fact the hall-house of Rosemarkyn itself. It is to be feared that he did not very seriously search for some hidden and remote refuge such as she had suggested. He himself returned to his principal dun and headquarters at Inverpeffery, partly for her reputation's sake and partly the better to deal with the situation that developed out of the changed conditions in the neighbouring Mormaordom of Moray. But he kept an eye on the young woman and her child, saw her fairly frequently, and made sure that Malduin, his seneschal, respected her needs and privacy. She asked more than once when he was going to find her a place of her own, but always he put her off.

She represented a problem, to be sure, and a major unsettlement. Even if he could keep her safe, there was no means by which he could enforce secrecy or prevent talk. All Scotland knew that the Mormaor of Ross held the Lady Gruoch. And all would draw their own conclusions.

On two more occasions he suggested marriage — and with a little more enthusiasm than before, although it had not really been he who had made the suggestion previously, but she who had forestalled it. The forbidden has its own desirability, especially when physically within one's grasp; and she was a highly attractive woman in more than just her beauty of person. So that he began to have a preoccupation with her — which was notably unlike MacBeth.

She did not spurn his tentative advances unkindly. Indeed, she was quietly friendly when they met, acknowledging her indebtedness. But ever with her guard up, as it were. Perhaps her guard was permanently in position.

Less personal but as persistent a preoccupation over these months of the year of Our Lord 1032 was that of the province and mortuath of Moray. He desired it also, inevitably. Not only because it would greatly enhance his power and status, but because it was the fairest and largest province in all Alba, his family heritage and where he had been reared, his childhood's home, the rambling island palace of Spynie in the Laigh. As a youth, twelve years before when his father Finlay the Mormaor had been slain by his own cousins Malcolm mac Maelbride

31

and Gillacomgain, he had sworn that one day he would avenge his sire and regain Moray. The vengeance had been taken by others, and both the brothers were dead. But now Moray lay awaiting him.

He could have simply mustered his fighting-men and marched in — as undoubtedly Thorfinn would have done and as Neil Nathrach and many another advised. But this would mean war. And although MacBeth did not shrink from bloodshed, where necessary, he did not wish to impose the inevitable battle, sack and rapine on his beloved Moray.

He could, and did, make all arrangements for a swift assembly of his Ross forces, however, so that he could have 1200 men on the march, if need be, at two days' notice.

MacBeth was, in the event, called upon to put his assembling procedures into practice unexpectedly and at sufficiently short notice, in the Ides of April, the call coming from an unlikely source. It emanated from Scone indeed, in Fortrenn, and from Malcolm the Second, King of Scots, in the form of a royal command of the Ard Righ to one of his lesser kings of the ancient Pictish realm, to march southwards in fullest strength and with all speed, to help counter the invasion of the kingdom by Knut the Dane, King of the English, known to the Sassunach as Canute.

This summons, needless to say, put MacBeth into a major quandary. His first thought was that it was a trap to lure him into Malcolm's clutches. But, in that case, would the Destroyer have invented so tremendous a threat as the invasion of the mighty Canute the Great, Emperor of the Anglo-Saxons and the Scandinavians, as he called himself these days? Or urged him, MacBeth, to come with all possible strength? Surely the armed strength of Ross would be the last thing that was desired, in any such trap?

On the other hand, Canute had been long making threatenings towards Scotland. Inheriting Denmark from his father Sven Forkbeard, he had conquered all England, some of Ireland, Norway, the south of Sweden and many of the Baltic lands. He was now claiming overlordship of Cumbria and Strathclyde, Teviotdale and the Merse, and likewise Lothian, all fairly recently incorporated into Malcolm's kingdom — although Lothian had been a Pictish province for centuries. So invasion was not improbable. But this was very sudden. Not that Canute was one to send out heralds before he acted. If it was true, the threat was dire, and MacBeth's duty clear. He put the mustering system into immediate operation, and sent his fastest birlinn northwards up the coast to Duncansby in Caithness, to enquire of Thorfinn — who, hopefully, had not yet set off on his hosting.

Two days later the birlinn was back. The Earl Thorfinn had gone to Orkney, assembling longships. But his sword-father, Thorkell Fosterer, was still in Caithness, the messenger reported. And there was no question about the English invasion. The Norsemen, indeed, had known it was to take place for many days before the King's summons to the Mormaor of Caithness arrived — they had their own links with Canute the Dane, of course. To MacBeth's demand as to what Thorfinn was doing about it, his informant could only shrug. Thorkell Fosterer had been less than explicit.

At any rate, MacBeth's own course was now clear. He would march the next morning. Meanwhile, he took time to pay a fleeting visit to Rosemarkyn.

He found Gruoch and the boy at the boat-stand, preparing to go fishing for flounders in a coracle. She was sufficiently relaxed with him now to invite him to accompany them.

"I thank you, no," he answered. "I have little time. We march at dawn."

"March . . . ?" Her lovely eyes widened. "March where? And why? To Moray?"

"No. Much further. To the south. Canute the Dane invades. From England. All must rally to the defence of the land."

"Canute!"

"Yes. It is what we have long feared. All must rally. I came but to say goodbye."

She searched his face. "So it is goodbye? So soon. This, this could be no light matter. Canute is powerful, fierce, with great armies."

"That is truth. But Malcolm, whatever else he is, is also powerful and fierce. As able a general."

"It may be so. But against the might of the English, Northumbria and the Danelaw, possibly even the Norsemen . . ." He could see the thought strike her, then. "MacBeth — what of Thorfinn?"

"I do not know," he said, at his flattest.

"He may side with Canute. They are of a kind. Almost kin, Vikings both."

He shrugged. "None ever knows what Thorfinn will do, save Thorfinn! All I know is that he is in Orkney, gathering longships. And has also received Malcolm's summons. For Caithness and Sutherland. But . . . he knew of the invasion earlier."

"So!" She shook her head. "You could be in great danger, I think — whatever Thorfinn does. Must you go? Could you not send another? Even in this peril, I do not trust Malcolm Foiranach. Nor Duncan. Send one of your thanes, with your force."

"*I* am Mormaor of Ross," he pointed out, simply.

"You may never come back to Ross!"

"You are too fearful, Daughter of Warriors!"

"I am fearful *because* I am a daughter of warriors — too many of whom have not returned to their places. I fear, yes — I fear evil for you in this."

He smiled a little. "You are not as was my mother, Donada nic Malcolm, burdened with the sight?"

She waved that aside. "Of such I know naught. But I see grievous danger in this. Evil for you."

"Take comfort from my mother's seeing, then. She dreamed that I would not fall by the hand of man until a forest itself rose up and walked! Birnam Wood, in Atholl. Until Birnam Wood marched to Dunsinane in Gowrie. So, perhaps I am safe enough!"

"Do not mock," she said. "You will take care?"

"I take too much care, Thorfinn says."

"I care not what Thorfinn says. It is you that matters, not that loud-of-mouth."

"I esteem your concern for me, Princess. Although I fear that it is concern for your future care and the safety of Lulach, which moves you."

"Think that if you wish, MacBeth."

"I have left orders, not only with my seneschal here but with the Thane of Affric, whom I leave behind, that you are to be cherished and given what you ask. If so be it that I do not come back, you will be safe. A secure house found for you. So fear nothing."

"My fears are . . . otherwise, I tell you. But, I thank you."

He eyed her levelly for moments on end, there beside the bobbing coracle. Then he nodded abruptly. "I go now. There is much to be done. God be with you."

"God speed," she said quietly. And added, "My friend."

*   *   *

They marched southwards, 1200 armed men on the shaggy garrons of the Highland hills, under the great red-and-white banner of Ross, crossing the Glass River at Kilmorack and into Moray. At Inverness the folk hid, and peeped and watched from doorways and corners, for fear that this might be the men of Ross coming against them now that their own men were away — for the Moray contingents under Crinan had marched off three days before. But MacBeth pressed on, at the heavy lumbering garrons' trot — which, although it appeared slow, was remarkably deceptive and could cover sixty miles in a day. They climbed the long ascent of Drummossie Moor to the Passes of Moy and the Slochd and into Strathspey. Then on through Badenoch and over the great and grim Pass of Drumochdar, out of Moray and into Atholl. At Dunkeld they were at Crinan's chief seat — for as well as being Mormaor of Atholl he was hereditary Abbot of Dunkeld which, in the Celtic Church, carried with it the Primacy of All Scotland. He was absent, of course, being on ahead with his own levies; but his wife the Lady Bethoc nic Malcolm was in residence in the large rath above the Tay, and MacBeth felt bound to call upon his aunt. She was a tall, angular, stern woman, unbending, very different from her late sister, the gentle and other-worldly Donada, and she greeted her nephew without enthusiasm. The call was brief. But she was able to tell him that the King, her father, had moved on with his army from Scone, his capital, to Stirling, to halt Canute at the crossing of Forth. Which meant that he had meantime abandoned not only Teviotdale and the Merse to the invader, but Lothian also, even part of Lennox.

It took the Rossmen another day and a half, through Fortrenn, Gowrie, Strathearn and Monteith, to reach Stirling, where the Forth narrowed sufficiently to be bridged. Or not exactly Stirling but the Haugh of Kildean and the causeway-head across the marshes, on the north side of the river, where the royal army waited. It was a bare mile but a barely passable mile, from the towering mighty rock on the other side of the flood-plain, crowned by the ancient Pictish fort of the Snow Dun, with its township of Stirling clustering round its flanks.

The Forth and Teith Rivers, the dividing line between the Northern and Southern Picts, between Alba and Lothian, between Highlands and Lowlands, made the greatest flood-plain in Scotland, possibly in all the Isles of Britain, their mean-derings forming a watery, swampy barrier five miles wide by over twenty miles long, a wilderness of mosses and meres, of lochans and bogs and scrub forest, all the way from the fierce mountains of the Lennox and Loch Lomondside to the Scottish

Sea, impassable for man and beast save by one or two secret, tortuous routes known only to a few. Except here at Stirling, just before the combined rivers opened out to the estuary and salt water. Here the bog was but a mile wide, protruding rocky hills narrowing it, the soft ground being on the north side only. The Romans, it was said, had bridged the river at Kildean and built the mile-long narrow causeway of timber and stone across the moss beyond, to firm ground, for their legions to cross, in their fruitless attempts to dominate the Caledonians, as they called the Northern Picts. That it had been a sorry business was evidenced by their name for the Snow Dun hill, *Mons Dolorum*. Eastwards from it was the widening estuary, westwards stretched the endless swamp. Here, then, Malcolm the Destroyer awaited Canute Svenson the Mighty, in the most strategically significant location in the land. The attacker could only do so by first crossing that bridge and causeway.

The Scots army had encamped in a vast crescent on the slightly higher ground above the marsh at the causeway-head, lapping up the skirts of the long rocky whaleback, sentinel on the north side, known as Craig Kenneth — for the great King Kenneth MacAlpin had likewise fought a battle here a century and a half before. On the crest of this, the King and his commanders had formed their present headquarters, with a farflung prospect all around save to the north, where the green Ochil Hills rose steeply. Only, today, the view southwards was less fair and distant than usual, obscured by great drifting palls of smoke.

MacBeth, used to assessing numbers, reckoned that there might be some 8000 to 9000 men gathered there, a great host, but none too many if Canute brought anything like his full strength against them. He saw the banners of Fife, Strathearn, Lennox, Angus, Mar, Atholl and Moray amongst them.

With some difficulty finding sufficient space for his men to encamp, MacBeth left them under Neil Nathrach, and with his thanes and lieutenants threaded his way through the lines and the evening cooking-fires and rode up the steep of Craig Kenneth by a twisting path. The higher they climbed, the more obvious was that great pall of smoke to the south.

There was a clump of trees on the grassy summit ridge, and there the High King's Boar banner flew in the westerly breeze. A rough table had been contrived, and round this sat a group of men, about a dozen, while others stood around respectfully. All watched the newcomers' approach, and as they came up, all the sitters save two rose to their feet. Remaining sitting were an old man at one end and a young at the other.

MacBeth and his party dismounted and strode forward to the table. He bowed to his grandfather.

"Sire!" he said. And to the others, "My lords." That was all.

The King was old, but only in years and wickedness. His person could have been that of a man thirty years his junior, upright, heavily-built and broad-shouldered, but without fat or flabbiness. His hair and beard were grey, but not sparse, his features handsome if long, his carriage carelessly proud. But it was his eyes that took and held the attention, hooded eyes but lively, strange, glittering, the most alive eyes MacBeth for one had ever seen in a man, with a life almost of their own. He was dressed unexceptionally, for war, in leather and scaled mail, with saffron kilt and shoulder-plaid, much less richly than many of his mormaors and thanes — but in that man's presence none would ever consider clothing of any importance. His great crested and crowned helmet was laid aside, but he wore a simple narrow circlet of gold around brows and hair.

He held out an imperious hand. "MacBeth mac Finlay — greeting!" he said. "Last come — save one! But none the less welcome for that, grandson." He had a deep, vibrant voice with just the hint of a lisp.

MacBeth dropped on one knee to take and kiss that firm, freckled, outstretched hand — and shut his eyes lest he would see scarlet blood on it as he did so.

"I came so soon as I might, lord King. This is a far cry from Ross. I have brought twelve hundred. Another five hundred from my westlands follow, under the Thane of Gairloch."

The King nodded. "Yes. You all I welcome, my friends. In this pass." He paused, as though perhaps the welcome might have been otherwise in different circumstances. "But where, grandson, is that other awkward brother of yours?"

"Neil, sire, is down at the camp, seeing to my people."

"I do not mean that viperish one, man! I mean the ravenous — Thorfinn, my Mormaor of Caithness."

"As to that I know not. I am not *that* brother's keeper! I have not seen him since the Feast of the Assumption. When *you* may remember that he came visiting me. And Moray. And you did not!"

The monarch's glittering eye glared balefully at this grandson for a moment. Then he turned towards the others at the table, and waved a hand. "You will know all here?"

MacBeth inclined his head. His glance ran over the Mormaors of Lennox, Strathearn, Fife, Angus, Mar and Atholl, and the Thanes of Glamis, Monteith, Gowrie and Breadalbane. And Duncan mac Crinan, now being styled Prince of Strathclyde.

"I know most, yes, and greet all. Although I do not know the priest. And this lord." he gestured towards a swarthy individual, richly clad.

"That is Echmarcach mac Ranald mac Firbis, King of Dublin. Claimant of my sub-kingdom of Man. If your Norse friends can be dispossessed! And the good Malduin is the new Bishop of St. Andrews. In whose gentle hands are all our souls!"

MacBeth was sorry for the new bishop, true primate of the Church, although the title of Primate of All Scotland still went with the hereditary Abbacy of Dunkeld. His predecessor, Alwin, lately dead, had had a sore road to travel with Malcolm Foiranach. He looked a mild and studious man, his Celtic tonsure, of the front part of his head only, adding to an already high and scholarly brow. The other, the swarthy Irish kinglet, was presumably a distant kinsman of Malcolm's — and therefore of his own — the King's mother having been a princess of Leinster. This Echmarcach was one of Thorfinn's most constant targets — as were most others whose lands fronted the Irish Sea. MacBeth bowed to them both, and then turned back to the King.

"What of Canute?" he asked.

"Aye, Canute." The royal voice went thinly rasping, like the scrape of steel. "The bold Dane! He . . . lingers, boy. He burns and slays his way through my Lothian, but does not hasten. His van is already at Stirling, facing us. But Canute delays. And slays."

"His numbers?"

"Some say two-score thousand, some more. English, Danes, Norwegians, Northumbrians. A mighty host."

"So many. So you wait? While Lothian burns. And, no doubt, the Merse and Teviotdale also."

"Could you do better, stripling? With a foe four times as many, and more. Led by one of the greatest conquerors in Christendom."

"Hear MacBeth, the Scourge of the North!" Duncan mac Crinan mocked, from the other end of the table. He was a pale, thin, reedy young man of twenty-seven years, the same age as MacBeth, good-looking but not in a strong way, hair so fair as to be almost white, but his skin of an unhealthy-seeming pallor. Indeed his by-name was Duncan Ilgalrach, the Bad-Blooded.

MacBeth ignored his cousin. "Perhaps not. But I might seek to bring Canute here the sooner. Coax him, that the land might be spared his burning and slaying. Make as though to move to meet him. Attack his van across the river. Not with your full force. How far off is he?"

"We heard last that he was at the Avon. Linlithgow," Lennox said, whose territory was nearest and who was providing the informants and scouts. "By now he could be at Ecclesbreac, or Falkirk as the Saxons name it." He pointed. "The smokes are sufficiently near for that."

"It is not too late . . ."

"No!" the King said. "Think you I have not considered this? We might not win back to this strong position. Be trapped beyond the bridge and causeway. It is not worth the hazard." That sounded sufficiently final.

"So you but wait?"

"We wait, yes. Let the Dane take the hazards. He can achieve nothing against us without crossing that bridge and causeway. When he does so, let him beware! You will perhaps learn, young man, to enlist the *land* to fight for you, when you lack men. If you live so long!"

"I but thought to bring some aid to your subjects of Lothian, Sire."

"If that other rebellious grandson of mine, Thorfinn Sigurdson, would but come, as commanded, and bring his longships into the Scottish Sea, I could make a sea-borne descent on the Lothian coast, behind Canute. And both give him pause and bring relief to the people. That is what I have been waiting for."

"Thorfinn is a treacherous Viking barbarian!" Duncan declared. "I said that we could rely on him only to fail us!"

"Thorfinn is his own man. And a better man than you, Duncan Ilgalrach!" MacBeth told him.

"Quiet, dolts!" the King snapped. "Thorfinn Sigurdson is *my* man, for Caithness and Sutherland. And he had best remember it. I gave him that mortuath, as a bairn. I could take it back."

It was on the tip of MacBeth's tongue to question any man's ability to do that; but he thought better of it and changed the subject somewhat.

"For a landing on the Lothian shore, could not MacDuff supply sufficient vessels?" he asked.

"I have only slow and unarmed fishing-craft. Canute will have his own longships — he always has. Attacked, these would be as lambs before wolves," Duncan MacDuff, sixth Mormaor of Fife and Fothrif, was a red-faced, bull-like young man, short of neck. His peninsular domain of Fife was almost an island.

"When you have finished teaching us our business, grandson, perhaps we may eat?" Malcolm said, and waved peremptorily to the waiting servitors, who had been about to present a meal of cold meats and ale when the Rossmen arrived.

As a grandson of the King, and one of those in line for the throne, MacBeth as of right took a seat near the head of the table — not too close to the monarch, for comfort's sake, but a goodly distance from Duncan mac Crinan, whom he loathed. With his so evident unpopularity with the King, there was no competition to sit beside him on the part of his fellow mormaors; but Glamis, one of Angus's thanes, came. He was a man of middle years, and one of the most renowned of Malcolm's generals, and so of sufficient independence to follow his own line somewhat and sit where he would.

"Greetings, MacBeth," he said. "Your father was my good friend. I rejoiced that Gillacomgain got his needings."

"You were there, friend? I cannot think it well done, nevertheless."

"The burning?" The other shrugged mailed shoulders. "It was not done prettily. Or as I would have it. But he is better dead. The Lady Gruoch — what of her?"

"She is well," he was told briefly. "And safe."

The other eyed him. "Aye," he accepted.

The King was watching them. Perhaps he could lip-read. "The woman Gruoch?" he said. "You hold her?"

"I give her shelter, sire. Only that."

"Shelter is as good a word for it as other! But — watch how you tread that bird, cockerel! She is dangerous."

MacBeth rose, pushing back the rough bench and all but unseating his neighbours. "Lord King!" he jerked. "That lady is fair. And virtuous. And has suffered. If you miscall her, I must leave your table."

"Ha — so that is the way of it! Tush, man — sit down and eat your meat." Malcolm, grinning, pointed a leg of lamb at his grandson. "Be not so delicate of skin! I but jested. Save your heat for Canute. Sit — and teach Glamis there how to fight battles!"

"That I would not think to do, sire."

"Forby, I agree with the Lord MacBeth. We should have sent a force across the bridge."

"The more fool you, then! Am I surrounded by fools? There is only one way to deal with Canute. Thank you your God that I know how to do it."

None might controvert that, and the meal progressed in more subdued fashion.

MacBeth excused himself as soon as he might, and went back down to his own folk. As far as was possible he would seek to keep his distance from his grandsire and his entourage.

Next day they watched Canute's main array arriving, hour after hour, company by company, some horse but mainly foot — for though this was in name an English army, it was Danish led, with many Norse contingents from the Danelaw and Northumbria; and the Norsemen were not really horsemen.

It was a strange sensation for fighting-men to stand there idle all the long day and watch the enemy mass grow in strength. Towards evening, the watchers on Craig Kenneth could see a group move forward from the centre of the English front to a point a little east of the bridge. It was too distant to distinguish individuals but the Scots leadership had little doubt that it was their enemy counterparts. Presently other men began to carry down what were evidently rafts to the muddy banks of the river. Clearly these were to ferry over probing parties.

"Now the Dane will learn his first lesson!" the King said.

Even at that range it was possible to perceive the chaos which developed as the raft-parties reached the north shore. Clambering up the steep banks of slippery mud in itself was barely practicable. But what followed was infinitely worse. Some of the marshland surface looked comparatively firm — until an attempt was made to tread on it, which revealed the greenery to be no more than a thin skin of moss and scum masking deep black mire beneath. There were tussocks and clumps of reeds, but though a man might be able to stand on one of these, to move to another was frequently impossible. Nowhere could anyone move more than a few yards in any direction, however agile. None of the probers got more than a hundred yards from the river, and few that far.

The English leadership group turned back towards the town. "Now they will try other points, upstream and down,"

Malcolm declared. "And will find none better. And tomorrow, Canute will assail the bridge."

Just in case the enemy chose to do this before waiting for the next day, part of the Scots army stood guard all night along the causeway.

In the morning, however, although the English preparations for an assault were evident, with the massing of men around the bridge-head, it was a small deputation under a flag of truce which presently came forward over the bridge, to where the first Scots ranks waited just out of bowshot from the south bank. The Scots command watched from Craig Kenneth.

In a little while a mounted figure came riding back, while the deputation waited in mid-marsh. It proved to be young Donald, son of the Thane of Doune, in command at the bridge-head. He announced that Canute, King and Emperor, requested speech with Malcolm Kennethson, in peace and amity.

The King spat out an oath. "Go tell Knut mac Sven that I know of no emperor save that of the Romans. That if he comes in peace to my realms, why does he bring scores of thousands of armed men? And tell him that I am an old done man and that if he wishes speech with me, he must needs come to me, not I to him. Across yonder bridge and causeway!"

In something over an hour the youth was back. "Sire," he panted. "The King Canute sends word that he will be happy to meet you in mid-causeway. He desires to speak with you on a number of matters of concern to you both. In especial your tribute to him for the Scots realm, of which he says he is over-lord. And of the benefits of belonging to his empire, along with the English, the Danes, the Norse, the Swedes, the Irish and others."

"Ha! Then go tell the Dane that if he desires tribute he must needs come and collect it, like lesser men. And that I will meet him in mid-causeway only with a sword in my hand. That is all."

Now there was major activity in the Scots camp — for Canute could scarcely ignore that. Companies began to pick their way down through the marshland, hundred upon hundred. From this north side there were firmer approaches, almost tracks, with cattle wading in the pools and water-meadows. From these it was possible to penetrate quite deeply into the swamp, although by round-about routes. The defenders had had plenty of time, and labour, to cut and lay miniature causeways and platforms of brush-wood, branches and tree-trunks, all leading to various sections of the true causeway, on either side, rather like the pattern of veins in an inverted leaf. Along these the Scots moved until they were flanking their fellows who lined the causeway itself for most of its mile in length.

Canute's attack was sudden, and fierce as it was unsubtle. At the blowing of a bull's horn, a mass of swordsmen and spearmen carrying painted cowhide shields, came racing down to the bridge, and across. The Scots defence was placed well back from the bridge-end, to be out of range of English arrows. The shield-carriers ran to as near these as they dared, and then flung themselves down on the causeway and into a rough formation, so holding their shields one above the other to create a fairly solid barrier, which arrows could not penetrate, so that the Scots archers were frustrated. Some of the enemy had already fallen to these, but most survived. Now another wave of the English came running out — or, since these were all bowmen, they may well have been Welshmen, the finest archers. These raced on, to the cover of the shields, where they crouched, strung arrows to their bows, and commenced to shoot without delay.

Now it was the Scots turn to fall back, lacking any such barrier of shields, and well within bowshot. As they did so, more enemy came on, in surges. When these were in position, the shieldmen made their next leap forward.

So that was to be the pattern.

It would have been an excellent pattern, for the enemy, had it not been for Malcolm's flanking forces out in the moss. These were unable to penetrate to the south end of the causeway, so that they could not affect the early stages of the advance. But as the Scots defenders fell back, every move brought them, and the English, nearer — as was the plan. Each retiral covered perhaps 150 yards. At the fourth, the range was right and the waiting men, crouching in bog and slime, could act at last.

It was arrows at first, and a hail of these winged in upon the enemy from both sides. They were now unprotected, with their shields facing only to the front, and insufficient by far to cover both elongated sides as well. Enfiladed, the English fell in scores.

Now both armies rushed in reinforcements. But the fact was that only those in the bog itself were really effective, for the causeway was so narrow that only a few on each front thereon could bring their weapons to bear; the rest could only wait to fill dead men's shoes. And to act as very prominent and easy targets for the men in the moss.

It was a skilfully laid trap.

When it became abundantly apparent to the foremost of the English that their position was untenable and that no further advance was possible, they had only one course to take, backwards. And now the third stage of Malcolm's plan was brought into action. The most southerly companies of the force in the moss moved in on the causeway from both sides, like great pincers. It was a difficult, almost desperate floundering business and not achieved with either speed or exactitude. But eventually, coated in mud and slime, the claws met, and all the enemy to the north of that point were trapped.

There followed a dire slaughter, Canute and his great host on the south shore powerless to intervene in time. Some fought fiercely to the end. But probably the majority jumped into the bog, preferring to take their chances there. Some of these undoubtedly managed to scrabble and plouter through the mires and pools to the river, through the Scots lines, and across. Others lay hidden under banks and in reed-clumps, until darkness might enable them to escape. But most died there, one way or another. And presently the causeway was again clear of the foe.

It was no great victory, to be sure. Probably not more than 800 or so were involved on each side, and the vast English army remained but little diminished and unblooded. But it was a resounding defeat for Canute the Mighty, and its significance as great as it was undeniable.

"He will not try that again, I think," Malcolm Foiranach commented. "Since we can repeat it."

The Scots stood to arms again that night, but the foe made no move.

Next day the two armies waited, a mile apart, in a strange hiatus, so much strength, might and hostility concentrated in so comparatively small area, facing each other, like fighting-dogs on leash, yet inactive. When King Malcolm was asked what he intended next, he replied curtly that that depended on what others did, since he was not the Lord God Almighty. None thought to question him further.

Then, about mid-day, a messenger came to the Scots camp from a look-out post on the hill of Clach Mannan some nine miles to the east, from which a good view down the Forth estuary into the Scottish Sea could be obtained. He reported that a great fleet of longships had come in from the Norse Sea and were now lying off Saint Serf's monastery at Culross, in

Fothrif. Scouts declared that the sails bore the black raven device.

"So — Thorfinn has come, at last!" Malcolm exclaimed. "But — you said he lies off? At Culross? Why lying off?"

"I do not know, lord King. But that is the word. The great host of ships lies offshore, waiting."

"Foul Fiend seize you, man! What do you mean, waiting? Waiting for what?"

"I know not, lord King . . ."

"MacDuff — this is your territory. Ride to Culross. At your fastest. Tell my grandson of Caithness that I require him here, forthwith, not idling there. His longships to be brought as near to this craig as may be. I have been waiting for him, and those ships, for too long. I require them for my next move. Bring him back with you."

"He may not heed me, Sire. Thorfinn Raven Feeder is a man of a high temper . . ."

"Satan scald you, man! Off with you."

It was evening before MacDuff of Fife returned — and alone. The Orkney fleet still lay off Culross, he explained, defensively. He had had himself rowed out to it, in a coracle, and told Thorfinn his, the King's message, but to no effect. The earl would say neither yea nor nay. But he would not come to Craig Kenneth.

"What do you mean, fool — neither yea nor nay? What is he there for? He has come south. In answer to my summons. What service to lie there? We need his ships. You, MacBeth — what is he at?"

"I cannot tell you. I did not know whether he would come, or no. He considers himself no man's liegeman, yours or Canute's. What he may intend I know no more than you."

"Mine or Canute's! Are you telling me, boy, that he admits no difference between myself and the Dane?"

"He holds the Orkneys of Norway."

"He is my daughter's son."

They stared at each other, enemies.

The day following, with no move of any sort evident from Culross, Canute at least ran out of patience. He sent another deputation, again suggesting a meeting, but this time he worded it differently. He did not demand but requested. And offered to come to Malcolm on Craig Kenneth, in view of his great age, if he would ensure safe conduct. They had matters of profit to both to discuss, he asserted.

45

When it became evident that Malcolm was disposed to accede to this, there was some upset in the Scots camp.

"Why concede him this?" Duncan mac Crinan did not often seem to counter his grandfather. "He cannot attack us. Let him seethe in the cauldron he has boiled!"

"Hark to the warrior Prince of Strathclyde!" Malcolm scoffed. "Winner of battles uncounted! Canute has lost less than a thousand men on that venture. And he has — what? Fifty thousand more. He is a hard man. If he chose to repeat that attack on the causeway again and again, how often could we defeat him? Four times? Five? Before we weary. Still he has two-score-thousand left. You are but babes, all of you! When you cannot win with your swords, talk, I say. If your enemy will be so kind! You — go tell the Englishmen that I will speak with King Canute here. At two hours past noon. That will give us time. Tell him that he has my royal word that he and his will return safe to his people. Meanwhile, we have work to do."

The work consisted of rounding up local people, even older children, women and old men, and forming them up in ranks and companies well back from the Scots camp, but seeming to be in extension of it, giving them a scatter of banners, shields, helmets and spears, so that at a distance they looked like reinforcements. Canute would not be within half-a-mile of the nearest, to perceive the deceit.

At length, a great blowing of bulls' horns heralded the English royal party, riding fine tall horses, so much more slender and longer in the leg than the Scots garrons.

"We must behave civilly towards England's king, curse him — even though he is no more than a Viking pirate!" Malcolm declared. "Someone must go meet him on the causeway. Duncan — you, I cannot think, would be sufficiently civil to the Dane. It had better be my other grandson, MacBeth, who loves Vikings! Echmarcach of Dublin will go with him. Lest he forget whose side he is on! Go, and bring this self-styled emperor to me."

As Duncan hooted, MacBeth tightened his lips but restrained his tongue. The Irish kinglet and he moved over to their horses and rode off down the steep track, silent.

They met the group of about a dozen, perhaps one-third of the way along the causeway, between the long lines of scowling Scots abristle with spears, swords and axes. Most of the on-coming party looked typical Vikings, with their great horned and winged helmets, shaggy bearskin cloaks and thonged and

46

banded breeches, although there were Saxons and Welsh lords amongst them also. Canute himself was easily identified, for he was the smallest, thinnest man there, on the largest horse. He was in his late forties, slight but wiry of body, narrow of feature, with long, lank hair, drooping moustaches and forked beard, keen of eye and very mobile of expression. His black helmet was encircled by a golden crown, and the armour scales of his leathern tunic were also dazzling, polished gold. He was waving an animated hand as he talked with his companions, clearly no careful maintainer of royal dignity.

MacBeth saluted him. "Lord King, I greet you in the name of my liege lord Malcolm. I am MacBeth mac Finlay of Ross. And this is Echmarcach, King of Dublin."

"Ah, MacBeth, yes. I knew your father. You are half-brother to my good Thorfinn Raven Feeder, yes?" He had an extraordinary deep voice for so slight a man. "The King of Dublin I have heard of. He is a long way from home! King Malcolm is well? For his years? Despite his inability to travel!"

"He is well. As you shall see. We take you to him."

Canute's darting eyes were very watchful as they rode, missing little; but he talked easily, almost companionably. There was no hiding his shrewdness, however.

"You also are far from home, MacBeth," he observed. "Malcolm the Destroyer must have deemed himself in dire need to bring you so far south?"

"I am one of his mormaors. It is my duty to answer his summons to arms. As must all others. With their fullest strength."

"Ah, yes. How fortunate is Malcolm in his lords. Mine, now, so often find other business of their own more pressing! Is that not so, my friends?" He looked round on his party, smiling.

"We, perhaps, have greater need of defence, sire," MacBeth suggested.

"You are scarce in a position to deny it! I have more men coming from my farthest bounds. As have others. They may be here this day."

Up on Craig Kenneth the two monarchs met, such very different men, yet both renowned warriors, both superb leaders, both ruthless. Malcolm, behind his table under the trees, rose.

"Knut, son of Sven," he greeted.

"Malcolm mac Kenneth — we meet at last! For this I have waited long. Too long."

"My hall door was always open, had you come in peace."

47

"I had hoped, expected, that it would be you who would come to me!"

"Why so?"

"To pay homage for your kingdom, what else?"

"Homage, Dane? The High King of Scots pays homage only to Almighty God!"

Canute controlled himself with an obvious effort. "I think your memory fails you. With old age, perhaps. But . . . I did not come here to wage a war of words, Malcolm. But to come to some agreement — if we can."

"Do I hear aright? Or do my so ancient ears betray me — like my failing memory? Knut the Dane come to talk peace? Sit you, sit you, man — before you change your mind!"

After a moment, Canute grinned, although with a modicum of humour, and sat down at the other end of the table from Malcolm. All others stood, silent, watchful.

Malcolm eyed the other with mock consideration. "Should we commence with prayer to God and His holy saints?" he asked. "I have my good Bishop of St. Andrews here, adept at the matter. I have heard that you have become uncommon pious of late. Since visiting the Pope of Rome."

"That will not be required," Canute said shortly. He had, two years earlier, led a most notable pilgrimage to Rome, unkind tongues suggesting that the accumulated weight of his oppressions having made something such imperative if he was to be able to sleep of a night. The King of Scots, as it happened, slept excellently well.

The older man shrugged. "We do not agree on religion. Nor yet on homage. Have you aught else to discuss with me, Knut Svenson?"

Canute removed his heavy crowned helmet and laid it on the table, nodding. "I have, yes. I have come a long way to see you. At some inconvenience. You will understand that I would not wish to return to Peterborough empty-handed. There is the matter of Lothian, the Merse, Teviotdale, Cumbria and Strathclyde. And . . ." He glanced over at Echmarcach, ". . . shall we say, Dublin and Man also?"

"Forgive me if I do not understand? Your interest in these principalities of mine seems to me to be obscure."

The other laughed. "Obscure, my friend? Do your aged eyes also fail you? Or is it caused by yonder smoke? Has it not come to your notice, Malcolm, that I *hold* these principalities? Or can hold them. And there is nothing that you can do to alter it."

"Hold? You mean that you have ravaged and burned a path through them to reach here? That is not holding them, Dane."

"Think you that you can drive me from them?"

"I can try. And will. Do you wish to spend the rest of your days in fighting the Scots?"

"If so *you* wish. But I think that there will be few Scots left to fight."

"All Scots are not in Lothian and the Merse. Nor yet in Cumbria and Strathclyde."

"No. But when we cross this Forth, we shall deal with the North as we have dealt with Lothian and the South."

"When! You cannot cross the Forth, man. Or you would not be here talking! Have we not proved that?"

"You have proved nothing — save that you rely on a mile of narrow track across a bog. Not much to save a kingdom! A few hundred you have repulsed. Think you that you will keep my full strength back, when I attack in earnest? That was but a trial, a testing."

"You will find the same reception, and the same bog, each time you test. However often."

"Nevertheless, we shall cross, in the end. And you know it. I have many times your numbers. See you — I would save the bloodshed. On both sides. We should come to an agreement."

"Save bloodshed — *Knut!*"

"Yes. Why should hundreds of men die, thousands it may be, for lack of a word or two spoken?"

"And the word or two? Homage? Fealty? The price of freedom itself!"

"Freedom? Freedom to do what? You would be none the less free in my empire. My yoke is not heavy. Ask these others. Indeed, you would gain much. And lose little."

"You waste your breath, Dane."

"You would condemn your peoples to invasion and slaughter, old man? For the sake of your own pride?"

"*My* pride? Think you my people have no pride? Ask these, my mormaors and thanes. Ask them if I should do you homage!"

A glance round the growling Scots present seemingly convinced Canute, for he changed his tune somewhat. "Malcolm — I am willing to go some way with you. To save the bloodshed. Lothian, the Merse and Teviotdale — these are not part of your ancient realm of Alba, of Scotland. You, and King Kenneth

49

before you, added these by conquest. From Northumbria and Cumbria. Part of *my* realms . . ."

"Of Edmond Ironside's realms! Whom you dispossessed."

Canute was patient. "Of the realm of England, if you prefer it. Now, I could take them back. You will admit, if you are honest, that you cannot prevent it. You dare not cross Forth yourself, against our opposition. And Thorfinn Raven Feeder waits, offshore."

"Thorfinn is my grandson, and one of my mormaors."

"And one of *my* earls! Why think you he waits there? Seek to move across this river and he will attack your rear. I tell you, I can take back and hold Lothian and the rest, with little trouble. But — I should be content with less."

"Less? Less than what?"

"Less than taking it from you wholly. Do homage to me, Malcolm mac Kenneth, for Lothian, Teviotdale and the Merse. These only. And I shall be content."

The older man stared at him, assessing.

"Do that, and I shall withdraw my armies. And accept that all Alba, all north of this Forth, is yours. Pay tribute of one serf, one cow, one horse, one bushel of meal, if you like. And our differences are over-past. I say it is an excellent bargain. For you."

"No!" That was Duncan, who hated all Danes. "It is a trick and a trap. Tell him to be off, sire."

"You say so, grandson?" Malcolm, who ever knew his own mind, seemed this time to require advice. "What says my other grandson? You, MacBeth?"

"I say that you, sire, will do only what is in your own mind. But, for myself, Alba is what is important. The rest less so. You are High King of Scots, not of Lothian or the Merse. War I am prepared for. But not over who claims paramountcy in Lothian."

"So says Thorfinn's brother!" Duncan exclaimed. "The jackal who waits outside to see which side will win!"

"We shall discuss that on another occasion, cousin . . ."

"Peace, bairns!" King Malcolm said, in strangely genial, grandfatherly fashion. He turned to Canute. "Knut Svenson, I accept your proposal. I will be your man for Lothian, the Merse and Teviotdale. But only these. For Alba, its High King is no man's man. Aye, and who knows — one day I may come to *you* for homage! For some of Cumbria and Tynedale!"

The other monarch drew a long breath. "In that day, we shall see, old one! But — I commend your wisdom. And that of

50

this MacBeth. The other requires . . . schooling! We shall be friends, now. And you may find my empire of service, I think. Now — have we a paper? And a scribe?"

"A paper . . . ?"

"To be sure. Have you not found, in this of being a king, that papers are useful? The sword may speak loudest, but the paper can last the longest! This bishop you spoke of — such always have paper, pens and ink. And never fear, friend — *you* shall decide the words on this paper. I but wish to have a paper, signed and sealed."

Malcolm shrugged. "Myself, I have little use for ink and paper. The pen is only of worth if the sword-arm behind it is strong. But, if you wish it. Bishop Malduin, come you . . ."

While the bishop and one of Canute's clerks teased out phrasing to suit the situation, the two monarchs drank ale and eyed each other like wary hounds. Malcolm made less fuss about the wording than might have been expected — perhaps significant as to how much value he put on signatures. When it came to signing, he appended his name with a stabbing motion which all but broke the quill.

Canute signed as though more accustomed to the task. But he demanded witnesses, two to each side. Malcolm looked around him.

"Duncan disapproves," he said. "So do some others. It had better be Echmarcach and MacBeth. These two will serve. They brought you here."

"I sign nothing which commits me to King Canute as overlord," the King of Dublin asserted.

"Tush, man — you are signing nothing anyway. Only being witness to *my* signing."

MacBeth witnessed the two copies without demur.

There was no false bonhomie about Canute the Mighty, however much he might be prepared to smile to gain his ends. Having apparently got what he had come for, he wasted no time in taking his departure. MacBeth conducted him and his party back to the bridge-head.

"When your grandsire dies, MacBeth, who will succeed to his throne?" the Dane asked, as they were parting. "You, or that Duncan?"

"Duncan, sire. He is the King's choice. Ever has been."

"A pity. I would have thought that Malcolm would have had more sense! Hear me then, young man. Should the time come when you might think to contest such clearly foolish choice,

51

remember Knut Svenson. I might be useful to Thorfinn Raven Feeder's brother."

"I do not desire the throne, sire."

"Then you are more fool than you look! And your realm the loser."

3

SINCE THERE WAS to be no fighting, MacBeth was no more anxious to prolong his stay in the Stirling vicinity than had been Canute. Malcolm's company and Court held no attractions for him. But the King, for some reason, insisted that he accompany him as far as Scone — which, since it was on his way, MacBeth could scarcely refuse. In fact, en route, Malcolm seemed to have little to say to him, and the younger man rode most of the way with his own thanes and those of Glamis and Cawdor.

Malcolm Foiranach was no sluggard, whatever his age, and it took the host only a day and a half to reach fair Scone, in its woodlands across Tay from Bertha at the mouth of the tributary Almond. MacBeth did not ford Tay, and took his leave of his grandfather here.

"I fear that you are a fool, boy," the King said. "I sorrow for it. But then, your mother Donada was a fool. And she disobeyed me and married your father when old Sigurd died. I cannot abide fools."

"Yet you abide Duncan!"

"Ah, but that is different! A fool who will do what he is told is to be preferred to a fool who will not! Forby, Bethoc is no fool. And she married him that I chose for her — Crinan. Crinan's line the throne needed. Finlay's it did not! And Duncan is their son."

"Yes. And many have had to die for that fact!"

"Death is ever with us, boy. With kings more than others."

"There is honest death and dishonest. Decent and cruel. You, sire, I think deal in the second!"

"Watch your tongue, MacBeth! Forby, I have a kingdom to rule. And may not be so nice as some would like."

"Have I your royal permission to leave, sire?"

"Go, then. Duncan will go with you. As far as Dunkeld.

Crinan — bide you with me, this night. I have matters to talk over."

"Sire — I have a long road to go. I would prefer to go on alone, and fast."

"Nonsense. Duncan will not hold you back. Is it that Gruoch you are in such haste to win back to? It is time that you bairns learned to live with each other instead of ever bickering. Duncan will go with you to Dunkeld, with the Athollmen. That is my royal command."

Fortunately the cousins did not have to see a great deal of each other on the further fifteen miles to Dunkeld. Each had his own leadership group and friends, and their hosts kept separate. But at the Birnam pass of Tay, a couple of miles south of Dunkeld, with MacBeth discussing with Neil Nathrach his mother's strange dream about Birnam Wood moving to Dunsinane, Duncan rode up from the rear.

"MacBeth," he said, without preamble. "We have had little cause to love each other. But we are kin, and there is no need for us to be unfriends. The King would have it otherwise. We near my father's house of Dunkeld and the day draws on. Bide the night there. My mother — your aunt — would welcome you."

MacBeth looked at him sidelong. "I thank you," he said stiffly. "But I called upon the Princess Bethoc. On my way south. And we could ride another score of miles on our way, tonight."

"It would please her. She often speaks of you. Come, even for a small while. A refreshment of wine or ale. It would be esteemed kindly."

MacBeth could be obstinate, even ruthless; but he was not the man to utterly reject an advance.

"Very well," he said. "For just long enough to pay my respects. And to drink a horn of ale." He saw Neil Nathrach scowling and head-shaking. "Neil, ride on with the host. I shall catch up with you before many miles."

His half-brother nudged his garron close, at the other side from Duncan. "Do not enter that house alone," he muttered.

The other nodded. "Duthac. Murdoch. Come meet the princess, my aunt," he said, to the Thanes of Alness and Oykell.

It was Duncan's turn to frown, but he said nothing.

At the green haugh of the Tay, below the towering crag on which rose the dun of the Keledei, the Castle of the Culdees or Holy Men — from which Dunkeld obtained its name — seat of the Hereditary Abbots, the Moray host camped, the Athollmen began to disperse and the Rossmen marched on. MacBeth and his two thanes, with a small bodyguard, turned off, to climb with Duncan to the dun.

Bethoc nic Malcolm showed no more signs of delight at her nephew's re-appearance than she had done earlier. Nor indeed in her son's return — though this was perhaps just her way. After only a fairly brief exchange they seemed to have exhausted all that they had to say to each other, and MacBeth was more than ready to depart. But Duncan had disappeared, presumably to see to the suggested refreshment. There was some uncomfortable waiting.

When his cousin returned, with servitors bearing trays of oatcakes and honey, wine and ale, he brought with him a child, a boy of about three years, a sturdy infant of somewhat lumpish build, reddish-haired with a notably large head.

"Here is my son Malcolm," he announced. "Meet your kinsman the Lord MacBeth, Callum." He patted the boy's head. "Is he not a fine lad?"

MacBeth had heard of this child, a bastard allegedly of a miller's daughter at Forteviot, of whom Duncan was said to be inordinately proud — which indeed he must be to have the boy reared here in his father's house. It was a strange circumstance for a prince unmarried, possibly some proof of his manhood. What Bethoc thought of it she did not divulge.

MacBeth, fond of children, stooped to speak to the boy, accepting it as a further sign that there must be good in his cousin so to cherish his illegitimate offspring. When he straightened up, it was to find Duncan himself holding out to him a great silver-mounted bull's horn, brimming with wine.

"Drink, cousin," he said. "Drink to the future of Alba and its reigning house."

MacBeth could not object to that, and sipped.

"Young Malcolm mac Duncan will recite his lineage back to Alpin, and beyond," the proud father declared. "Callum — tell the Lord MacBeth the names of the kings you come from."

But the child grew shy, embarrassed, and despite much coaxing, could not be cajoled into speech.

"Drink up, man," Duncan urged. "It is good wine. From France. I will fill up the horn . . ."

"Enough! I shall not finish this, indeed."

"Callum — Malcolm son of Duncan, son of . . .?"

At length they got away, Duncan almost effusive in seeing them off.

"The Lord Duncan was . . . notably kind," Duthac of Alness observed. "Kinder than his usual."

"Kinder to mormaors than to thanes, perhaps!" Murdoch of Oykell said. "My lord got wine. We got only ale."

"We must not be too hard on the man," MacBeth said. "He is scarce used to dispensing hospitality, I think."

They caught up with Neil Nathrach and the main Ross force at sundown, in the pass of Killiecrankie, and camped for the night just beyond its northern jaws.

Feeling unaccountably weary and slightly sick, MacBeth rolled his plaid around him early, and sought sleep.

He wakened in the night lathered in sweat and writhing with pain.

Presently his groaning attracted a sentry. When this man could get no sense out of the mormaor, he woke Neil.

That man had some skill as a physician, with knowledge of herbs and simples, passed on to him by his mother. He felt his half-brother's brow, his pulse, his heart-beats. Then he probed strong fingers at the stomach.

"God's saints, man — your bowels are in knots, just!" he cried. "You are fevered . . ."

But MacBeth was only semi-conscious now, and lashing out.

Calling for help, Neil bound his arms with his own golden sword-belt, declaring that his brother must have eaten something foul and should be made to vomit it up. But how to achieve that in present circumstances? Tickling the throat with a feather was scarcely practical behind clenched teeth. And he had no brews here to use as vomitories. Nor could he try bleeding, lacking equipment.

"What shall we do?" Murdoch mac Leod, who had wakened, demanded. "He is very sick. He, he looks like to die on us!"

"He is sick, yes. But he will not die yet awhile, pray God. He is strong. What can this be? It is like . . . poison! Aye, poison!" The thought struck him. "You — you do not feel sick, my lord Thane?"

"No. I am well enough. Why?"

"You also ate in Duncan mac Crinan's house! Did my brother eat differently?"

"No. Oatcakes, honey, ale, wine . . ."

"Wake my lord of Alness. See if he is well . . ."

Duthac of Alness, although dazed with sleep, could find nothing wrong.

"God knows what it is, then," Neil said. "But — we must get him first to salt water. Then home. Then . . ."

"Salt water! Nowhere in all Alba are you further from salt water than in mid-Atholl!"

"Salted water, then. Water with salt in it. To make him vomit. Somehow I must get it down his throat. A house, with salt. To bring up what is poisoning him. Then home, where I can treat him. Starting forthwith."

"Home, man! To Inverpeffery? Have you thought how far that is?" Oykell demanded. "Eighty miles to Inverness. Over twenty beyond."

"Even so." Neil paused. MacBeth was talking, but incoherently, raving. "Even so. Tie him in a litter between two garrons. Ride day and night, without stop. A score of hours? Less. It can be done. And must."

Neil Nathrach had his way. He bound his half-brother in his plaid, and with another two contrived to form a litter slung between two horses, roped so that they could not pull apart, he left the Ross host there at Killiecrankie, and with a small group and spare garrons, set off northwards into the night, without delay and at highest possible speed.

Houses with salt were not to be looked for in any numbers in the Central Highlands, nor indeed anywhere. Neil recognised that he might waste much vital time searching; so he waited until, in the early dawn he saw a larger establishment than the usual cabins and cot-houses of the clansfolk, a small hall-house within its group of huts, at the crossing of the Atholl Garry at Struan. Without compunction and amidst a great barking of dogs, he knocked up the owner in the name of Crinan, Mormaor of Atholl — uncle by marriage, after all, to the casualty. An old man eventually answered the summons, without enthusiasm. Asked, from his bed, to provide salt for complete strangers, and not Athollmen at that, he was scarcely to be blamed. But salt was forthcoming, and water was to be had in plenty. Getting the solution between the now unconscious sufferer's lips was less difficult than Neil had feared, because now the teeth were unclenched.

They rode on, with further supplies of the salted water, Neil close at his brother's side. When, presently, he heard MacBeth all but choking, his heart lifted. He halted the garrons and raised his brother to a sitting position, and praised his Maker and all saints as the bile oozed and belched out. It was likely to be a long way from any real cure, but it must surely help. Whatever evil thing was in MacBeth's stomach and bowels must be got out somehow. He would give him more salt water in a mile or two.

The sunrise began to glow above the mountain ridges to their right as they trotted steadily on up the long rise to the pass of Drumochdar, at the garrons' mile-eating pace. Ninety miles to go.

4

MACBETH WAS SWIMMING, gasping, struggling for air, in a heavy, surging sea of vivid, clashing colour, jetty black, flame-red, violent green, orange-yellow. He was tired, tired, for he had been fighting those dire waves for long, and he doubted whether he could keep it up for much longer. Yet he knew that if he gave in, even for a moment, that foul sea would overwhelm him and he would sink down, down — but not into mindless oblivion to be welcomed but into eternal torture and pain. He *had* to stay afloat somehow, anyhow.

Despite the terror of the red waves and the green, the black ones were the worst. They were *heaviest*. They weighed him down. They choked him. And they spoke not so much of pain and death as of evil, the nameless evil of the ancient ones. Each wave was whispering at him as he fought it past, whispering a message, always the same message, as they swirled by. "Birnam Wood!" they hissed. "Birnam Wood!" The black waves were certainly the worst.

The hand, white but strong, when it reached for him was the most lovely thing that he had ever seen. If only he could grasp it . . . Once he touched those fingers, cool, firm — but could not hold them. He went down and down again, but fighting now, furiously, angrily. To have been so near to salvation — for he knew that if he could but grip that hand he would win out of this savage sea.

He was coming up again, up through the black and the red and the green, up, up — and there, praise God, was the hand, still outstretched for him. With the supreme summoning of his all but expended residue of strength, he reached out and still out, and grabbed. And his clawing, burning fingers closed on that cool strong firmness, and held, held. Safe, secure at last. In a surge of sheerest thankfulness he let all else go but that white hand, and sank away this time into blessed peace and unknowing.

When next MacBeth opened his eyes, it was to see, instead of heaving, menacing waves of colour and darkness, the timbers of a ceiling painted with Pictish beasts and symbols, strange of design but familiar all his life. Then a face swam into his vision between him and the symbols, a face pale but lovely, close to his own, the eyes kind, kind.

"Gru . . . och!" he whispered.

"Hush, you," she murmured. "Hush you, my dear. All is well." She pressed his head back, gently, wiping his brow with a cloth. "No words, MacBeth, *a ghraidh*. Gather your strength."

He closed his eyes — for the effort to speak had taxed him greatly. But he opened them again when he felt a stirring at his fingers. He found that she was seeking to release her hand from his grip.

"Let it go, *a ghraidh*," she said, smiling. "You do not need it now. It is numb."

He relinquished his grasp only reluctantly — for somehow he knew that hand had meant the difference between life and death to him. She wriggled her fingers painfully.

"You have a fierce grip for a sick man!" she said. "You have clutched it tightly for hours."

"It . . . it saved me," he got out.

He must have drifted over to sleep after that — without wishing to — for when next he was aware of his surroundings, it was his half-brother Neil who sat beside the bed.

"Och, Beda!" Neil said, brokenly. "Beda, lad!" It was his childhood name for his brother.

"Where is she?" MacBeth strove to sit up, urgently. "Where is she, Neil?"

"Quietly, man — quietly! She has not gone far, never fear."

"Where? Where is she . . .?"

"She has the chamber above. That was Morag's. She has dwelt here since she heard that I had brought you home. Scarcely left your side, day or night. She is tired."

MacBeth stared at him.

"It has been . . . a close thing, Beda. Many times we feared for your life. Praise God you have come through it."

"She . . . held out . . . her hand."

"Eh?"

58

"She held out her hand. To me. Saved me."

"Aye. No doubt. See, now — you must try to eat."

The next sleep was a long one, for when he awoke it was the middle of the night. A single candle flickered in the drift of air. The darkness and the flame was too reminiscent of past horrors and MacBeth started up, alarmed. But a hand touched his bare shoulder and he sank back.

"Gruoch!" he said, with a sigh of thankfulness.

"All is well," she assured.

"Yes," he agreed. But he held out his hand. She took it and clasped it and he was content.

But not for long. "Why are you so good to me?" he asked, presently.

"Can you call it that?" she wondered. "I have sat by your bed. To relieve Neil Nathrach. That is all."

"You have cherished me. For long. Neil told me. And you saved me. Your hand. I could not have lived else. Your hand . . ."

"You talked much of a hand, yes. In your fever. To be sure, you gripped mine sufficiently hard! If it was my hand that helped you, I am glad, glad. A very ordinary and weak woman's hand."

"Sufficiently strong to save me."

"You must not say that. It was Neil who saved you. He ministered to you, brought you home in a litter all the way from Atholl, as fast as beasts could run, day and night, never halting. Bursting the hearts of eight garrons, they say. Since when he has bled you, physicked you and watched over you. I have but aided him. Sat here, and prayed. Prayed for you, and for God's vengeance on Duncan mac Crinan!" That came out almost on a hiss.

He began to shake his head, but desisted from dizziness. "I do not love Duncan," he said. "But he scarce deserves that, I think . . ."

"You were poisoned. And he is a poisoner. You had just left his house, had you not?"

"Yes. But I cannot believe this."

"He has poisoned others. Gillacomgain often spoke of it. With the deadly meiklewort. It is said that he poisoned two Danes with meiklewort. Neil says this was poison. With you."

MacBeth was silent.

"He besought you to enter his house, Neil says. After showing you no love. And soon thereafter you fell sick. Would have died,

59

had it not been for Neil. It was the wine that was poisoned."

"We cannot be sure . . ."

"We can. I *know* it! They desire your death, Duncan and his grandsire. As they desire mine. As they have slain many. Tell me of this wine. Did it taste nothing amiss? Did any other drink it?"

"Duncan himself had some. Not the others. It seemed good wine."

"He would drink from his own cup, not yours?"

"Yes. He brought me a large bull's horn. But I did not drink much of it. The child was there — Duncan's son, Malcolm. I was talking to the child. I did not drink much of it."

"Did he urge you to do so?"

"Ye-e-es. But only as any man would."

"If you had drunk more, then I say that you would have been dead now, MacBeth. Oh, thank God!" She clutched his hand.

"Thank Neil also! And thank *you!* You came from Rose-markyn. Did Neil send for you?"

"No. I think that he resented my coming, at first. When I came unbidden. He loves you, that one. But he came to accept me, when I would not go away."

"You would not go away? Why, Gruoch?"

"I could not leave you in dire need. I could offer a woman's care. You were good to me, took me in when I needed help, cherished me and Lulach. Think you that means naught to me? I could do no other." She sat up ."But, see you — this will not do. All this talk. Neil was very strong on this. You are not to talk much. You are to rest. Sleep. Regain your strength. Only that. Sleep again now, *a ghraidh*."

"You say *a ghraidh* — my dear!"

"It, it slipped out. I meant . . . my friend. Shut your eyes. No more talk meantime." •

"You will not go away, Gruoch?"

"No. I shall bide here."

"Give me your hand. I mislike the darkness. Voices. Birnam Wood. Ill voices. Your hand . . ."

He drifted off, and she settled herself back in her chair, her hand gripped still.

Presently, she leaned over and lit a new candle from the old.

At some unspecified time later she opened her eyes. MacBeth was sitting straight up, staring in front of him.

". . . three," he was saying. "Three of them. Women. Hags. Strange women. They pointed at me . . ."

"Hush you — it was but a dream. Nothing to fear."

"They pointed, I tell you. All pointed. One said, 'I see the Mormaor of Ross.' One said, 'I see the Mormaor of Moray.' The last said, 'I see the King!'."

She eyed him, silent.

"You hear, Gruoch? That is what they said."

"It was a dream. You are not yourself. Still the poison works within you." She pressed him back. "Sleep again."

"No. I want no more of that. If these are dreams, I want none of them. The other I have often. Of the moving forest. Birnam Wood . . ."

"Yes. You have said that. It was but another dream. Of your mother's."

"She had the sight. Perhaps I have, also?"

"Do not distress yourself. It is the poison in you. Setting up these humours."

"Perhaps. But it is no evil thought to be Mormaor of Moray, at least. If you will but wed me . . .?"

"I told you — you can be Mormaor of Moray now, if you so wish. With my blessing."

"It is more than your blessing I want. It is *you*. Your hand in marriage." He was sitting up again, eagerly.

"But . . ." She shook her head. "Lie back now, my dear. It is no time to be speaking of such things."

* * *

Neil Nathrach was a stern physician, and it was days before he would permit his patient to leave his bed and venture out into the blossom-time orchard on the terrace, above the marshland between the estuaries of the rivers of Peffery and Conon. Here MacBeth was allowed to sit, sheltered from the breeze, watching the first martins and swallows and listening to the cuckoos calling endlessly from the stunted thorn-trees of the peat-bog and salt-marsh. It was a strange place for a dun, but the site was strong nevertheless, protected by water and marsh as effectively as though on any crag or ridge. The orchard was a familiar place indeed for MacBeth, for to this house he had been brought as a boy on his father's death.

Now, although he saw much of his brother, many of his thanes and chiefs came to visit him, and even young Lulach played on the grass beside his hammock, the one he wanted to see, Gruoch, seemed to avoid him — or at least to avoid being alone with him. He was not yet dining in the hall, with all the dun's company, and she usually ate with him either outdoors or in his room; but never, it seemed, alone. He fretted over it, in his still-weak state. It seemed evident that she did not wish to be questioned further on the subject of marriage.

There were, to be sure, other questions and problems exercising his own mind and those of his friends. In especial the possibility of his poisoning — although all others seemed to take it as a certainty and no question. And if it was so, what was to be done about it? The accepted opinion was that Duncan had deliberately coaxed MacBeth into his father's house to poison him with the wine; but that he had been put up to it by King Malcolm — whom Neil and the thanes remembered as having insisted that Duncan accompany him northwards, despite reluctance. It was just one more murder-plot by the old devil, to clear the way for Duncan's eventual accession. But as such it could not be forgotten any more than forgiven. Nor, as it were, shrugged off. Vengeance, retribution, battle — these were the demands being made, the courses being urged.

The victim reserved judgment meantime. Not that he lacked spirit or his due measure of human resentment. But he preferred to make his major decisions on proven information, or if that was not possible, at least on sound reasoning. Not on hearsay, prejudice and conjecture. He and Thorfinn had often found cause for disagreement on this score; now he was equally at odds with his other half-brother.

Besides, his physical weakness still affected his mind and will. And he had more than sufficient for his somewhat overstretched emotions and attentions to cope with meantime — for he found himself to be most directly and totally enamoured of Gruoch nic Bodhe, in a fashion he had not thought possible and to the exclusion of almost all other considerations.

So, since she would not come to him, alone, he must go to her. He climbed the winding stair to her room, which was directly above his own in the main tower of the dun, the third evening of his release from bed, and knocked at her door.

She came to open, needlework in her hand, a tapestry of vivid Pictish designs. Clearly she was distinctly put out to see him there.

"My lord!" she said. "You, it is. I, I . . . you should not have climbed the stairs."

"I needs must, if I am to see you, Gruoch. And you named me my dear, before, not my lord!"

"A slip, my lord. I talk much with Lulach, and so call him. I would have come had you sent for me."

"I would not *send* for you, for what I have to say. May I enter?"

"It is your house. But — we would be better below, I think, in the hall. Lulach sleeps . . ."

"What I have to say, Princess, is scarcely for the hall either! And I shall not shout, to awake the child!" He pushed past her into the room.

It was not large, and simply furnished, as was his own, with a great bed, in one corner of which the boy slept, arms wide, two or three chests, a bench and a stool, sheepskin and deerskin rugs on the floor and coloured hangings to cover the bare stone walls. She had been sitting in the window-seat, where were the wools and shears for her work.

"You have been avoiding me," he charged, walking over to the window. "Keeping your distance."

"Not avoiding, no," she demurred. "I dine at your table, do I not? Walk in your orchard . . ."

"Not alone. Never alone with me. Do not let us play with words, Gruoch. Although you nursed me close as your own child, now you seek not to be alone with me."

She did not speak.

"I know why, to be sure. You fear that I will speak of marriage again. Why?"

"I told you before. I have had sufficient of marriage."

"To Gillacomgain, yes. But I am different."

She mustered a small smile at that.

"It is true, Gruoch — is it not? I am not like Gillacomgain, am I?"

"You are not like Gillacomgain," she agreed.

"Well, then. Marriage with me would be quite different."

"Perhaps. But that is not to say that I must needs embrace it."

"No. But — it is suitable. You need a husband. To protect you and the boy. To give you a home fit for a princess. And, and you are young yet. And beautiful."

"All this you have told me before."

"But it is true."

"And it all means that I should wed MacBeth?"

"Why not? Am I so ill a match? So displeasing?"

"Not so. You are sufficiently personable! And, save in some respects, well spoken of. I am sure that you would make a fair enough husband. Were I looking for one!"

He frowned at her, biting his lip. He looked tougher, sterner, than he knew.

63

She sat down, beside her wools. "You cannot conceive of a woman not wishing to wed you? No?"

"No!" he exclaimed. "That is nonsense! Folly!"

"Hush — or Lulach will awake."

"A plague on Lulach! If you think so ill of me, why did you come from Rosemarkyn to save me?"

"I did not save you. I told you — it was Neil who saved you. And the saints of God."

"*You* saved me," he said heavily. Then a thought occurred to him. "You said, back there, that I was well spoken of. Save in some matters. You said that — save in some respects. What did you mean?"

"Few men are well spoken of in all things . . ."

"Do not cozen me. What tales have you been listening to?"

"I do not listen to tales, MacBeth. But the Mormaor of Ross has a certain . . . reputation. Like other men of rank. It would be strange if he had not. There is, see you, the matter of the Lady Annabella."

"Ha! That! There is nothing to that. A, a passing fancy only."

"Sufficient to upset two thanes, I am told. Her father and her husband."

"Both fools!" he asserted strongly. "She is Breadalbane's daughter. I was young — we both were young. I found her . . . friendly. Then she was married to that oaf, the Thane of Kyle. I did not see her for years — Kyle being in Strathclyde. Then we met again. At a council at Lochaber. Kyle was drunk — as ever. She, she sought me out."

"Sought you out sufficiently to run off with you! Or so I heard."

"Who has been telling you all this? Neil? That serpent! It was nothing. Came to nothing. She is a woman of, of sudden passions. Blows hot and cold. I took her back to Kyle. He scarce noticed that she had been gone, I swear! And that was two years back."

"She might seek you out again, this woman of passions!"

"I think not. Nor would I meddle with her again. She has a child now."

"Yours?"

"God's death — no! I, I — see you, do I ask *you* all these questions? Of before we knew each other?"

"Perhaps you should. Marriage being a serious matter. For the woman, at least!"

He bit that lip again, staring at her.

"Other reputation MacBeth the Mormaor has — apart from his way with women!" she went on. "I am told that, though in general quiet, patient even, he can be harsh, ruthless. If offended, a terror!"

"Who said that? I punish wrongdoers, persistent wrongdoers. As must any mormaor and thane. *You* know that. But I seek to be just, fair. Only an unfriend could say otherwise."

"Unfriend? I wonder! Did you not once have a man's tongue cut out?"

"He slandered two honest women. Of malice."

"And another's right hand cut off?"

"It was that, or his head. I gave him choice. He had slain a man, in robbery, and should have hanged. But he had a wife and five bairns . . ." He paused. "These things I think only one man could have told you. I do not see the Princess Gruoch listening so to servants! It must have been Neil, my brother?"

She did not answer.

He looked away. "I counsel you to consider well how much heed to pay to Neil Nathrach," he said slowly. "He has great virtues. He would die for me, yes. You yourself have said that he loved me but was loth to accept your aid in nursing me. Do you not understand? He loves me and watches over me — but feels, I think, that I *belong* to him! As I do not! Others must not, cannot, love me as Neil does. He was my father's bastard, you see. Three years my senior. Had our father but wed his mother, *he* would have been the mormaor. He cannot forget it, I fear."

"I see. So — he is not called Nathrach, the Serpent, for nothing?"

"Do not mistake. He is the loyalest of all. But — he judges some things differently. And he has a strong will. So I must needs watch him. Always."

"All men require watching!" she commented.

He wagged his head. "Can you think of any other, and better, reasons why you should not wed me?"

"It is scarce so much why I should not, surely? But why I *should!*"

"It would be fitting. Appropriate. Convenient. The answer to many problems. It may even be expected of us, situate as we are."

"Then we should change that situation. And promptly. Since we must not disappoint expectations, must we? It is time that I left your house."

"No!" he cried. Leaning forward he grabbed her shoulders,

actually shook her. "Woman — will you stop such talk! How can I reach you? I love you, dote on you, need you! You are all I want, all I shall ever want. You are the beat of my heart, the blood in my veins, the light of my life. You are the fairest, most beautiful woman God ever made, and I cannot live without you! I love you beyond all telling and all things. And you, you but mock me!"

She swallowed. "Mock — never!" she got out.

"Mock, yes. Put me off. Say me nay."

"But — why did you not tell me this before?"

"I have been telling you. For days."

"No. Not this. Not of love. And caring. Of need and, and true loving. Only of suitability. Of convenience. Of what would be best. Of my great need of a husband. Even of gratitude. Nothing of love."

He was still gripping her shoulders. But now she had risen from her window-seat and was therefore standing very close to him. He gazed into her eyes.

"What of it? You knew I loved you, surely? I have never hidden it."

"You never said it."

"What difference would it have made?"

"Oh, you fool, you fool!" she all but sobbed. "Can you not see? I am a woman. Not just a princess, an heiress of kings. I need love, caring. The rest — it counts for little . . ."

"You are saying that you have been waiting? Waiting only for this? A few words! To say that I loved you?"

"Of course, of course. What else? How could I tell?"

"Then, then — if I had said so, at the first? Told you how it was with me. What then?"

"Then it would have spared us both much pain and distress, heart of my heart!" she said simply.

"God be good — you mean . . .? Gruoch, you mean . . .?"

"My dear, my dear!" she cried, and flung herself into his arms.

Almost unbelieving, he clutched her to him, wordless.

"My heart's darling — how could you be so foolish, so blind?" she demanded. "I have been yours, from the start. For the taking."

*   *   *

They were married within a few days, on the Feast of Saint Cyr. Neither were of a nature for fuss or delay. They might not have waited for even those few days had it not been for two men, whom it was advisable to have present, or politic, at any rate — the Abbots of Applecross and Deer. These were not to perform the wedding ceremony — that was done by the old Bishop Dungal; but it was scarcely thinkable that a Mormaor of Ross should marry without the witness of the O'Beolain of Applecross; or the widow of Moray and mother of the heir of line, without the Abbot of Deer. These two, between them, demonstrated much of the state of the Celtic Church, which was very different from and quite independent of the Romish polity. It was the Columban Church, based on a monastic system of government, not a diocesan. The great Columba himself had been first Abbot of Iona, the fountain of the faith, and no bishop; and on abbots he had founded the Scoto-Pictish Church five centuries before.

Unfortunately there had been degeneration — as in other branches of Holy Church. Marriage was not forbidden to priests and presbyters — although it was not encouraged — and as the churches and monasteries accumulated lands and influence, certain priestly families began to adhere to them, generation after generation, and in time they became hereditary fiefs, the abbots powerful nobles. Such were the O'Beolain Abbots of Applecross, on the Wester Ross Hebridean seaboard — as were the mormaor family of Atholl, Abbots of Dunkeld, calling themselves Primate. Deer, in North Buchan, however, founded by a Mormaor of Moray, was still a true monastic centre, a notable place of scholarship and learning, its abbots churchmen first and foremost, however influential.

The wedding took place at Rosemarkyn, the main church of Ross, before quite a large and distinguished company, despite the call for simplicity. Neil Nathrach acted groomsman for his brother, with modified enthusiasm. MacBeth would have wished Thorfinn to be present, but his whereabouts were unknown, hosting in the Hebridean or Irish Seas.

For her part, the bride made no complaint.

5

THE MORAY SITUATION, of course, was not forgotten, never forgotten. While MacBeth had certainly not wished to give the impression that his marriage had anything to do therewith, he was much concerned. Gruoch herself indeed had to be, since the mortuath, in any honest assessment, belonged by rights either to her son or to her husband. The King, whilst anything but discreet, had not attempted to appoint any new mormaor. Crinan, Duncan's father, was still nominally in charge of the territory.

MacBeth by no means sought warfare, any more to win Moray than to gain vengeance on his alleged poisoner. But weighing up the situation that autumn of 1033, he came to the conclusion that the chances were that he might not have to fight to gain the mormaorship. None of the Moray thanes were in any good position to claim it for themselves; and moreover were still more unlikely to unite in favour of any one of their number. Crinan was equally unlikely to attack unless spurred on by the King. And when MacBeth heard that Duncan had gone courting in Northumbria, almost certainly on his grandfather's instigation, he felt fairly sure that there would be no call to arms against him meantime. He decided to make a move into Moray.

Perhaps he might have thought twice about any such venture, so soon after his wedding, and preoccupied as he was with the delights of love, had it not been for the fact that he might take Gruoch with him — indeed, not so much might as ought to. For he planned a progress rather than any sort of invasion. They would both go, and young Lulach with them, with a sizeable company but no army, and show themselves to Moray and its people as the rightful inheritors thereof. But a strong host would be mobilised, and wait behind, just across the Ross border, in case of trouble.

They set off from Inverpeffery on the Nativity of Saint Mary, a fine and colourful mounted company about 200 strong, men and women, with flags, banners and symbols, even a party of priests under the Abbot of Applecross and Bishop Dungal, to emphasise the peaceful nature of their visit. Neil Nathrach remained behind, with a large armed force ready for swift action.

Inverness was not the traditional centre and capital of Moray, which was much further east, at Spynie on Spey, in the Laigh. But Gillacomgain, like his brother before him, had made it his headquarters, finding Spynie much too close to Thorfinn's Moray toehold of the Borg-head of Torfness, for comfort. Approaching the town where the unhappiest years of her life had been spent, needless to say was something of an ordeal for Gruoch; but she was not the sort to make any fuss. Their reception here might well be significant, and she had an important role to fill.

MacBeth had made no secret of his intentions and journey, and nothing was more sure than that their arrival at the mouth of the Ness would be no surprise. In the event, as they approached, they could see that the town area was packed with people.

Inverness was an only slightly less strategic site than was Stirling, 150 miles to the south. Glen More, the great and deep valley system which clove through high Drumalbyn, the mountain mass of Highland Scotland, reached salt water, in the north-east, here, at the Moray Firth. Twenty-five miles of that cleft was filled with the deep and mile-wide Loch of Ness. The short but strong and broad Ness River ran from the loch-foot to the firth, six miles, with only the one bridge or practical crossing — at Inverness. So that for over thirty miles there was no way across Glen More, from the southern Highlands to the northern, save here. Unless by boat, and boats were kept notably well guarded.

The town straddled both sides of the bridge; but most of it, and the oldest part, lay on the south side, where the river-bank was flanked and dominated by a long curving ridge, of no great height but sufficiently steep to command the crossing. On the crown of this ridge, at the eastern, seaward end, rose the old stone dun, on the site of the one-time fort of the Pictish King Brude — for this was the capital of ancient Pictavia. This was the strongest position. Next to it were the blackened ruins of Gillacomgain's rath and Gruoch's former home, timber-built, clay-coated, within its broken stockade. And nearby was the church and monastery of Saint Baithen or Bean. Below, the town spilled down the slopes in terraces and steep lanes, and lining the river-bank.

A bell was ringing from the saddle-roofed tower of the monastery, no doubt to warn all of the Rossmen's approach. At the far side of the bridge a great crowd waited. So far as the newcomers could see, they were not armed, or not aggressively so.

MacBeth reined up. With women present, he was taking no unnecessary chances. He sent forward the priestly group, Bishop Dungal's coigreach or crozier prominent, an acolyte ringing Saint Maelrubha's famous hand-bell from Applecross.

A somewhat similar clerical party came out across the long wooden bridge from the other side, also displaying a crozier — indication that Bishop Malise of Inverness was present. The two groups met, conversed briefly and then came back over the bridge together.

Bishop Malise, a younger man with a leonine head and fine features, raised his hand. "The blessing of Almighty God upon you, MacBeth mac Finlay — if you come in peace," he declared strongly. "And to you, Lady Gruoch. I hope I see you well? And the Lord Lulach. My lord Abbot — I greet you."

"We come in peace yes, Bishop," MacBeth agreed. He pointed. "These assembled there? Who are they?"

"The thanes, my lord. Of Urquhart and Cawdor and Lovat. And the good folk of this town and country. To welcome you."

"Urquhart? And Cawdor?" MacBeth glanced at his wife. Morgund of Urquhart was married to Gillacomgain's sister; and Hugh of Cawdor had been a close friend of the late mormaor. "How honest, think you, is *their* welcome, Bishop?"

"So be it you come in peace, wholly so, my lord. Or so I believe."

"How many armed men have they, man? Hiding out of sight?" That was Farquhar O'Beolain.

"Only each his own small guard, my lord abbot. This I know."

"Very well. We shall go speak with them," MacBeth decided. "And try these thanes' honest welcome."

They crossed the bridge.

The three thanes and the town's notables stood on a slight rise, in from the bridge-end, backed by the crowd, watchful, silent. No cheers greeted the Rossmen. It might be a welcome, but it was a wary one.

A big burly man of middle age, small-eyed and fleshy-featured, richly dressed, the central of the three thanes, spoke.

"Greeting, my lord mormaor. We all wish you well. And hope that you are fully recovered from your sickness. Which we all heard of with sorrow. And much concern."

"I thank you, Morgund of Urquhart. I am well." MacBeth spoke coldly, however. This man, Gillacomgain's brother-in-law, had been no friend to Gruoch in the past. He had a reputation for cunning and ambition. He was calling MacBeth mormaor now, but that might be only in reference to Ross. It would do him, and the others, no harm to be made a little more uneasy. "But — should not your first concern be with the Princess Gruoch, the lady of this mortuath? And with your late lord's son, Lulach? Whom you did nothing to aid, when in need."

That had the desired effect. Urquhart turned to the other thanes, who looked equally upset. Something like a sigh rose from the crowd.

"To be sure, my lord," Cawdor said. "We are devoted to the Lady Gruoch. And to the Lord Lulach. We sorrow for their misfortunes. But rejoice that she has now found so sure a shield and protector as yourself." He was a lean, dark individual with a beaked nose and trap-like jaws.

Gruoch inclined her head but said nothing.

"We could do nothing against the King," Lovat said unhappily, a weak man in a delicate situation.

"*Against* the King, no! I do not advocate treason!" MacBeth told them, sternly. "But *for* your lady and young lord, you might have done something. I did, with the less duty. They had to escape alone, unaided, like hunted creatures. From murder and burning. And you stood by." It was unfair, of course, deliberately so. But it was important that these people should be confused, uncertain of their position or his intentions, apprehensive.

"What could we have done . . .?" Urquhart began, but MacBeth cut him short.

"Enough of this. Do we stand here all day? I see that my wife's house has not yet been rebuilt. After more than a year."

"We, we knew not who was to be Mormaor of Moray, lord. Until we knew . . ."

"My Lord MacBeth," Bishop Malise intervened firmly. "Refreshment awaits you at my cashel of Saint Baithen. There is no need to stand here."

"Very well. Lead the way, bishop."

As they climbed the hill between the cabins and cot-houses, picking their way past the rooting pigs and pecking poultry, Gruoch looked at her husband assessingly.

71

"I am seeing a new MacBeth!" she observed.

He shook his head. "No. But this is necessary. A lesson taught now, to these, could save much teaching elsewhere."

"I pray that *I* may never need such lessons!"

He smiled. "In our house, you do the teaching!"

Passing the burned-out hall-house in its wrecked stockade, Gruoch averted her eyes, and kept the child in talk and looking elsewhere.

Nearby they came to the cashel, the Celtic Church's name for a monastery. It was a wide turf-walled enclosure, the walls not crowned by a defensive paling of pointed tree-trunks like the rath, the spacious interior dotted with many wood-and-thatch buildings. Most of these were small and all were simple. The majority were the sleeping-cells of the monks and brothers, mere huts, the bishop's no different from the others. The two largest buildings were the dining-house — it could hardly be called a hall — and the guest-house for visitors, itself sufficiently modest. The church of Saint Baithen was on the same scale, with no more pretensions than a cottage. Compared with any Romish religious establishment, in dressed stone, pillars, stained-glass and ornament, it was all humble indeed, some might say laughable. But the Celtic tradition was a notably different one, outdoor, non-hierarchal and non-territorial, with the emphasis on teaching, conversion and baptism, healing. Buildings were considered of much less importance than holy wells, sacred spots and streams, carved stone shrines and crosses, saints' bells and the like.

In the dining-house a simple meal was provided for all who could squeeze in, although most were catered for outside. There was much milk and cheese, oatcakes and honey, bowls of curds laced, since it was the Feast of the Nativity, with the Highland spirit, whisky.

The thanes were careful now as to what they said, and paying elaborate if awkward attention to Gruoch and young Lulach. MacBeth all but ignored them for a while, talking with Bishop Malise — whom indeed he found more to his taste than old Dungal of Rosemarkyn, a man of character and intelligence. Eventually, he paused, turned, and raised his voice.

"My lords — I would have your attention. And, it may be, your advice. Who, say you, should be Mormaor of Moray?"

There was a profound silence as men eyed each other uncomfortably. None was going to be foremost in answering that awkward question, so baldly put.

But MacBeth was insistent. "Morgund mac Morgund — you are senior here, I think. Who say you?"

The big man moistened thick lips. "I . . . it is not easy, MacBeth mac Finlay. He, Finlay, was mormaor here. But . . . died. And you are his son, his only son. But Malbride and Gillacomgain have been mormaors since. Malbride left no child. And this, the Lord Lulach, is Gillacomgain's son . . ."

"I did not ask for a history lesson, man! I asked you who you say should be mormaor now?"

"My lord, it is the King's choice . . ."

"Not so. The King confirms, he does not choose or appoint. Not unless there is no rightful heir. He is Ard Righ, King of Kings, not *Maker* of Kings. Are you saying that there is no rightful heir here?"

"No, no . . ."

"Then who, man?"

Urquhart gnawed his lip, looked over at Gruoch, and remained silent.

"So! Cawdor — how say you? Since Urquhart is insufficiently bold to venture an opinion, perhaps you may have more spirit?"

"I say, my lord, that the question is best answered by the Lady Gruoch. Since the choice lies between her husband and her son."

"None other?"

The thane hesitated, eyes darting. "I am aware of none other," he said then, carefully. "None other with right as heir."

"Ah."

"Others might come forward, claiming other right. Of the sword, perhaps."

"And such might be . . . ?"

Cawdor considered the knuckles of his fist, gleaming rather noticeably white. "There is the Earl Thorfinn, my lord. Who already has a grip on Moray land. At Torfness. Or there is the Earl Gillaciaran of the Sudreys, Thorfinn's uncle — who has taken over certain Moray glens down by the Western Sea. Since Gillacomgain died. Again there is MacDowall, Lord of Galloway, who has conquered some of Dalar and Argyll. And pushes ever inland towards Moray-land. All these."

"These are not heirs. Only possible *takers*." It was no part of MacBeth's strategy to indicate that Thorfinn would *not* seek to take over Moray. "As for takers, there might be others, nearer home who might so aspire?" He paused significantly. "But I spoke not of such. I asked you, Cawdor — who by *right* should be Mormaor of Moray?"

The other made his choice. "*You* should, my lord."

"I should? Then — you would dispossess the Lord Lulach?" He patted the boy's head.

"My lord. And lady! Since it must be one or the other, it had better be yourself. It is possible that Lulach might have the first claim. But he is only a child. He could not *hold* Moray. For many years to come. You, I say, are the tanist — the nearest in blood best fitted to hold the inheritance together. It is a wise system."

"I could be captain. Hold the mortuath *for* Lulach."

"Better to be mormaor yourself, lord. If my lady will agree? At least until the Lord Lulach is of full years. Men, I say, would be less like to assail Moray if it was yours than if it was a child's. And you but captain. The Earl Thorfinn, your half-brother. I think that he would not seek to take *your* mortuath. But he might think to take Lulach's, who is no kin to him."

"Aye. So there we have it! It is the Earl Thorfinn you fear. And I am the best guard against my Viking half-brother. Is that it?"

Cawdor was silent.

MacBeth looked round the group. "Were it not for Thorfinn Raven Feeder, someone else might be sitting Mormaor of Moray now, I think! With your blessing. Who? You, Urquhart? You, Cawdor?"

Throats were cleared, heads were shaken. Major discomfort reigned.

Conal of Lovat — who of course could have had no ambitions for the mortuath — found words first. "Hugh of Cawdor is right, lord," he asserted earnestly. "You should be mormaor. Your Ross protects Moray on the north. The Earl Thorfinn, if it is yours, will protect it on east and west, from the sea . . ."

"And in the south? Crinan of Atholl and Gartnait of Mar. Do they love me? Crinan, father of Duncan!"

"My lord." Urquhart recovered his voice. "The Lord Crinan does not desire Moray — that is clear. When you were sick, like to die, we feared invasion. We approached Crinan. But he did nothing. He has . . . enough. If Duncan, Prince of Strathclyde, desired Moray, would he not have taken it, when he was here? With the King. Forby, he is gone courting the Northumbrians to wed the Earl Siward's sister, they say. So he is too busy. And his father will not contest your taking of the mortuath, I swear. As for Gartnait of Mar, he has no concern in the matter."

"I see. So, when you thought me dying, you would have handed over the mortuath to Crinan or Duncan, with no thought for Lulach here, the rightful heir!"

"Not so, lord. But . . ." Helplessly Urquhart shook his greying head.

MacBeth decided that it was enough, the lesson sufficient. "So be it," he said. "You all would name me as mormaor? Here, before these many witnesses. Above all others? That is your considered advice? You, Urquhart?"

"Yes."

"You, Cawdor?"

"I do."

"You, Lovat?"

"To be sure, my lord. That I have held, from the first."

"Very well. If the other thanes of the mortuath think as you do. And if my good wife agrees. I shall accept the Mortuath of Moray. Until Lulach shall be of age to hold it himself. Do you agree, my dear?"

Gruoch nodded. "I do. It is best so."

"Good. We shall sound the other thanes. In a progress. All of us." He paused, to let that sink in. "It is understood?"

Only one voice was raised, that of his own Farquhar O'Beolain of Applecross. "And if the King disapproves? Will not confirm?"

"My grandsire may not greatly love me, my friend. But he is a man much concerned with realities. What he cannot alter, he accepts with what grace is in him. This, I think, he will accept — since he can do no other. Lacking traitors in the camp!"

That pause was pregnant.

MacBeth rose, and assisted Gruoch to her feet.

Later, in the spider-hung guest-house, handed over for their exclusive use, Gruoch chid MacBeth gently.

"You can be as hard a man as any, I have learned this day."

"Would you have had me otherwise? It got the matter settled to good effect."

"Oh, yes. To excellent effect! But — so sly, so cunning!" She smiled, however. "When it was to be that Morgund who was the cunning one."

"That one has less wits than he is given the name for, I think. Hugh of Cawdor has more, it seems. Although I would trust neither of them!"

"Yet you so worked it that it was they who gave you the mormaorship! Or seemed to."

"To be sure. It was . . . advisable. So now they are committed. To me. Before many witnesses. And will be more so before we are finished. A man, or a mormaor . . . or a king, must use the tools that come to his hand."

"A king . . . ?" she whispered.

*   *   *

Next day they set off up Glen More with a much enlarged company — for MacBeth insisted that the three thanes accompanied them, with some of their people. Moray was a vast area, the largest mortuath in the land, and it was out of the question to visit even any major portion of it. But certain key districts and thanedoms they could show themselves in, with advantage.

They rode up the north shore of long Loch Ness, Urquhart's own thanedom, this, requiring no attention. But at the far loch-head, at Kilchumin, they entered the territory of the Thane of Lochaber, a highly important individual of mixed loyalties, whose west coast sea-lochs were much at the mercy of raiding Vikings and Islesmen. MacBeth felt that here was a man who would quickly perceive where his best interests lay.

In the morning they moved on up the River Oich to Loch Oich, still in the mighty Glen More, halfway up the side of which they reached Invergarry, where Ewan of Lochaber had his dun. As MacBeth had anticipated, this youngish and somewhat harassed noble was more than happy to accept the Earl Thorfinn's half-brother as lord — since it ought to ensure him relief from the Orkneymen's raids, at least. If he could translate the situation into actual protection by Thorfinn, then many of his problems would be solved. For the Viking presence in the Hebrides and the West Highland coastal regions was as comprehensive as it was terrible — and of all the Viking pirates, jarls and raiders, Thorfinn was the chief. MacBeth was not a little amused, privately, over how much he was using his half-brother's name and reputation as lever in this business — but was in no least doubt that Thorfinn would do exactly the same in similar circumstances.

Turning back north-eastwards they took the south side of Loch Ness, then southwards, climbing now, up into and over the heather moors of Meallmore and down beyond into Strathdearn, they proceeded to the pine-forest country of Badenoch, where the Thane of Rothiemurchus was important.

At length, satisfied, MacBeth turned away due eastwards for the Laigh, the low-lying, fertile plain near the coast, heart of the province and its most populous area. He had little fear for his reception there, where his family's influence was still strong. Moreover Thorfinn's base of Torfness was so situated on the coast thereof as to menace, if need be, most of that rich and pleasant land. It would be a bold thane or chieftain indeed who rejected Thorfinn's brother in the Laigh.

Out of the Highlands of Braemoray they came down to Elgin, the ecclesiastical centre of Moravia, a most holy place supporting no fewer than four cashels and six churches. Here the aged senior bishop, Congal, now almost blind, actually wept on MacBeth's shoulder. He had christened him, after all. There was little need for any demonstration or angling for support here. Only the one more call now, he told Gruoch — Forres. For Nairn, a little further to the west, was Cawdor's town, and could be omitted meantime.

Forres, a dozen miles west of Elgin, near the head of the Laigh was the traditional capital of Moravia, where the great bay of Findhorn came close to the foothills of Braemoray. Here, after the fall of the Pictish monarchy at Inverness, the royal power of the Scots had been established, and a large Pictish fort transformed into a straggling palace of sorts. Here so much had happened in the story of the North that the chroniclers and sennachies for once had not required to invent and romanticise. Here great battles had been fought, great treacheries hatched, evil spells cast, notable feats performed not only in arms but in poetry, piping, racing and athletics, in design and stone — and wood-carving, in painting and sculpture. For here were schools of music and the arts, of dance and mime, of weaponry, even of falconry. Here no fewer than three kings had died evilly — Donald the Second, slain; his son Malcolm the First, slain; *his* son, Duffus murdered, allegedly by witchcraft. Presumably the witches were also responsible for the fact that when this third king's body was hidden under the bridge of Kinloss, the sun did not shine until it was discovered, weeks later. Here Thorfinn's ancestor Earl Rognvald defeated the Mormaor Malbride, and riding into Forres with the dead mormaor's head hanging from his saddle-bow, was scratched by the latter's protruding tusk-like tooth, on the thigh, and died in poisoned agony. Here the present King Malcolm Foiranach had suffered defeat by Sven Forkbeard, Canute's father, and only escaped with his life.

The Thane of Brodie was the local chieftain and distantly

related. But it was important that he should be reliably of MacBeth's persuasion, here at the centre of the mortuath. So MacBeth, Gruoch assisting, made a point of being specially forthcoming, going to the trouble of occupying the dusty and neglected old palace for a couple of days, for appearances' sake, and making much of Brodie. Then, satisfied at last, he sent home all the thanes, chiefs and clerics whom he had collected, including his Ross contingent, with his thanks and general instructions.

Relievedly he turned back, east by north, with only Gruoch, Lulach and a small group of servants.

And now he was a different man entirely, sloughing off the stern, watchful, calculating dynast and reverting to his old self of quiet, contained, self-sufficiency, mild of manner, friendly. He was going to show his new wife his favourite place on the face of the earth and, he hoped, her future home.

*   *   *

Spynie was a strange place to find on a seaboard of cliffs and rocks and lofty sand-dunes, a great loch trapped behind the dunes, shallow, irregularly shaped, four miles long by almost three across, flanked by quite steep little oak- and pine-forested hills on the landward side, and dotted with islands, large and small. Once, long before, some north-easterly storm had blasted a gap in the barrier of dunes, and the sea had got into the Laigh, to flood and fill the hollow pastureland and hillocks behind. For a while it had been an almost landlocked tidal bay, with even fishing-havens, rather like the somewhat similar Findhorn Bay some miles to the west, nearer Forres. Then the sand had gradually reasserted itself, and the dunes had built up again and the bay became a loch. For, during the sea's prevalence, it had eaten back and back, to tap the course of the Duffus or Black Water of Spynie, which now flowed in here instead of debouching on the main coast, replacing salt water by fresh, trapped. So here, in the heart of the fair and fertile Laigh of Moray, called the Garden of Alba, where frosts were little known and summer lasted three weeks longer than anywhere else in Scotland, was a great fresh-water loch, where fish abounded, wildfowl flocked and flighted and deer swam out to graze on the islets. It had been a boyhood paradise for the young MacBeth, and would never lose its grip on him. He had been only fourteen when his father was murdered, and his mother had had to flee with him to Ross. It would probably be true to say that the loss of Spynie had taken longer to heal in the boy's subconscious than had that of his father.

Gruoch was amused but also touched at her husband's eagerness that she should gain the best impression of his beloved Spynie at the first viewing, his almost boyish anxiety that she should like it. And it would have been strange had she not done so. Surmounting the oak-forested Hill of Findrassie, after some miles of woodland, suddenly the loch opened before them, serene, fair, that golden day of early August, the calm water deeply blue, with green islands, yellow sandy bays and inlets, dark rush-beds and white banks of meadow-sweet, all rimmed with forested banks to the south, braes of pasture and tilth to the east, and to north the long barrier of sandhills range upon range. Near the centre of this south side, some three hundred yards out from the shore, was the largest of the islands, artificially enlarged with tree-trunks, stone and soil, so that it was half a crannog, to cover about four acres. On this, amongst orchards and bowers and gardens, rose a long low hall-house similar to that at Rosemarkyn but larger and not cluttered with stables, byres and other domestic offshoots, timber-built but clay-coated and whitewashed. On other islands nearby were the domestic offices — the Hounds' Isle, where the hunting-dogs were kennelled; the Horse Isle, with the stables; the Ice Isle, where food was stored underground in artificial ice-caverns, the ice brought in winter from the Heights of Brae-moray. Further away was St. Ethernan's Isle, where was the church, and the Isle of Spirits where the dead were interred. And away at the western end of the loch was Rose Isle, where there was a Keledei college. All the domestic sites were connected by an elaborate system of stone causeways some two feet below the surface of the water, so that access was not dependent on boats. Over all seemed to hang an air of abiding tranquillity.

Gruoch gazed all but spellbound, in delight — and looking from that prospect to his wife, MacBeth had to swallow his emotion at the sheer beauty of both.

"It is beyond all lovely," she breathed. "A dream of peace, of content. So quiet, so sure. No evil thing ever happened here, I swear!"

"If it did, I never heard of it," he said. "My mother, Donada, called it the *Dorus Neamh*, the Gateway of Heaven. And she had the sight."

She nodded. "The sight, yes. How strange that this should have been the haven of Malcolm the Destroyer's daughter!

Oh, thank you, my love — thank you for bringing us here."

"It is yours from now onwards, my dear. All yours. Come."

They rode down to the shore, telling the servants to wait behind with Lulach — for this was only for themselves. As he urged his garron into the water, he warned her, "Ride close behind, and turn only when I turn. This causeway twists and bends like any serpent. So that none shall gain the island who do not know it. But — the route is not something that *I* shall ever forget, I think."

Picking their zigzag way out to the Hall Isle, MacBeth eyed the house a little anxiously, now that they were coming to close quarters, afraid of dilapidation.

"I should perhaps have sent men to make good any damage, clean all, before I brought you," he said. "Thorfinn keeps watch on it, when he comes to Torfness. She was his mother also . . ."

"No," she assured him. "This is as I would have it. *Our* place. I would cherish it, clean it, with my own hands. This is not for others . . ."

Seen close to, the house had lost some of its clay plaster, swallows nested in the thatching, the orchard and gardens were overgrown. But there was nothing that a little time and energy would not put right. And the interior proved to be dusty, with some bird-droppings, but undamaged. For none were likely to misuse or even enter a house that Thorfinn Raven Feeder watched over.

He carried her in over the threshold in the old tradition, not omitting to kiss her comprehensively in the process.

"This is where we start a new life, Gruoch nic Bodhe mac Kenneth!" he told her.

"Yes, Mormaor of Moray and Ross. And start you by fetching me wood and peats and tinder and flint. I want fires burning on every hearth. And water, much water. And cauldrons and pots and cloths, many cloths."

"Yes, Princess . . ." he said.

*   *   *

Six happy, full and busy weeks they spent in the House of Spynie, or *Dorus Neamh*, setting it, and themselves, in order. They cleared up and refurbished the old house and filled it with satisfactory things, like the scent of cut flowers, dogs and puppies, the aroma of peat-reek and birch logs, and love, love above all, and laughter. Even Lulach, a quiet and reserved child, blossomed out. They had servants to help them, to be sure, especially in the gardens; but the important things they did themselves. MacBeth had to be much away, in Forres and Elgin and elsewhere, naturally, seeing to the affairs of the mortuath — for he was concerned that these should not be allowed to intrude on the peace of Spynie; but he endeavoured to be home each night — save for the one brief visit he paid to Ross and Neil Nathrach at Inverpeffery, for an assize of judgment. He had never known such fulfilment and happiness.

It was not all work and domestic activity. They hunted deer in the forest, hawked for wildfowl and herons in the reeds and marshes, fished in the loch and the sea, explored the cliffs and caves and sand-dune country.

One day MacBeth took Gruoch to the Borg-head of Torfness, which lay only five miles to the west. Indeed, they could just glimpse the tip of its tower from Spynie, at the far end of the sand-dunes. It was remarkable by any standards and an unlikely place to find on that open Moray seaboard and in the same vicinity as Spynie. A great red rock outcrop thrust from the sands here, rising to quite a height and projecting out to sea in the form of a half-mile-long ness or headland, Torfness — actually Thorfinn's Ness, called after Thorfinn Skull Cleaver, a mighty ancestor of the present earl. Here the Jarl Rognvald, first Earl of Orkney — he who had died of tooth-poisoning — had built a borg, and used the ness as a breakwater and haven for his longships, on the site of a Pictish fort and cashel, as a base for terrorising fair Moray, fortifying and garrisoning it strongly. His successors had maintained and extended this menacing outpost of Orkney, so that now there was a small town here, supplied almost wholly by sea, self-sufficient, having no relations with the surrounding country — save for the occasional minor raid — but secure because of the threat of Thorfinn's name and fame. Three longships were always stationed in the harbour. Here Gruoch had fled from the pyre at Inverness.

MacBeth had no difficulty as to entry, of course, and found the captain of the borg, old Gunnar Hound Tooth, gruffly amiable and remarkably well-informed as to what went on in Moray and further afield. He had no word of his master Thorfinn, however, last heard of operating in the Irish Sea. The couple were well entertained, and MacBeth showed his wife the sights of the place, the beacon-light which was the key to a whole chain to rouse the entire coast; the ramparts of the old fort, now incorporated in the borg's defences; and, best of all, the extraordinary underground baptistry cavern and well-chamber, with a magnificent pool, ten feet square and four feet deep cut in the living rock, fed by an ice-cold spring, in which crystal font the Keledei had immersed their early Pictish converts. The famed Pictish bull carvings, too, were unique, their meanings now lost.

It was almost six weeks to the day from their arrival at Spynie, in late September, that their idyll at the *Dorus Neamh* was shattered — although that is perhaps an unkind way to describe the arrival of a brother. But when the Earl Thorfinn appeared on any scene, peace, quiet, tranquillity, fled. Especially when, as on this occasion, he had brought lively company — and not just Thorkell Fosterer and his usual uncouth crew.

He arrived quite unheralded and unexpectedly that quiet September evening, in a riot of noise and laughter, of bulls' horn wailings and bellowings, the cruder and more boisterous for having a woman with him. He yelled his greeting as he came splashing hugely across the causeway, roaring joyously when one of his Vikings fell in, not following the zigzags with sufficient care. He made no attempt to ensure that the lady immediately behind him did not do likewise.

"Come you, come you, MacBeth mac Louse!" he cried, to his half-brother who stood on the island shore watching. "You have married a wife, I hear. Come, meet mine! A plague on you, man — must you stand there? Fearing to wet your feet! Come meet your good-sister, Mormaor of Moray-land. Where have you hidden that Black Gruoch?"

MacBeth stayed where he was, wordless, astonished. Thorfinn married would be something for the sennachies and saga-mongers to rhapsodise over.

She was a big blonde woman, tall, large-breasted, splendidly made, with long plaited yellow hair, round laughing features and notably blue eyes, comely rather than beautiful — and strong-thighed and calved, for she had her skirts kilted high, although her splashing was soaking her just the same. The Vikings who came behind were loud and basic in their praise, comment and advice.

Thorfinn climbed out on to dry land and shook himself like a dog, before coming on to grasp and pummel his brother — without troubling to turn and assist the lady.

"Son of Life — at his most lively!" he exclaimed. "Are you a man again? After your sickness? Smile, man — laugh! At the sight of this great heifer of a woman! And Thorfinn Sigurdson wedded! Look at her — Ingebiorg Finn'sdotter, from Zetland. Where they mate with whales! Is she not an armful?"

MacBeth pushed past him, to meet the flushed, breathless, soaked but entirely cheerful young woman. "Lady — welcome to my house, to Spynie, to Moray, to my family. You are very fair — wasted, I think, on this bear, Thorfinn. But here, at least, you will find us better!"

"Devil roast you — who has been teaching you that sort of talk?" Thorfinn growled. "That Gruoch? Perhaps I should never have brought her to you! Or taken her myself. Then this one would not be so pleased with herself!"

"Lord MacBeth," the young woman panted. "I have heard much of you. And nothing ill. Although this Orkney bull bellows ill of all others! How did the same mother bear you both?"

"She was mild and gentle, lady — like my own self! I think that the Earl Sigurd the Stout must have been a terrible man."

"So! That will be it. Perhaps when he breeds on *me*, Orkney will do better?"

MacBeth smiled. Clearly this woman would be able to look after herself.

Thorkell Fosterer came up. "What think you, MacBeth, of the Countess Inge?" he demanded. "*I* chose her for him. Not many would have had him, you see. But I did my best . . .!"

Gruoch arrived, a basket of fruit on her arm. The contrast with the other young woman was remarkable, dramatic. They sized each other, amidst the comments and witticisms of the Vikings — but it was noticeable that these were a deal less outspoken and scurrilous towards Gruoch, a little wary even.

The two women, after a moment or two, embraced, seeming to accept each other. The earl might almost have shown traces of relief.

They trooped into the hall-house for refreshment.

They had to hear, of course, a quite unbelievable version of how Thorfinn had won the hand of Ingebiorg, daughter of Finn Arnison of Zetland, a Norse noble and formerly of Galloway. What had made him fall at last into the trap and trammels of matrimony, he admitted that he did not know — he must have been drunk, presumably. It was indeed really Thorkell's fault — which he would not forget! But soon he would have her whipped into shape. Although she was shapely in a lumpish fashion already, was she not?

Ingebiorg hooted laughter.

It was the quite irrepressible Thorkell Fosterer who broached the subject of Moray. "We heard that the great MacBeth had won over the whole of Morayland by smooth words and cunning talk. Not a sword drawn, not an axe raised! Is this truth? Or some dastard's tale!"

"How think you, Pirate?" his host answered. "Is only bloodshed how you measure success?"

"Success will call for more than words, I say. You may have *got* Moray so, but to hold it you will need swords!"

"Perhaps. And am I not the fortunate one, then, in having Thorfinn Raven Feeder and his sworders to help me hold it? I made great use of that fact in my much talking."

"Ha!" Thorfinn said.

"Yes. Words, used heedfully, can effect as much as swords, on occasion. Even silence may work wonders. As *you* proved, off Culross in the Scots Sea. When you drew no sword, raised no axe. Yet caused both Malcolm and Canute to think again." He had not seen his brother since then.

"The swords were there. To be used if required," Thorfinn pointed out.

"To be sure. And *I* had Neil Nathrach and 2000 men waiting behind the Glass River, when I went into Moray. Had they been required."

"You took a chance, man. You could have been set on and slain long before your Viper could have reached you. *I* risked nothing."

"Save offending both kings."

"For kings I care that!" Thorfinn snapped his fingers. "Great and small, they suffer from the same disease — self-importance."

"Unlike earls and mormaors!" the Countess of Orkney commented.

Gruoch smiled, and replenished drinking-horns.

"Why are you here?" MacBeth asked.

"Why but to come see my new good-sister. And let Ingebiorg meet the Scots."

"You did not come all the way south to Moray for that, Brother."

"Also I wanted to find out what you had been doing here in Moray. And what were your plans."

"Plans? What plans should I have? Save to rule my two mortuaths in peace. And . . . and cherish my wife."

"Tcha! See you, man — you now control Moray and Ross. With Lochaber. *I* control Sutherland, Caithness, Orkney and most of the Hebrides. Dalar and Argyll are more like to heed you and me than, say, Malcolm Foiranach. Finn Arnison, in Zetland, and kin in Galloway, is now my goodsire. See you what this means? *We* rule all the North, not Malcolm. Once there were two kingdoms. Of the Northern and Southern Cruithne, or Picts. There could be again."

"Who is scorning self-important kings now!"

"I care nothing for kings. But kingdoms are different. A Northern kingdom. Do you not see it?"

"I see trouble in that kind of thinking, Brother. I say forget it." MacBeth looked over at his wife.

She changed the subject, easily. "Tomorrow you men should go hunting. We shall require a full larder to feed so many large Vikings. Ingebiorg and I shall talk women's talk."

"And from all such preserve us!" Thorfinn prayed.

"Yes. We shall hunt the woods of Findrassie and Ardgilzean," MacBeth agreed. "And see what you Orkneymen can do lacking a hatchet . . .!"

6

AUTUMN WAS TURNING to winter and the mountains which rimmed the Laigh on all but the seaward side, near and far, were already white with the first snows, above the deep brown of the faded heather. Thorfinn, his bride and his Vikings, had long since sailed back to Brough in the Orkneys, to feast and drink and sing and procreate and sleep the winter away. So far there had been no really hard weather in this favoured Garden of Alba, although elsewhere there had been snow and ice. Life at Spynie was pleasantly full, with the last of the honey-running, fruit-preserving, fish-smoking and the like filling the shortening days. This, when the news reached them — Malcolm the Destroyer was dead. Slain, by treachery, at Glamis, it was said.

At first none could quite believe it. The old King had been a dark shadow, yet also a shield, over the land for so long, reigning for thirty-one years, no less. It was almost inconceivable that the shadow and the shield should be no more. Although a new shadow was there to take its place — but no shield.

If the news, which came via the Keledei at Rose Isle — who seemed to have their own sources of information, like all churchmen — was received with incredulity, it was not long in being confirmed. A royal messenger arrived at Forres and was sent on to Spynie, from Duncan mac Crinan. Malcolm mac Kenneth was dead, and the Mormaor MacBeth mac Finlay was requested to attend the obsequies at the Abbey of Colum-cille at Iona on the Ides of December.

This was normal practice — although December was a bad month to get corpse and mourners to a Hebridean island. But the body would scarcely keep until spring. All the Kings of Scots were taken on this last journey to the most sacred spot in the kingdom, in many kingdoms, for burial; and it was traditional that the Ard Righ should be accompanied by his lesser kings, the mormaors. Only thereafter would the new King be proclaimed, and taken back for enthronement on the Stone of Destiny at Scone.

MacBeth, then, was part-prepared for the summons; and although Gruoch was uneasy and full of warnings, there was no question but that he must go. This was the first major parting from Gruoch since their wedding, and a sore business. She was pregnant.

With the Thanes of Brodie and Darnaway — Cawdor claiming indisposition — he rode off westwards two days later, all wrapped tightly in their plaids against the chill December rain, which would be snow on the high ground. And they had much high ground to cover, however carefully they picked their route, across wide Drumalbyn, the lofty and fierce roof of Scotland. They had five days to reach Iona, and in these conditions it would take them all of that.

It took them five days exactly to reach, not Iona but Nether Lorn, and the rendezvous for the funeral crossing. There was a recognised procedure and itinerary for these royal progresses. The dead monarch was always brought to Kilninver, at the foot of the Braes of Lorn near the mouth of Loch Feochan, to commence the seaward passage to the Isle of Mull. Often there was a considerable wait here, for suitable weather conditions on a notoriously storm-prone seaboard, and a chapel had been built on a green hillock, where the mummified corpse might lie, watched over by relays of mormaors and thanes, until the voyage could be started. The hillock was known as *Carraig nan Marbh*, the Rock of the Dead.

MacBeth and his little party arrived at Kilninver in the early dusk of the 13th, or Ides of December, to find the cortege already there, with quite a large number of men encamped in what shelter they could find, against a blustery, north-westerly half-gale, lords in a barn and the coffin in the chapel. Searching around, MacBeth quickly came to the conclusion that the weather had delayed more than himself, for he could perceive very few of the faces he expected to see. At length he found the Thane of Glamis huddled over one of the many fires.

"So MacBeth at least has come!" that tough campaigner commented, mouth full. "I feared that you would be like the rest."

"Many will be delayed. Snow and flooding. It is ill weather for travel!"

"Oh, yes. Indeed, yes. So — many do not travel! What more simple? But it is ill done. *He* would not have done it, for all his sins!" And he jerked his grizzled head towards the chapel.

"You mean . . . ?"

"I mean that it is not delay, my lord. Snow and flood and ill travel. They are not coming, that is all. Lennox is the only mormaor here — save for yourself."

MacBeth stared at him. "But — Duncan? His father? MacDuff? Mar? Angus? The others?"

"They bide at home!"

"God's Grace! Duncan — his favoured one! He sent *me* word to come . . .!"

"No doubt. That is the style of him! You should know him by now." Glamis recollected. "Yourself, my lord — you are well recovered? Of your sickness."

"Yes. But this, this is beyond belief! Not to come to the King's entombment. Did he tell you why — Duncan?"

"No. He came to Glamis. Saw the King dead — the body. Told me to have the corpse embalmed and coffined. Then to escort it to Iona. Lennox would come. He mislikes Lennox. Then he left, without saying more. After but an hour or so."

MacBeth shook his head. "How did the King die?" he asked.

"Well may you say it! He died at my dun. Suddenly and strangely. He came to Glamis in the evening. From Kincardine in the Mearns. With a small company. Within the hour he was rolling on my floor. In direst pain. Two hours more and he was dead. That was Saint Katherine's Day."

"Dear God! The, the same as . . .!" He paused. "You think — poison?"

"What else? An old man, he could not fight it. Like some!"

87

"Who . . . ?"

"In the stir, four men who had come with him rode off. From Glamis. Nameless men that I knew not. When I heard of it, I sent after them. Fast. But my men did not catch them. Seeing that they were pursued, they thought to take the shortest, most level, route. They were strangers, to be sure, to Angus. They did not know that Forfar Loch was there. Frozen over, with a covering of snow. They rode hard across — until the ice cracked! We shall never know who they were, I think. Forfar Loch is deep, deep!"

For a little there was silence between them. Then MacBeth said, "You said that Duncan came, thereafter. From where?"

"From Kincardine, also. Next Day. From Malcolm's summer palace."

"And these men, who failed to cross Forfar Loch — they could have been heading back to Kincardine?"

"I think it likely."

They exchanged glances.

"I should go see him. My grandsire," MacBeth said heavily. "Where is Lennox?"

"I will take you . . ."

That night MacBeth took his turn at the vigil beside the King's bier in the little draughty chapel, a chilly, eerie business, with the wind howling and whistling and the single lamp flickering and casting weird shadows. One noble must always stand at the head, and a common soldier at the foot, while a priest muttered endless prayers at the altar. Because so few nobles were present, MacBeth had to stand three hours before handing over to Brodie. The King, although he might have died in agony, showed no signs of this on his carven features. He looked, indeed, almost nobly sardonic, as though the final victory, amusingly, was with him, the wavering lamplight seeming to give life to his expression. He had been an evil man, an object of terror for most of his long reign. Yet he had been a strong king, and his realm had known that it could rely on him to protect it from all but himself. Standing looking down at the dread face, his mother's father, MacBeth was aware of much trouble in his mind, confusion of spirit. What was the meaning of it all? What of all the untimely deaths this man had caused? In order that a treacherous weakling should inherit his throne — Duncan, who had not even troubled to come to his interment. What of all those who had paid the price of this folly? And yet, Malcolm Foiranach had been no fool. What had driven him on? In his twisted way he must have loved Scotland. What of his Scotland now . . .?

The following day the wind still blew strongly, and the boatmen would not hear of risking the passage to Mull. Although it was only seven miles, the Firth of Lorn, which they had to cross, was a most dangerous water.

The Thane of Lochaber, whom MacBeth had sent to summon on his way over, arrived just before noon, in a rain-squall, with sleet behind it.

An hour or so later there was a great outcry and much pointing. Sweeping round the southern headland into Loch Feochan came five low, lean longships, sails furled on account of the gale, oars flailing in clouds of spray. The breathless chanting of their serried rowers came fitfully on the gusting wind.

All were agog at the sight, and in such weather, speculation mixed with alarm. Who travelled the most dangerous seas in the world in winter storm, and why?

The leading vessel drove in to the anchorage and ran its fierce dragon-head prow up on to the weed-strewn strand, men with ropes leaping down into the white-capped breakers of the shallows, cold or none. The craft's great square sail was momentarily unfurled, long enough to display the black spread-winged raven device of Orkney.

"I thought so," MacBeth observed, amidst the exclamation, and went downhill to greet his brother.

They met on the beach, Thorfinn all dripping bearskins and salt-tarnished armour.

"What brought *you* here — to bury the man you so hated?" his brother asked. "You would never come to him while he lived!"

"I am a Mormaor of Scotland, as are you — when it suits me! You would not have me to fail in my duty? Besides, what happens after the burying will signify the more."

"You will find that others have failed in their duty, then! Too many."

"You say so? Who?"

"Duncan, for one."

"Duncan? That rat is not here?"

"No. Nor others . . ."

Lennox and Glamis came down, somewhat doubtfully.

"Who are these?" Thorfinn demanded, at his most arrogant.

"Aluin mac Gillachrist, Mormaor of Lennox. And Cormac mac Eochaid, Thane of Glamis."

"Ha —Glamis! Where Malcolm died? Did you slay the old devil, then? Not before time!"

"I did not, my lord earl. But someone did. Evilly."

"Who? Think you he deserves the thanks of us all?"

None answered that, Lennox coughing uncomfortably. "You have come a long way to attend the King's burial nevertheless, my lord," he said.

"So I have, man — so I have. Further than any here, I swear. But then — is it not a cause for celebration? It is not every day that we get rid of such as my grandsire! No?" Undoubtedly he knew that he was embarrassing them, but cared nothing. "But — you said burial. I thought that it was to be at Iona? Or have you put down roots here?"

"The weather, my lord. We are delayed . . ."

"Weather?" the other demanded. "What is that? What are you? Lily-maids, afraid of a puff of wind? I went to Iona, and found that you had not come. They told me that you would be here, or at Loch Spelve in Mull. So I came to fetch you."

Lennox, a quiet man, swallowed. "You have *come* from Iona? In this, this storm?"

"This is no storm, man, A breeze! How many are you?"

"Over one hundred. The boatmen said that they dared not chance the passage. In this . . ."

"Boatmen! Are you Scots lords, or mice! To wait on the pleasure of idle boatmen! See you — get your people down here and into my longships. And fetch the body. I will have you in Iona by dark. If you make haste."

No excuses were accepted, of course, and despite manifest reluctance the embarkation commenced. The royal corpse was brought down with more haste than ceremony and lashed down on the stern platform of Thorfinn's own ship — received with less reverence by the crew than some thought suitable. Most of the funeral party however were so concerned about their forthcoming voyage as to fail to notice such minor details.

Thorfinn, now very much in charge, allowed no wastage of time — he had thirty-five sea miles to go before dark, and was shouting to cast off almost before the last of his passengers were aboard.

Thorfinn's shipmaster, Biorn Bow Legs, was a massive, shaven-headed gorilla of a man who appeared to manage his craft with a drawn sword, which he wielded mainly to beat time on a great bronze gong beside the steering-oar. This clanging beat seemed almost to be the motive power of the ship, the timing by which the oarsmen drove their long sweeps, and to which they and the reserve crew sang and gasped their curious chant as they rowed, a fierce stirring refrain, endlessly repeated. Despite the cold, the oarsmen threw off their skin jerkins, to row half-naked.

It was choppy enough even in these sheltered waters; but once they cleared the twin headlands into the open firth, the half-gale hit them like hammer-blows and the waves reared high in hissing menace, the surface all but completely white with spume. Immediately the long low vessels began to toss and twist like live things in a see-sawing motion of major and dizzy proportions — but strangely enough to roll but little. The passengers, clustered together in pretty general misery however, clinging to each other for support in their shivering — for they were all soaked to the skin in moments — little perceived the advantage of this.

The normal procedure for a royal funeral was to sail across the seven miles of the Firth of Lorn from Kilninver to Port nan Marbh, the Haven of the Dead, on the Loch of Spelve on Mull, and thereafter to resume the land journey for some thirty miles, crossing that large island and down its long peninsula of the Ross to Fionnphort, where another ferry took them over the mile-wide Sound of Iona. But Thorfinn rowed directly for Iona, using the long, cliff-girt southern coast of Mull as shield and breakwater.

So they kept as close inshore as the reefs and skerries of that savage coast would allow, thrusting their way through the boiling seas in a fury of spindrift, some of it, alarmingly, now coming from the rocks and even cliff-foots, where the great seas smashed themselves into soaring towers of spray.

Something over two hours of this, and with the light beginning to fail, they reached the end of the Ross of Mull's shelter — if so it could be called — and had to turn northwards round the Isle of Erraid and its multitude of outliers towards the narrow Sound of Iona. For the space of some three hectic miles they were wholly unprotected from the full force of wind and ocean, and the seas they had encountered hitherto were of minor size and virulence, the gale screaming. Fortunately they were now heading directly north-west into it, which made the business less dire for the oarsmen. Biorn Bow Legs banged his gong the harder, the chanting jerked and panted, Thorfinn roared great laughter and the passengers clutched each other, groaned, spewed and suffered.

91

This last was only a short ordeal, however, and quickly they were into the quieter waters of the Sound. Through the mists of spume they could see the scattered buildings of the Abbey of Columcille, the most sacred site in all Scotland.

The Abbot Malmore mac mhic Baithan, Co-Arb of the Celtic Church and titular Superior of the Abbey of Kells in Ireland, seventy-seventh in descent from Columba himself, a cheerful and vigorous old man with no fewer than five bishops, greeted the newcomers kindly and herded them off to guest-houses, peat-fires and cauldrons of hot water, with plaids to warm them while their clothes dried. Also ample food and drink. Abbot Malmore seemed to be on particularly good terms with Thorfinn — which was strange, considering that the Vikings for centuries had been the plague, almost the end, of the Abbey and monks. Nine times the Norsemen had sacked and burned it. But apparently the earl and the abbot had come to some sort of satisfactory arrangement — although the former was scarcely a religious man. Indeed now Thorfinn was obviously looked upon as in charge of the funeral arrangements and all else, rather than Lennox, Glamis or MacBeth.

The Abbey was a far-flung establishment within a broken rampart of turf, which covered many acres, consisting of innumerable small buildings, some disused and ruinous, no less than seven of which were in fact churches. None of these were large, and the holiest almost the smallest, actually Saint Columba's own cell on the summit of a small eminence called Tor Abb. The sleeping-huts of the brethren or "family" of Iona, some eighty in number, were dotted about haphazard, amongst a great scatter of variously-carved saints' crosses. There was a tall, circular outlook-tower on another rocky eminence, a mill, kiln, barns, cowhouse, guest-houses and the like. All around, where the island soil permitted, were patches of tilth, and sheep and cattle wandered at large. Blown sand from the innumerable cockle-shell white sand bays, mixed with spindrift, filled the air.

It was outside the Tor Abb church next morning, with the wind happily much abated, that Malmore and his bishops held the burial-service for Malcolm the Destroyer. Considering how many hundreds of difficult miles the body had been brought for this, it was a very simple ceremony. But the Celtic Church did not go in for elaborate services any more than elaborate doctrine. Christ's teaching was considered to be sufficient for ordinary men, even kings. There was no sermon, no oratory, no resounding list of the dead monarch's achievements — as well, perhaps; the only item to take up time was the lengthy recital, by the chief sennachie, of the late King's genealogy, on the Scots side seventeen generations to Fergus Mor mac Earc and before that through unnumbered Irish kings to the semi-legendary Fir Bolg royal line, to the Horseman of the Heavens, Eochaid, and the goddess-spirit of the Lightning, Bolg herself; on the Pictish side it went even further, through half-a-dozen Brudes and Nechtans and other practically unpronounceable and almost certainly mythical ancestors. Lesser men shivered and stamped their feet, while Vikings drifted off with unflattering comments. This over at last, Malcolm mac Kenneth mac Malcolm mac Domnell et cetera, was bundled into the cavity awaiting him in the Relig Oran, the crypt where Oran, last of the Druids and first of Columba's converts lay, along with forty-six or so of Malcolm's just enumerated ancestors, and his heavy grave-slab lowered upon him. Then all returned, without delay, to the Abbey eating-hall, where such feast as was available on the island awaited them.

The meeting of mormaors to confirm and appoint the next king should then have been held. But with only three present this was ruled out — although Thorfinn made not so much a speech as a statement that, since Duncan mac Crinan was incompetent and a known poisoner, and he himself had no interest in becoming King, therefore Malcolm's remaining grandson MacBeth mac Finlay was the obvious and only choice for the throne — to the embarrassment of MacBeth but the cheers of most of those present, notably from Glamis and Lennox.

All this having taken up no great time, by noon Thorfinn was fretting to be off. Abbot Malmore had envisaged a much longer stay and made suggestions as to activities — although there was not a great deal to do on so small an island in winter save eat, drink and pray. But the earl declared that he and his were for off. He was prepared to take the other mourners back to their horses at Kilninver if so they desired. If not, they could find their own way. With the sea much moderated, none thought to refuse this offer, and hasty leave-taking ensued. It must have been the most abbreviated royal interment Iona had ever experienced.

Although it was a cold and far from pleasant voyage, there was no comparison with the outward journey. With the sails available to assist the oarsmen, they were back to Loch Feochan in two hours, with still sufficient light left for most of the company to make a start on their homeward roads. The Vikings barely allowed time for orderly disembarkation before they were off again, northwards up the Firth of Lorn, with 250 miles to go.

Thorfinn's farewell to his brother had been eloquent. "We will meet again, Son of Life, shortly, at Scone. And see who will sit on the *Lia Faill*, the Stone of Destiny, next!"

Watching the gong-clanging longships drive out to sea again, Cormac of Glamis summed up the general reaction. "There goes a man that I would sooner have my friend than my enemy!" he growled. "The pity that Malcolm loved the wrong daughter!"

As so often, MacBeth said nothing.

Frost made the journey home to Moray less of an ordeal than the wind and rain, and MacBeth was back at Spynie in time for Yule. Gruoch, after the first joyous reception, greeted him with significant news indeed — again via the Keledei at Rose Isle.

"My dear," she said, "Duncan has deceived and wronged you once more. He held his Council of Mormaors at Scone, whilst you were at Iona. And was appointed and enthroned King of Scots, on the Stone, the next day, MacDuff placing the crown on his head."

He looked away and away. "So-o-o!" he said at length. "I should have guessed. That is Duncan, yes. It was all a ruse. How does one deal with such a man? Ah, well — it settles that problem, at least!"

"That crown should have been yours, my heart."

"Scarcely that. Duncan is son of the elder sister. *Could* have been mine, shall we say? Had I desired it."

"*Should* have been," she insisted. "Through me, your wife. I had more right to it than had Malcolm. Certainly more than Duncan. And through me, Lulach. While he is a child, you, my husband, should have the rule. And I should be Queen. Not Queen Consort, but Queen!"

He looked at her searchingly. "And did you want that, my dear?"

She flung herself into his arms. "God knows!" she sobbed. "God knows — for I do not! But, but . . . that is what should have been. For you. To think of that Duncan, King! Yes — I wish it! I wish it!" She gulped. "Your dream. Do not forget your dream. They said — I see the Mormaor of Moray. I see the King!"

Troubled he smoothed her dark hair. "It *was* but a dream, lass. And we are happy here, are we not? Happier, I swear, than on any throne."

94

"Perhaps. Yes — we are. But . . . can we deny our blood, our destiny?"

He did not answer.

"You will accept it, then? Accept this wickedness? Do nothing?"

"What *could* I do? Even if I desired it? It is too late. He *is* the King now, crowned and seated on the Stone of Destiny. Nothing can change that. The thing is done."

"Thorfinn would say otherwise, I think."

"Should you have wed Thorfinn then, after all?"

"No! Oh no, my dear, my love, heart of my heart. Never that . . .!"

"Then hush you, woman. And forget Duncan the King. And Thorfinn the Earl. And all others who would come between us. You have MacBeth mac Finlay, for better or worse. And I have Gruoch nic Bodhe. And I, for one, am content . . ."

7

FORGETTING DUNCAN, OR for that matter Thorfinn, was comparatively easy in Moray for the rest of that winter, and life at Spynie was little spoiled by the dynastic situation — especially as Gruoch's pregnancy progressed and more domestic preoccupations prevailed.

But if either of them had imagined that Duncan's shadow could ever pass them by, placed as they were, they were destined for disappointment. Word, and ever more ominous word, of the new King's activities grew with the year. The first was innocuous enough, namely that he had married the lady he had gone to Northumbria to woo in the autumn, the Lady Sybil, sister of the Earl Siward of Deira. Siward was a Dane, indeed nephew of the late King of Denmark and cousin of Canute; and governed Northumbria for Canute, although there was a Saxon Earl Eadulf thereof, who seemed to lie fairly low, advisedly. On the face of it, therefore, Duncan's marriage was unexceptionable and might even be wise and advantageous — after all, Malcolm had presumably approved the match. But scarcely were the nuptials over than Duncan announced a claim to overlordship of Northumbria; this on the flimsy grounds that after the Battle of Carham nineteen years before, when Lothian was ceded to Scotland in total, the overlordship of Northumbria itself was included in the settlement. If Malcolm, the victor of Carham, had himself ever so asserted, he had never been so rash as to seek to do anything to enforce it. Nor had he sought to bring it forward in his negotiations with Canute. Now Duncan was demanding what his warrior grand-sire had not dared to do. Rumour had it that Canute was sick with jaundice; and it was conceivable that Duncan was relying on the fact, and had struck some bargain with the Earl Siward on marrying his sister. But by any standards the thing was folly, playing with fire.

A further and possibly greater folly followed. The King sent a demand to Thorfinn for tribute and tax to be paid to him forthwith for the mortuaths of Caithness and Sutherland — or so old Gunnar Hound Tooth at Torfness reported. He did not report on the earl's reaction — but that was scarcely necessary.

At this stage Gruoch was delivered of a fine boy, and for the time being, at least at Spynie, the follies of princes receded somewhat from consideration. They christened the child Farquhar, amidst great rejoicings.

Six weeks later a courier arrived from Orkney, via Torfness. The Countess Ingebiorg had also produced a son, to be named Paul. Thorfinn's message added that undoubtedly the prodigy would go down in saga as Paul the Bellower. He made no reference to Duncan or his demands.

It was Saint Moluag's Day when the new King's first actual communication with MacBeth arrived at Spynie, by the hand — or, rather, the mouth, since it was no letter — of the young Thane of Stormounth. It was a command for the Mormaor of Moray and Ross, in company with the Earl Thorfinn of Caith-ness and Sutherland, to proceed with all expedition and fullest force against the rebel MacDowall, Lord of Galloway, presently troubling the King's provinces of Dalar and Argyll and the western seaboard, and to take whatever steps were necessary against him, for the realm's good.

To say that MacBeth was surprised would be an under-statement. He looked at Stormounth unbelievingly. "But . . . this is crazy!" he cried. "Does he know what he is asking? He wants me to go to war, on his behalf. After, after all that he has done!"

"On the realm's behalf, my lord. MacDowall is a rebel and

man of blood. He sides with the Northumbrians against Strathclyde and Cumbria."

"Perhaps. But that is not my concern."

"It is a royal command."

"One which I cannot obey. This is a matter for sea attack. Ships. I have no fleet of warships to carry a host . . ."

"The Earl Thorfinn has."

"And think you that Thorfinn will fight Duncan's wars for him?"

"He has been sent command to do so."

"Saints save us — Duncan mac Crinan has run mad! If he is so anxious to do battle, let him do it himself. Tell him so, from me . . ."

"He is to do so, my lord mormaor. He intends to invade Northumbria. That is why you are to engage MacDowall. So that he cannot come to the aid of the Northumbrians."

"Attack Northumbria! Has he taken leave of his wits entirely? War with Canute!"

"Canute is sick. A failing man. And Siward will make only a show of fighting. When Earl Eadulf of Northumbria is defeated, Siward will assume the earldom under King Duncan. As well as his own York, or Deira. And when Canute, his cousin, dies, he will be in a strong position to take the English throne, in place of Canute's weak sons. It is all well planned."

MacBeth was speechless.

"So Cumbria and Strathclyde, on the west, must be made secure. And MacDowall of Galloway is the greatest danger. The King has made his young son Malcolm, Prince of Strathclyde, for the folk to rally to. You are to attack in his name . . ."

"God in His Heaven — did I hear you aright? You say that he has made the boy Malcolm, Prince of Strathclyde? His *bastard!* He of the big head — Canmore?"

"Yes. He much loves the lad . . ."

"But — loves or not is nothing to the point, man! The child is a bastard, born out of wedlock. And Prince of Strathclyde is the title and position of the heir to the throne! Is Duncan planning to make this Malcolm, the Forteviot miller's daughter's son, tanist? Heir to Scotland! A fine tribute to pay to his new Queen! To prefer his bastard to any child she may bear him!"

The young Thane shrugged. "He is the King . . ."

MacBeth sent Stormounth away with a non-committal reply to Duncan, intending no action. Then, two weeks later a messenger arrived from Thorfinn saying that he would be coming with his fleet to Torfness in ten days time to pick up MacBeth's force against MacDowall. That was all; no comments or questions, just the bald statement. And as big a surprise as Duncan's own command.

MacBeth, in a quandary, gave reluctant orders for a small force to be readied, and waited.

When Thorfinn arrived at Torfness, two days early, it was in major strength, with some score of longships and almost 3000 men. He came to Spynie in high spirits. MacBeth was at Elgin, on business of the mortuath, and when he returned home it was to find the Vikings in noisy possession. Thorfinn had brought Ingebiorg and the baby, to keep company with Gruoch while their men went campaigning. An infant under each arm, he shouted greeting from the causeway-head. Where were the forces of Moray and Ross?

His brother, who was not much of a shouter, reserved his reply. But he had his own charges to make, when presently Thorfinn had got rid of the babies.

"I scarce expected *you* to obey Duncan's command!" he said. "You who scorn kings."

"Ha — but there are commands and commands, brother. This one I rejoice to obey."

"Did you send Duncan his tribute, then?"

His brother hooted.

"Why this, then?"

"Why? Because I mislike MacDowall. I have many bones to pick with him. Also I find Galloway to my taste, and have long thought of making a try for it. A fair province, wasted on such as MacDowall. Thought of it the more since I wed Ingebiorg. Indeed — do not tell her — but that was one of her attractions!"

"Ingebiorg? Why?"

"Did you not know? Her father, the Earl Finn Arnison, married a sister of Kenneth, Lord of Galloway, whose son Malcolm this MacDowall slew and took his lordship. There is a cousin, Sven — or Suibhne, as they call it there — in Galloway still. I have been considering how best to bring MacDowall down and take Galloway. Now your Duncan orders me to do just that, by royal command. Shall I disobey the King of Scots?"

"I see. I did not know of this. But — MacDowall is strong."

"I am stronger."

"Then you do not require my help to bring him down."

"That is true. But it might serve you none so ill to come in with me. Duncan's messenger said that you also were commanded to this. It will be his first call upon you? As King. A pity to fail him! When you also could gain by it."

"What should I gain in this, man?"

"Much. I want Galloway. And an end to MacDowall's raiding in my Hebrides. But there is much else that he has stolen and held — the isles of Arran and Bute. And the Cumbraes. Taken from Strathclyde — Duncan's own now. These could be yours."

"I do not need them. On the other side of Scotland."

"Never refuse the chance of good land. If you do not need it, you can always use it as bargain for something you do want." Thorfinn paused. "Forby, I say that it is time that you showed that you can use a sword, Brother. *I* know that you can. But many do not. For too long you have stayed at home. Not gone warring, hosting. Cherished Ross and now Moray, like any father. You won Moray with words. I have nothing against words, see you — but most men pay less heed to them than to swords. If you wish to hold your mortuaths in peace, as Thorkell told you one time, then wield the sword now and again. A simple rule!"

MacBeth remained doubtful.

Strangely enough, Gruoch agreed with Thorfinn for once. She was not a hating woman, but she hated Duncan. She saw this adventure as a means to beat Duncan at his own game. Seem to obey his command, she said, and in doing so, establish a presence on his flank, in his own Strathclyde indeed, with Thorfinn. It would be an ever-present threat to Duncan's peace of mind thereafter. Make him rue the day when he had made his bastard Prince of Strathclyde.

It was this more than anything which weighed with MacBeth. He had been grievously offended by this appointment of the child Malcolm Big-Head to the position traditionally reserved for the heir apparent of Scotland. Whoever should be King after Duncan, it should not be a bastard. The Celtic system of tanistry enjoined that the most suitable and able close member of the royal house should be tanist or heir. Meantime, that was himself, undoubtedly; and later, Lulach. But even if this was denied, Duncan could yet have sons by his new Queen Sybil. To make his bastard Prince of Strathclyde was insufferable. He must be made to realise it. The thing was accepted. MacBeth, with two thanes and 400 men, would join the Orkney expedition.

99

For the life of him MacBeth could not feel other than a holiday atmosphere to prevail, rather than any warlike passion, as the fleet drove its way northwards up the Sutherland and Caithness coasts in the late July sunshine. On the dragon flagship at least high spirits obtained — perhaps they always did when there was any prospect of fighting ahead — Thorfinn in great fettle. He seemed to see it all as expressly designed for his delight and advantage. And he was clearly and sincerely rejoiced at having his half-brother with him on a venture, something that had not happened for a long time. Thorfinn Raven Feeder, the happy Viking.

The passage of the dreaded Pentland Firth, or Pictish Sea, between Scotland and Orkney, was comparatively smooth for so ominous a water, where the great Western Ocean met the North Sea in a confined strait. The wind was directly in their faces here, and always strong, so that it was oar-work all the way. But once, after seventy miles of it, they turned southwards again into the coloured Sea of the Hebrides, it was all plane-sailing, with the oars little required and the most lovely prospects known to man for their delectation, an endless panorama of islands and skerries, white cockle-shell sands, soaring hills and cliffs, many-hued seaweed strands and waters the clarity of which had to be seen to be credited.

Throughout almost 150 miles of the Nordreys, the carefree atmosphere maintained. Then, passing the great thrusting promontory of Ardnamurchan, they entered the Sudreys area, and a change came over the Norsemen. They remained as cheerful as ever, but now they were keenly on the alert, watchful, anticipating. MacDowall seldom ventured so far from Galloway as the Nordreys, but the Sudreys were a favoured summer stamping-ground — when he was not raiding Man or the Irish or Cumbrian coasts.

Thorfinn headed now for Coll, a long, narrow island, fifteen miles by three, where his uncle and lieutenant for the Hebrides, the Earl Gillaciaran, had his headquarters. Thorfinn had no especial right to the Hebrides, of course, other than conquest, like his fathers before him; but that was as good a right as any, so long as he could hold them. Gillaciaran was Celtic, as his name implied, with a Norse wife, Thorfinn's aunt, and the true lord of the islands. But he was well content to act deputy, rather than to oppose the mighty Thorfinn.

He was a stout man of middle years, lazy but effective enough when it came to the pinch, with two stalwart sons, the elder of whom, Somerled, was a fire-eater. He kept eight longships at the ready always in Coll's wide natural harbour of Arinagour. It made a packed anchorage when the Orkney fleet joined them.

Gillaciaran had fairly recent news of MacDowall, for Somerled was just back from chasing him away from the coasts of Islay. There had been no real fighting on this occasion, for MacDowall preferred not to take on Gillaciaran unless he could not avoid it, finding easier game more profitable. Somerled, although having only five longships against the other's nine, had chased him for forty miles, into the mouth of the Firth of Clyde, where he felt his responsibilities to end, and had come home for reinforcements.

He had these now, with a vengeance. Leaving Gillaciaran with only two stand-by ships, Thorfinn added the six Coll vessels to his fleet, under Somerled, and set off south-eastwards at top speed.

Nightfall overtook them just north of the Mull of Kintyre, a dangerous lee-shore if ever there was one. Thorfinn, giving the menacing Mull itself a very wide berth in unpleasant cross-seas, carried on eastwards in darkness, feeling his way through Sanda Sound and into the wide Firth of Clyde — here, more properly, the mouth of Kilbrannan Sound. Then, sheltered by Kintyre's mighty breakwater, they slipped past the Isle of Davaar into the large landlocked bay of Kilkerran, and there lay, five nights out from Torfness.

MacDowall might not still be in the Firth of Clyde, of course. The short night over, at first light Thorfinn sent out two of Somerled's craft to search, whilst he let his own crews and warriors go ashore to stretch their limbs after their cramped quarters aboard.

They had an entire forenoon to relax before one of the Coll vessels came back with the news that they had located the enemy some score of miles up the east coast of Kintyre, at Cour, where they had seen the smokes of their burnings a long way off. His galleys were lying in the quiet deep bay of Cour, opposite Catacol on Arran. Somerled was watching, hidden behind Eilean Cour, just to the south.

Thorfinn was having horns blown to recall his men before ever the report was finished. His force would be divided. Half he would take directly up the Sound of Kilbrannan. The other half, under one of his captains, Harald Cleft Chin, would sail round the *east* side of Arran and, if necessary, into the Sound

101

from the north. If MacDowall bolted north-about, they might trap him between them.

So, in a short time, they were thrashing up Kilbrannan in a cloud of spray, fourteen longships in close order, the great mountains of Arran towering on their right, the lower green hills of Kintyre on their left — to which coast they kept close. Long before they reached the Cour area, halfway up the long peninsula, they could see the brown smoke-clouds rising high into the afternoon sky, to speak eloquently of burning villages and cot-houses, of ravishment and death.

The problem, of course, was the impossibility of an unseen approach for so large a squadron. MacDowall was no fool and would certainly set a watch. Thorfinn therefore crept up the Kintyre shoreline, for cover; but their best hope was that the raiders would have probed sufficiently far inland as to require some time, after warning, to get back to their ships and away, giving the fleet opportunity to come up.

In the event, they had just connected with Somerled's craft behind a small island, when, something like two miles in front, nine galleys shot out of Cour Bay, to turn away northwards in haste. Cursing, Thorfinn yelled for more speed. The chase was on.

MacBeth, for one, had never seen such a fury of energy and determination as the dragon-ship's oarsmen put into their sustained effort, Biorn Bow Legs' gong increasing its rate of clang to an extent that was even painful to listen to, the accompanying chanting more of a rhythmic groaning, punctuating the thrash and creak of the oars. The rowers were fresh, to be sure, and the south-westerly breeze enabled the sail to help them. But the same conditions applied to MacDowall's oarsmen, and clearly they were no sluggards. Thorfinn gained on them, but only slightly, outdistancing all but one of his own ships in that process. Somerled's birlinn. It would be a long chase in these circumstances.

Much depended now on the reserve Orkney squadron beating its way up the other side of Arran. Almost certainly MacDowall would turn eastwards round the top of Arran, through the Sound of Bute, and into the Firth of Clyde proper, since to continue on up the Kilbrannan Sound would lead only into Loch Fyne — which, though the longest sea-loch in Scotland, was a dead-end. But if MacDowall perceived the squadron waiting for him, he could turn away northwards instead, round Bute and into the network of narrow straits, sounds and lochs known as the Kyles of Bute, where his vessels could split up and lose themselves.

Sure enough, the fleeing ships swung eastwards towards the Sound of Bute, cutting the corner of Arran so dangerously tightly that the pursuit might gain no advantage. Still more than a mile behind, Thorfinn was shouting mighty imprecations, naming his oarsmen laggards and the sons of snails and appealing to his Maker for justice at least, if not favour.

There were only about three miles of the Sound of Bute to cover, and all on the dragon-ship, save the oarsmen, held their breaths as MacDowall's craft cleared its eastern end. Would they turn south, or north? They were close inshore, so they would not get any wide view down the firth until they were well out. And if, catching sight of the other squadron then, they turned back northwards, Thorfinn would have gained some small advantage, at least.

But no, the Galwegians swung southwards, and continued on that course until out-of-sight behind the mighty headland known as the Cock of Arran. Those who had breath to cheer on the dragon-ship did so.

Rounding the Cock, they saw the enemy ahead — but no others. Harald Cleft Chin, a seasoned campaigner, must have had the wit to keep close inshore also, and hide himself in one of the eastern bays of Arran. Which was, of course, excellent — but it did mean that when he came out, to intercept the enemy, he would not have much time to get into any blocking position across the width of the firth.

MacDowall certainly knew how to handle his ships, taking major risks, and advantage of every headland, islet and reef. Thorfinn was still gaining, the rearmost Galwegian now only half-a-mile ahead. But the rest of the Orkney squadron was now strung out well behind, save for Somerled's birlinn, which kept up strongly.

Then, at last, they saw developments. Harald Cleft Chin's vessels came out from Brodick Bay about a mile in front of the enemy. MacDowall's reaction was swift, unhesitating. His nine ships parted company, fanning out each on its own course. Harald's vessels had no option but to single out individual targets and seek to head them off. Thorfinn swung off after the flagship.

The diversion had enabled the pursuit to make further precious advance. And the avoiding action occasioned by the interceptors, aided further. Soon only hundreds of yards separated the two leaders' craft, yells and challenges ringing out.

It became a personal duel of wits and seamanship — although one other Galwegian ship stayed close to MacDowall's own, unfortunately. Twisting and turning, they sought to shake off their pursuer, and when that became obviously impossible, to prevent him coming alongside. The Vikings, however, were adept at this process and anticipated MacDowall's every move. Skilled oarsmen on both sides made for intricate and astonishingly swift-changing manoeuvre; but there were dangers in this, also, for those serried oars could be shorn off as though by a knife, by the sharp cutting prow of an enemy — and the Viking ships were equipped with a special blade-like ram for just such purpose. And shearing off the oars could effect direst bloody havoc amongst the rowing crews. In such grim business the advantage tended to lie with the aggressor holding the initiative and being able to select his approaches.

MacBeth had some bowmen amongst the Moraymen on the dragon-ship. But the sea-raiders, Norse or Celtic, did not go in for archery in any large way, heaving and unsteady decks not being the ideal bases for such marksmen. The Moray archers did manage to do some damage at this circling and tacking stage. But Thorfinn was quickly impatient of this finicking arm's-length warfare, and concerned himself solely with close-quarters tactics. Time and again he made a run-in at the enemy, but on each occasion was skilfully eluded — amidst roars and yells of fury and hate on each side. He had to be always on the look-out for what the second Galwegian ship might do to aid its leader — for unfortunately young Somerled had come across another enemy craft which showed fight, and was now engaged in a running battle half-a-mile away. So the dragon-ship meantime was one facing two. Not that that worried Thorfinn Raven Feeder; but it did mean that he had to watch his flanks all the time in his assaults on MacDowall.

MacBeth suggested that his bowmen could concentrate on this second vessel, to make it keep its distance, and his brother agreed.

At last Thorfinn saw his opportunity, as in turning away from one running on his port side, MacDowall was, for a brief spell, directly stern-on to his assailant at only a ship's-length, and with his speed much reduced. Roaring to his oarsmen, Thorfinn raced up the central gangway between the benches, from stern-platform to bow, sword high — and in answer, the dragon-ship surged forward in a burst of power, and, actually ramming the other craft's hull, drove rasping on up the starboard side of the enemy, snapping off the long oars like twigs and hurling their rowers into screaming broken ruin — whilst the Norse oarsmen on that side raised their sweeps high, out of the way, the men on their starboard side continuing to row strongly.

Even as the ghastly grinding connection was made, Thorfinn leapt from one ship to the other, sword flailing, jumping over the shields and the sprawling mangled bodies of the Galloway oarsmen, and followed by a stream of axe- and sword-wielding Vikings, yelling hate. It was a chaotic, wild affray, for there was little foot-room on rowing-benches and gangway, and what there was was slippery with blood or cluttered with bodies. Rowers and sworders stumbled away before the boarders, seeking a firm stance and room to fight. Up on the bow-platform MacDowall and his chieftains stood crowded, ready, but unwilling to leap down from their advantageous position. MacDowall himself, wearing a pointed helmet and chain-mail tunic, red with rust, was readily identifiable, a dark, hatchet-faced man in his forties, thin but wiry, with long down-turning moustaches. Thorfinn shouted at him to come to grips.

MacDowall, needless to say did not do so. But Thorfinn had his hands full, nevertheless, there being no room on the platform for all the Galloway crew, so that most of these formed a solid mass below it, at which the Norsemen had to hack. They were no mean fighters, either, although too cramped for good swording.

MacBeth saw his opportunity, and took it, urging the dragon-ship's prow forward until it was level with the other's bows, and then, backed by his Thanes of Brodie and Darnaway, leaping directly on to the Galwegians' platform, using a Viking shield as a sort of battering-ram to gain space for a foothold and to use his sword. His Moraymen poured after him, in more danger of being pushed over the side by pressure of bodies than from actual assault.

In the midst of this chaotic struggle MacBeth suddenly became aware of what was happening at the far side of the bow-platform. The second Galloway ship had come up, there, come close, and men were jumping, not from it to the flagship but in the other direction. When he perceived that MacDowall himself, astonishingly, was one of those leaping to the other craft, he realised that this was not some manoeuvre to gain advantage but that the Lord of Galloway was going to make off in this second ship. He yelled this warning to Thorfinn, who, fighting at a lower level, could not see what was going on; but in the uproar he was not likely to be heard. Anyway, what could his brother do? The second craft drew off, after only moments, leaving the flagship to fight its own battle, and swung its bows in a south-easterly direction, oars flashing.

The situation changed swiftly and drastically thereafter. The Galloway flagship's crew, abandoned by their lord, lost heart and began soon to throw down their arms. Thorfinn perceived the situation and, bellowing his rage and disappointment, turned to push his way back through the press to his own vessel, many of his people with him. Leaping on to the dragon-ship, he shouted to MacBeth to take over the other ship as prize, and in the same stentorian breath ordered Biorn Bow Legs to cast off and pursue the fleeing MacDowall.

To do all that took time however, inevitably, with few of the Orkney crew still at their oars and some confusion as to who should stay with MacBeth and who should go. So, by the time that Thorfinn was on his way, the fleeing vessel had got most of a mile's start. MacBeth could almost feel his brother's wrath pulsing across the waves.

The deserted Galwegians proved little trouble now, and MacBeth was able to keep an eye on the further situation. MacDowall was obviously now heading straight across for the other side of the firth and the nearest point on the Ayr coast, some seven miles away; and the chances were that he would reach it before Thorfinn could catch up. Elsewhere the main Orkney fleet had now reunited, and most of the running fights were over, although one or two of the enemy ships appeared to have got away.

MacBeth had the prize ship tidied up, the blood washed away and a new crew at the reduced number of oars, when his brother got back, in a towering rage. The wretched MacDowall had escaped him, landed on the Ayr shore near Ardrossan and scuttled off into the woodland with his crew — no doubt to win back to Galloway overland. Was there ever such a dastard, such a dunghill cock! To leave his host, with scarce a blow struck! It was beyond all belief. When he got him — as get him he would, by God's Eyes — he would teach him how to die, at least!

They ascertained that of the nine Galloway ships three had escaped, two were sunk and four captured. They had taken some 300 prisoners, many of them wounded. The dead had been disposed of overboard, uncounted. It could scarcely be called a victory, but it might serve as a warning to the province of Galloway — where they were going now.

One slight delay Thorfinn did accept. They paused, some thirty sea miles on, at the mighty soaring crag of Ailsi, down near the mouth of the firth, and, at the tiny and only eastern strand thereof, unloaded their prisoners on to that inhospitable rock. There was a hermit in an eyrie of a chapel high up the cliff, water to drink from his well and solan geese to eat. They would harm no one there — even if they did not live so well as when raiding the Hebrides. They were left, boatless.

The Mull of Galloway was only another forty miles southwards.

*   *   *

Galloway was a huge province, mountainous inland but jutting in great low-lying peninsulas into the Irish Sea. MacBeth had never had occasion to visit it, but Thorfinn had raided there often. MacDowall was known to base himself on Kirk Cuthbert's Town on the Dee estuary, well to the east. But Ingebiorg's cousin Suibhne mac Kenneth, or Sween Kennedy in the Galloway speech, retained a small corner of territory in the remote area of Soirbuy, in Wigtown Bay, further west. Thither Thorfinn headed first, for the sake of appearances — his own appearances. King Duncan might say that this expedition was being conducted in his name; but the Earl Thorfinn had other views.

Sween Kennedy greeted the invaders warily from his dun of Sliddery, above Cruggleton Bay, between Saint Ninian's Candida Casa at Whithorn and Wigtown, a very strong cliff-top hold in which he roosted uneasily. He was a strangely diffident and indecisive young man to be the descendant of the fierce ancient Kings of Galloway and of the Norse rovers who had conquered them, a quiet and scholarly individual as different from his cousin Ingebiorg as was possible to imagine. Clearly Thorfinn thought little of him, but was prepared to use him. Whether or not Sween wished to be used was beside the point.

The fleet sailed back down Wigtown Bay, a major arm of the sea despite its name, and round the knobbly hillocks of the Borgue peninsula, some score of miles, into the Dee estuary. This was a much shallower firth, and the tides here, as on much of the Galloway seaboard, were difficult, ebbing and flowing over great distances and drying out to vast sand and mud flats at low water. Fortunately the longships were of shallow draught, and down the centre of all the major bays, which were really estuaries, rivers ran through the mud flats, so that they might still navigate up these. But it could make a slow and twisting progress — and in single file the great Orkney fleet, with its captured additions, was strung out ridiculously. It was only half-tide when they pushed up the Dee estuary. Thorfinn had been in some doubts as to whether to lie off until full tide, when they might go up at speed; but since it was on the ebb, that would hold them up for hours — and what was more important, allow the entire countryside to take warning, since the fleet could by no means be hidden. Posts driven into the mud and projecting above the water showed the course of the river-channel at such half-tide conditions.

So, feeling almost foolish, the leadership headed a mile-long column of vessels, winding and turning the six miles to Kirk Cuthbert's Town, which had superseded ancient Wigtown as the main centre of Galloway. As a result, by the time even one-third of the Viking host had disembarked at the narrows of Dee, most of the townsfolk had fled inland, and the fighting-men had moved over into the security of MacDowall's fortress area.

This was far from being the usual hill-top dun or fort. There was little outcropping rock or heights on this fairly level coastal plain, and the fort was in effect an island in marshland, some way south-west of the township, using an inlet of the estuary to flood the surroundings, with a single underwater causeway across. Within was a fairly extensive area, square, with turf-walls and redoubts at the angles. It was a strong place only because of its position. MacDowall himself had not devised it; probably had not the ability to do so. The tradition was that the Romans had established this post during their short-lived occupation of Galloway.

Thorfinn ordered the town to be fired forthwith, as a suitable declaration of intent, and then went to look at the fort situation.

It was unfortunate for the defenders that the assailants were under leadership which knew Spynie so well — for the defensive system was so very similar. A fairly well-defined path gave away the hidden approach through the marshland to the underwater causeway; and by crouching low at the water's edge it was possible to trace most of the latter's course and zigzags.

Thorfinn wanted immediate action. This Kirk Cuthbert was to be an example for all Galloway — to save much trouble for all concerned. He actually sought his brother's advice as to how to get his men across that marsh and moat without unacceptable casualties.

"I would say smoke," MacBeth told him. "To cover your assault."

"But the wind is blowing the wrong way, man. From the south-west." He pointed behind them to the burning town, where the great smoke-clouds were rolling away from them, in an easterly direction. And at the other side of the fort was the estuary, with nothing to burn.

"Fire-arrows. To burn the thatch on those huts in the fort."

"Ha! But they will know that we will be crossing on that causeway, and could concentrate their defence."

"No. Cozen them. Fetch thatch from the town roofs — such as are not already burning. Straw. Hay. Cut reeds. You have plenty of men. Bring it to throw into the marsh, all round here. For standing on. Parties working all along this side. But not at the causeway-end. As though you did not know of it. Bring timber too, from the houses. Lash it together, to make rafts. To carry out over the straw and thatch to the water's edge. At many points. They will believe you intend to attack on these. Then I will get my bowmen to shoot the fire-arrows. All will be covered with the smoke. You press out, then — along the causeway."

"By the Powers — you can use that head of yours when you must! It is worth trying . . ."

With more than sufficient men, the various tasks did not take very long to perform. The materials were to hand in plenty, and only had to be transported. Meanwhile the Moray archers were collecting and tying tinder to their arrows. Shouted challenge and abuse at the fort's defenders went on all the time, as a matter of policy. There was about 150 yards of swamp and then a hundred yards of open water to cross. It was impossible to say how many men were massed in the fort — many, but hundreds rather than thousands.

A fire had been lit, and at a signal from Thorfinn, MacBeth gave the order to shoot. The bowmen dipped their tindered arrows in the flame and then took aim for the various hut roofs some 300 yards away. Not all the tinder tufts remained alight for the flight, but none missed such easy targets, and sufficient were still burning to set alight the thatching in mere seconds, for it had been a dry month and summer. Great yellow-brown clouds of smoke came billowing across. Soon all, fort and attackers, were lost in acrid, eye-stinging obscurity, men coughing, choking.

But all was urgent and disciplined activity on this side nevertheless, with companies moving purposefully in on Thorfinn, who led the way out through the marsh to the causeway, swords drawn.

MacBeth waited with his bowmen in case the smoke gave out and more archery could be valuable. Most of the fort area was just within bowshot.

This was not needed. The smoke of the burning huts lasted sufficiently long for Thorfinn and the head of his column to win out over the causeway unobserved, however slowly they had to creep and feel their way. Once over, the surprise seemed to be complete. The sounds of battle suddenly arose and maintained.

It was at this stage that a Viking left in charge at the town sent word that his scouts reported a massing of men in woodland on higher ground a mile or so to the east. Who these were, and their numbers, was not obvious. They might be locals rallied from this area; but on the other hand, it might be MacDowall himself arrived for the defence of his homeland.

MacBeth sent the messenger, with a guide through the smoke, to cross the causeway and inform Thorfinn. Also to tell him that he, MacBeth, was taking a force to investigate.

He took his 400 Moraymen, with young Somerled's 200 Hebrideans as well, and hurried back to Kirk Cuthbert, streaming-eyed and coughing as they went. There they learned the location of the reported Galloway force; and adding another couple of hundred Vikings to their strength, with scouts ahead, set off in that direction.

As the ground rose, inland, the cultivated lands and pastures of the coastal area faded out and scrub woodland took over, amongst low green hills. In such country, of course, it was difficult to see any distance ahead or to discern any concentrations of men. MacBeth went warily, moving forward slowly on a wide front.

They began to catch glimpses of men, in ones and twos, retiring before them. Presently their own scouts brought one of these back, whom they had managed to capture.

With a little persuasion the man, an enemy scout himself, talked. He admitted that it was MacDowall, Lord of Galloway, who was ahead, who had just arrived from the north, overland, and had hastily gathered together a host of about one thousand, with many more sent for, messengers going out into many parts of the province. Pressed, the man did not think that MacDowall was eager to fight, meantime, preferring to wait until more of his people had assembled. He was based, for the time being, on the hill-fort of Culcaigrie, near Culcaigrie Loch, some seven miles to the north west.

MacBeth sent back this information to Thorfinn, and added that he would keep his present force between Kirk Cuthbert and the enemy, until informed of his brother's intentions.

He spaced out his men along a wide front, just within the scrub forest, with advance patrols well forward. And waited.

In a couple of hours Thorfinn sent a courier to say that the fort had fallen satisfactorily, and that MacBeth should leave a screen of a hundred or two men in his present position to guard against any surprise attack — although that seemed unlikely. He and the bulk of his company might as well return to Kirk Cuthbert.

The fires had all died away, save for pale wisps of blue smoke, though the acrid smell of burning was everywhere, when they got back to the town area; and the Vikings had established a large camp to windward — from which better smells emanated, entire newly-slaughtered Galloway cattle being roasted on spits over cooking-fires, by the dozen.

But welcome as this provision was for hungry men, the effect, for MacBeth at least, was somewhat spoiled. For near Thorfinn's own fire, he had a quite large squad of men very busy, mainly prisoners but under careful supervision. They had a huge pile of heads there, cut off the slain in the fort battle, a messy, bloody and fly-buzzing heap; and they were hard at work washing and cleaning up these, combing out the tangled hair and beards and trimming off neck skin and the like, preparatory to hanging them up individually on posts as a sort of frieze all round the perimeter of the township. There were between three and four hundred of them, Thorfinn calculated, sufficient to make a good and effective showing.

When MacBeth protested that this was an unnecessary barbarity, his elder brother reproved him sternly, suggesting that he used his own head while still he had it. He, Thorfinn, was a great believer in avoiding unnecessary bloodshed, he pointed out; and this procedure would undoubtedly greatly aid in that. There was nothing like severed heads for dissuading folk from taking up arms and opposing due authority. He had found it very efficacious in the past, in making people think

111

twice about getting in the way of Thorfinn Raven Feeder. Galloway would thereby suffer the less. These men had died anyway, at the fort fight, so it cost nothing extra. And they were past caring what happened to their heads. Whilst their widows and families would be much convenienced by being able to identify them properly, cleaned up like this — much more readily than in an untidy heap of slain bodies. While the burial would be simplified likewise — and the remainder of the car-cases could be left to feed his renowned ravens.

MacBeth, although far from over-delicate of stomach, and eating as far away from the heads as possible, still found his appreciation of the roasted beef impaired.

Thorfinn was concerned that the hosts of Galloway should not be given time to rally to the support of MacDowall. So the night's rest was cut short, and before dawn the Viking host was on the march. They moved up to the higher ground northwards, to their forward line, to be in a position to advance at first light.

So, in the early morning mists they moved on, in force, through the forest of scattered birch and thorn scrub, as silently as they might — thereby surprising and annihilating one forward company of Galwegians. But these were able to sound the alarm, and thereafter the defending forces retired north-westwards before them, keeping just out of contact. That is, until they came to the now narrowed River Dee, in the Tongland area, where it was sufficiently shallow to ford. This crossing MacDowall was prepared to contest. In the riverside meadow-land the two hosts could now see each other plainly. It was clear that, so far, MacDowall had only about half the invaders' numbers. Despite this, it was equally apparent that any opposed crossing of the Dee would be costly. Thorfinn had local prisoners brought before him, and after threatening them with unpleasant death, extracted the information that there was another ford, at a monks' cashel, about a mile upstream, at Clochan. So, while seeming to press ahead with preparations for a major crossing here, in the face of the enemy, he secretly detached a small force of about 300 to make their way unseen up the river, to take and hold this ford.

When word was brought back that the second crossing area had been found undefended, the Viking army was gradually withdrawn from the Tongland ford and sent north. This process could not long be kept from the enemy across the hundred-yard-wide river — and then it became a race for the second ford. But, since Thorfinn did not remove all his men from the lower site, MacDowall was forced to leave roughly half his force still on guard there. In the event, the Vikings got sufficient men across the upper ford to form a strong bridgehead on the west bank, against which the Galloway men dared not commit themselves. So MacDowall had to give orders for retiral again, losing both fords — and moreover having his army split in two.

Now it was more or less headlong flight and pursuit, north by west, into low hills. There was still another river to cross, the Tarff, but in this dry summer it was not a major obstacle and no attempt was made to defend it.

Two or three miles of this and the running battle still in two sections, they came out into a sort of amphitheatre of the hillocks, in typical Galloway cattle country. The knobbly green heights around did not reach much more than 400 feet, here cradling a marshy plain over a mile across, in the centre of which was an oval, reedy loch. And near the top end of this, on the west side, was an isolated mound, steep but flat-topped, crowned by the hill-fort of Culcaigrie, MacDowall's redoubt area.

It so happened that, owing to the configuration of the land, the two retirals and pursuits reached the loch area almost a mile apart, one to the south-west of the loch-foot, the other halfway up its east side. Thorfinn, leading the northern chase, swiftly saw his opportunity. He sent a third of his force racing north-about, to cut off flight in that direction, thereby pinning this half of the Galloway host against the loch itself. It is probable that MacDowall himself would not have allowed this to happen to him, being an experienced campaigner — but he was with the southern half. The leader involved — who had been detached merely to try to hold the upper Dee ford — did not know what to do, and turned at bay. Most of his men fought well enough, but they were beaten before they started, out-numbered and out-manoeuvred and with the terrible person of the Raven Feeder against them. Many fell, including the leader, but more melted away into the marshland and even took their chances in the waters of the loch itself.

MacDowall meantime was hastening up the west side, pursued by MacBeth, Harald Cleft Chin and Somerled. He would perceive that he had lost his second force. He would have barely 600 men left. His only chance, undoubtedly, was to reach and hole up in his hill-top fort and hold out until his full Galloway manpower rallied to his aid.

But even that was not so simple, with Thorfinn, before his waterside battle was finished, sending his same fleet-footed detachment running round the north end of the loch to try to reach the fort-hill before its owner. They did not quite manage this, but got there in time so to disrupt the ascent of the steep slope that MacDowall had to turn there and fight them off. This was the position when MacBeth came up.

It was no place for a powerful attack; but on the other hand it was too steep for any co-ordinated defence either — not fighting terrain at all. The defenders were able to roll down some loose rocks, which did cause casualties amongst the Vikings; but otherwise it was a case of catch-as-catch-can, every man for himself.

With their enemy so close behind, there was a further complication for the Galwegians when they reached the top of the hill. The fort, being constructed to keep attackers out, had high walls of stone topped by iron spikes, and only one narrow entrance. Now these defences proved to be almost as much of a problem to the Galloway men as to their assailants. They had to queue up to get in at the gate. In consequence, fierce fighting developed just outside. This was still in progress when Thorfinn arrived, in panting wrath.

That was enough for MacDowall, already inside. He had the massive gates slammed shut and barred — leaving those of his folk outside to their fate. Clearly he was a man with very definite priorities. One way or another he had lost all but a hundred or two of his host.

The invaders were now faced with an intractable problem. This fort was strong, in its position and structure as in defensive system and theory. Almost certainly it would have its own draw-well, deep as this must be. MacDowall might have left most of his people outside, but that might even be to his advantage now since he would not have to feed them. So long as he had sufficient men to man the walls — which seemed likely. Smoke would not be apt to serve here — although it might be used to screen part of an all-out assault.

At least, MacDowall did not appear to have any bowmen. The Viking host sat down around the fort to consider the situation — most of it at the bottom of the hill since there was no room for them at the top.

MacBeth, who possessed a clear mind in most matters, put the position to his impatient brother and the others. "Time in this is important for us only in one respect — that the Galloway men do not come to MacDowall's rescue in too great numbers. Time for them to muster. Were it not for that, we might starve him out. We have no great need for haste. If we can prevent the Galloway hosts from coming here, or even assembling together, then MacDowall will have to yield."

"Any fool could see that. But how is it to be done, man?"

"Go to them, instead of waiting for them to come to you. Send out your envoys. Guarded by companies strong enough to protect them — a hundred or two. You do not require a great many here. You could send eight or ten parties. The Gallowaymen would be loth to attack the like, with your name on them, without themselves being strongly mustered. Use Sween Kennedy. Send them to all towns, centres, properties. Proclaiming that you have put down MacDowall in the name of King Duncan. That Sween here is now Lord of Galloway again . . ."

"Sween — no! *I* will be Lord of Galloway. Sween can act my deputy — only that." Thorfinn grinned at Kennedy. "Eh, Cousin?"

That young man shrugged.

"As you will," MacBeth went on. "But send out your parties. As though you had already conquered Galloway. Forthwith. I think that these people will not rally against the Earl Thorfinn if they believe the fight lost already. And Mac-Dowall will be left to fall like a ripe apple."

Thorfinn could think of no better strategy, so the thing was agreed. And no sooner that than he was organising it. The grass was never allowed to grow under the Raven Feeder's feet. Bands were sent out to capture sufficient of the sturdy Galloway ponies in which the land abounded. His envoys should ride, not march. Prisoners were questioned as to the whereabouts of the main towns, villages and populations of the province, spokesmen selected and instructed. The first were on their way before nightfall, leaving the invading host encamped around Culcaigrie Hill.

So commenced a strange interlude, an almost unreal period of quiet and inactivity in the warm August days, an experience practically unique for the Vikings and a major trial for Thorfinn Sigurdson, who swore that he had never spent so long in one place during a hosting, and hoped not to do so again. He did not, in fact, sit idle. He ranged the country round about, on a small Galloway horse, looking rather ridiculous with his long legs trailing the ground. He rode with his scouting parties. He visited the nearest townships. He went hunting, fishing. And morning and evening he climbed the hill to shout at MacDowall to surrender. Or else to come out, like a man and settle their differences in single combat, by sword or axe or bare hands. If he, MacDowall, won, by any saint he cared to name, or Thor and Odin if he preferred it, Thorfinn swore that he should march away where he would, unmolested. He achieved never a word in reply.

So passed four days and four nights. And on the fifth day, the unexpected happened. Guards at the top of the hill came running down to announce that there was uproar within the fort. Thorfinn was off ranging the land, and MacBeth climbed up to see what was to do, after putting the camp on the alert. Shouting was still going on inside the walling; and presently men appeared at the wall-top, gesticulating, calling out, to the besiegers. They apparently were anxious to come over, to desert the fort. But understandably were afraid of their reception. MacBeth called reassurances.

About a score of men got over, dropping down from the wallhead, before the move was stopped from within. Some died in the process, many were wounded. Their story to MacBeth was one of resentment. MacDowall was a harsh master. He executed men for the slightest fault. He had abandoned their comrades outside the fort. Conditions within were bad, particularly as to water. There was a well, deep under the hill, but the dry weather had sapped its supply and there was only a muddy trickle coming up in the bucket — and this was being reserved almost wholly for the lord and his wife and children, who had been brought into the fort earlier. In pleading for their lives, the deserters revealed that there was a structural weakness in the defences. A portion of the stonework at the north-west corner was in danger of collapsing at the base — probably again owing to the dry weather and the consequent erosion of the soil there, at the edge of the steep slope. They were having to shore it up inside. But it might be quarried away from the outside.

MacBeth moved round the hill to the point indicated, to investigate. Sure enough, the masonry of the fort there, where it came close to the edge, was crumbling away, with something like an incipient landslide of the underlying earth. But even as he peered and probed, stones and rocks were hurled down from the wallhead, so that he had to make a hasty retreat. He returned to the hill-foot to consider the matter.

When Thorfinn got back later in the day, his brother had a

scheme to propose. They should contrive a number of large shields, shelters, made of thornwood branches covered in cowhides, with supports — rather like tables. These would be held up, under the walling, by men, whilst others worked under their cover to loosen and break down the stonework. They would require to be strong, to withstand the battering of rocks from above; and many would be needed, to provide adequate protection some way down the slope. Working conditions would be difficult, in that steep place, but not impossible.

Thorfinn, enthusiastic, sent men off to collect tough branches, and skin cattle, straight away. They would work through the night.

In the morning, while the main host set up a great diversionary noise all around the fort, the shield-bearers and stone-quarriers went to work at the north-west corner. They were quickly discovered, of course, and assailed with rocks. But the threat of action elsewhere undoubtedly preoccupied the defenders — and probably the fort's weakness having obviously been divulged, this affected the morale also. Moreover, the shields worked very well and the men beneath were able to operate steadily, with a constant stream of dug-out masonry and filling rolling away down the slope. There were few major casualties.

In only a short time more men were appearing at the wallhead, eager to desert. Thorfinn shouted welcome to them all, and added insults and dire threats towards MacDowall. He also advised the would-be surrenderers to open the fort gate and let them in, to save further trouble.

They did not do this. But thick as the walling was, relays of workers had a sizeable gap made at the angle before long. This would be defended strongly inside, no doubt; so the attackers built fires around it, where they could, at the head of the slope, adding reeds from the marsh to set up clouds of brown smoke. The updraught, the westerly wind and the formation of the ground, caused much to pour in at the gap.

Thorfinn himself led the way in, through the thick smoke and the gapped masonry. Once inside, however, there was little resistance, most of the garrison being content to throw down their arms in a hopeless situation. But there was a small central redoubt, on the hill's summit outcrop, walled around, and to this the attackers saw that MacDowall, his family and two or three others had retired. Thorfinn bellowed eloquently as to what he would do to his enemy when he got up there. The Lord of Galloway shook his fist, wordless.

The earl, and all others, were unprepared however for MacDowall's ultimate move. As the Vikings began the last short ascent — and it was abundantly clear that nothing could stop them — he suddenly turned on his three children with his sword, as they stood near, the eldest no more than ten years. Three mighty swipes, without pause between, and he had decapitated them cleanly, expertly, with scarcely a sound out of them — for he was a notable executioner. Then he swung on his cowering, staring wife. Her outstretched hands did not save her. This time he clove right down through the skull to the very breast-bone. As she collapsed in red spouting ruin, he turned again, grimacing, to face Thorfinn and the nearest Orkneymen, now faltering in their climb in something like horror. Tearing off his armoured tunic, he thrust out his dripping sword, hilt first, to one of his chieftains standing there, commanding him to hold it firm. Then, yelling curses on Thorfinn and all his kind, he ran forward, to hurl himself upon the sharp point with all his strength. He was not dead when the earl came up to bend over the twitching body, but almost so.

"You die better than you lived, man," Thorfinn said, deep-voiced. "We will settle our differences another day, perhaps, hereafter!"

The other's glazing eyes closed.

*   *   *

The very next morning the messenger from Thorkell Fosterer arrived at Culcaigrie, via Kirk Cuthbert. He had come 400 miles, at the top speed of a fast birlinn, with his news. Duncan the King had deceived them once more. Scarcely had the earl left the Pentland Firth than Duncan had sent an army north. He had actually made his sister's son, Matain mac Caerill, the Thane of Buchan, Mormaor of Caithness and Sutherland in Thorfinn's stead, and sent him up with some 3000 men to take over the two mortuaths in the Earl's absence.

Thorfinn's explosion of wrath was frightening to behold, even for his own brother.

Thorkell Fosterer had gathered together a scratch force of Vikings in Orkney, brought them across the firth, and caught Matain mac Caerill near Thurso; and after a tough fight defeated him. But the invading host had been split at the time, with a large section away raiding in the west, in Sutherland. Matain had fled, to rejoin these, with the remnant of his troops; and Thorkell, having suffered heavy casualties, and himself wounded, was in no state to seek to inflict a second defeat. He urged Thorfinn's immediate return.

Such urging was scarcely necessary. The earl was planning his moves even as the courier spoke. He would sail from Kirk Cuthbert with 2000 men, just as soon as he could get them there and embarked. His oarsmen would have him back in the Pentland Firth inside three days and nights if they burst their hearts doing it, and he would cleanse his lands of the Thane of Buchan and all his crew — aye, and then deal with Duncan mac Crinan. MacBeth would stay here, with the other thousand, to widen and deepen their hold on Galloway.

His brother demurred. If Matain had marched north from Buchan, he would have to have passed through Moray and Ross. God knew what havoc he might have created there. Duncan loved him, MacBeth, no more than Thorfinn, and would not have instructed his nephew to spare his lands. He was for returning home as quickly as any. Duncan had fooled them with this Galloway expedition, to get them out of the way, both of them. He had to go back. Thorfinn would have to leave somebody else in charge in Galloway.

In the end they left Harald Cleft Chin and Somerled mac Gillaciaran. With MacDowall's death they should have little difficulty in consolidating the Viking hold on the province.

8

THANKFULLY MACBETH FOUND all well at Spynie, with no troubles to report. The Thane Matain had indeed marched through Moray, Neil Nathrach agreed, but had been sufficiently discreet about it to choose an unobtrusive route through the uplands of Braemoray, and seemed to have kept his men under control. Probably he was a cautious man, and did not want the land hostile behind him in case of any forced retiral. Neil had not felt strong enough to deny him passage and to provoke major fighting, in MacBeth's absence. Forby he had come in the name of the High King. He had not announced his business in heading north, but it was apparent that it must be against Thorfinn.

Gruoch and Ingebiorg had been perturbed, of course, but not unduly so, since they seemed to have infinite faith in their respective lords. Now that the brothers were back in the north, the wives were flatteringly reassured. MacBeth suggested that Ingebiorg stay on at Spynie meantime.

He had parted from his brother at Duncansby, Thorfinn's main Caithness seat and anchorage, at the eastern end of the Pentland Firth, where they had found Thorkell Fosterer waiting for them, wounded but far from subdued. Matain was still in Caithness, he had reported, westwards on the Sutherland border around Reay, waiting presumably for reinforcements. He was said to have some 2000 men, at least. Thorfinn commented grimly that he would deal with the situation at once. He gave MacBeth three of the captured Galloway ships to transport his 400 Moraymen home, scornfully rejecting offers of help.

A week and a day later Thorfinn arrived in person at Torfness, come for his wife. His greetings were as boisterous as ever, his humour as ponderous. MacBeth had to ask him as to the position regarding Thane Matain.

His brother shrugged. "That Matain is dead. Like all his host. I slew him my own self. And not before time!"

"His host . . .?"

"We took no prisoners," Thorfinn said simply. "Caithness and Sutherland are *mine!*"

MacBeth forebore to question further, meantime, in front of the women.

But in the evening, strolling under the apple-trees and slapping at midges, Thorfinn talked seriously. "Duncan," he said. "What is to be done with Duncan mac Crinan, Brother?"

MacBeth took his time to answer. "Would to God that I knew that! I have thought on it, long. There is no easy answer. He is the King . . ."

"He is a dastard, a cheat, a liar and a poisoner . . ."

"All that. But still the King. High King of Scots."

"And that means that you will lift no hand against him?"

MacBeth frowned. "I can advise against, even *work* against his policies, where I conceive them to be wrong. You might say that it is no less than our duty, as mormaors. But to lift hand against his person — no!"

"I say that is weak folly, man! You said that same of Malcolm Foiranach. That I accepted, because you had taken an oath to sustain him. But you have taken no such oath for Duncan Ilgairach, who gained the crown by murder and deceit."

120

"He still sits on the Stone of Destiny. Placed there by most of the mormaors of Scotland. That Stone is the touchstone of our ancient throne. It is the talisman of our race and realm. Whoever sits on it rules Scotland, of right."

"Half the men who have sat on it — more — have been slain. And by their own people, our forefathers. Did it save them?"

"Perhaps not. But I do not judge my duty by the failures of others."

"Spoken like, like a self-righteous monk! You should have been a churchman, Brother. Duncan tried to murder you — and you turn him the other cheek. He will do so again. He has tried to steal my birthright . . ."

"Duncan the *man* I might seek out to slay, if I could — for I am no monk. But Duncan the King is otherwise."

"If *you* were King . . ."

"I should not expect my mormaors to rise up in arms against me."

"Then you would be a fool — if you had offended them."

"We shall not agree on this, Thor."

"One day we may. When even MacBeth will turn. If Duncan does not get him first! But — at least *I* am not to be bound by your weakness."

"No. I had not thought it. What are *your* plans?"

"I had it that we should strike at once. Both of us. I would take my full strength, by sea, to Galloway. Duncan would learn of it. But would think only that I came to strengthen my hold on that province. You would march the strength of Moray and Ross south, to Fortrenn. I would strike north-eastwards from Galloway. We would have him nailed between us. My ships to go back, north-about again, and down this east coast, while we marched. To support us from the sea. Eight days, ten, and he would be ours. And *you* would be King of Scots. Sit on your Stone!"

MacBeth shook his head, wordless.

*　　　*　　　*

Autumn passed into winter, with MacBeth busy. The rule of two mortuaths was a major responsibility for a man who took his duties seriously; and when they were such large territories as Moray and Ross, covering between them a quarter of all Alba, much travel was involved, even to hold the mormaor's seasonal courts of justice. Sometimes he took Gruoch with him. Even

Lulach was taken on occasion, out of policy. He was a strange, withdrawn child, as though ever watchful, wary. The baby Farquhar was left at home.

In March they heard that the Earl Eadulf of Northumbria, for whom Siward the Strong was "governor", had made a serious raid on Cumbria, no doubt in retaliation for Duncan's claim to be overlord of Northumbria and demand for tribute. There had been bound to be trouble over that foolishness. There was much slaughter and burning before Eadulf was repulsed. Siward, although now Duncan's brother-in-law, did nothing. He might even have arranged it all, for certainly Eadulf could not have done it without his knowledge.

There was no word from Galloway or Thorfinn.

Then came the news that Canute the Mighty had died. For a while men could scarcely believe it. He had been ruling England, and so much else, for over twenty years, and with so strong a hand. Bloody, savage, cunning at first, he had become pious, wise even. He had changed the face of England, Norway, Denmark and Sweden. He had introduced regular taxation, standing armies, the rule of law — Canute's law. Christendom would be a different place without Knut Svenson.

It was a high summer day of July when a young fisherman from the nearest haven to the *Dorus Neamh* came to inform his lord in haste that there was a fleet of ships beating northwards only a mile or so off-shore. MacBeth rowed across Spynie Loch in a coracle and climbed to the sand-dune ridge, to investigate.

There were eleven ships-of-war strung out in line, now some way to the north, not Viking longships but galleys, taller, heavier vessels. They flew banners, but it was too far to distinguish the emblems.

He puzzled as to who it could be, and could not reach any conclusion. These large ships could each hold many men, far more than longships, so it was a major expedition. He ordered the warning beacons to be lit along the coast, so that the smoke-signals could be seen on the Ross side of the Firth.

The fleet did not turn into the Moray Firth however, but continued on up the coast, past the bold headlands of the Sutors of Cromarty. It was Caithness or Sutherland then — or Orkney itself. Three longships slipped out of Torfness harbour, one to shadow the fleet, two to head directly seawards. It would be a surprising matter if these two were not at Orkney first.

Precisely a week later, on Saint Blathmac's Day, the galleys began to come back. Look-outs reported two of them sailing south. Then a third. Then, after an hour or two, another pair. No more.

"Eleven ships went up," MacBeth said. "Five returned, wide-scattered. It needs no seer to tell what that means. Whoever they are."

It was only a few days more when the great fleet of longships arrived at Torfness, and Thorfinn came hot-foot to Spynie.

"Up, man — up and be doing!" he cried, whenever he saw MacBeth. "Work to do. We shall have him, once and for all. Put an end to his folly."

"Which folly is that? I can name a few fools."

"Do not play the clever man with me — for I am no fool! Duncan Ilgairach's folly, to be sure. He is delivered into our hands. He came to destroy Orkney, with his galleys and his thousands. Thinking me to be still in Galloway. To harry and slay and burn my islands. Then, no doubt, to do the like for Caithness and Sutherland. But I had returned. I was sailing between Deerness and Copinshay with but six longships when we sighted him coming up. Eleven great galleys, he had. Slow, heavy craft, filled with men. My heroes herded them like sheep! You should have seen us! We sank five before they had had enough, and fled. We got another after that, too . . ."

"So it was Duncan himself. For all his cunning, he is . . . unfortunate!"

"And will be more so. I have 3000 men with me, and go to teach him his lesson. Come, you."

"You have sufficient to deal with this, without me."

"But you will be the next High King, man. Or do you want the young bastard Big Head to be named monarch?"

"No. But — we have spoken of this before, many times. I will not raise hand against the King."

"You would have him put down. But someone else must do it — for MacBeth to have the crown!"

"Have it that way if you will."

"You are an awkward, stubborn son of sin . . . !"

The Viking host moved off southwards next morning. Thor-finn said that all would be disorganised in the South, after Duncan's defeat. Now was the time to strike back. MacBeth and Gruoch watched the fleet sail from Torfness, the former set-faced.

"You wish that you were going with them," she said. "Despite your stand, you desire to be sailing against Duncan."

He breathed out heavily. "I am none so noble, I fear. No

virtue in me. I can hate as well as the next. Were Duncan not the King! . . .!"

"He is a bad King. Bad for the realm, a danger to all Scotland. Is there not a duty to put him down? For the benefit of all?"

"Temptress! Think you I have not asked myself that a score of times? So have said all who contemplated treason. No. If the High King cannot depend on his lesser kings' loyalty, then our whole ancient system of government falls. Thorfinn does not see it so — but Thorfinn is a law unto himself."

"Thorfinn has been attacked by Duncan. Twice."

"Yes. Perhaps if I was attacked, it might be different. If I had to fight in self-defence."

"You *were* attacked. Poisoned . . ."

"That is supposition, no more. We have no proof of it."

She looked at him with a mixture of love and exasperation.

Thorfinn came back after three weeks, his people glutted with loot, blood and fulfilment. They had not caught up with the fleeing Duncan himself, but had wreaked their vengeance on his domains. They had raided right down the east coast, harrying far and wide. They had showed that there was no place in Scotland safe from Thorfinn's vengeance.

9

MACBETH'S SECOND CHILD was born in March, on the Eve of Saint Patrick, another son. They named him Luctacus. He was a happy, easy-going infant, from the first. With three children it was now a lively household, and Gruoch quietly happy. The *Dorus Neamh* was a wonderful place for a family to grow up.

There was no news from the North but plenty from the South, most of it coming via the Keledei. England, following on the death of Canute, was in a poor way. He had left his kingdoms to his three sons, but his so-called empire to none; Norway to his eldest, Sven, Denmark to Hardicanute, and England to Harald. None of them was of the stature of their father, and of the three Harald Harefoot was probably the weakest. There were many who grudged him his throne, including his Saxon half-brothers, Alfred and Edward Atheling, sons of King Ethelred the Unready — for Canute had married Ethelred's widow, Emma. There were also their nephews, the dead Edmund Ironside's sons. Perhaps most dangerous of all was the Earl Godwin of Kent, married to the Atheling's sister, and a great warrior — which the others were not. So, although the Witan, or council of the realm, had appointed Harald, as Canute had ordained, the country was full of rumours and alarms.

Seeking advantage in this, the ineffable Duncan took it upon himself to invade Northumbria, in retaliation for the Earl Eadulf's raid on Cumbria — despite the fact that his queen, Sybil, had just presented him with a fine son, Donald — Donald Ban, or the Fair, they were calling him, to distinguish him from various other Donalds. This Northumbrian venture was no mere raid but a full-scale invasion in major force, which drove south from the Merse and by sheer weight of numbers did not halt until it reached the great Saint Cuthbert's Town and fort of Durham on the Wear. Further than this even the rash Duncan dared not go, for beyond Durham was Deira, or York, Siward the Strong's earldom. He was taking a large risk as it was. He besieged Durham — in which Eadulf was reputed to have taken refuge — but anyone with any experience of warfare could have told him, and probably did, that he had neither the equipment nor the expertise to capture any such walled city. After two weeks of siege, with Siward oddly silent, Duncan had to give it up — by which time, of course, the Northumbrian forces had had time to rally, and they sorely harassed the Scots army all the way back to the Merse and beyond, causing heavy casualties. So ended a profitless adventure.

The effect on MacBeth of these tidings was to make him wonder ever more about his cousin Duncan's state of mind, even his sanity. He had been no sort of warrior at all, the reverse indeed, until his grandfather died; now, as King, he was seldom not on one kind of campaign or another. And however cunning the timing and preliminary planning, these were all without exception misconceived, recklessly carried out and unsuccessful. He seemed to be consumed with a fever to prove himself a great soldier, greater than his grandsire Malcolm, greater even than Thorfinn, certainly greater than MacBeth the rightful tanist. And as a result he was proving a disaster for Scotland.

Duncan's follies were by no means at an end. Warning came secretly to Spynie from Cormac of Glamis. The King was assembling a great army, greater than ever before. He had sent for all the forces of Strathclyde, Lothian and the Merse, as well as those of Alba proper, and from as far west as Kintyre and Dalar. Also Echmarcach of Dublin and his Irish. He was gathering shipping to form a large fleet. It was no secret that it was aimed against Thorfinn. But the whisper was that MacBeth also was to be taught his lesson. This was to be once and for all. Part of the army was to march north, not over the high passes but by the east coast lowlands, by Angus, the Mearns, Mar and Buchan; the rest to sail in the ships. There was a rumour that they would join at Torfness, in the Laigh. He, Glamis, would have to provide his share of the Angus force; but like many another, he would be a reluctant fighter. This warning, at least, he could send.

MacBeth, it seemed, was to have his hand forced, his mind made up for him. Grimly he ordered a full muster of his forces, and sent urgent notice to Gunar Hound Tooth. His brother, almost certainly, would be away hosting by now, if not at his new lordship of Galloway. But he was a swift mover, and once informed, he would scorch the sea itself in his haste.

This was late June. Fortunately Duncan in fact gave them ample time. That would not be his intention, but he would be waiting for the Irish and other remote contingents. Also he might well be wishing to ensure that the Orkney fleet was well away on its summer sailing. At any rate, Thorfinn arrived at his borg of Torfness in mid-July, in furious style with exhausted oarsmen, spoiling for a fight, to something of an anti-climax, with Moray lapped in high summer peace, bell-heather blooming and the harvest beginning to ripen. MacBeth all but apologised.

His brother was not critical. Time he required. He had only a dozen longships with him and less than a thousand men. Thorkell Fosterer would be bringing on the main Orkney strength in a few days. Let Duncan delay.

Although MacBeth still would not commit himself to actual fighting, they planned strategy in the event of an attack on Moray itself. The Moray forces were divided into three groups, to play a watching and flanking role. The main body was based on Forres, one division was on guard in the Fochabers-Dundurcas area a dozen miles to the east, to defend the crossings of Spey; and the third, smaller, sent to the high inland passes of Badenoch, in case Crinan of Atholl elected to aid his son by coming up behind them, in a back-door assault. Thorfinn commended these arrangements, but argued that the principal

126

assault would almost certainly be by sea — for Duncan was a lazy man in his person, however ambitious, and was unlikely to choose the long wearisome marching by land if he could sail comfortably in a ship. On the other hand, after his complete defeat off Deerness, he would not be apt to risk another sea-battle against longships; so the chances were that he would disembark somewhere along this Moray coast — if indeed he was aiming at MacBeth, before proceeding on to Caithness and Sutherland, and then over to Orkney — and he would, of course, be concerned to join up with his overland forces. But the Moray coast, with its endless miles of shelving sands, interspersed with fierce cliffs and reefs, was a difficult seaboard to land an army on, save perhaps from longships which could run their prows up on to the strand. There were few havens, at the mouths of Spey and Lossie and Findhorn, with Torfness the best, of course. They should have their forces placed so as to contest landings at these points therefore, in the first place — but watching their backs. Glamis' reference to Torfness itself did not necessarily signify anything. After all, it was the best-defended position on the east coast of Scotland.

This seemed sound reasoning, and the available manpower was redistributed.

Thorkell Fosterer arrived with almost 3000 Orkney, Caithness and Sutherland men in the main Viking fleet — and almost at the same time word was sent from the Spey that an army estimated at as many as half that again was approaching through Strathbogie and Strathisla, from Buchan. Much now would depend on timing; but clearly the campaign was on.

The vast majority of the longships were sent away from Torfness, to hide themselves in the great landlocked bay of Findhorn, with many of their people disembarked. All forces were alerted, and arrangements made to switch men from one front to another swiftly, as necessary. MacBeth declared that still he had no certainty that he, or Moray, was Duncan's objective.

That evening, as the light was fading, a scattered fleet was reported off the mouths of Spey. In only hours now they would know what the future held.

*　　*　　*

Glamis had been right in the rumours he had intercepted. Torfness was the first target. It seemed a strange choice, the most heavily defended feature on the entire seaboard. Perhaps

Duncan thought that he could overwhelm it, by surprise, in the first assault, with Thorfinn himself presumably elsewhere; and once taken it would give him an excellent harbour and base, and deny the same to the Vikings. At any rate, at sunrise he attacked from the sea, with diversions along the beaches to east and west — and without waiting for his overland army, which was presumably being held up by the Moraymen, under the Thanes of Brodie and Alness, at the wide barrier of Spey.

Thorfinn, waiting on the little hill amongst the wide woodlands of Kinloss, near Forres, could scarcely believe his good fortune. He had not many more than the usual garrison in the borg and township of Torfness, and these had instructions to seem to give ground a little, to encourage the enemy, at this stage — although never to allow penetration of the fort itself, of course. Now he waited, allowing old Gunnar to seem to work out his own salvation.

After a while, he turned to MacBeth. "Are my people to do all the fighting here, or are you convinced this time, brother?" he demanded. "Duncan has landed in Moray, without your leave. Do you require more?"

"Torfness is yours, not mine. All know that. It is in Moray, but scarcely of it."

"And what of the host seeking to cross Spey? Is that not your territory? You shall have to make up your mind."

"Yes."

It may be that Thorfinn deliberately delayed his counterstroke so that Duncan would advance further around Torfness, into what was indisputably MacBeth's terrain — although he said that it was to get the maximum numbers of the enemy force committed — before he had the beacon lit on Kinloss hillock to send its smoke-signal to his fleet-captains, hiding in Findhorn Bay, to throw themselves into the attack. At the same time he ordered his Viking host to advance from the woodlands to the east, where they had remained hidden. The serried ranks of the Moraymen were held back. They were in reserve, they were told — to their chagrin. MacBeth himself, however, went forward with his brother.

Thorfinn's timing was excellent. His marching men covered the three miles or so to the neck of the half-mile-long Torfness peninsula just as the longship fleet appeared off its point. The noise of the battle for the borg-head area was loud and fierce, but by no means all the King's troops had yet disembarked — for although it was a good and fair-sized haven, the heterogeneous

128

southern fleet was so large, and with few shallow-draught vessels, that they were having to queue for landing facilities.

Duncan had managed to get some of his smaller craft to land round the west side of the peninsula, as far as halfway along, so as to put in an attack on the borg from behind — so these people were between Thorfinn and Gunnar. He pointed it out cheerfully to MacBeth as a further invasion of Moray territory. Not that these would survive for long, he assured.

It made a curious battle and battlefield, a long, narrow tongue of land with fairly steep sides, jutting into the sea, with the Viking forces attacking north-westwards from the land and south-eastwards from the sea, Duncan's people doing much the same but having to turn and face the assaults behind them, and the borg defenders in the middle, now themselves turning to the attack. Numbers would be approximately even although fully one-third of both hosts were still in their ships.

Thorfinn, as ever, led his men into the fight well in the forefront, wearing a gilded winged helmet, sword in one hand, stabbing spear in the other, a gigantic and fearsome figure, yelling challenge. Immediately behind him a brawny standard-bearer carried the great raven banner of Orkney. It was strange indeed that there was never any lack of volunteers for this honour, for the tradition was that this terrible flag spelt victory for him over whom it was carried but death for the carrier. It was not always so, needless to say; but Thorfinn's father, Earl Sigurd the Stout, having grasped it from the dying hands of its bearer at the great battle of Clontarf, had died himself moments later, still holding it. Because of his enormous stature, Thorfinn always required a tall flag-carrier, or the banner's folds got in his way. Not for him the cool and judicious control of battle from some commanding centre. He was, in fact, no general but a brilliant captain. MacBeth, with much more of the mind of a general, stood aside meantime.

The first impact, inevitably, was overwhelmingly in the Vikings' favour. They had the numbers concentrated, the impetus and the fact that their enemies were aligned to fight in the other direction. It was not long until these, occupying the shaft of the peninsula, broke and were swept aside.

The Orkney fleet, now, had made contact with the King's ships which still lay off, and near-panic and confusion prevailed, considerably distracting the forces already landed. Some vessels were burning, and an onshore breeze blew their smoke further to confuse the fighting at the borg.

This fort was very strong, both in its position, size and fabric, crowning a rocky eminence — the original Jarl Rognvald had ensured that, strengthening the already mighty defences of the earlier Pictish stronghold with the three rings of vitrified stone ramparts. The invaders had managed to take most of the town, but were making little headway against the citadel itself, into which Gunnar had withdrawn his people. The descent of Thorfinn and his horde, of course, transformed the situation — and the fact that the King's troops were marshalled to surround the borg much handicapped them now. They had to regroup under attack — and Gunnar was ready, as they did so, to counter-attack from above.

It would have taken a much better and more experienced commander than Duncan mac Crinan to regain control of that situation. His men fought well and lacked nothing in courage; but they found themselves split into five different major groupings and many smaller ones, with little linkage. Moreover the sea-battle preoccupied them grievously, as well it might — although it was no real battle in fact, but rather a massacre of shipping, with the longships efficiently savaging what was basically only a vast flock of transports.

MacBeth, watching it all, was in a state of agitation. Every instinct urged him to be in there with the rest, fighting. To stand idle in a battle, watching one's friends, was of all things most soul-destroying for any man of spirit. And he knew that his own troops, drawn up back there in the Kinloss woodlands, would be feeling the same, and cursing him, possibly despising him. On the other hand, he told himself that obviously Thorfinn did not require his aid. If he had done so, he knew that he would have gone in. What then of his principles?

He was so cogitating with half his mind, whilst the other half concentrated on the fighting, when one of Brodie's men reached him, panting. The inland royal army, under the King of Dublin, had broken through all their attempts to hold it, at Spey and elsewhere, he reported. They were four or five times Brodie's numbers. Now they were streaming westwards through the Laigh, by Innes and Meft. They could be as near as five miles, by now.

At last, there was no more hesitation and faltering on MacBeth's part. An invading army was marching through his Moray, assailing his own forces — and under Echmarcach of Dublin, to whom he owed nothing and whom he did not like. Moreover, on the line it was taking it would pass close to the

130

Loch of Spynie and his Gruoch and children. That was enough for MacBeth mac Finlay. He hurried back to Kinloss and set his waiting host in motion, eastwards, amidst cheers.

They marched through his own familiar territory, along the south shore of Spynie Loch, by Kintrae and Findrassie. Passing the Hall Isle, he sent a messenger to reassure Gruoch and to tell her that if there was any danger, or worsening of the situation, he would come to her.

He was making for a specific spot — and hoping that he was not too late to reach it. The River Lossie, which had partly created this loch, now, because of blown-sand movement, had found its way to the sea about a mile east of the loch-head, making something of a dog's-leg bend. That mile between was swampland, former salt-marsh, and together with the river itself formed an effective barrier. After the line of the larger Spey, it was the best place to try to hold up an advancing army in all the eastern Laigh.

Despite his haste over the six-mile gap, he was concerned, as he neared the head of the loch, to see much activity ahead, this side of Lossie. However, closer approach proved it to be his own people, Brodie's force, preparing to make another stand here.

MacBeth had almost 2000 men there, all told, to face something over double that number, reputedly. He was told that King Echmarcach was proving a fairly cautious general, however — and possibly was being somewhat restrained by Glamis, whose banner was prominent amongst the many in the opposing host and who was the most experienced commander Duncan had. His reluctance for this adventure could be an important factor here.

Any commander who was not a fool would be cautious approaching this position, of course. The Lossie was not so deep here as to prevent determined men from crossing; but it was still tidal at this point, and like many tidal rivers, it had steep, and slippery mud-banks through the marshland.

MacBeth could see the enemy front now, clearly enough, stretched across the sandy scrubland, armour and spears glittering in the sunlight, flags and banners innumerable, rank upon rank. Scouting parties were nearer, probing the soft land but keeping well out of bowshot.

In the interests of further delay he sent across a deputation under the Thane of Oykell and a flag-of-truce, using two coracles, to ask who dared to cross Morayland without the Mormaor of Moray's leave, what was their intention and where

131

were they heading? Oykell was instructed to take as long about it as possible.

In fact, it was the best part of an hour before he came back — and all the time the tide was making. Perhaps Echmarcach himself was well enough pleased to let time elapse, to see how things went with the royal force at Torfness. For although he had been arrogant and brusque, he had not hurried Oykell away when Angus and Glamis and Lennox had prolonged the interview quite noticeably. Oykell had been told to inform MacBeth that all were here on the High King's business and that he was required to give them undisputed passage to join Duncan who was disembarking at Torfness — that was all.

After a suitable interval, Oykell was sent back, to declare that even the High King was expected to inform his mormaors of entry into their territory — as any of the mormaors with the King of Dublin would confirm. And until such approach was made, MacBeth would feel obliged to deny passage to all armed men. If the visitors would care to lay down their arms, however, it would be different. Would they so do? King Echmarcach might like to come and discuss this matter personally?

It was while they were awaiting an answer to this new delaying tactic that an urgent message came from Thorfinn. Duncan, with the battle still undecided though going against him, had fled the scene, leaving most of his force still fighting strongly, and abandoning his shipping, or such of it as survived. He was heading at speed eastwards, with some six or seven hundred of his best men as bodyguard. He could be making for Spynie. Or seeking to join Echmarcach's force. Or both.

MacBeth acted immediately. He dared not take too many men from the Lossie line, outnumbered two to one as they were already. But he might spare, say, 300. Summoning Brodie to take command at the central apex, he left him his banner, so as not to give Echmarcach warning that he had gone, and set off again westwards with his tight company. It was a strange battle — and as yet he had not struck a single blow.

Could Duncan be making for Spynie? Or had Thorfinn suggested that merely to spur him into precipitate action? Was it not much more likely that he was merely seeking the security of his second army? Yet he would know that the island was MacBeth's home. That Gruoch would be there. And Lulach. Important threats to his position, so long as they lived. He had sought to grasp them before. It was the sort of thing that he might do, that man. Use them as hostages, if not worse . . .

The two companies could scarcely miss each other on that strip of low land between the wooded hills and the loch. But when MacBeth saw the others, expected as it was, he was perturbed. For the King's party — and it could only be that — was halted at the lochside, and at the end of the causeway opposite the Hall Isle, or nearly so. Something seemed to snap in MacBeth's carefully disciplined mind. His enemy was there, within only a matter of yards of Gruoch and their children. King or not, he must be assailed.

Yet, in the event, it was Duncan who actually attacked. When he saw the party advancing from eastwards, half the size of his own, he ordered his people into action forthwith. Whether they had been intending an assault on the island was uncertain; but there was nothing uncertain about their intentions now. Shouting hate, brandishing swords, axes, spears, they hurled themselves forward against the newcomers.

If the entire battle was a strange one, this detached struggle was particularly so. Where the rest had been carefully planned and directed, this had not. Both parties had left their main forces and were presently entirely on their own. Yet they contained two of the three main protagonists, their enmity direly personal. And there was bitterness here, antipathy, fear, elementary emotions. And no generalship at all.

Headlong the two sides clashed, in basic, furious and completely unrefined hand-to-hand fighting, as Thorfinn indeed was wont to do, MacBeth now foremost of his company, shouting for Duncan. His cousin, however, saw his role differently, as no doubt a king should, and remained well within the circle of his warriors, although encouraging them vigorously enough by word of mouth. The noise and shouting, there on the quiet green shore of the loch, was fearsome.

MacBeth, supported as he was by hard-smiting close companions guarding his sides, had only one objective — to hack his way through the infuriating protective cordon to get at Duncan. He fought skilfully enough — for he was no mean swordsman — but almost subconsciously, his mind preoccupied with two concerns, his cousin and his wife. Gruoch would be watching this, there across the water, fearing for her own and her children's safety. For his own too, perhaps.

How many men he slew or grievously wounded in that fierce, single-minded progress, he neither knew nor cared. He was wounded himself slightly, twice, in forearm and shoulder, glancing sword-cuts, but he scarcely realised it.

133

Duncan sought to keep a good belt of swordsmen and axemen between himself and that savagely determined smiter; but it was not easy, all men not necessarily being concerned with laying down their lives to ensure their liege lord's. Avoiding action was all too apt to be taken — leaving shameful gaps which his fanatical cousin might exploit, and did.

The struggle, as a whole, was a ragged one, with much ebbing and flowing of advantage. Because of MacBeth's own fiercely determined assault at the centre, with its personal support, that sector tended to do better than the rest, pressing much further forward. For the same reason, human nature being as it is, the opposition was less eager to be involved there, and was consequently more aggressive elsewhere. So the affair was uneven, to say the least, with the superior numbers of the royal contingent slowly beginning to tell. Save at the centre, which had become almost a separate conflict.

MacBeth, in fact, was not really leading his company at all. He was concerned with nothing but reaching Duncan. More than once he managed to get so near that only a single line of defenders were between him and his goal — but always some attack, some eddy of the fight, or some expert manoeuvre by Duncan, frustrated him. He was now bleeding from a grazed brow, and somewhat dizzy from the blow, the blood getting into his eyes; but still pressing his attack with little diminished vigour.

Then he saw his chance. Two men were between him and the King. But in avoiding one of MacBeth's figure-of-eight left-right slashes, the one cannoned into the other and both stumbled and fell to their knees. For a moment or two there was a clear gap between the two cousins, only a yard or so apart. MacBeth kicked savagely at the two fallen men, tumbling them right over, and leapt in, sword high.

Duncan had a sword drawn too, although he had used it little. Now he thrust it forward in a jabbing motion, low, foreshortened, for MacBeth's belly. That man brought his own broad blade slashing down just in time to smash the other's steel aside, only brief inches from its mark. Now, close together, staring into each others' eyes, it was a question of which could control his weapon best and fastest, bring it back up to a striking position and then strike. MacBeth, more fit, more active, although wounded, won by split seconds. Recovering balance and purchase of his sword, he drove it down on the other's sword-arm shoulder just as he reached a position to lunge again. With a yell, the King crumpled at that side, dropping the sword from nerveless fingers. In a swift change of stance, MacBeth drew back sufficiently to thrust violently, with all the residue of his failing strength. The other's armour-scales deflected the blow from his heart upwards, but the point penetrated the leathern tunic above, and ran him through below the left shoulder. Mouth wide, Duncan mac Crinan sank to the bloody grass.

MacBeth was reeling, staggering. His men closest to him, perceiving all, and his danger, clustered round him in a tight knot, to part-support him, part-hustle him back from the thick of the fighting. That they were successful in doing so was in no small measure due to the fact that the word of the King's fall was immediately shouted aloud, and everywhere men hesitated, faltered. Some continued to fight as lustily as before, but many did not, on both sides. With MacBeth being led aside, stumbling, the point seemed to go out of the contest for most of them, with little desire for death when the issue seemed to be decided anyway. Quite quickly the fighting tailed off. The sides, by mutual consent, drew apart, taking their wounded with them — including the King. A lot of dead were left lying.

MacBeth, whose blow on the brow had affected him more than he had realised, sought to pull himself together and take charge of the situation once more. But his head was spinning so badly that he required to be held in order to stand up straight. Presently, sitting down heavily on the trampled grass, he relayed jerky orders for his people to cluster in a tight knot by the lochside, at the end of the causeway, in case the enemy rallied and tried to attack the island. They could hold the causeway against all comers.

But it became apparent, even to MacBeth, that Duncan's men, far from thinking of resuming the struggle, were preoccupied with something other, something behind them, westwards. Hastily, in fact they began to stream away and up into the hillside woodlands south-eastwards, carrying the King and most of their other wounded with them. Soon only the dead and mortally injured were left to share the battle-ground with the men of Moray.

It was the first of the Vikings coming from Torfness, sent by Thorfinn to aid his brother. Coincident with their arrival, a coracle was paddled across from the Hall Isle by Gruoch herself. Exclaiming at the sight of her blood-soaked husband, she ran to him. Thereafter there was an interval of considerable confusion,

135

with MacBeth urging the Norsemen on, to go reinforce Brodie at the Lossie, and explaining to Gruoch that he was only scratched and perfectly able to continue in command of his forces — to counter her insistence that he must come back immediately to the *Dorus Neamh* and her nursing — and hearing through it all that the Torfness battle was to all intents over and a complete victory for Thorfinn, although with fairly heavy casualties. Out of all this din of words, some order and decision was at length reached.

The Viking vanguard should go on the mile or two to the Lossie line. Garrons would be brought across from the Horse Isle for MacBeth to ride thither also — with Gruoch, it seemed, since she would by no means leave him now. More Norsemen would be along soon, Thorfinn had promised. Meantime Gruoch alternated between bathing and binding up his wounds with her clothing, making endearing noises, and scolding him heartily.

The horses had come and MacBeth was secretly wondering just how he was going to manage to mount, not to mention stay mounted thereafter, when Thorfinn himself arrived with another large contingent. His shouted triumph was somewhat muted at sight of his bandaged and unsteady brother, his ribaldries dying away.

Sympathetic expressions were brief, however, like his assurances to Gruoch that MacBeth had a head of iron, to match his heart, and would be none the worse after a good meal and a night's sleep. There was no need for him to go on to the Lossie again. He, Thorfinn, would see to that. But — where was Duncan?

"I wounded him," his brother said thickly. "They took him away." And he gestured in a vaguely upward and south-easterly direction.

"You wounded him? Only *wounded!* God's Eyes, man — you did not kill him?"

"He could have been dead. When I struck him down. But . . . he was not."

"And you let him go? You had him — and you let him go!"

"He was wounded also. Can you not see?" Gruoch said, sharply.

"Where did they take him? How long ago?"

MacBeth pointed again. "That way. Through the woods. Over the Hill of Spynie. To join the others, no doubt. Echmarcach."

136

"When?"

"I do not know. Sufficiently long. But they have the Lossie to cross. . ."

Thorfinn wasted no more time, but swept on.

Gruoch took her husband over to the *Dorus Neamh*.

His brother was back with the sundown of a long day, satisfied save in the matter of Duncan's escape.

"When he saw who he was facing now, that Irishman drew back," he reported. "He has the elements of wisdom in him, that Echmarcach! He left a screen of men to guard the river-crossings. But we will leave that, for tonight. My heroes are weary. And hungry. Tomorrow we shall see. How are you now?"

"Stiff," MacBeth said.

"To be sure. I hope that Duncan is stiffer! Your bed — that is the place for you, Brother."

"Yes, my dear," Gruoch said, pleaded. "Come to bed. Nothing more that you can do tonight . . ."

*　　　*　　　*

In the morning, aching but clear-headed, with word that Echmarcach's army was still standing by inactive a mile or so behind the Lossie, MacBeth discussed strategy with Thorfinn over breakfast. Despite Duncan's defeats and losses, he could still muster a large force, its inland section as yet all but un-blooded. And now that the King was injured, incapacitated surely, it might well indeed be under wiser and better direction. The Vikings had suffered quite heavy losses — although the Moraymen had not. MacBeth believed that negotiations might now prove more fruitful. His brother, predictably, was con-temptuous of negotiations.

It was at this stage that Gruoch came to announce a visitor under a flag-of-truce — Cormac of Glamis.

That grizzled veteran marched into the hall escorted by Darnaway. He raised his hand in salute.

"Greetings!" he jerked. "Duncan mac Crinan is dead." He paused. "Dead," he repeated, deep-voiced. "He died of his wounds. At dawn. At a smith's hut. Bothgowan, near to Pitgavenny. They have taken his body to the abbot at Elgin."

"Dead! He is *dead*? I, I killed him!" That was MacBeth, all but croaking.

"His blood was bad. Always was so. Duncan Ilgalrach, the Bad Blooded. It would not stanch — the blood. So he is dead."

137

His hand rose again. "Hail MacBeth, High King of Scots."

Eyes widening, MacBeth stared at him, as the others drew long breaths.

Glamis strode forward, to drop on one knee and reach out both hands to take MacBeth's between them, in the traditional gesture of fealty.

"I Cormac mac Eochaid, am the first to give you my allegiance, my lord King!" he said.

MacBeth shook his head, slightly, then desisted at the pain of it. He looked over at Gruoch. "I am not King yet," he said, slowly.

"Who else is there?" Thorfinn asked, rising to come and clasp his brother strongly, producing more pain. "MacBeth the King! Son of Life, by God!"

10

IT WAS AN extraordinary transformation, by any standards. From organising a battle to organising a state funeral, in the course of mere hours. The fact that MacBeth was suffering from wounds and dizzy spells was immaterial. The first duty of the tanist to the Scots high throne was to arrange the funeral to Iona of the dead King. And whatever Duncan had or had not been, he had been King of Scots.

At least there was no longer a problem of hostilities and armies to complicate proceedings. That was what Glamis had really been sent under the flag-of-truce to say — that, with Duncan dead, there was no longer anything to fight about, any real opposition to MacBeth. The campaign had all been wholly at the King's will. Echmarcach, apparently, had been undecided as to making this move, Fife likewise; but the other mormaors with the inland army had persuaded these that there was no point in remaining in arms against MacBeth — although Thorfinn's position was rather different.

However, they had to swallow Thorfinn — and were enabled to do so with rather better grace in that he promptly offered to transport all concerned to Iona in his longships, an offer few thought to refuse, in the circumstances. The long and difficult journey across Highland Scotland and through the Hebrides appealed to none, at this stage — especially as, in this warm summer weather, the body would have to be conveyed quickly.

So, within three days of the Battle of Torfness, the main protagonists were heading north, in at least superficial amity, in a group of vessels flying the raven banner of Orkney, leaving the fighting-men behind, the dead king inconspicuous, rolled in sail-cloth. It would be inaccurate to suggest that they made a happy, comfortable or congenial company, or that any large proportion of the mormaors, thanes and chieftains were fully at ease in MacBeth's presence — much less Thorfinn's. MacBeth, head and arm bandaged, endeavoured to be conciliatory, or at least civil towards all, his brother making no attempt to be one or the other. However, Thorfinn made sure that only Glamis and Lennox and Angus, with the Moray and Ross thanes, abbots and bishops, travelled in his own dragon-ship, the others distributing themselves as they would in four other craft. Echmarcach of Dublin, with some of the Lothian and Strath-clyde lords, was left behind, it not being any affair of theirs. They would lead the southern army on its homeward way.

MacBeth had given orders that he was to be treated only as Mormaor of Moray and Ross. He was not King yet, and might never be so. Nevertheless there was a new attitude towards him evident on all hands; even his own thanes less easy with him. He was uneasy even with himself, indeed. Whether or not he became the King, nothing could alter the fact that he had *slain* the King — he who had been so loth to raise hand against the Ard Righ. Nothing would change or undo that. He, MacBeth mac Finlay, had killed the crowned occupier of the Stone of Destiny. He had no doubt that one day destiny would call him to account.

Old Abbot Malmore and his bishops and "family" greeted the invasion philosophically, although they had scarcely envisaged another royal interment quite so soon. Nor were they evidently censorious as to the manner of the royal death. This time, at least, there was no need for such haste as heretofore — although the body was beginning to smell. It was put in a cave, meantime, on the west side of the island, while the monks made a suitable coffin. The mourners sought to adjust themselves to the circum-stances and the suddenly changed tempo of events.

There were five mormaors present, in addition to MacBeth and Thorfinn, Lennox, Angus, Strathearn, Fife and the Mearns. Mar had been slain at Torfness, and Crinan of Atholl was

139

absent. There was a total of twenty-one thanes, seven abbots, hereditary or otherwise, and three bishops other than the Iona ones, with a selection of chiefs, toiseachs and captains of clans. Earl Gillaciaran and his sons were there, from Colonsay. It was a vastly more representative gathering than on the last occasion.

Since feasting was in order, Thorfinn sent his men scouring adjacent Mull for the wherewithal, with instructions that, since it was ostensibly for the benefit of Holy Church, they should not just take all in normal Viking fashion, but pay for it. Whether they did or not, ample provision was quickly produced, sufficient indeed to keep the brethren well victualled for many a day after the visitors were fed and gone.

Although he did not deserve it, as Thorfinn proclaimed loudly, Duncan received a fuller and more dignified burial ceremony than had his grandsire, despite his brief reign. All must be done properly and in order, MacBeth insisted. There being no cold wind to hasten the recital, even the genealogy sounded more interesting, and one King's name longer. The coffin was lowered beside its predecessor in the Relig Oran, with not a single damp eye.

Afterwards, at the interment feast in the Abbey eating-hall, the more vital part of the proceedings took place. MacBeth had some difficulty in dissuading his brother from taking the lead in the matter, asserting unsuitability. Lennox assumed the duty. A quiet non-controversialist, he spoke formally and undramatically.

"When we, the mormaors and lesser kings of Alba, have buried one High King, it is the custom here in the Abbey of Columcille to name his successor, before the gathering of his thanes and officers. It was not done at Malcolm's burial through . . . mischance. Better that it should have been, I say. But that is past. Today there is but one man who should succeed to the high throne — MacBeth mac Finlay . . ."

Thorfinn vociferously led the cheering — although not all actually joined in.

"He is undoubted tanist," Lennox went on. "He is grandson of King Malcolm the Second and . . ."

"So is Maldred mac Crinan," MacDuff of Fife put in heavily.

Thorfinn hooted his opinion of Maldred, formerly called Prince of Cumbria, before Malcolm Big Head had been made to supersede him, Duncan's diffident and retiring brother.

Angus spoke up, a sad-faced man of middle years, with a

lachrymose eye. "None has ever considered Maldred for King. He has not himself, I say. He has not the quality for it. Any more than, than . . ." He did not finish that.

"The Lord MacBeth has to wife the Lady Gruoch nic Bodhe, who was son to Kenneth the Second," Lennox resumed. "Had she been a man, she would have had better claim to the throne than any. For this reason also her husband should be King."

There was a long growl of agreement. Much of it came from the thanes present. They had no say nor vote in this matter but at least they could make their preference known to their lords, the mormaors.

"There is only one other, close, of the royal line, and of age." Lennox glanced over at Thorfinn. "The Earl of Orkney. But he declares that he has no wish to wear the crown . . ."

"I prefer to be Earl of Orkney," that man interjected. "I may make kings, or unmake them. That is enough for me!"

MacBeth turned his bandaged head to look thoughtfully at his half-brother.

There was a pregnant silence.

Then MacDuff spoke again. "The King — Duncan — has a son. Donald Ban."

"What of it?" Strathearn demanded, a thin, cadaverous-looking man. "We do not seek bairns for our High King."

"I but remind all." Even MacDuff would not dare to mention the bastard Prince of Strathclyde and Cumbria, Malcolm Big Head.

Lennox cleared his throat. "The issue is clear then, I say. I name to you MacBeth mac Finlay as our next High King."

"As do I," Angus put in.

"And I," Colin of the Mearns added.

With four of the mortuaths held by MacBeth and his brother, it did not demand any deep calculation to perceive that the thing was settled.

"I also," Strathearn muttered, if without enthusiasm.

MacDuff of Fife grunted something which might be taken as assent.

As a great sigh swept the company, Thorfinn rose to his feet and, without the normal necessity of standing on his seat, lifted one mighty leg to place his foot on the table-top itself. So standing he held high his drinking-horn.

"To MacBeth mac Finlay, High King of Scots!" he shouted. "Health — and a sharp sword!"

There was a considerable noise as men rose and forms were

pushed back. Only the other mormaors present might stand on their seats, feet on the table, but all the rest of the gathering stood, horns and beakers raised.

"MacBeth the King!" they shouted. "Hail the King! Hail the King! Long live MacBeth!" and drank deep, each to empty his cup to the dregs. MacBeth alone remained seated.

When at length the hubbub subsided, the mormaors climbed down and all resumed their seats, he rose slowly, having to steady himself with a hand on the table — for the dizziness was still there. Thorfinn banged a mighty fist on the board for silence.

"My friends, I thank you all," he said, husky-voiced. "You do me too much honour. But . . . I accept your naming. In my wife's name as in my own. I can do no other. But — you go too fast, to hail me as King. I am not the King until I am crowned at Scone. This is only nomination. Until I am seated on the Stone I am only mormaor, selected and named. No more. Let none forget it, as I do not. Then will be time enough to hail me. I shall travel to Scone as soon as is possible. With the Princess Gruoch. For she will share the throne with me. Not merely as wife and consort, but as reigning Queen. For she is the true heir-of-line. Being a woman she could not be tanist. Whether she could sit on the Stone I do not know — but it has never been done. But she can *share* the throne, and will do. That I swear."

The reaction to that was mixed, some applauding, some nodding but as many looking doubtful or expressionless. The Celtic tradition made much of women in story and song, as inspirers of heroism and mothers of heroes — but not in authority, not on thrones. A woman should not be the Fount of Honour, it was felt, since she could not hold knighthood. The King must be of knightly status. Yet there was no law which said that a Queen could not reign.

Thorfinn slapped his knee — but in amusement rather than in acclaim.

MacBeth went on. "I shall seek to be a true and good King, honest, just, a protector of the weak, and as strong as God in His wisdom allows." He looked slowly, deliberately all around the great ring of faces, seeming almost to miss none, certainly not his own brother's, over which he actually appeared to linger a moment. "The high throne is the symbol of the greatness and enduring glory of our ancient race. I shall maintain it so, with God's help — let none mistake, foe or friend. While I am High King — if so I become — none other shall usurp or over-shadow my part and calling. Even though he be better man than

I am. I promise — and warn — all here. You have still time to change your nomination, before Scone. Think well! For the rest, I am grateful to you all. I am in your hands."

He sat down, in silence.

Presently a medley or talk and comment, question and discussion arose, by no means all of it favourable-sounding.

Thorfinn leaned over. "That was strange speaking, Brother," he said, and did not seek to lower his strong voice.

"It required to be said."

"Perhaps. But — to whom?"

"To *all* who heard me. Did I not say? Foe and friend alike."

"So-o-o! It is that way, is it?"

"That way," MacBeth nodded. "If I am to sit on the Stone. If you mislike it you may still claim the throne, Thor. You might have new allies now, Elder Brother!"

The other looked at him through narrowed eyes for long moments. Then he laughed aloud, and slapped a huge hand on MacBeth's shoulder, making that man wince.

"Son of Life!" he cried. "Live on!"

11

THEY CAME TO Scone, in the Stormounth, on the banks of Tay, almost a month later, on the Eve of Saint Cuthbert. Scone was accepted as the place of greatest significance in Fortrenn, or Southern Pictavia, for here was the highest point on Tay reached by the tide, where the salt waters with their powers of death were turned back by the living waters of the river. The great Abbey of Scone was situated on a terrace above a bend of the wide river, a fine place amongst open woodlands, centring on a large partly-artificial mound called the Moot Hill. No doubt, there had been originally a circle of standing-stones there in the Druid era, for it had always been a sacred place, and was extended for present ceremonial purposes. There was a stone church, much more commodious than in the generality of Celtic abbeys and cashels; and this was the resting-place of the *Lia Faill*, the famous Stone of Destiny, talisman of the race, the Abbot of Scone its keeper. The normal scatter of subsidiary buildings surrounded, but these were much more extensive than usual, to cater for the large numbers who thronged here on great occasions. Otherwise it was a typical Celtic monastery, functional and unadorned.

The MacBeth family had travelled southwards slowly and in state, with a large company from Moray and Ross. They were far too many to put up within the abbey, so they had to be sent over to the township of Bertha across the river, for the present vastly extended with tents and pavilions. There was no palace at Scone, the royal residence being some seven miles to the north-east, in the Sidlaw heights, at Dunsinane. But MacBeth felt that it was unsuitable to go there before he was officially monarch, so he and Gruoch and the children put up meantime in the abbey guest-house, asking no more than any other visitor.

Abbot Cathail, to be sure, fussed over them like a hen with but one chick.

It was customary for the monarch-to-be to spend some portion of the night before his coronation in a vigil of prayer and meditation. MacBeth, with Duncan's death on his mind, might well have spent hours in the quiet and dimly-lit chapel before the altar, had Gruoch not put her foot down strongly and dragged him off to bed. For so beautiful and spirited a woman she had a strong vein of practicality.

All the following morning the nobility and high clergy of Alba, Lothian, the Merse, Strathclyde, Dalar and Argyll were arriving. Thorfinn, bringing Ingebiorg with him, was one of the last to appear, from longships brought as far up Tay as was possible — MacBeth having wondered, indeed, whether he had been offended by the nomination speech sufficiently to absent himself altogether. Perhaps he did delay until the last moment deliberately, to arouse just such a fear — it was the sort of thing that man might do, Neil Nathrach said. He was cheerful enough on arrival, however, and Ingebiorg her usual uncomplicated self.

The Primate of All Scotland, Abbot of Dunkeld, should have been in over-all charge of the ceremonies; but this was, of course, Crinan of Atholl, and he was the only mormaor not present. His place probably should have been taken by the Abbot and Co-Arb of Iona, Saint Columba's successor and senior cleric of the Church; but he was an old man, frail, and had moreover already given MacBeth his blessing at Iona. It would have been a long and difficult journey for him. So the duty was to be performed by Malduin, Bishop of St. Andrews, *Ard Episcop*, High or King's Bishop, assisted by the Abbot of Scone, Keeper of the Stone.

The coronation ceremony was a mixture of the ancient Pictish and Scoto-Irish inaugural proceedings, with the original pagan basis overlaid by Christian rites and additions. Most of it still was conducted in the open air before the assembled people, as was proper. Indeed the initial service in the abbey-church was more in the nature of a personal preparation and extension of the night before's vigil than any vital part of the coronation itself, attended only by the monarch-to-be himself, his family, the mormaors and officers of state. Then, to the sweet chanting of a large choir of men and boys, the procession filed out into the midday sunlight, led by the master-of-ceremonies, the Great Sennachie, the clerics, the principal guests and the mormaors, these carrying variously the crown, the sceptre, the sword-of-state, the Book of Laws and the purple robe. MacBeth and Gruoch came last, except for Neil Nathrach with Lulach and little Farquhar now four. The baby Luctacus had been left at Spynie.

Only the Sennachie, the two officiating clergy, the mormaors and the royal couple climbed on to the top of the Moot Hill, or *Tom a Mhoid*, the Hill of the Vows. Here, in the sacred grove where the ancient kingdoms of the Northern and Southern Picts joined, Druidical worship had given way to Christian, King Nechtan in 710 accepted the amended dating for Easter and Kenneth mac Alpin had brought the Stone of Destiny from Dunstaffnage in Dalar in 844, on uniting the thrones of Picts and Scots. Now the *Lia Faill* formed the centre-piece of the day's ceremonial, together with a lesser stone, a mere boulder this, lying nearby.

The *Lia Faill*, the most revered object in the land, had been brought out of the abbey-church to stand on a three-stepped plinth on the summit of the hill. Various origins were assigned to it. Some said that it was the stone which Jacob had used as a pillow at Bethel when he had his vision of the angels ascending and descending, which later fell into the hands of the Pharoahs of Egypt at the Captivity, and was brought first to Spain and then to Ireland by Scota, daughter of a Pharoah — who gave name to the Scots. Others said that one Simon Brec, a son of a King of Spain in the Celtic days there, had brought it to Ireland. And from Ireland Fergus mac Erc, King of Antrim had carried it to Dalar or Argyll when he formed a new kingdom in what was to be Scotland — Dalar-rioghd or Dalriada. Some averred that it was in fact Saint Columba's portable altar-cum-font, made out of a meteorite which had fallen at some auspicious occasion. Others that it was the font from which Saint Boniface had baptised King Nechtan, made out of an early Roman altar from the Antonine Wall, later decorated with Celtic carving. Whatever its origins, it had been the crowning seat of kings for many centuries.

MacBeth, as he walked past it, Gruoch on his arm and adjusting his stride to her's, eyed this palladium of his people. It stood seat-high on its plinth, black, gleaming, the intricate interlaced Celtic carving, with which it was adorned, reflecting the sun — for it was made of some very hard, dark stone susceptible to polish, probably indeed a meteorite. Some had called it the marble chair, although it was not of marble. It was oddly-shaped, rounded at base but squared-off at the top to the oblong, with curving volutes at the two ends to facilitate carriage, these also finely carved. It would be very heavy. The top, or seat, had a hollow in the centre, which could well have been used to hold holy water. Mysterious, unique, it stood there in the sun, symbol of power and majesty down untold generations.

The other stone, a few yards to the west of it was vastly more simple, merely a lump of natural grey granite in which the imprint of a man's right foot had been cut to the depth of over an inch. Nothing more than that.

The Sennachie, Bishop and Abbot led the little procession past the stones, to the west, where all halted, to turn and face the east — not, it is to be feared towards Christ's birthplace but in a still older gesture of worship, towards the sun's rising. The six mormaors, Thorfinn towering above the others, lined up in a crescent, in the midst of which MacBeth and his wife placed themselves, flanked by Malduin of St. Andrews and Cathail of Scone. The High Sennachie — none other than Farquhar O'Beolain Abbot of Applecross — stepped forward. All this while the cheering of the crowds all but drowned the choir's singing.

The O'Beolain held up a hand for quiet. As both shouting and chanting died away, acolytes blew lustily on bulls' horns in a long wailing ululation. Thereafter he spoke.

"I, Farquhar O'Beolain, appointed High Sennachie of this realm, do declare to you all, high and low, noble and simple, that following upon the death of Duncan mac Crinan, High King of Scots, the mormaors of Alba, as was their undoubted

146

duty, and theirs only, have selected and chosen to occupy the vacant throne MacBeth mac Finlay, Mormaor of Moray and Ross, grandson of King Malcolm of potent memory. Moreover, I declare to you that the said MacBeth will reign hereafter in concert with his wife, the Lady Gruoch nic Bodhe mac Kenneth, of royal descent, as King and Queen of Scots, not as King of Scots and consort. This to be known and understood by all. In token whereof I now do rehearse to you their true and lawful descent, as proof of their right. Thus. MacBeth son of Donada, daughter of Malcolm the Second, son of Kenneth the Second son of Malcolm the First. And Gruoch daughter of Bodhe, son of Kenneth the Third, son of Duff, son of the said Malcolm the First. And thereafter, jointly, thus . . ." Once again came the long recital of names back and back into the mists of antiquity, far enough back to reach the mythical ancients of legend, the point being to demonstrate that the new Ard Righ Albann was descended from the primordial gods of the race, and so sacred in his own person.

If this lengthy enumeration wearied the huge company, none showed it — save perhaps the Earl Thorfinn, whose patience for more than genealogy was apt to be quickly exhausted. A resplendent figure, he fidgeted, tugged his forked beard, scratched his head and stared around and even behind him.

At length O'Beolain was finished. "I now present to you the Lord MacBeth," he said.

That man bowed deeply to the east, north, west and south, and then to Gruoch, who curtsied low.

It was now Bishop Malduin's turn. Stepping in front of the royal couple, he administered the oath, MacBeth repeating after him, hand on an illuminated book of the Scriptures, that he would maintain the true worship of God as appointed by the Church, protect the realm from all its enemies, uphold the laws of the land, do justice without fear or favour, cherish the widows and orphans, the poor and the weak, and be in all things a loving father to his people. Then, signing to the pair to kneel, the Bishop placed a hand on each lowered head. His own eyes upraised towards heaven, his lips moved in silent prayer — and everywhere men and women all but held their breaths. The Laying on of Hands in the apostolic succession was a vital and most significant rite in the Celtic Church, without which none of the rest of the coronation service could proceed. In a loud voice he cried, "In the name of God the Father, God the Son and God the Holy Ghost, receive ye the Holy Spirit.

The Spirit come upon you and the power of the Highest over-shadow you. Receive ye the spirit of wisdom and understanding. Receive ye the spirit of counsel and might. Receive ye the knowledge and the fear of God. In the name of the Father, the Son and the Holy Ghost."

As a long sigh rose from the gathering and the couple rose, the Abbot of Scone moved over to lay a coverlet of purple silk on top of the *Lia Faill*. Then coming back, bowing, he held out his hand to MacBeth, who took it, and was led slowly forward and up the two steps, there to stand and face the huge company.

A hush fell on all, any ripple of movement ceasing. This was the moment of destiny. The man who stood there, so utterly simply clad in the *leine croich*, the saffron kilted linen tunic, with the gold-linked mormaor's belt its only mark of distinction, was still only a man amongst men, a great noble yes, but one of many. But when he sat . . .

For long moments he stood so. Then, leaning forward and up — for the abbot was a small man — Cathail pressed a hand on each of the broad shoulders. MacBeth sat.

The shout which rose and maintained echoed to the very surrounding hills. The trumpets which blew a triumphant fanfare were barely to be heard nor was the traditional clashing of shields, so deafening was the acclaim of thousands. On and on it went. The Scots had a King again.

The bishop brought Gruoch to stand behind the Stone.

MacBeth knew an extraordinary exultation of the spirit, allied to a profound sense of unworthiness. It was not so much the realisation that he was now transformed from subject to king, but the fact that here he was actually sitting upon the Stone of Destiny, the lawful and accepted incumbent of the *Lia Faill*, that mystic and enduring token of authority — and would, must, continue so until his life's end, for there was no abdication or surrender from that seat. He was all unworthy. But, to be sure, unworthy men had sat on this Stone before him, the last probably the most unworthy of all. God aiding him, he would do better. That he swore to himself. He had taken the solemn coronation oath, yes, made his public promises. But this was his own personal and private oath. He would not debase the Stone of Destiny and what it stood for.

His heart full, he half-turned to grasp his wife's arm.

When the abbot thought that he could make himself heard, he raised his hand, to declaim the time-honoured words:

"The Scots shall rule that realm as native ground,

Wheresoever shall this Stone be found."

As this also was acclaimed by the crowd, Cathail beckoned to MacDuff of Fife. That bovine, high-coloured young man paced forward, frowning, bearing the simple golden crown of Scotland on its cushion. There had been some doubts as to whether he, who had put the crown on Duncan's head, should do the same for MacBeth whom he had made no secret of disliking. Indeed Thorfinn had himself wished to do the crowning, as suitable. Others had suggested that Bishop Melduin should do it. But MacBeth had insisted that it must be MacDuff. Fife was the second mortuath of Alba, after Moray; and since Moray had usually been the seat of the reigning family themselves, the holder of Fife was traditionally accepted to be the rightful man to be Hereditary Inaugurator. MacBeth had determined that all should be done in due order, without innovation save for Gruoch's part. Moreover, it might be wise to have MacDuff seen by all to be positively involved in the crowning, for the sake of united support of the throne.

So MacDuff came and placed the crown on MacBeth's head, with minimum ceremony, bowed briefly, and returned to his place with the attitude of an unpleasant task dutifully accomplished.

Thereafter one by one the mormaors came over, Thorfinn with the great sword, which his brother took in his right hand, the others giving him the sceptre, the Book of Laws placed on the Stone at his side, and the purple robe of royalty draped round his shoulders. Then Cathail brought Gruoch round from behind the Stone to the front, where Bishop Malduin placed another circle of gold, specially made, on her head.

MacBeth rose to his feet, still holding up the heavy sword and the light sceptre, beside his wife. So they stood together, while the trumpets blared, the cymbals clashed and the very Moot Hill itself seemed to shake to the shouts of "Hail the King! Hail MacBeth! Hail the King and Queen!"

But all was not done yet. The second stone had its part to play. Laying sword and sceptre on the *Lia Faill* and flanked by his mormaors, the new monarch paced over to the granite boulder. There each of the mormaors drew from some pocket a small pouch or bag and, led by Thorfinn, proceeded to open these and each pour a dribble of soil into the deep carved footprint, earth from each of their mortuaths. Kicking off his right sandal, MacBeth placed his bare foot on the top, pressing down the symbolic earth of his provinces — save, in this instance,

149

Atholl unrepresented — High King of Scots and of Scotland too, there being a difference.

There remained the homage, a lengthy procedure, wherein all the principal men, officers and land-holders of the kingdom filed up on to the Moot Hill to kneel before the monarch and make their oath and gesture of fealty, hands within hands. First the *grad flaith*, the territorial nobles led by the thanes and lords, then the clan chiefs, toiseachs and captains, followed by the smaller landowners and lairds, the judges and officers. It took almost two hours, and MacBeth sat on the Stone throughout, Gruoch standing at his side, Lulach and little Farquhar brought up to stand there likewise, a tiring business. But at last it was done, ceremonial over, and it was time for rejoicing, entertainment, feasting.

When the company was replete and the wine and ale flowed freely, the O'Beolain beat on the high table to demand silence for their liege lord. The High King would make the first address of his reign.

MacBeth rose, and bowed formally to Gruoch at his side.

After he had given his general thanks to the assembly, he paused and looked round. "In especial, I have to declare the mighty aid given by my own good half-brother, the Earl Thorfinn of Orkney, Mormaor of Caithness and Sutherland, whose stout heart, strong arm and great sea-power have been my unfailing support. Whether I could be standing here *without* that support, I do not know. I hope that his support may continue. But this I say to you, and to him. That hereafter it can only be accepted where it is offered freely and given without price demanded. I say this hard thing that all may know that this kingdom, or any part of it, shall not be traded for the strength of any, brother or other, while I sit on the Stone of Destiny. You all hear me, MacBeth — and I say it out of a full heart. The Raven Feeder knows it. Now so do you all."

At first only Thorfinn himself dared applaud, as men eyed each other doubtfully, even in something approaching alarm. But the earl's hooted acclaim, slightly ribald as it was, set others beginning to nod their heads and murmur about wisdom, prudence and the like.

"For those who supported me, then, my thanks. They will not find me otherwise ungrateful. To those who did not support me, I say that it is the realm which is important now, not what is past. I shall not seek to punish or revenge. That would be empty foolishness. Some will have to be replaced in their office, but there will be no ill-usage. With the late King's close kin I have no quarrel — after all, they are my kin also. The Mormaor Crinan, my aunt's husband, is not present, but I wish him no ill and would have him my friend. His son Maldred likewise and his grandson Donald. The Lady Sybil shall be provided for if she chooses to remain in Scotland. As for the boy Malcolm, whom they call Canmore, the miller's daughter's son, he need fear nothing from me — save that he cannot remain, as he should never have been, Prince of Strathclyde and Cumbria. That title and position now goes to my stepson, Lulach mac Gillacomgain — whom God preserve."

There was a corporate gasp throughout the hall at this declaration. The King was naming as his heir-apparent not his own son Farquhar, but his wife's son by his late enemy. Nothing could more clearly emphasise his belief that she had the greater right to their throne, and that his insistence on their joint reign was no mere token.

Gruoch reached up a hand to grip his arm, wordless.

"Other appointments I shall make in due course," he went on, level-voiced. "But two I give you now, since they also are personal to me. The Earl Thorfinn to be Lord of Galloway and Carrick, and also Governor of Strathclyde and Cumbria for the Prince Lulach. And my foster-brother Neil, to whom I owe my life, to be Thane of Cawdor, in room of Hugh, reduced."

He had to raise his voice above the hum of comment at this indication that he could strike as well as overlook.

"Finally, my friends, it is enough if I say that it shall be my endeavour to seek peace with all my neighbours and with all the princes of Christendom. This with all my powers. Yet, I shall not hesitate to draw the sword in defence of any and every of Scotland's rights and interests, against whomsoever, foe or friend. I seek no territorial gains for my kingdom — but will yield none." He paused, and for the first time smiled a little. "Enough. Since I am now of the priestly order, made so by the Laying on of Hands, I finish by saying — God bless and keep you all!"

He sat down.

Thorfinn jumped up, to still the applause by slamming fist on the table to make every dish and beaker and drinking-horn jump.

"You have a man on the throne of Scotland again!" he shouted. "A man, I say. I may not love all that he says and does, now or hereafter — and nor may you! But, by God, he will say and do it just the same! For he is a King indeed. On your feet, I say, and drink to MacBeth the King, and his lady. MacBeth the King!"

Thorfinn Raven Feeder must ever have the last word, as Ingebiorg pointed out.

12

ALTHOUGH NOT AS lovely a spot as Spynie, Dunsinane was a pleasing place in aspect and character. It was one of the two principal royal residences of Fortrenn, the other being Forteviot. Malcolm Foiranach had chosen to reign from Forteviot, as also had Duncan. So it was almost inevitable that MacBeth and Gruoch should prefer Dunsinane, which had been her grandfather Kenneth the Third's palace.

They found it to be more of a fort than a palace, however. It occupied the summit of a grassy hill at the western end of the famous and lovely vale of Strathmore, just over 1000 feet above the Tay, an eagle's-nest of a place, with views to catch the breath.

The views and its defensive potential, were probably the best of it — that and its name, *dun-sithean*, the mound or fort of the fairies — for the accommodation, although covering a wide area within the strong ramparts, was inconvenient, in some respects almost primitive, more like a scattered township within a wall than a palace. The great hall, for instance, although large enough, occupied a building by itself, as did two lesser halls, with no sleeping-quarters under the same roof. The royal apartments were little to be distinguished from the garrison's. If at first sight Gruoch's heart lifted, at second it sank — even though she did not say so. Thorfinn and Ingebiorg who, with her father, accompanied the royal couple from Scone to see them settled in, were less inhibited. They exclaimed loudly that the place was impossible, no better than a robbers' hold, and no lodging, much less a residence, for the King of Scots. They should get them over to Forteviot in Strathearn right away, whether that Duncan had defiled it or not.

But there was an obstinate strain in MacBeth, and the more

152

they decried Dunsinane — supported for once by Neil, Thane of Cawdor — the more determined he was to stay.

He did not add, but nor did he fail to remember, that his mother's dream had linked him with Dunsinane, never with Forteviot. Her strange warning about Birnam Wood could scarcely trouble him now that he was here to see the place. Her dream, after all, had been that he would prosper *until* Birnam Wood came to Dunsinane; and Birnam lay fully fifteen miles to the north-west, in Atholl. His first glance, on reaching the hill-top, had been in that direction, and he had been relieved to see that the hills of Auchtergaven and the high Moor of Thorn rose between, not to mention the unseen valley of the Tay itself. For Birnam Wood to come here would demand powers no man possessed. The dream, then need not be a premonition or caution at all, but in fact an encouragement. Here at Dunsinane he would stay — for such time as he must reside in the south part of his kingdom, for he and Gruoch had every intention of maintaining Spynie as their home.

Most of the duties which now fell to him, MacBeth could take in his stride. But quite quickly after the coronation he was faced with a situation demanding more than mere mormaoral judgment. It concerned the mortuath of Mar, and the thanage of Buchan therein. Gartnait of Mar had died at the Battle of Torfness, leaving only a fifteen-year-old heir, Martacus. Matain mac Caerill of Buchan, Duncan's brother-in-law, he who had aspired to be Mormaor of Caithness and Sutherland and whom Thorfinn had slain, had left no child but only a younger brother, one Lachlan .This Lachlan was now seeking to take over Mar by main force, declaring that the fifteen-year-old Martacus was too young, lacking in wits and incompetent to rule a major mortuath; and in this he was being supported by Matain's widow, the Lady Cathula nic Crinan, and one or two of the thanes of Mar. It looked as though open war might be near. The widow of Gartnait, mother of Martacus appealed to the new monarch.

MacBeth accepted that the decision was properly one for the High King, but recognised the dangers, especially at the very start of a new reign. He would consider the case. But instead of summoning the contenders to Fortrenn, he would go north to Mar to hear the matter on the spot, where local conditions and witnesses should make for fair judgment. Moreover, this would all help forward a strategy he was determined to pursue, to seek to shift at least some of the power of the throne from the South, where it had been concentrated for too long, back into the North — for it was, after all, a Northern dynasty. Also, it would provide an excellent excuse to return to Spynie for a spell.

So, in breezy autumn weather, leaving a triumvirate of Lennox, Strathearn and Glamis in charge at Fortrenn, MacBeth, Gruoch and the children rode away eastwards down the great vale of Strathmore.

Mar was one of the most extensive provinces of Alba, comprising the vast basins of the Dee and Don and Deveron, all the coastal plain to the verge of Moray, and inland some of the highest and wildest mountains of Scotland.

It took them two full days of major riding, as much as the children could stand, to reach their objective, the renowned and ancient Abbey of Deer, founded by Saint Drostan, one of the Brethren of Columba, amidst spreading oak-woods. Its Abbot Malbride had blessed their wedding, and they were most warmly welcomed.

MacBeth had already sent out summonses to both parties and their witnesses to appear before him here in two days' time, and although not a man for display, he decided that it would be politic to manage this, his first major royal occasion, to some effect. With Abbot Malbride's co-operation he had the abbey's eating-hall prepared. It did not have a dais, so a makeshift platform was contrived at one end, from the monks' table-boards, covered by sheep and deerskins. On this the establishment's two best chairs were set, side-by-side, as thrones, decked with purple vestments. The hall itself, severely plain like all Celtic religious buildings, was decorated for the occasion with birch and pine branches, the former now beginning to turn a delicate pale gold, much more attractive than the seared oak. There was no other seating; but even with all standing the hall would not hold any large proportion of those who had come, so the main door was left open, that some of those outside could at least hear what went on. All had to be assembled well before royalty put in an appearance.

The abbey could produce no trumpeters, so they had to be content with horn-blowers. A group of these sounded off loud and long, their curious wailing notes echoing from all the surrounding green hillsides. A procession of monks, chanting, led in Deer's three bishops and other clergy, to range themselves behind the improvised platform. Then Abbot Malbride brought in the Mormaor Colin of the Mearns and Farquhar O'Beolain of Applecross — who was making his way home-

154

wards with the royal party. These three mounted the dais, to stand behind the thrones, as assessors and advisers. O'Beolain, in his capacity as High Sennachie, took charge, raising hand to halt the chanting and all talk and stir.

"Silence for the King!" he cried. "The Lord MacBeth, High King of Scots. And the Lady Gruoch, Queen of Scots. The Appointed of God and the Protector of Holy Church."

Into the profound hush the royal couple paced, side by side, each with a plain circlet of gold around their brows and a purple cloak over their shoulders, but otherwise simply clad. At their back came the princes, Lulach and Farquhar, Prince of Strathclyde and Cumbria and Mormaor of Moray and Ross. MacBeth and Gruoch seated themselves, a boy at each side. The family aspect was to be emphasised, for more than dynastic reasons. There was much improvement in the image of kingship necessary after Duncan's reign and the latter part of Malcolm's. This of a royal family was important.

O'Beolain raised his voice again. "Hail to the lord King!" he cried. "Hail the King and Queen!"

Loud, deafening, the company's response rang out. Young Farquhar actually looked a little frightened at the din.

At length MacBeth brought them to the nub of the matter.

"Your late Mormaor Gartnait mac Donald fell in battle at Torfness in Moray. He was fighting in the train of the King of Scots, as was his duty. So no blame attaches to him or his, in this matter." MacBeth paused, to let that sink in. "His lawful son, Martacus mac Gartmait, is aged only fifteen years. But others have succeeded to mortuaths at an even earlier age. I myself became Mormaor of Ross at sixteen. And my half-brother the Earl Thorfinn was appointed Mormaor of Caithness and Sutherland at the age of five years, by King Malcolm himself. So youth of itself does not debar Martacus. Let that be accepted."

Another pause, amidst some shuffling of feet.

"However, Lachlan mac Caerill, now Thane of Buchan, supported by some others, makes protest against this succession. As likewise is his right, as thane, so be it his objections are well-founded and honestly held. He claims that Martacus is unfit to hold the mortuath of Mar, not only by reason of youth but through lack of full wits. This is a hard matter, and difficult of proof and decision — for, to be sure, Martacus and those who know him best, maintain that he is in fact of clear mind and in full control of his wits as any youth of fifteen years. If it could be shown that this is not so, then it would be my duty to declare him unfit to be a mormaor, by our ancient custom and the laws of tanistry, which provide for such circumstances, in favour of good governance. Martacus mac Gartnait, having no uncle or brother nor close male kin, Lachlan mac Caerill declares that he, as senior thane of this mortuath, should be mormaor. This is the issue. Does any here claim otherwise, or that I have stated it unfairly?"

None were so bold.

"Then, since it would be unkind as unsuitable for any, boy or man, to appear before us all, at the start, to defend the quality of his wits, and moreover unfair to have a mere youth to testify first, before all, I call upon Lachlan of Buchan to show cause, firstly why Martacus is unfit to hold the mortuath; and secondly why he himself should be mormaor rather than other. Thane of Buchan, stand forward."

A darkly good-looking young man, keen-eyed, with something of a hatchet face, stepped out, and bowed. He had a confident, not to say arrogant, way with him.

"My lord King," he began strongly, "I declare to you, before all . . ."

MacBeth held up his hand again. "Thane of Buchan," he said evenly. "The Queen of Scots sits at my side. Have you not perceived her?"

The other's face fell. "I . . . I . . . my Lady Gruoch!" He bowed, more deeply. "I meant no disrespect."

"Proceed," the King said briefly.

Put off his stride considerably, Buchan faltered. "It is my . . . in this matter I make claim, my lord King — and Queen Gruoch — that it is common knowledge that Martacus mac Gartnait is lacking in wits, and always has been. I . . . "

"I am not concerned with common knowledge, my lord, but with facts," MacBeth interrupted, at his sternest. "You make a grave assertion. Make it good."

Buchan moistened his lips, frowning. "How may I do that? With words? Try him, I say, Highness. Try him, and see."

"In due course. Meantime we await *your* persuasion. Tell us wherein the Lord Martacus has shown witlessness."

Lachlan shook his head. "I cannot," he admitted. "Only he can do that. But on your second point, my lord King, I *can* show good cause — why I should be mormaor. Buchan used to be a mortuath on its own. It was not part of Mar. Indeed, it could be that at one time Mar was part of Buchan! It is sufficiently large — larger than Strathearn or Lennox or the Mearns. I can name you Mormaors of Buchan right back to the days of the sainted Columba. This Abbey of Deer has a book in which my forebears are named as far back as Beatha the Pict, who welcomed Columba here in the year 575. He was Mormaor of Buchan."

"A proud boast, my lord. You are to be congratulated. But is not this to argue that you should be Mormaor of *Buchan*, not Mormaor of Mar?"

"My lord King — I say that the present house of Mar are usurpers. They come of heathen Norse pirates, who, who . . ." He hesitated, recollecting the King's Norse half-brother, but went on regardless. "They are Ivorach, of the line of Ivor Flatnose, the Viking, Norse King of Munster, who invaded these coasts with fire and sword and slaughter over a hundred years ago, and made himself lord both of Buchan and Mar, by force. They are not of our own race, but foreigners, and should not hold a Scots mortuath. Norse-Irish Vikings. The dead Gartnait's father, Donald, fell fighting for his kin, the Irish, at Clontarf, a score of years ago." That was vehemently said.

"That may all be so, friend," MacBeth acceded. "But I have not heard that to have Norse or indeed Irish blood unfits any man to be a Scots mormaor. Or indeed king! If it does, then I can name sundry whom you would have unseated! Including, to be sure, the Earl Thorfinn. And was not the late King Malcolm's mother Irish-Norse, from Leinster? Also the former Lords of Galloway were Norse, for four generations."

"My claim is that the Ivorach seized the two mortuaths unlawfully and should never have been accepted as mormaors. I represent the ancient line of one of them, perhaps both. In this pass, with a child heiring Gartnait, I say that it would be just that I should have the mortuath."

"Because he *is* a child? You did not make so bold while Gartnait nor yet Donald were mormaors!"

"My brother Matain was then Thane of Buchan."

"I see. Very well, my lord. You have made your position clear. Now we shall hear others in your support. Who speaks for Lachlan, Thane of Buchan?"

"I, Cathula nic Crinan, do," a clear cool voice declared, and a woman stepped forward, to stand beside Lachlan. She was of striking appearance, not beautiful but with a fine presence, holding herself proudly, about MacBeth's own age, and richly dressed.

157

"Ha, Cousin," he said. "It is good to see you."

She inclined her head — it certainly was no bow — and neither smiled nor spoke. Not that he blamed her. After all, he had slain her brother, and *his* brother slain her husband.

Gruoch leaned forward in her chair. "Greetings, Cousin," she said quietly.

When there was no response to that either, MacBeth shrugged. "You wish to support Thane Lachlan, your good-brother, Princess? Do any others?"

"I do, Highness. I, Formartine."

"As do I, Fyvie, lord King."

"I say that we need a strong mormaor here, such as we have not had for long," Formartine asserted.

"I thank you. Now we shall hear the other side. Who speaks for Martacus mac Gartnait?"

"I do — Kintore." A burly middle-aged man said heavily. "And speak for many more than myself, King MacBeth."

"I can believe that. Speak up then, my lord."

"I say that the lad Martacus is well enough, of mind as of person. I can remember Lachlan mac Caerill himself, at fifteen, as but a weed of a youth, with spots!" There was a titter at that. "There is nothing amiss with the Ivorach line. I myself fought with Donald at Clontarf — a stout warrior and great man with the axe. If Gartnait was scarce so well-doing, and ill-advised enough to fight against Your Highness at Torfness, he was yet no weakling. He fought at King Duncan's command. I say that there is no reason why Martacus should not be Mormaor of Mar, as is his right. Many would rally to him who would not rally to Lachlan of Buchan — Kintore amongst them!"

MacBeth nodded. "That I can understand. Does other wish to speak?"

"May I, my lord King?" a soft voice asked. "Martacus is my son. But perhaps I know him best."

"Ah yes, Lady Ailie, to be sure. Let us hear a mother's voice."

The Lady of Mar was small and plump and rosy, as different from the Princess Cathula as was possible to imagine, and not only in looks. She was diffident, mild-seeming, and spoke with the slightest lisp, this forcing of herself into prominence here clearly an ordeal, yet her determination to speak on behalf of her son as evident.

"Martacus is a good boy," she asserted nervously. "He speaks but little. He is easily tongue-tangled, shy, but, but so am I.

158

There is nothing wrong with his wits, lord King. He thinks before he speaks, perhaps over-long for some. So that when talk is swift, he may say little, or nothing. I . . . I am like that, my own self. But he listens and heeds. And acts well enough. Indeed he is more scholar than was his father or any kin of mine. He reads much, too much perhaps. And he is kind of heart, would hurt none. But not weak, no." Biting her lip, the woman shook her head in a gesture that was more eloquent than she knew. She said no more.

"Thank you, Lady Ailie," the King said. "You make me wish to meet this son of yours. For *I* too was slow of speech, as a lad — some say I still am. And the Prince Lulach, here, is something the same. Is Martacus mac Gartnait here?"

Out from behind larger folk a boy was pushed, small for his age and most obviously reluctant. He was sturdily built however, stocky, open-faced with freckles and curling hair, holding his head somewhat forward as though possibly short-sighted. Coming to stand between his mother and Kintore, he bobbed two quick bows towards the thrones. A hand reached out to grasp his mother's.

"Ha, Martacus of Mar," MacBeth said, conversationally. "We have not met, but we are kin of a sort, for your great-grandsire wed my grandsire's sister." He spoke slowly but not loudly. "We shall talk more privately hereafter. Meantime I am not going to harry you with questions — for it is an ill thing for anyone, man or boy, to have to stand before many and give account for his wits. So fear nothing. I but wish to speak with you, as one kinsman to another." He smiled. "You understand?"

The boy, who had been listening intently, tensely, lips slightly parted, now moistened those lips, and after a moment, swallowing, said,

"Yes, King."

"Good. You live at Kildrummy, on the Don, I have heard? I have never been there. Is it a great dun? Or a rath? Or a hall-house perhaps, your Kildrummy?"

Martacus's pink tongue-tip appeared, and he looked over at his mother, as though suddenly agonised. Presently he whispered something, but to her only.

MacBeth leaned back in his chair, at ease. "Lady Mar — if he prefers to speak to you, rather than to me, I do not know that I blame him!"

"It is not that, Highness," the mother stammered. "It is that

159

he does not wish to seem to mis-speak you, to contradict you, the King."

"Contradict? How that? Tell me, Martacus — and contradict if you will."

Hesitantly, jerkily, the lad spoke. "Kildrummy is . . . not any such, King. Not dun or rath. Or hall-house. It is a fort. Of the old people. The Cruithne. On a hill. Many houses. Within ramparts. Many ramparts."

"Ha! A Pictish fort converted? To be sure. I know the sort. Indeed I have inherited one just so, with this new crown of mine! Dunsinane, the name. Kildrummy is so? Do you like living on the top of a hill?"

A nod.

"This fort of mine, Dunsinane, has its difficulties. As a house. On top of its hill. The Queen, here, I think, esteems it but lightly as a home."

Gruoch spoke. "Yes. It may be very strong, secure. But living on a hill-top could be uncomfortable, I think. Fine prospects, yes. But draughty. And cold in winter. I do not know if I should like it, Martacus."

Whether it was the feminine intervention or merely the subject that interested him, Martacus found his voice.

"No," he said, with something like assurance. "Living on a hill is good. None may creep on you unawares. And in winter it is better. For the water does not freeze."

"I should have thought that it would freeze more readily?" Gruoch objected, but smiling.

"No." The boy was almost scornful, of this feminine ignorance. "Water does not flow up on to a hill-top. So a deep well has to be sunk. Down to where the water is. And there, deep under the ground, it never freezes." He spoke slowly, picking his words, but with entire authority.

MacBeth coughed. "Now that I had not thought of!" he said. "You advise a hill-top house then, Martacus? What of having to carry up all the fuel, peats and wood, for the fires?"

"Peats and wood will dry more quickly on high ground than on low. And it is easier to make stout ramparts."

"How so?"

"The wind is stronger. The stone may be melted by burning, the better."

"Ha-a-a! So you can melt stone, young man?"

"Yes. The old Cruithne did it. They built their ramparts of stones and logs and turf and peats. Leaving holes for the wind,

between all. Then set it all afire. The hill-top winds birl, just."
The boy waved his hand in a circular motion. "The peats and
the wood burn very hot. The stones melt and run together. So
the ramparts become hard, hard. They cannot be breached by
ram nor pick. Nor yet burrowed through."

Still speaking conversationally, relaxed, MacBeth raised his
voice somewhat. "Did *you* know that, Thane of Buchan?" he
asked.

After a moment Lachlan answered. "I have heard something
of the sort, I think."

"To be sure — something of the sort. I see that I must consult
Martacus mac Gartnait over my fort-building hereafter!"
MacBeth paused. "*Non potest urbs occultari supra montem
posita!* How say you, Martacus?"

The boy flushed, gulped, and then came out with a halting,
"*Nec tamen facile hostis cius urbis civis inopinantes opprimet.*"

"Good. Your lady-mother said that you were something of a
scholar." Again the raised voice. "My lord Lachlan — do you
agree with that?"

Stiffly Buchan answered, "I did not hear what was said."

"Hear? Or understand? We spoke in the Latin."

"I, I was not trained for the Church, my lord King!"

"Was I? Very well, Martacus — we shall talk more of this
later."

"Thank you, my lord of Mar, for enlightening *me*, at least!"
Gruoch said. "I knew nothing of this, of the melting stone."

MacBeth raised his hand. "Enough has been said on which
to base a judgment," he declared, more formally. "I have three
counsellors here, whom I shall consult. And then give our
decision." He murmured to his wife and then turned to the trio
behind the chairs, who bent their heads to listen and speak.

The talk in the hall and beyond swelled.

The discussion on the dais did not last long. The O'Beolain
signed to one of the horn-blowers to sound a blast, and into the
ensuing quiet cried, "Oh, people — hear you the High King's
judgment."

"We are all agreed," MacBeth announced. "Martacus mac
Gartnait appears to us to lack nothing in wits. We see no reason
why he should not be Mormaor of Mar. I now so declare him,
before all. So the Thane of Buchan's cause fails on the first
point. But I have been concerned for his second point. Buchan
was formerly a mortuath, yes, and is over-large to be merely a
thanedom. Beatha the Pict, or Cruithne, was to be sure Mor-

maor of Buchan — as I should know, for he was a forebear of my own. My name, indeed, is taken from his. It is, I think, unsuitable that Buchan should be only a thanedom of Mar. And Mar is great enough without Buchan. So I do hereby ordain that it shall be again a mortuath of my kingdom. Lachlan will, I am assured, make a good mormaor. As, in a year or two, will Martacus — both to the good support of this realm. This is my royal judgment. Hail, Martacus, Mormaor of Mar! Hail, Lachlan, Mormaor of Buchan!"

Loud and long the cheers resounded for what was clearly a most popular decision, with both sides well content.

After the eating and drinking and entertainments which followed the judgment were over, and they could be alone in the abbot's simple house, Gruoch questioned MacBeth.

"That judgment, my dear, so very wise — good enough for Solomon! I think that you had made up your mind to it before ever you entered that hall! Confess it!"

He shrugged. "Not quite. I believed that this would be the best decision, yes. But until I had seen both contestants and estimated their quality, I could not be sure."

"Suppose then that we, your advisers, had counselled otherwise?"

"Then, my heart, the King would have had to weigh up for his decision who he could least afford to offend! And make judgment accordingly."

"I see. So that is kingship! Not justice but expediency?"

"Perhaps. That, I am finding, is where a king may have to be different from other men. But, at least, I have now two more mormaors on whom I probably can rely for support. Which is important."

"I would not rely too strongly on Buchan — if he weds that Cathula! *She* will never forgive you the deaths of her husband and her brother. And more her brother than her husband, I think!"

"It may be so. But it is not so much Cathula as her father who concerns me."

"Crinan? You are troubled over Crinan?"

"I do not say troubled. But concerned, yes. He did not come to the coronation, although summoned. I have sent him two letters — but he has not replied. He has sent his son Maldred and the boy Malcolm Big Head to take refuge with Siward of Deira — which I take but ill. He sits there in Atholl hating me."

162

"He is but one mormaor in many. Nine now, is it?"

"Yes. But he is Primate of the Church, Abbot of Dunkeld also, and could sway many. MacDuff of Fife does not love me either. If these two joined forces . . ." He paused. "But — enough of such talk, lass. Enough for the day. Today has gone well. And tomorrow we ride to Spynie, and forget this of kings and queens and realms for a space — if we may. The *Dorus Neamh* my love — only fifty miles away."

"Blessed place," she said. "My dear — do you wish that you had never accepted the crown?"

"No-o-o," he answered. "No. It had to be, I think. It . . . was fated."

"What else is fated, then?"

"This — that we two shall be all in all to each other. Till the world's end, my love. Inseparable, through light and dark. That whenever men hereafter think of MacBeth they shall think also of you. Is that enough?"

"It is enough," she said.

13

THE FIRST MAJOR shadow to darken the new reign was cast, however, not by Crinan nor yet MacDuff but by Thorfinn Sigurdson no less.

Early that winter Siward Biornson of Deira, the Dane, slew the Earl Eadulf of Northumbria, and now ruled most of the North of England. Perhaps more significantly, as far as Scotland was concerned, he had married the inoffensive and gentle Maldred mac Crinan to his wife's sister, Aldgitha, a woman much older than himself. Siward was not the sort of man to arrange such things without sufficient reason; and taken with the fact that he now had his own sister, Queen Sybil, Duncan's widow, back in his care, and her stepson the boy Malcolm Canmore, it looked as though he visualised uses for them all. As young Malcolm had been Prince of Strathclyde and Cumbria, and Maldred his governor there, it might seem ominous for Cumbria — which of course neighboured Northumbria on the west.

At any rate, Thorfinn, who was taking his overlordship of Galloway — which was considered part of Cumbria — seriously, and was spending much time in the area, perceived the threat. And being Thorfinn, he did not long delay action for consultation or authority, but sailed the following spring, as early as conditions allowed, across the Solway Firth and invaded Cumberland proper. There he inflicted two minor defeats on his fellow-Viking Siward's forces, before MacBeth heard about it all.

MacBeth was perturbed and angry. He had made Thorfinn officially Lord of Galloway and also Governor of Strathclyde and Cumbria for the young Lulach, the Prince. So any attack by him thereabouts represented the authority of the Scots crown. He, MacBeth, was anxious that his reign should be, as far as possible, a peaceful one. Yet here was his half-brother, so early in that reign, challenging Siward the Strong and risking full-scale war, and without troubling to ask permission or even to inform anyone. Siward was a danger, yes, and a powerful one; but all the more reason to deal with him cautiously.

MacBeth left Gruoch at Dunsinane, and with a small hard-riding party set off across Southern Scotland for the Solway.

They went by Stirling and Lanark, Douglasdale and Nithsdale, to Dumfries, in just over two days' fast going — one part of MacBeth revelling in the opportunity for urgent physical action after all too much dignified kingliness. At Dumfries, head-town of the eastern portion of Galloway, he learned that the Earl Thorfinn was still believed to be in Cumberland, just where uncertain but last heard of near the Northumbrian border in the Gilsland area. More alarmed than ever, he rode on eastwards and crossed Sark and Esk into Cumberland.

Cumbria, the former kingdom of the Cymric Celts, incorporated in the Scottish realm for almost exactly a century, stretched south as far as Lancaster, where it marched with the Cymric principality of Wales. Although in theory Scots now, Southern Cumbria, or Cumberland, was so in fact little more than nominally; and comings and goings, save with Galloway, minimal. Certainly it was not worth going to war over.

At Caerluel, near where the Eden entered the south side of Solway, they had firmer news of Thorfinn. He had, two days earlier, annihilated a roving band of Northumbrians, near Gilsland on the Irthing, some fifteen miles to the east.

The border between Cumberland and Northumberland in those high moorland areas was a very uncertain entity; but

164

where the great Roman Wall itself was concerned, it was clear enough — and Gilsland was right on the Wall, and inside Northumberland. So much MacBeth learned. It speeded his progress the more.

It was at the site of a former Roman camp near Denton, on the Irthing, a mile or so on the Cumbrian side, that he eventually came up with Thorfinn's encampment by the riverside.

His brother was not present, meantime, being off prospecting the vicinity eastwards apparently — that was, inevitably, inside Northumberland. The veteran Harald Cleft Chin had been left in charge of some 500 Vikings here, who were filling in the time of waiting with eating vast quantities of slaughtered beef, drinking stolen ale and playing their own uninhibited games with a large number of underclad women, whether captives or local volunteers was not clear. Harald greeted MacBeth heartily, with no suggestion of concern for his new kingly status. He was loud in his acclaim of the earl's, and his own, exploits hereabouts.

Thorfinn arrived back with the sinking sun, and at sight of MacBeth emitted a great shout of joy, dropped the handsome if bloody head he was carrying by the long hair, and came running to embrace his brother in a mighty bear's-hug, armour, bearskin, blood and all.

"Son of Life!" he cried. "God's Eyes — yourself! Here's a sight for singing. What brings you to this benighted spot?"

"You do!" MacBeth got out, struggling to free himself. "You, man. You had to be stopped. And I knew that you would heed none other than myself."

"Stopped? Stopped what?"

"Stopped your endangering of my realm, Brother. Stopped making war on Siward. Stopped invading . . ."

"Tush, man — are you out of your mind? It is this Siward Biornson who has got to be stopped. Before *he* makes war! Do you not know what he is about . . . ?"

"I know enough of what you both are about to bring me hotfoot here from Fortrenn, to halt this folly. If it is not too late."

"To late for what, by the Wounds of Christ? I am governing this Cumbria for you, am I not?"

"Is *that* governing Cumbria?" MacBeth pointed to the fallen head. And, turning, gestured towards the skirling, screaming women.

"Tcha — they are doing none so badly! And that — that is

165

no Cumbrian. That is a Northumbrian brigand. One Ulf, chief of a rascally crew of raiders that I broke up two days back. He escaped — but I got him today. *He* will trouble your Highness's peace no more!"

His brother drew a long breath, and shook his head, next to helplessly. "See you, we will speak of this later." He looked around at the circle of grinning Vikings, many of whom also carried heads.

"Yes — let us eat first, of a mercy! An empty belly, they say, breeds wind and wrath both! We shall eat, lad — and talk the better sense thereafter."

Despite ample eating and drinking, however, identity of views remained as elusive as ever. Avoiding a head-washing and hair-combing session at the riverside, MacBeth led his brother along the Irthing bank, in the dusk, away from the camp.

"Thor," he said, seeking to be patient, "Why did you not inform me before crossing Solway and invading this Cumberland? Seek my agreement and permission?"

"Invade? Permission? I am Governor of Strathclyde and Cumbria, am I not? How can I invade it? Or require permission to enter it?"

"You know as well as do I that Cumbria is not as the rest of my realm. Parts of it, Galloway and Eskdale, Annandale and Liddesdale — these are part of Scotland, yes. But this southern country, called Cumberland, is a *dependency* of the Scots crown, no more. Malcolm the First gained overlordship of it, to the River Derwent, by a bargain with the English king — who did not control it anyway, for it was then an independent kingdom. That was in 946 or thereabouts. Malcolm did not conquer it. Since when it has adhered to the Scots crown, in name — not because we hold it fast, or because its lords love us, but because if they do not accept the Scots suzerainty they know the English will step in and take them. They are all but independent, but prefer our light hand to the English heavy one . . ."

"I know all that. These Cumbrian lords, then, should be grateful to me for protecting them from Siward. For he intends to take Cumbria and Galloway. And later to name Maldred mac Crinan King of Scots — but himself rule Scotland through that weakling. That is Siward Biornson! Thinking to do what Canute could not do."

"You have no proof of this."

"I have as much proof as I need. Think you I have not put men to the question — these Northumbrian chiefs I have

166

captured? Before beheading them! That is Siward's intention, have no doubt."

"It may be what he eventually hopes for. But meantime he has not raised his hand against Scotland. Or Cumbria. Or Galloway. This that you are doing could provoke him to do so, provoke outright war. And I do not wish for war, am not ready for war."

"Then leave the warfare to me, who am ready!"

"No! I am King of Scots, and if war there is to be, *I* will decide on it and declare it."

"Tush, man — you can spare yourself that sort of talk, with me! I shall not stand by and see Cumbria, much less my own Galloway, threatened, and do nothing."

"In Scotland, if I say so, you *will*, Thor."

They had turned to face each other, there in the half-dark, two determined men.

"So that is how the cock crows, Young Brother!" Thorfinn said, great voice quivering. "To *me*, who put you on your throne."

"That you did not. You helped me *towards* it, yes. Weakened Duncan, yes. Hastened his end, no doubt. And I am grateful for some of it. But you did not put me on the throne. Do not ever say it, Brother, if you would keep my regard and affection."

"Ha! Your new crown makes your head swell, I swear!"

"Swear it if you will. But let me be clear on this, Thor — and you — now and for always. I, and I alone, made the decision as to whether I would accept the crown. And accept it not from you but from the Council of Mormaors. *I* now sit on the Stone, for better or for worse. To be a worthy King of Scots, I must *rule* as well as reign, in Scotland. I cannot allow myself to be forced or pressed or overborne by any — even by my brother the Raven Feeder! In Orkney and Zetland, which are yours, not Scotland's, and in your hosting outwith my realm, you will do what you must and I will not attempt to interfere. But in my kingdom you will do as I say. Let me never have to say it again, Thor."

They marched on along the riverside path, the very air almost vibrant between them, and quickly Thorfinn's enormous striding took him well ahead. But presently MacBeth found his brother waiting for him.

"You know, do you not, that I could tear your precious kingdom out of your grasp, and sit myself on your throne — as easily as that!" And he snapped his fingers.

"You could try, yes. But I do not know that you would succeed. And I would fight you to the death, Thor."

"I could take over your land bit by bit, man. Your provinces and your mortuaths. Already I control Caithness and Sutherland, Galloway and the Hebrides and much of Dalar and Argyll. Think you you could stop me taking the rest?"

"Yes. For I sit on the Stone."

"Your Stone did not save Duncan!"

"Duncan was unworthy. It will be my concern to be more worthy. I have sworn the oath and received the hands. Do not forget it — for *I* do not!"

Again they strode on, Thorfinn once more swiftly moving ahead.

Presently MacBeth slowed, turned, and went slowly back whence they had come.

He was almost back to the camp when his brother caught up with him again.

"Fiend seize you — you ever were a difficult, obstinate devil!" he burst out. "God knows why I suffer you, and support you. And, and love you, the saints forgive me! I must be growing old! But, curse you — yes, have it as you will. MacBeth the King! Let it stand."

"Difficult, I accept. Obstinate, perhaps. But the King, yes. And always. You have the choice. I have none. I have sworn the oath." He half-turned then. "Is it a compact, then, Thor?"

A massive arm encircled his shoulders. "Have it *your* way, lad. A compact, yes." And they gripped hands.

"I am glad." That was simply said. And, after a pause, "Tomorrow you will return to your galleys and sail back to Galloway. And bury those heads!"

"Precious Soul of God!" Thorfinn exclaimed.

14

THAT SUMMER WAS an uneasy one. If MacBeth's own enemies, or those of his realm, were indeed going to strike, it seemed probable that they would do so sooner, at the beginning of his reign, rather than later when he was likely to be settled on the throne. Siward's manoeuvrings were obvious enough in all conscience; and Crinan's behaviour sufficiently ominous. And King Harald of England had died suddenly, after a weak reign of only four years, to be succeeded by his brother Hardicanute, King of Denmark, Canute's second son, who was little of an improvement; and moreover delayed his coming over from Denmark to take up his new throne, so that there was a hiatus in the rule, with the inevitable consequence of the English nobles, Danish and Saxon alike, taking the opportunity to increase their power and wealth at the expense of weaker neighbours, Siward by no means alone in this. Anything might happen in these circumstances, MacBeth realised only too well.

Nearer home there was a further preoccupation. Old Malmore, Abbot and Co-Arb of Iona died, leaving a significant gap to be filled in the leadership of the Celtic Church.

MacBeth consulted Abbot Cathail of Scone, who declined the suggestion that he himself should stand for election, but proposed the late Malmore's own assistant at Iona, Robartach by name, a vigorous but modest man in his late thirties, who had latterly been carrying much of the abbatial burden in any case, and was refreshingly unconnected with any of the rival groupings and influences within the Church at large. MacBeth remembered the man as quiet but effective and reliable. Anxious lest Crinan should insinuate some nominee of his own into this important position, he agreed to throw his weight behind the nomination of Robartach.

These preoccupations were the background to the summer period. But in the foreground were very different problems — and for these Gruoch was largely responsible. MacBeth had come back from Cumberland to discover that his wife had not been idle during his absence, having taken the opportunity to plan out her own answer to the Dunsinane accommodation difficulties. She had found an alternative and improved site nearby, on another green hill-top three miles to the west. Here she had already mapped out and planned the house she wanted. She was not asking for a great new palace. It could be quite modest in size — but it must be comfortable, and with larger chambers than this barrack at Dunsinane.

MacBeth was nothing loth. He accepted her site and plans gladly. But he decided to make something of a political virtue out of a domestic necessity. If this was to be a royal house of the High King, he said, palace or none, then it should be built, as it were, by the nation and not by himself only, though in the

169

main he would pay for it. From the moment he had decided to accept the crown, he had, at the back of his mind, the need to improve the image of the throne, sadly tarnished of late years, to seek to emphasise the unity of the kingdom.

So the call went out to all the mormaors and greater thanes, as an exercise in kingcraft and solidarity. All were invited to assist. If they lived too far away to make a personal appearance practical, they could send expert craftsmen, materials, furnishings, transport animals.

Oddly enough, the notion caught on remarkably, and something of a social element was introduced, aided by Gruoch's suggestion that all should be encouraged to come along and bring their wives and womenfolk with them — unheard of hitherto. As a result, MacBeth got to know his nobility, by and large, almost better than any King of Scots had done before him; and they him.

Deliberately MacBeth summoned young Martacus of Mar to assist with the rampart-building of the outer fortress, to apply his theory of stone-melting. And to keep Lachlan of Buchan happy, a personal invitation to him to supply timber from his inland forests. He accepted cheerfully, but the Princess Cathula, to whom he was now married, made her excuses.

In fact, something like the beginnings of a Court developed at Dunsinane that summer — and the inadequacies of that draughty establishment were thereby brought home to the visitors, to excellent effect.

But there were some notable absentees. It was scarcely to be expected that Crinan would contribute, although invited to do so; and MacDuff of Fife, although next to Strathearn the nearest neighbour of all, made no move in the matter either.

Vast quantities of materials, stone, timber, turf, peats, had to be dragged from near and far to the hill-top site; and innumerable teams of oxen were used for this task. A certain competitive spirit had already developed amongst the teamsters, from various districts and mortuaths, and wagering on speed and prowess was good for progress and morale. This gave Gruoch the notion that there could be a major and set contest, to see which could drag a given load over a given distance to the site, already being called Cairn Beth, in the fastest time. Already teams belonging to the two Fife Thanes of Lindores and Kinross were involved in the work. If urged to support an all-Fife effort, MacDuff could scarcely refuse without offending his own people. MacBeth set a day, before harvest, and ensured that the word of it reached Kennochy, MacDuff's principal seat in central Fife, not as coming from himself but from his thanes.

The chosen August day, the Eve of the Assumption, was distinctly warm for the business. Great crowds assembled from near and far, large numbers lining the route to be taken and taking up their stance on the slopes of the palace hill itself, which made an excellent grandstand. The starting-point was at the edge of Druids' Scat Wood, one of the main dumps for the building materials, and exactly a mile from the site. Here no fewer than eleven loads had been built up, all exactly the same, meticulously weighed-out, consisting of quarried stone, sawn logs, cut peat and turf, and beside each load an identical heavy wooden sled. The number of oxen to be used was left to each team. Basically the more numerous the animals the less manageable, so it was a question of seeking to balance power, pace and ease of handling.

As to the teams themselves, only five men were allowed for each, and the captains were to be the mormaors or chief thanes themselves — this ordained by MacBeth, who was reverting to being Mormaor of Moray for the occasion. This way MacDuff had to take part — since he had indeed risen to the bait. Lulach was being allowed to captain the Ross team in place of young Farquhar.

Needless to say the land had been scoured for the best and strongest oxen, and many a small farmer and husbandman had done well out of the search. Most teams had plumped for eight beasts, the traditional span for an oxgate on the plough; but two had ten and one, Buchan, actually was going to use twelve. Fife was one of the tens.

MacBeth, in good spirits and laying aside kingliness for the occasion, indeed stripped to only his short saffron kilt and brogans, greeted all comers, and made a point of being especially affable towards MacDuff — although he got little response from that hot-eyed, hulking individual.

The Thane of Glamis, who was not taking part in the Angus team, acted as starter. He called all to order and explained the procedure. At the blast of a horn the race would commence. Teams could choose in what order they wished to harness up the oxen, load the sleds and set off. Also select whichever route they cared to the objective. No deliberate bumping, impeding or entangling was permitted. If loads collapsed or fell off, on rough ground, they had to be built up in total before proceeding.

171

The winner would be the first team to deliver its full load in proper order at the gates of the new palace.

The eventual wailing of the horn ushered in a state of what looked like utter confusion. Sixty men and almost double that number of animals had to struggle, manoeuvre and sort themselves out in a comparatively confined space. Oxen at the best are slow, ponderous brutes; and all the men involved, particularly the captains, were not necessarily expert in handling them or in loading and stacking heavy goods. Indeed most of the mormaors were little better than in the road at this stage, and the parties which got on best were those with most professional teamsters included. Some set about harnessing and inspanning the oxen first; others got the loads stacked on the sleds in solid fashion, roped and secure.

MacBeth had deliberately chosen to have his Moray team placed next to the Fife one, and he was interested to see that MacDuff was working like a Trojan at the loading, heaving logs and stones about with fierce energy, even if his actual loading technique was erratic and much of his work had to be rearranged by his team-mates. He gave the impression that he intended to win this race — which was strange in view of the fact that the oxen he had contributed were amongst the poorest there.

MacBeth was probably wise in leaving most of the loading and spanning to the professionals; at least his sled was loaded before MacDuff's — and others. He aided with the inspanning of the animals — and having only eight against Fife's ten, they made a little time there also. Not that he was anxious to beat MacDuff — the reverse rather.

When, two-thirds of the way to the foot of the hill, MacBeth saw that he was leaving a glowering MacDuff behind, and moreover that Buchan was now catching up fast, he recognised that something would have to be done if Fife was not to be actually last in the race. He realised that he would have to take his team into his confidence, and ruefully told them that they must hold back, somehow, seem to take a mistaken route and then turn back, so as to let Fife catch up. His men did not hide their resentment, but did as they were told. Fortunately the Lothian team just in front lost part of its load and fell behind.

MacBeth, making what seemed to be an ill-advised detour round a patch of soft ground, came back level with MacDuff. He thought to try what a little raillery might do.

"Ha, MacDuff!" he cried. "How fares Fife? Are you weary? Or saving all for the final hill? That you plod so!"

"We shall see," came back. "Who are you to speak?"

"We are just getting into our stride, man! Your beasts are not trying. I swear! Is Fife but a poor place for oxen?"

"There is nothing wrong with my oxen. We had a bad start."

"It's your beasts, friend. They lack muscle. *You*, now — a great bull of a man like you could pull your sled better! I vow, if you harnessed yourself in place of the lead-ox, you would beat us all!"

MacBeth's grin, as he called that, faded before the sheer fury and hatred on the face that MacDuff turned to him.

"Curse you, MacBeth!" he exclaimed. "Curse you — you will pay for that! God help me, you will!"

"A mercy, man, I but . . ." MacBeth stopped himself, reminding himself that he was the King and must not seem to make unnecessary apology. "No ill meant," he jerked.

MacDuff kept his head turned away now, and gradually MacBeth's team moved apart and ahead.

When eventually MacBeth joined Gruoch and her son at the palace-gate, to accept considerable laughter and mock condolences, and himself to congratulate Colin of the Mearns, the winner, it was to perceive that though the Fife team was itself now nearing the hill-top, MacDuff was no longer with it. Raising his glance, MacBeth saw a single distant figure striding back, as it were against the tide, back across the route for the starting-point.

That night, in their own bedchamber, Gruoch kissed her husband. "A successful day, my heart — save for MacDuff. It has done more than anything yet to endear you to your people, noble and simple, I swear."

"Yet it was for MacDuff, in the main, that it was devised. The man is an oaf and a fool. But . . . I blame myself. So thin of skin, I should have handled him more carefully."

"Care nothing, my love. It is not so great a matter. He is but one amongst many. And he will get over it."

"He is the foremost mormaor of my realm. And powerful. With Crinan against me, I cannot afford MacDuff's enmity."

"Crinan is old and lazy. And MacDuff a fool. Never heed, my dear . . ."

15

In crisp golden October weather, MacBeth organised and led a sort of pilgrimage to Iona, late in the season for such as it was. The idea had been simmering in his mind all summer — but he could not contrive it earlier, for the decision on who was to be the new Co-Arb and Abbot there had not been decided. However, the choice was now made, with Abbot Cathail of Scone having had his way, and Robartach, old Malmore's assistant, appointed by a handsome majority of abbatial votes. To mark the occasion, and his own approval — also to mark the defeat of Crinan the Primate, who had sponsored a kinsman of his own — MacBeth announced that he would attend the inauguration in person. That this would tend to bind most of the Church closer to the Crown was not the least of it. To emphasise this essential unity of Church and State — as also to help to change the notion that all government of the realm must centre around Fortrenn, Scone and Dunsinane — he ordained that his first High Council of State should be held at Iona, at the same time. All mormaors, thanes, abbots and sundry bishops were summoned to attend, with representatives from Lothian, the Merse, Teviotdale, Strathclyde, Dalar and the Hebrides. It would be inconvenient for many, admittedly, so MacBeth was seeking to make something between a holiday and a pilgrimage out of it all.

The main party sailed in three galleys from Alclyde, under the shadow of Dumbarton Rock, the capital of Strathclyde. This was the most convenient method of getting to Iona from mid-Scotland — provided storms withheld. MacBeth would have liked to have had Gruoch with him, but galley accommodation was scarcely comfortable for women, especially if the weather roughened as was highly possible, and Gruoch was pregnant again. He did take Lulach however, now a slender boy of eleven. As heir to the throne, MacBeth was anxious to bring him into prominence, although he was still a shy and silent lad.

MacBeth was glad to see a number of longships already lying in the shelter of St. Ronan's Bay in the Sound of Iona, when they arrived, including Thorfinn's unmistakable dragon-ship. He had been rather afraid that, after the strong line he had taken with his brother in Cumberland, Thorfinn might elect to keep his distance for a while.

There was certainly no hint of anything like pique about the earl's greeting thereafter — even if the hugging, backslapping and bellowed laughter was scarcely the normal reception for a monarch. Nevertheless, MacBeth hoped that their leave-taking might be as hearty.

Neil Nathrach, Farquhar O'Bcolain, the Abbot Malbride of Deer and Bishop Malise of Inverness were also already here, with sundry Dalar notables. Likewise the Earl Gilleciaran from Colonsay. So there was a good representation from the North. Indeed the attendance altogether was encouraging, the only important absentees being Crinan of Atholl and MacDuff of Fife.

In the morning Robartach was installed as new Co-Arb and Abbot of Iona in the open air, in the Columban tradition — anyway, the church would not have held half of the assembled congregation. Robertach made a short speech of affirmation and promise, the psalm was sung and communion dispensed, in both kinds, to all. That was all, not taking above twenty minutes.

There followed a still more informal little ceremony. The late Abbot Malmore's old garron, Moses, on which he had covered much of Scotland and of which he had been very fond, had died two days before. Now it was to be buried in the animals' cemetery, with benefit of clergy — the Celtic Church being concerned for the lesser creation — and thereafter a prayer said over the grave of its master, the Church being likewise much concerned for the departed's onward progress towards a better and fuller life. MacBeth elected to attend this moving little interment, conducted by the new Co-Arb. It was perhaps the first time that a King of Scots and most of his nobility had graced the funeral of a horse.

That was the forenoon's programme. In the afternoon MacBeth held the first full Council of his reign, in the abbey eating-hall.

After welcoming the company and bidding them speak out, without fear, he paused. "Before we commence our discussions, it is suitable that an appointment be made. Indeed three appointments. Whilst I, the High King, must preside over my Council, it is wiser that other than the monarch conducts it. In a secret council, that is the duty of a secretary. But having made decisions, it will be necessary that they are carried out thereafter. For this the High King has to be assisted and reminded by one well qualified so to act. Who must needs be a man used to conducting large affairs, with scribes and clerks at his hand, able to put into effect the laws and statutes which we shall make. This is the function of a chancellor. I say that it is reasonable that such Chancellor of the realm should also be the Secretary of the Council. There has been no Chancellor for long, by title. But the late King Malcolm used Malduin of St. Andrews, his King's Bishop, for some such duties. I therefore propose that Bishop Malduin be appointed Chancellor of the realm. Does any make objection? Speak."

None spoke.

"Very well. Bishop Malduin — come forward and take your seat at the small table, and bring your scribe, to write fairly what is decided here!"

The little bishop, and a tall gangling monk with sundry rolls of paper, quills and ink-horn, came up to the dais and sat opposite Lulach.

"The two other appointments may as well be considered now likewise," MacBeth went on. "Since our decisions will almost certainly require them. The realm requires a High Constable and a High Judex, if its laws are to be upheld and administered honestly. For High Constable I name you Cormac, Thane of Glamis, the most experienced soldier in this kingdom, than whom none is better fitted to carry the sword of the law and see that it is obeyed by all, without fear or favour."

A spontaneous cheer broke out. Glamis was one of the most respected figures in the land, and moreover had been, like Malduin, as close as anyone could be to King Malcolm, so that continuity was maintained.

"For Judex, different qualities are demanded," MacBeth resumed. "Since he administers the laws he must be learned. Also wise and fair. After much thought I have decided on Ewan, Abbot of Abernethy, as the best man for this position. Does any assert otherwise?"

There was a strong murmur, now, amongst the packed benches, as men commented. This was a clever move. Ewan was one of the hereditary abbots, and so that influential faction was complimented — which might have looked towards Crinan. But he was a studious man and scholar, taking an active part in Church affairs. Moreover he was a kinsman of MacDuff's, Abernethy being in the northern corner of Fothrif, part of Fife. Much other than good justice might be achieved by this appointment.

When there was no contrary voice raised, MacBeth signed to Bishop Malduin to take over.

The new Chancellor cleared his throat. "I would say that I am honoured by the High King's favour, and I hope, the trust of all here," he said. "I shall endeavour to serve him, you all, and the realm, honestly and to the best of my poor abilities in all duties of the chancellery, with the aid of Almighty God. I hope that you will bear with me, at first, when I fall short." He consulted a paper. "The first business before the Council is, as suitable, the security of the realm. As all must know, the situation south of our borders is not good. The new King of England, Hardicanute of Denmark, still lingers in that realm. As a consequence, England is in much unrest, and violent men work their lawless wills. To our especial concern, Siward, Earl of Deira, now Earl of Northumbria also, through the murder of young Earl Eadulf, is in a position to threaten our borders and peace, with no higher power in England to restrain him. It behoves this Council, therefore, to consider what steps shall be taken."

There was silence, apart from a derisive hoot from Thorfinn, on the King's right.

"My lord of Glamis, High Constable," MacBeth said easily. "This is within your province, is it not? What is your advice?"

Glamis took his time to answer. "The threat is there, my lord King. And Siward is not by-named The Strong for nothing. He has claimed that Lothian and the Merse should be his, now that he is Earl of Northumbria. But I have heard of no great mustering of men, as yet, in Northumbria or Deira. Our Teviotdale folk have much coming and going with the Northumbrians and they have no word of assembling of forces in strength. I have made it my concern to find out. And the season grows late for warfare campaigning. I think that Siward will not reach for his sword this year."

"My own view, my lord," MacBeth said. "But with the spring, he might?"

"Yes. So we must be prepared. And let him see that we are prepared. Muster some force of our own. Place it along the line of the Tweed and Teviot, Esk and Liddel. Not a large army sufficient to threaten Siward, but sufficient to guard all the fords and show that we are ready, if need be. And make plans forthwith for a full muster of all our strength, so that it can be brought together swiftly, in Lothian."

There were murmurs of agreement, interrupted by Thorfinn's snort of disgust.

"Not seem to threaten Siward, by God!" he cried. "What is

this? This upstart Dane claims Lothian and the Merse and Teviotdale. Aye, and threatens Cumbria and Galloway, all Strathclyde. And you fear to threaten *him!*"

"Not fear, my lord earl, but advise that we do not," Glamis answered heavily. "We are not ready for war — even if we desired it."

"And so give him time to build up his strength against us, man? What will putting off serve you? Why think you he has gathered Maldred and the bastard Malcolm and the rest into his grip? Siward the King, the Gentle! I tell you that he intends to proclaim Maldred as true King of Scots, and Malcolm still Prince of Strathclyde and Cumbria, and he their protector. Use this as excuse to march on Scotland. And you — you would not threaten and provoke him! Give him time. I say strike now. Strike *before* he is ready."

"We are not prepared, not fit for war . . ."

"*I* am. Always I am. I could have fifty longships off the coast of Northumbria in two weeks, with 4000 men."

There was a quivering silence in the eating-hall.

"We are grateful for the Earl Thorfinn's advice and stout offers of aid," MacBeth said carefully. "Who can tell when we may need to call on such good help. But not yet, I think. Any such attack would, I say, be seen as an assault on *England*, not just on Siward. It would bring Hardicanute hastening from Denmark. And serve to unite the squabbling English lords, Dane and Saxon. We might, for a time, defeat Siward. But thereafter have on our hands outright war with England. I did not ascend this throne to attempt what even King Malcolm dared not endeavour. I prefer my lord of Glamis' proposals."

Again silence, men loth to involve themselves in what was clearly a struggle between brothers, and potent brothers.

There was one man present who suffered no such inhibition. Neil Nathrach spoke up from the thanes' benches.

"I say that before we spend our time considering the danger from Northumbria we should first consider the danger nearer home!" he said strongly. "We here discuss the security of the realm. There are those within this realm who endanger it more immediately and closely than this Dane Siward and a few exiles."

There was further hush. The King's brothers were proving embarrassing councillors.

"I think, my lord of Cawdor, that none within my realm so threaten it that its safety is at stake," MacBeth said.

"Then why are Crinan, Mormaor of Atholl and MacDuff, Mormaor of Fife, not present?"

So the thing was out and names were named. MacBeth tightened his lips in displeasure, and Thorfinn grinned widely. Everywhere others muttered, sighed or shrugged.

"Lord of Cawdor," MacBeth said sternly. "Neither of these mormaors have said a word or lifted a hand to endanger the peace and security of the realm. Remember it."

"Nevertheless, lord King, these two are powerful, and your enemies," Neil went on, unabashed. "One the father of the late Duncan, the other his friend. If these two worked together, and with Siward, then the realm could be in danger indeed."

"Ha — the Serpent hisses to some point, for once!" Thorfinn exclaimed.

"Chancellor — I cannot have members of my High Council accusing my mormaors of possible treason, in their absence," MacBeth announced. "I ask you to declare the Thane of Cawdor unheard. And have your clerk to unwrite what he has said."

"I so do," the little bishop said unhappily.

"My friends," MacBeth went on steadily. "High Councils are called to advise and aid the High King in the better governance of his realm. But the King it is who takes the decisions. Let none forget it. All may speak — but what they have to say must be well considered and of *help* to the monarch, not hindrance. I have heard what has been said as to the security of my kingdom, and I will consider it well. Has any other anything of import to raise which has not yet been spoken on? Any other threat to the realm? If not, I will ask the Chancellor to move on to the next business."

Thankfully the bishop consulted his papers again. "There is the matter of due provision for widows and female dependants," he said. "Also of orphans. The King's Highness is concerned."

"I am so concerned," MacBeth agreed. "But this is a matter I raise on the Queen's behalf. Although I fully approve it myself. It is a matter which should have been dealt with long since. At present, when a man of any property or standing dies, his son, brother or other male heir inherits all. No provision need be made for his wife, his daughters or his sisters if they are dependent upon him. This is manifestly wrong and unjust. Especially as frequently the wife has brought considerable property to the marriage in the first place. The Queen, my wife, cites her own case. When she married Mormaor Gillacomgain

179

of Moray she brought him large lands. Yet when he was slain, she was left with nothing. The Prince Lulach here could have claimed, in due course, his inheritance. But she, the widow, had no claim as to law, even of her own former lands. When we married, I settled her own lands on herself again. But no law said that I should. And had she had a daughter by Gillacomgain, instead of a son, that child would have had no rights in her father's land or wealth soever. All our women are in this case. She, Queen Gruoch, says, and I say, that it is manifestly unjust and should be put to rights. Do any disagree?"

No man raised his voice in dissent. But neither did any cheer or show elation. There was indeed complete silence.

"If your not speaking means assent, my friends, am I to command the judges and clerks to make up a suitable law to right this wrong?"

There was a shuffling of feet.

"A man's property is his own," Strathearn said, on the King's left. "None can command him to leave it to any. Save his tanist and heir. Woman or other."

A murmur of agreement ran through the hall.

"My lord of Strathearn is only partly right in what he says," MacBeth observed. "A man's property in goods, cattle, silver and the like, is his own entirely. But his land is not. The land is the Crown's, in the first instance — all the land of the realm. Not the King's in person, but the Crown's. Never forget it. This must be understood. Every transference of land requires the Crown's assent. And this meeting is the Crown-in-Council. Therefore, as far as land is concerned, the greatest source of wealth, this Council can advise the King to make laws. I have consulted the greatest authorities on this matter. I say that the Crown has the power to act, and must do so in justice."

Thorfinn chuckled — but he was the only one so to do.

"This is a hard matter, lord King," the Thane of Breadalbane complained. "Much is in it affecting us all most grievously. I say that we must consider it, consider it well. And return to the matter on another occasion."

There was no doubt, from the reaction, that this had the approval of most present, even of the clergy.

"I recognise, my lord, that this is a large mouthful for you to swallow at one gulp," MacBeth said. "All I ask today is that you agree that the present situation of women is unjust and that this be remedied in law. I will have the matter fully worked out for the next Council, when all can be considered more closely.

180

Does that content those lords who question justice for women?"

Put that way, men could scarcely say more. Breadalbane alone raised his voice.

"We shall see," he said.

"Yes, my lord, we shall undoubtedly see!" the King commented, and there was steel in his deliberate voice now. "And let me remind you, lest any forgets, that this is a Council to advise the King. It is not a Witenagemot of the Saxons, nor a Thing of the Danes, nor yet a Senate of the Romans. Scotland has none such — as yet. The King hears the advice, and heeds — if he will."

There was a prolonged pause.

In somewhat lighter tone, he went on. "Whilst on the subject of women, I would remind all here who are of the knightly order — and that is many — that they have all taken vows before God to protect and care for women and children, and in especial widows and orphans. In my realm such vows shall be respected. Chancellor — will you proceed?"

"Merchants and husbandmen," Malduin read out, hurriedly. "The King's Highness is also concerned for the state of merchants and husbandmen in this realm. As are many others, in especial Holy Church. For long, these and others like them, millers, fishers, smiths, craftsmen, have suffered much, with none to protect them. They have been scorned and misused, robbed and imprisoned at the hands of more violent men. Their labours have been made of no avail, their corn trampled, their beasts carried away, their goods stolen. And they, they have not always had the support and protection of their lords and thanes and magistrates. Nor indeed, of the Crown. For the weal of the realm, this must be put to rights. The King would have this Council's advice on how best this may be achieved."

"Merchants, husbandmen and millers!" Thorfinn exclaimed. "Some of the greatest robbers I know are millers! And merchants none so far behind!" A shout of laughter. "Such cattle are necessary, I have no doubt. But scarcely fit to waste the time of the High Council of Scotland!"

From the reaction, clearly he had most of the secular members, at least, behind him in that.

"Does my brother of Caithness and Sutherland say, then, that my realm consists of its lords and land-holders, while such as merchants, millers even carls and bondsmen are not part of it?" the King asked.

"Not so. I but say that this Council has better things to do

181

than to spend its time on their affairs. It is the duty of the magistrates and justiciars, yes. If these are failing in their duties, let them be warned. We have appointed a High Judex. Let him see to it."

Again the murmur of approval.

"I say that the King's Highness is right," the Abernethy MacDuff said, a lean, dark and cadaverous man in his late thirties, with the stoop of a scholar. "Such folk require Crown protection. And deserve it. They well serve the realm, but are the prey of many. Freemen, they are often worse off than are carls and serfs."

"Well said, friend. What then should we do here to cherish such?"

"First charge the High Constable with their protection. That he appoint his officers in every mortuath, thanedom and community. More magistrates and judices to be appointed also, and of better quality, supported by the constables . . ."

"Who pays for all these?" someone shouted.

"*They* do, I say — the merchants themselves. See you, these traders and craftsmen and millers and the like — they have been shorn like sheep for long. We all know it. Because they create wealth, which others are greedy for. Think you that they would not gladly pay for their own protection? I say, bind them together, in companies and guilds. Each trader will pay something to belong to his company. And the companies to make payment to the Crown. So that it becomes the Crown's business to protect the traders and pay the constables and magistrates."

There was considerable interest and comment on this ingenious proposal, though by no means all favourable.

"Forby," the abbot went on, "there is more advantage in this of companies and guilds than but the payment. These could be charged with maintaining good standards of craftsmanship and work. We all know how much goods can vary, how often we find poor workmanship, scamped labour, bad weights, high charges. Make the companies responsible for their own people's standards. I have heard that this is done in Hamburg and Bremen in Saxony."

"That would take a deal of contriving," Strathearn said.

"No doubt, my lord mormaor. But if others can do it, we can."

"Excellent, Ewan mac Gillachrist," MacBeth praised. "All will now see why I chose the Abbot of Abernethy for Judex. I commend his policies. More particularly in that it touches upon

182

another subject which I would raise. This is the matter of training in useful labours and crafts. There are over many idle folk in the realm. We all know it. Not all are vagabonds. Some are honest and could be useful, but lack skills. Most lack the will or understanding to *seek* training. Training in crafts and trades. Schools should be set up — craft-schools. Many monasteries have such — but these are for their own church folk. What better than the good Abbot Ewan's trade companies and guilds to establish such training schools? To pass on and improve the skills and standards he spoke of?"

Since this did not appear to be going to cost those present anything, it was agreed, however sceptical the majority.

"That is the end of the King's proposals for this Council," the Chancellor said. "Does any present have other matter to raise, for the King's guidance?"

"I have," Bishop Malise of Inverness announced. "It is the matter of droves and pasture. Our cashel of Inverness, like many another of Holy Church, sends droves of cattle from our Highland pastures to the low country in autumn, and to markets. In the past, these droves have always moved freely on green and drove roads, as on the highways, all over the realm. But of late certain lords, thanes and land-holders have been halting the free passage of the droves and demanding toll, or payment for grazing consumed as the beasts pass through their territories. Is this not contrary to the law and ancient custom of our land?"

Most of the churchmen supported that, strongly.

"My understanding of the matter is that it is an age-old law of the land that all cattle and stock on the move, with their drovers, can halt for one night anywhere, without payment, save on land enclosed by a dyke or wall, on growing corns and hay meadows," MacBeth said. "So in my mortuath courts of Moray and Ross I have always upheld. High Judex — you have made study of the laws. How say you?"

"That is correct, Highness. With this addition — that no beasts may be pastured overnight within four stones'-throw of any vill, hamlet or township. And that all are properly herded and controlled. Such is the law."

"Then I pray that all land-holders present will hear and conform," Bishop Malise said. "Or I, and many another, will come to you, my lord Justiciar, for redress."

"Do that," the King said.

No further complaints or issues being forthcoming, the Chancellor closed the session, with the declaration that another

Council would be called in due course, within the year, or earlier should events make it advisable. Reports would then be made as to how the decisions taken this day were being effected. Almost relievedly the Council stood, as the High King and his mormaors left the hall.

In the abbot's lodging thereafter, where they were quartered, MacBeth looked at his two brothers.

"I rejoice that you both are my friends!" he told them. "For God help me if you were my enemies!"

Thorfinn laughed. "You should rejoice rather that you have such honest councillors. You need the like, Son of Life. All men do, but kings in especial. Notably kings strangely besotted with merchants, candlemakers, women and the like!"

"I have different notions of what is required of the King than have you, Viking."

"Clearly, yes. You might have made a passable bishop."

"And you, Raven Feeder, one of the idle robbers and sorners who could do with being taught an honest trade!" Neil Nathrach declared.

"Hark to our household viper! He who prefers war to be fought on his own doorstep rather than on the enemy's."

"I do not. But traitors should be rooted out before they stab better men in the back."

"I am not to suffer from lack of advice, then," MacBeth commented. "But of a mercy, could I ask that my brothers at least offer it to me a mite more privily?"

Part Two

16

It was the fourth summer of MacBeth's reign, and the fourth good harvest in succession. Men were saying that God Himself must be with the King, for in the memory of the oldest such a succession of excellent seasons could not be recollected. The barns were full, the girnels overflowing, the mills busy, the hay-stacks like regiments behind all the rigs, the brewhouses and maltings never so productive. The cattle, too, were fat and sleek, and the milk rich and plentiful, for the pastures had been as good as the rest. And not only had these been years of plenty but of peace likewise; for, almost unheard of as it was, there had been no war, no sizeable resort to arms even. King Mac-Beth had said that he intended his to be a reign of peace; and somehow, whether it was by his achieving or a higher power's, peace there was, within all his borders.

There were those who attributed this happy state of affairs to Divine Providence directly, and only incidentally to the present monarch, as an immediate result of MacBeth's cherishing of Holy Church. For he had gone out of his way to support and work with the churchmen to a degree hitherto unknown in Scotland — or for that matter in most other lands, although Saxon Edward, England's new king, who was gaining the by-name of The Confessor, was religious almost to the point of mania, but showed it not so much by working with the Church as by dominating it. This MacBeth did not attempt, being far from pietistic. But he endowed the Church with lands and property, and employed many churchmen in his processes of government, with remarkable results.

MacBeth was indeed attending a conference of churchmen at St. Andrews, with his Chancellor Bishop Malduin, when cou-riers arrived hot-foot from Dunsinane with the grim tidings. The Mormaor Crinan of Atholl had risen in arms, denounced MacBeth as usurper and murderer of his son, and called upon all true men to rally to his standard and to proclaim his other son Maldred king. Crinan's force, already large, was marching southwards from Dunkeld.

MacBeth was, in fact, utterly unprepared for this development. There had been no least warning nor hint of trouble. He had no significant number of men mustered in arms — nor could he possibly assemble any army locally, in time to meet this Atholl host. Here, at St. Andrews, in the East Neuk of Fife, forty miles from Dunsinane, he was on markedly unfruitful ground for raising troops; for although MacDuff himself was not there, having fled the country, and thought to be with Maldred and Siward in Northumbria, his Fife people had not suddenly attained any marked love for the King, most of his thanes keeping their chilly distance. And before MacBeth could reach areas where he might successfully muster men, Angus to the north or Strathearn and Lennox to the west, Crinan would be between him and the last two, and occupying the Fortrenn central region.

There was one comfort. Gruoch and the young people were in the north, at Spynie, where they sought to spend most of the summer months. So they would be in no danger meantime.

MacBeth made up his mind quickly. There was little that he could usefully do here — apart from sending out urgent calls to the mormaors and thanes to muster. There was much shipping at St. Andrews, for the churchmen did a considerable trade in the products of their farms and mills, looms and brewhouses. He would take ship forthwith to Moray, where he could raise many men quickly from his own mortuaths, and bear down thereafter on Crinan from the north. It would mean largely sacrificing the south, with Fortrenn, to his uncle's occupation meantime — but that was the lesser evil.

Requisitioning the swiftest vessel in port, a converted galley which stank of a variety of cargoes, and leaving the Chancellor to send out the orders for mobilisation, MacBeth embarked and set sail with the first tide across the mouth of the Firth of Tay, within four hours of the arrival of the news.

By water the journey was a bare 160 miles, and with summer seas and a south-westerly breeze they made good time. He reached Torfness in under the twenty-four hours, borrowed horses from Gunnar Hound Tooth and was home at the *Dorus Neamh* an hour later.

Gruoch's joy at seeing her husband was tempered by her wrath at Crinan and her indignation with anyone who would support him — as presumably many must be doing if he had an army strong enough to challenge the King. She was a woman of spirit and vigour with nothing meek about her. In the past she had held that MacBeth should have dealt with his soured uncle in no uncertain fashion and in his own time, instead of leaving him alone, isolated in Atholl, she holding much the same opinion as Neil Nathrach — and indeed Thorfinn. Her husband's reasoning that Crinan was getting to be an old man, known to be lazy, and that there had been more than enough blood shed in her family already — and moreover that it might well produce the feared violent reaction from Siward — she held to be mistaken. Now, however, she refrained from any I-told-you-so attitude, but asserted that Crinan must be crushed once and for all.

MacBeth needed no urging to action. He sent for Neil, from Cawdor, and all the other Moray thanes and chiefs, requiring immediate mobilisation and a meeting of the leaders at Forres in two days time. He rejected Gruoch's suggestion to send for Thorfinn's aid, however. He was not going to go running to his half-brother whenever he was in trouble. Thorfinn thought that he could not govern Scotland without him, and must be shown otherwise. Besides, Thorfinn would almost certainly be away at his summer hosting — possibly why Crinan had chosen to strike at this moment — and he was not prepared to ask Thorkell Fosterer for help in the affairs of Scotland.

Two days later — which was the very minimum time allowable for his chief men to assemble from so wide and difficult an area, and such as O'Beolain, for instance, would be unable to make it from Applecross by then — the council-of-war was held in the old palace of Forres, over a score of the leadership of the two mortuaths attending. There was, in fact, one unexpected participant, in the person of Gunnar Hound Tooth, from Torfness, uninvited but determined to be involved, the old Viking declaring that he was as much concerned as any of them in ensuring that the wretched Karl Hundison, as he called Crinan, should not be allowed to upset a situation satisfactory for himself and his master. Crinan had always been anti-Norse.

MacBeth explained the general situation to all, pointing out that it was possible that by now Crinan might have been joined by a force from Northumbria, under Siward or one of his lieutenants, even under MacDuff.

"Will Crinan know that you are here, in Moray, my lord King?" the Thane of Brodie asked. "Will he be prepared for an attack at his rear?"

"That I cannot tell you. I commanded the Chancellor and the others at St. Andrews to keep my departure by ship secret. But

189

whether they could do so, who knows? We must reckon with Crinan knowing that I am here."

"Then he could make our march south difficult. We have to go through near fifty miles of his Atholl, and by a score of passes. Any of these, held strongly against us, could much hold us up. In especial Drumochdar, Killiecrankie and Dunkeld itself. These, strongly manned by Athollmen, could cost us dear to force. If they did not halt us altogether."

To murmurs of agreement, MacBeth nodded. "I know it. Therefore I think that we must march otherwise. Not by the routes he would expect us."

"Let me send to the earl. Or to that ape Thorkell," Gunnar put in. "At Orkney. Give me five days, no more — and you may *sail* your army south in two-score longships, which no passes nor ambushes can halt."

"I thank you friend — but no. We must not be dependent upon the Earl Thorfinn's shipping. Moreover, we might have to wait for many days more than five for sufficient ships, if my brother is away hosting, or in Galloway. We must strike at once. I plan to march tomorrow, with such force as is already assembled, leaving the rest to follow on, so soon as may be."

"March where, Highness?" Duthac of Alness asked. "If the passes are held against us?"

"Crinan cannot hold every pass in Drumalbyn, with most of his Athollmen with him in Fortrenn. If he expects me to march, he will I think seek to man the main passes on the main routes. So we must use others. Where he would not expect us."

"What others are sufficient to take hundreds, thousands, of armed men?" Neil demanded.

"I can name you not a few. They are not strung on any one road. So it will mean much marching and counter-marching. And over difficult country. But nothing that Moraymen and Rossmen cannot master. It will take us longer, yes — but not longer than in waiting for ships. Or being held up in defended passes."

They waited doubtfully.

"We cannot hide a march of thousands," Neil objected. "Crinan will learn of our coming, our line of march. And move men to halt it."

"Not if we go only through the highest, emptiest uplands where no men are. There is much of such country in our Drumalbyn, especially in Atholl. We could not do it in winter. Nor in any other season than high summer, and after four good years. It will be sufficiently dry, the peat-bogs firm. There will be the summer shielings of the high pastures, yes. But the herders and lassies at the shielings are scarce the sort to send off hurried messengers to the glens and townships so fast as to get word ahead of us. I say that we can surprise Crinan. And then fight him on ground of *our* choosing."

He had their interest, even some enthusiasm now.

"How do we start?" Brodie asked. "Which way, Highness?"

"I have thought out some possible routes. But others — the Thane of Rothiemurchus here — may better them. He will know the northern parts better than any, I think. We make for the Spey and up to Rothiemurchus. Then turn up Glen Feshie instead of Glen Truim or even Glen Tromie. Feshie will take us fifteen miles through the southern Monadh Ruadh, unseen. Then over the high backbone of the land to Glen Geldie. There we are on the borders of Atholl and Mar. We could go down Tilt — but better down to the head-waters of Dee. Follow Dee down to Glen Clunie in Brae Mar. Gathering some Marmen as we go. Then up Clunie and over its mounth and down Glen Shee beyond, to Strathardle and Strathericht. That is East Atholl, and settled country, so we would have to choose some side glens to bring us down into Gowrie, near Blair or Drumellie. Then we will be at Crinan's back, whether he is in Fortrenn or Dunkeld."

Gillapatrick of Rothiemurchus, a young Highlandman of dark good looks and smouldering eye, nodded. "It is well considered, Highness," he said. "Until we win to the Braes of Mar. Then it could be better. A short way up Glen Clunie, takes Glen Callater off to the east. And over the Toll Mounth to the head of Isla. I have taken cattle-droves that way, to the low country, avoiding Atholl's tolls. Down the long Glen of Isla, all the way to Alyth in Strathmore, but five miles east of Blair in Gowrie. In Angus all the way from Mar, just outside Atholl, and land less peopled."

"Good. Excellent. That will aid us. Aye, and enable us to link up with the Angus thanes, in especial Cormac of Glamis. You all agree?"

There was no dissent now, even Neil Nathrach's doubts resolved. Only the Viking Gunnar had a question.

"I have five longships at the Borg," he declared. "How shall I best use them, in this?"

MacBeth shook his head. "It is kind, old friend," he said. "But this is not *your* war. Bide you at Torfness . . ."

"You call me friend and yet reject the hand I hold out, King MacBeth! I think poorly of that — as will the earl."

"Do not so, Gunnar. I esteem your friendship. See you, if I need your aid, your ships, I will send for them . . ."

"Lord King," Murdoch of Oykell intervened. "There could be good use for ships, fast ships. Send messengers by sea to Lachlan of Buchan and Martacus of Mar. Aye, and Colin of the Mearns, Cormac of Glamis and the rest. Acquaint them of your march south. But not the route. Have them to muster forthwith. Secretly as far as possible. But not to move until you send word. Then they could be waiting for us, in force, when we reach Strathmore. It could be to double our strength . . ."

"Yes. Yes — you are right, Murdoch. That is well thought of. Will you do that, Gunnar? Your fast longships as messengers. . .?"

So it was settled. MacBeth and the vanguard would march the next day — and the longships be gone before then.

* * *

It was a well-armed and fast-moving force of some 2000 that set out for the Spey, mainly mounted on garrons although with some 300 running gillies from the Braemoray uplands. More than twice as many would follow on, but these had not had time as yet to assemble and come from the distant glens of Lochaber, Moidart, Knoydart, Kintail and Wester Ross. The Highland-men were no hindrance to the horsemen as regards pace. On firm and straightforward terrain and beaten tracks they held on to the beasts' manes or the riders' sword-belts, plaids or even legs — for most men rode barebacked — as they ran, seemingly effortlessly. But much of the time they followed their own and more direct routes, over marshland, outcrops, screes and steep mountainside, where horses must detour.

Up the long and fair strath of Spey they went for a score of miles, after crossing the high moors of Braemoray and Dava, and into the great pine-forests of Nethy, Garten and Rothie-murchus. At this last they picked up another 400 Highlanders from the upland thanedoms, Clan Chattan men and noted fighters. More of these would follow, also.

Where the foaming, boiling Feshie rushed down to join Spey, they turned due southwards, to follow that lovely glen deep into the mighty mountain mass of the Monadh Ruadh. In the upper reaches of Feshie it was the running gillies who had to wait for the horsemen, amongst the fallen pines, the boulder-strewn haughs and the winding, climbing deer-paths. Up and up they mounted, by lonely ways which never before had seen a great armed force, almost to the very roof of Drumalbyn, the trees left behind, with the heather beginning to colour the brown and black of the peat-hags, the bog-cotton dancing in the breeze and deer herds and cloud-shadows adrift across the limitless wastes. The third night out they camped on the lofty watershed between west-flowing Feshie and east-flowing Geldie, at nearly 2000 feet above the sea, in as wild, desolate and empty a country as was to be found in all Scotland. Weary, hungry, coated in peat-mud, men knew now what MacBeth had meant when he said that he would surprise Crinan by the way he brought them. He surprised them all, marching them through this savage although beautiful waterlogged wilderness of the high places. Yet they had averaged over a score of punishing miles a day since leaving Forres; and their monarch had driven himself as hard as he drove them all. They were actually in the very north-eastern corner of Atholl here, with Mar ahead and Moray behind.

Next day they came down, thankfully, to the headwaters of Dee, which rose some eight miles and almost 3000 feet higher to the north, on the summit plateau of towering Braeriach itself. In the pleasant Braes of Mar country they were en-heartened to find reinforcements awaiting them, 600 no less, under young Martacus of Mar himself, now nearing nineteen years, and though still a quiet and studious youth, to be named lacking in wits by none. He brought word that his old enemy Lachlan of Buchan would bring on as many again in a day or two. Gunnar Hound Tooth had lost no time in his message-carrying.

This accession of strength inevitably delayed the march a little so that, despite the easier country, they did not cover quite so great a distance that day, camping at the junction of Glens Clunie and Callater. It was here that they turned off south-eastwards from MacBeth's original projected route, to avoid the more populous lands of Glen Shee and Straths Ardle and Ericht, to probe instead into the high, vacant fastnesses of the White and Toll Mounths, to the headwaters of the fine River Isla, over into Angus. This was almost as trying and tough going as the Monadh Ruadh traverse by Feshie, rising for a few miles almost to the 3000-foot level. They covered little more than a dozen miles that march — but climbed 2000 feet in the process, unusual activity for an army of thousands. Deep in the trough of Glen Isla they halted at Tulchan, with stragglers coming in for some two hours. None here would carry the word to Crinan. It was only some fifteen comparatively easy miles now down to the green levels of Strathmore, at Alyth, itself but the same distance, as the crow flew, from Dunsinane in Fortrenn.

Messengers from Cormac of Glamis were awaiting them at the township of Alyth. Their information was that their master was secretly mobilising the Angus levies — the Mormaor of Angus was elderly and sick. It had to be done secretly, for Crinan was at Dunsinane with some 8000 men, and any obvious mustering would bring him down on them in crushing strength. He suggested that the King waited, hidden, in the mouth of Glen Isla, for a few days until he could join him with the Angus force, and possibly with the Mearnsmen also, under Colin mac Phadruig.

MacBeth respected the old warrior's experience and advice; but on this occasion he thought that he could do better. Hiding in Isla was all very well; but a body of over 3000 men could not in fact remain hidden for long from an enemy only a dozen miles away. However loyal and favourable the Angus folk might be to his cause, someone would be sure to carry the word to Crinan. Having gained the initiative, MacBeth hoped, by his epic march over the mountains, he was determined not to fritter it away and lose the great advantage of surprise. He felt that some swift stroke now, with fewer men, would be more advantageous than delaying to accumulate reinforcements.

Not that he was rash. That was not his nature. He recognised Crinan's strength in numbers. At best, he himself could not expect to total anything like 8000 in a few days. He had something over 3000 now, and with the Angus and Mearns contributions, and Buchan's if he came in time, he might reach 5000. Even with his own Moray and Ross second force, when it arrived, he would still have less than Crinan's total — and his uncle might well be able to summon more meantime. Moreover the question of aid for the rebels from Northumbria was never far from MacBeth's mind. It seemed likely, to say the least, that such would be forthcoming. Therefore his policy should be to defeat his uncle as soon as might be, before it came — assuming that it was not already present.

To achieve success with small numbers, more than mere surprise would be required. Somehow Crinan's forces had to be split — yet without, if possible splitting his own. That might not be easy. But he reckoned that he had two advantages — one, in his uncle's attitude and character, the other in the lie of the land itself. Crinan was intensely preoccupied with Atholl in general and Dunkeld in particular, his mortuath and hereditary abbacy. Any direct threat to Dunkeld-in-Atholl would undoubtedly much provoke him. It so happened that here, at this Gowrie end of Strathmore, there was as it were an inconspicuous side-entrance to the Dunkeld area, through a series of shallow, heavily-wooded valleys and a strung-out chain of lochs linked together by the Lunan Water, to the north of the Stormounth and west of Blair-in-Gowrie. The chances of this being held in force were remote, with Crinan's main army so near, at Dunsinane, and no threat presumably anticipated from Gowrie. MacBeth therefore could make a secret march on Dunkeld from here, and probably get most of the way there, some sixteen miles, before being discovered. Then, almost certainly, Crinan would hurry north to give battle. But if, meantime, another and more open threat had materialised here in Strathmore, aimed directly at Dunsinane, he would be unlikely to leave the capital area defenceless. So he might split his strength.

So MacBeth sent the messengers back to Glamis. They were to tell Cormac to make his muster open and obvious henceforth, indeed to flaunt it, and to send as many men as he could marching up Strathmore towards Dunsinane. They need not hurry, but to make their approach very evident. Tomorrow, the looked-for reinforcements would back him up. Meanwhile the royal army would be heading secretly for Dunkeld. The Strathmore force would probably never have to fight. Its duty was to constitute a threat.

That night, then, in the August dusk, MacBeth led his troops out of the Glen of Isla and turned due westwards along the hillfoots that hemmed in the strath to the north, a strong scouting party under Neil Nathrach out in front. Skirting the populous area of Blair, where Strathmore trended away south-westwards, they headed into the shadowy woodlands of the Stormounth, closer country where they could by no means hurry, especially at night, but where they ought to remain undiscovered meantime.

It was an awkward march indeed, different from any hitherto but as trying, in the darkness. There was a road of sorts, to be sure; but it was narrow and twisting, winding through the wet forest. For this was a notably watery area, a system of narrow valleys draining extensive uplands on either side, but itself with little natural drainage, so that a string of marsh-fringed lochs took up much of the valley-floor, linked by the sluggish stream of the Lunan Water. To get thousands of men and horses through this elongated obstacle-course in fair order at night was no minor task. Before long, the force was strung out for miles. Fortunately there was no need for special haste.

At least they encountered no opposition. There were no real villages or townships.

They had covered most of the distance by dawn — or the front of the long column had — and MacBeth reckoned that they were less than five miles from Dunkeld. But here, at a widening of the curious valley formation, where the glen of the Buckny Water came in from the north, was the woodcutters' township of Botharstone. This could not be avoided, for Botharstone Loch filled the valley to the south, and the still larger Loch of Lowes to the west. However, MacBeth required word to be conveyed to Crinan, now, as to this presence and threat, so he made no attempt to prevent the cottagers from sending messengers southwards with the news — as almost certainly they would do. He *was* concerned, however, that warning should not be sent directly ahead of them; for, only some two miles on, was known to be a dangerous tactical position, not exactly a pass but a narrow gorge and river-crossing, where a few men could hold up a hundred times their number, allegedly. Neil of Cawdor was sent ahead, with some 200 men, to attempt to surprise it before word could reach there from Botharstone — since it was scarcely conceivable that so strong a position, so near to Dunkeld, would not be manned in time of war.

But while the main body rested at Botharstone, to allow the long straggling tail to catch up, and to eat the raw oatmeal washed down with water, and such cold meat as had survived thus long, Neil himself came back with the news. The position at Drumbuie ahead was not only manned but vigorously held against them, and by quite an effective force. There could be no surprise here. And the place was stronger even than they had feared.

He explained the position. The Lunan Water, which had strung together the entire valley system, here swung away northwards into the hills and its source in a group of high lochs. It entered this main valley by a kind of gorge, sure enough, steep but not really rocky, which had to be crossed. But that was not the worst of it. Beyond the Lunan, and coming down the same side-glen, was another quite major stream, issuing from the same hill-mass, and only about 300 yards away, the two running more or less side by side but with a broken wooded ridge between, to form a sort of double moat — the ridge which no doubt gave Drumbuie its name. Beyond again was a belt of marsh, which would be flooded in winter; and behind all rose the steep wooded sides of Crieff Hill. This all-but impassable gullet was almost a mile long. At its south end it opened directly into the Loch of Craiglush, and to the north it split into two difficult bog-floored glens. The road crossed the two streams and their troughs by narrow wooden bridges, strongly-held — and which could be easily demolished.

Clearly Neil considered that his royal brother had been too clever by half in choosing to come this way.

MacBeth called for his horse, and with a small group of his nobles accompanied Neil back to the site, reserving comment.

The Drumbuie position proved to be fully as awkward as reported. Indeed Neil's 200 had spent the interval investigating and assessing further, and without joy. They saw no way of making an opposed crossing without enormous losses. It was hard to gauge how many Athollmen guarded the position, because of the woodlands on all sides; but there seemed to be ample for the task.

MacBeth stoutly maintained that there was no defensive situation, natural or man-made, which patience and ingenuity could not turn.

An hour or so's inspection, with the forenoon sun dispersing the morning mists, and the King sat his garron, very thoughtful.

"It is difficult, I grant you," he told his lieutenants, at last. "Complicated. But not impossible, I think. The door is only as strong as its lock and bar. The lock, here, is the defending force. Weaken them, and we may open the door. We cannot reach them, to fight. But we can disperse them, thin them out. Their weakness is lack of numbers, compared with ours. We must use our numbers to stretch them, so that they are thinned, every-where. Then we choose our own place to cross in strength. These woodlands can hide our numbers and moves, as well as the enemy's."

Doubtfully the others eyed him.

"See you." MacBeth warmed to his theme. "We have 3000 men. I doubt whether they will have 300. Crinan would not dispose large numbers here, when he has so much to guard — all the northern passes, where he would look for us. There is much that we can do to thin out their defence. There is a mile of this gully and trough beyond. Not all of it could be crossed but we can force them to line most of it. Then there are the boggy glens to the north. We can send some hundred up there, to try to turn their flank. We may not achieve it — but it will mean the Athollmen sending more to prevent it. Then, at the other side, the south, is this loch — Craiglush, covering that flank. There is wood everywhere around. To make rafts. When they see us building these, they must detach more men to guard the loch-shore . . ."

"Rafts!" Neil exclaimed. "Saints save us — that will take an age of time! To fell and drag and build sufficient to carry hundreds . . ."

"None so long, man. We have plenty of axemen — war-axes, but they will serve. Plenty of horses to draw the wood. Ropes from twisted bracken. Besides, we have the time. Our main object is to split Crinan's army, draw part of it up to Dunkeld, then defeat it. We must give him time to come to us — since we do not mean to go to him! *We* choose the battle-ground. He has to come fifteen miles, and the Tay to cross — and will not yet know that we are here. The fight may not be until tomorrow. We have time and to spare."

Young Martacus of Mar, who was seldom far from MacBeth's side, spoke up hesitantly and yet eagerly. "Trees," he said. "F'fallen trees close g'gorges and choke valleys, in winter spates. F'fell many trees. Not only for rafts. Trim them and roll them down these steep banks. Some will float away, but more will catch and hold. Pile up. Fell scores, hundreds. Roll them down at many points. They will build up. Choke the gullies. And men may cross over. Like bridges, lord King — like bridges." He stammered a little breathlessly, in his excitement.

"God's sake, Martacus — you have it!" MacBeth cried. "A notion, indeed. Man — you have a head on those shoulders! We shall make my uncle's trees fight for us. Back to Bothar-stone then, and bring on our people. The axemen are going to be busy . . ."

So that sunny August forenoon the Wood of Drumbuie resounded to the chop of axes, the crash of falling trees — mainly birches — and the shouts of men, with little of the atmosphere of war about it all. Garrons dragged the logs to roll down the banks, or took them to the loch-shore, parties probed up into the hills, and all along the mile-long trough there was activity.

There was little sign of the enemy, apart from a group of about two-score who waited near the first bridge-end, presumably the leadership. These were equipped with bows, and every now and again shot a few arrows across, as warning to their opponents to keep their distance. Clearly the far end of this bridge was prepared for swift demolition, with ropes tied to props and supports, which could be dragged away from a safe distance should the royal troops try to rush it. Elsewhere men could be glimpsed amongst the trees, now and again, but no other grouping was evident save up in the glens to the north where the ground was less thickly wooded and considerable movement could be seen amongst the scrub.

MacBeth kept riding to and fro along the entire two miles or so of this front, from the heights to the loch-shore. The marshy edges of the latter were far from ideal for raft launching, with a state of more mud than water rapidly becoming established. But quite a number of figures could be seen watching from the far shore half-a-mile off. Up in the glens the prospects for any real attack were still less auspicious, with the floors so water-logged that any crossing against opposition, especially against archers, would be scarcely practicable. It was the central sector that encouraged him, where Martacus's log-jams were proving effective. Five points had been chosen for the tips, two below the bridge, three above, well spaced out. The ravine had an enormous appetite for tree-trunks and branches admittedly, seeming to swallow up vast quantities of timber with little evident result. But they had, after all, hundreds of woodcutters, hundreds of horses, and no lack of trees. Gradually the heaps and piles down at the river-level began to grow, partly damming up the water itself. And there was nothing that the enemy could do to halt the process — since any attempt at clearance on their part would expose them to MacBeth's archers. Some of the logs were carried away by the current, of course, but most of these finished up adding to lower jams. Two of the tips began to look promising, and the major efforts were switched to these.

It was in the early afternoon that a messenger came down from the glens with the information that the Athollmen there seemed to be withdrawing from their defensive positions, as far as could be seen going right back over the side of Crieff Hill. MacBeth immediately sent a runner down to the loch-shore for news from there. He came back presently with the word that the watchers on the far side of Craiglush had now disappeared.

"How say you?" the King asked his nobles. "Do they retire?

199

Or merely concentrate their force at these log heaps, which soon we shall be able to cross?"

He had his answer shortly afterwards. A horn sounded somewhere to the west. The Athollmen at the bridge-end began to pull on their ropes, and in only a few seconds the entire structure collapsed into the ravine with a crash. Then, without further demonstration, its former guardians turned and hurried off into the woodlands westwards.

"Gone!" MacBeth exclaimed. "They are off. They see that they cannot hold all these log-piles. Martacus — you have won the day! Without a drop of blood spilt. This, I say, the sennachies will sing of, hereafter!"

The young man flushed, wordless.

It was as MacBeth judged. By the time their advance parties had won across the awkward, makeshift bridges, there was no sign of the opposition anywhere. The way to Dunkeld was open.

*   *   *

By the time that they resumed their march MacBeth was already preoccupied with the next and principal problem — the choice of a battle-ground. For it never crossed his mind that his uncle would not come hot-foot to the rescue of Dunkeld. As he rode round the base of Crieff Hill, he could see the great River Tay now, smooth and dark, and beyond it the vast Wood of Birnam which climbed the steep Hill of Birnam. It was on that far side of the river that Crinan was almost certain to come, by the direct and quickest route — for there was no practical crossing of the Tay above the ford at Kinclaven, a dozen miles down, to the ford at Dunkeld, save for a boat-ferry at Caputh, useless for an army. Inevitably that name of Birnam repeated and repeated itself in MacBeth's mind. On this occasion, however, it was Dunsinane that would be coming to Birnam, not the reverse, so he had no foreboding. There was a Pass of Birnam, where the steep hill sent out a great buttress thrusting towards the Tay. But he was not looking for an ambush, however successful. That would not serve his purposes. It had to be a full-scale battle. He had to inflict a major military defeat, not win a skirmish. Or it all would have to be done again. He might lose that battle, of course — in which case he would be unlikely to survive for any second attempt.

Nevertheless, the Birnam Pass situation might have its uses. North of the pass the valley opened out again for almost a mile, to Dunkeld and its ford, and here there was something of an amphitheatre of fairly level ground, haughland and rig cultivation strips and the common grazings of the townsfolk, flanked on the east by the broad Tay and enclosed in the west by wooded hillsides. A killing-ground.

MacBeth decided that he would keep an open mind meantime. But if he did not perceive a better site, this would probably serve.

They expected to find Dunkeld itself held against them; but Neil, scouting ahead to the very edge of the town area, reported no opposition evident. Halting his force half-a-mile off, MacBeth rode forward with only a small leadership-group and escort — for he well knew the effect of an undefended town on an army such as his own. Before entering the place, he sent off Neil and his scouts again, to cross the ford — which they could see was not defended — and to probe southwards inconspicuously, looking hopefully for the advancing Crinan.

Dunkeld looked entirely normal in the afternoon sun, a sprawl of grey cot-houses with their thatched roofs and blue columns of woodsmoke, clustering round the abbey and cashel area at the riverside, and the fort and rath perched high on the crag above. But as MacBeth and his party cautiously made their entry, it was to discover only a few old folk and young children there, amidst signs of recent hasty departure. The place was abandoned by all who could get out, evidently having left at mere minutes' notice, fires left burning, pigs and poultry rooting about, even doors open. The visitors rode on to the cashel by the riverside, with its small stone abbey-church, where the clerics at least had not bolted.

The King dismounted and went forward alone to a group of silent, waiting churchmen. "I am MacBeth mac Finlay," he said. "I greet you, in peace. The good folk here appear to have fled from their King. Where have they gone? And why?"

One of the clerics, glancing at his fellows, spoke. "We . . . they did not know . . . who came. Did not know, lord King, that it was yourself. How could we? The word was but that a great armed host was bearing down on us. We, they feared an assault."

"Why?"

The spokesman moistened his lips. "Armed hosts are seldom gentle."

"No armed host has ungentled Dunkeld during all my reign. Why now?"

The other did not answer.

"So much for ill consciences! Are you Bishop Donnan?"

"No, Highness. The Bishop is up at the rath, yonder. With the Princess Bethoc."

"Ah. My aunt feels the need for the protection of Holy Church? She at least has not fled? Where is her husband?"

Silence.

"So be it. I shall go pay my respects to the Lady Bethoc. Meantime, my men are hungry. Of your goodness, prepare food, much food. And drink. This is a rich abbey — you will have a sufficiency. Be prepared to share it, I charge you. The Thane of Brodie, here, will arrange for it to be carried to our host."

MacBeth climbed the steep twisting track to the Dun of the Keledei. He had not been here since the day when Duncan had given him wine to drink. His thoughts were grim. So much had stemmed from that last visit. The rath or fortified hall-house stood within the ramparts of the ancient Pictish fort crowning the soaring, rocky crag, like some eagle's nest. Today, the great outer gates were shut, and all inaccessible, for it was a strong fortress.

The King drew sword and thumped on the heavy gate-timbers with its hilt. Men could be seen peering from behind the ramparts.

"Ha — porter!" he cried. "Open! Open, I say! I am MacBeth the King. I would speak with the Lady Bethoc. And the Bishop Donnan."

There was no reply. But some of the heads disappeared from view.

They had to wait a considerable time before a youngish cleric appeared on the bastion beside the gates, to stare down at them.

"You are MacBeth mac Finlay?" this man said doubtfully, as though he could scarcely credit it. "The King?"

"None other. And you are Donnan mac Colin?" The Bishop of Dunkeld was Crinan's brother's son, and ruled the abbey on behalf of his uncle. "We share an uncle I think, Bishop?" These two had never met.

"I, I greet you, lord King."

"Aye — but from a distance, it seems! Where is the said uncle?"

"He is, ah, from home."

"I had heard a whisper to that effect! How far from home, Bishop?"

"I am unsure, Highness. He has been gone . . . for some time."

202

"You say so. But — would it not be more comfortable to say so from closer at hand? Instead of keeping your monarch standing outside your door, shouting?"

"I . . . yes, Highness. I am sorry. But the Lady Bethoc my aunt, *your* aunt, orders that the gates remain shut. This is not *my* house . . .'"

"Very well. Go tell my aunt that I seek word with her."

Thankfully the bishop turned and went.

But he was soon back, his relief evaporated. "I regret it, Highness," he called down. "But the Lady Bethoc is, is otherwise occupied. She says that she has nothing to say to you, in the absence of her husband. She says to tell you that, that she has not forgotten her son Duncan! I am sorry, lord King."

MacBeth nodded. "So am I. But I understand. Tell her that I, too, have not forgotten Duncan mac Crinan! I bid you good day, Bishop. Perhaps we shall meet again in better comfort, before long."

It was late afternoon, and MacBeth was eating his share of the less than sumptuous provision hastily scraped together by the Friends of God, as the Keledei were styled, when Neil's courier arrived hot-foot. A great host had been sighted marching from the south, crossing the extensive Muir of Thorn. It was some six miles off, three miles beyond the far mouth of the Pass of Birnam. The Thane of Cawdor was keeping it under observation, hidden in the woodlands.

Before the man had finished MacBeth was calling for his horn-blowers to sound the alarm.

Having thought of no better plan of operation, he put his original scheme into immediate action. His force was divided into three unequal portions. 400 were sent to block the Pass, Neil to be recalled to command; 600 to go beyond, swiftly but on foot, to hide in the tree-clad hillsides along the line of the road southwards. The remaining 2000, with all the horses, MacBeth himself took to rim the great amphitheatre of open ground between the pass area and the ford of Tay — Dunkeld town being on the north side of the river. These he disposed amongst the trees of Birnam Wood. There was a sufficiency of cover, at any rate, in South Atholl, for any tactician. All his commanders knew their tasks, having been well briefed beforehand, in case no better project presented itself. Which was as well, for time was now short.

Having spread his men in a huge semi-circle just within the trees, MacBeth left Brodie in command there meantime and hurried off southwards, to the Pass itself, where his brother now should be installed, with Murdoch of Oykell in charge beyond, with his 600.

The situation at the Pass of Birnam was straightforward. Birnam Hill projected a wooded but steep shoulder eastwards to within 200 yards of the river, which here was forced into a major bend by the configuration of the land. The road, the main highway north and south through Atholl, threaded this narrow neck. Neil was already placing his troops above the road, as near as the cover would allow, hastily adding to that cover with birch and pine branches and uprooted juniper-bushes.

MacBeth had only just arrived on the scene when a messenger from Oykell warned that the advance-guard of the rebel force was close at hand. Soon they could hear the clop of hooves and a mounted party about a hundred strong came into sight, trotting along the road. Crouching low behind their cover, the northern men watched them pass, unsuspecting, Neil pointing out that they were led by the Thane of Breadalbane.

There was a tense interval as the sound of these faded amongst the trees. Then a new noise grew from the south, larger, more complex, not only horses' hooves but the murmur of many men, the shuffle of feet and the clank and chink of steel. The waiting men all but held their breaths.

Presently, under a group of banners, the enemy leadership rode into view, clustered round a noble-looking elderly man, heavily-built, grey-bearded, proud, in silver-scaled armour on a tall, white horse, no Highland garron — Crinan mac Duncan, Mormaor and Abbot. A dozen or so thanes, toiseachs and chiefs supported him, under the red and silver banners — and MacBeth at least was glad to see them there, even though the presence of some he much resented, since if they were here at the front they could not be dispersed through the host.

This host came on, marching only three-abreast, for the road here did not allow of more. The great majority were on foot, Highlandmen — for Atholl, being all a land of mountain and forest, was not rich in horses, as were the mortuaths of the coastal plains. But they were well armed, and looked a formidable force. And there were a lot of them.

This impression of numbers weighed much with the watchers — and in files of only three they seemed to take an endless time to pass. Everywhere around him MacBeth could sense impatience, anxiety to be up and at them, fear that they were risking disaster by thus delaying. He himself knew the same urgency, although *his* anxiety stemmed from the fear that the enemy leadership might get so far ahead that they would reach the ford and Dunkeld itself, before battle joined, and there choose to take refuge in the fort and not be involved in the fighting at all — which would ruin all. Yet he had to delay, to allow sufficient numbers past, to meet his plan of action. Premature assault could risk defeat.

The King was, in fact, roughly counting the files as they passed. He had no means of knowing his uncle's total strength present, but he imagined that it would not be less than half his reported army of 8000. Ideally, then, if there were 4000 on this march, he would wish to cut the column in half. But that would mean allowing something like 700 files to pass below. And at say two yards between each file, it would mean that the leaders might be most of a mile ahead before he struck — practically at Dunkeld. He dared not wait so long. Fortunately there seemed to be few men of rank scattered throughout the lengthy column — which meant that the extensive tail would be left largely leaderless. Clearly Crinan — who was not much of a warrior — had marched to defend Dunkeld rather than to seek a battle *en route*.

At barely 500 files MacBeth could delay no longer, afraid now that others would move if he did not. Slapping Neil's shoulder, he rose to his feet from behind their bush, sword held high. Silently, as commanded, the waiting 400 jumped up, and hurled themselves down upon the marching Athollmen.

This part of the action, although vital to the whole, was the most uncomplicated and easy. In the circumstances, it could scarcely fail. 400 men charging downhill on a narrow front upon a column of men on the march, and unprepared, were bound to have the best of it. Because of the bend of the road, the effective front was only some 200 yards long, so that less than seventy files of three were involved; and these pinned between the hillside and the riverbank had no room to form up or manoeuvre. In fact, most of them were swept right into the Tay by the rush — and even one or two of Neil's men tumbled in after them, unable to halt on the slippery bank.

Now the less simple stage began, and with the enemy north and south of the 200-yard gap warned and in shouting alarm. Neil had to rally his men swiftly, on the road, split them 300 and 100, and throw the two sections headlong at the disorganised ends of the column, the larger group to the north. Because of the twists of the road and the density of the flanking woodland, few of the enemy could see what had happened before or behind them. All the files concerned could know was that they were being attacked, by what numbers they could not tell, and that their comrades had disappeared. Without authoritative leaders, they tended to panic. Noise from further south now indicated that on that side there was trouble also, where Oykell's men had gone into action. The Athollmen were not to know that this was *mainly* noise, bluster — for 600 were not to be expected to match themselves against possibly 2000 and more, and where the ground was less propitious than at the Pass.

MacBeth, who had not joined in the downhill charge, waited only long enough to assure himself that all was going according to plan and that the two ends of the column were being, as it were, rolled up. He turned then, and ran for his horse, hidden higher in the wood, to ride as fast as he might for his main force.

When he reached Brodie and the others, it was to find them in as great a state of frustration and agitation as had been Neil's company before the assault. They could see the amphitheatre of open ground, and the confusion that prevailed there — yet the King had insisted on no attack until he ordered it in person. He was met, therefore, by a clamour of advice and demands for instant action.

Angrily he silenced them, and sought to make a swift but comprehensive survey. The enemy was disorganised and at something of a loss, but not in real chaos and demoralisation. The leadership group had turned back and were riding through their own files of foot. Most of these were turning also, but the fighting was still in the Pass woodlands and they would be able to see nothing of what went on. So far, none seemed to be crossing the ford to the town, and none looking towards the flanking forest and the hidden host, across the haughland.

MacBeth was, of course, concerned with the mounted leadership. He wanted them as far south, as far from safety, as represented by the ford to Dunkeld, as was possible. So he waited — but far from patiently himself. For he dared not delay for long. The southern portion of the rebel army was very much in his mind. It might be largely leaderless, and still more uninformed and confused than the forward section; but it was likely to be the larger, and might not take very long to discover that it was being assailed by only 600 or so from above, and a mere 300 in front. When it learned that . . .?

It was only a brief minute or two, however long it seemed, before MacBeth gave the signal. And like hounds released, the waiting Northerners burst out from their cover to hurl themselves across the level pastures upon the milling foe. But not in any wild, disorganised rabble. Each company knew its task. The majority were mounted, but by no means all — for the Highlanders much preferred to fight on foot, as did many of the others, horses being for transport, not battle. MacBeth had tried to instil his mormaors and thanes with the notions and opportunities of cavalry tactics, but with only limited success. He recognised that, however daunting the massed horsemen must seem bearing down on the strung-out, unprepared foe, most of his men would fling themselves from their mounts once amongst the enemy, and fight as they were accustomed, on foot. But one group, under Brodie, were specifically enjoined to remain mounted, and to remain also, as far as possible, in recognisable formation — an inverted V formation. This squadron, about a hundred strong, had an alloted task — to reach swiftly and wipe out at once the rebel leadership group, ignoring all else.

That MacBeth himself did not lead this arrowhead was a sore trial to him. But he told himself that he was a king, not a captain of cavalry, his part to direct the battle with his wits and authority, not to smite with just one more sword or axe, a bitter mouthful to swallow. He had retained a hundred or two men, mounted and foot, as reserves, to throw in where most required, and these likewise found their role unpalatable, all but shameful.

The initial clash was sufficiently dramatic and effective, at least, with the Athollmen given little time or opportunity to form up into any sort of defensive posture. Smashing through the already disordered columns, any possibility of the enemy forming a unified and coherent battle was lost — although admittedly this meant that the royal force likewise had to split up into small groups to deal with the consequent fragmentation. All semblance of formation on both sides therefore was quickly lost, and instead of a battle, dozens of small fights developed.

Brodie's tight arrowhead squadron was able to bore through the enemy foot like a knife through cheese. Crinan's group saw them coming, of course, but hemmed in as they were between the ranks of their own folk and the river, they could not do a lot about taking evasive action. This group of thanes and chiefs were all mounted, but not with any tactical intention, merely indicative of their rank. They did not attempt to put themselves into any defensive formation or hedgehog, but sought rather individually to get out of the way of that determined, menacing charge. Some achieved it, others did not — but as a leadership-group it disintegrated. The impact could be heard from MacBeth's stance.

From that distance the King could not make out who had got away and who had not. Most of the banners had disappeared in the first rush, but sundry horsemen were still milling around. Two quite clearly were making a dash northwards for the ford, riding down friend and foe alike in their headlong rush. Urgently MacBeth despatched young Martacus with a score of horsemen to head them off, if possible. The pair had distinctly the shorter distance to cover, but through the midst of the fighting, whereas the interceptors had a clear run.

In that confused scene it was hard to tell how the main struggle went — except that, broken up and without leadership, the enemy could scarcely win the day, on this sector. At one point, a larger number of the Athollmen seemed to have coalesced, and formed themselves into a rough defensive circle, which seemed to be holding its own. Against this MacBeth sent another wedge of some two-score horsemen, with curt instructions not to draw rein even for their own encircling men but to bore right through all, at whatever cost, and split that enemy ring by sheer weight of horseflesh. It must be destroyed before it could serve as a rallying-point for the rest.

When this manoeuvre was successful, and the circle shattered, and when the King saw that the two fleeing horsemen had been cut off and evidently disposed of, he decided that his duties as general had been sufficiently performed. He sent off the remainder of the reserve southwards, to the aid of Murdoch of Oykell and Neil, and drawing sword, rode off with Alness and a few others to join the fray.

In fact, they were too late for any significant part in the fighting. Everywhere the royal forces were gaining control, the enemy surrendering or throwing themselves into the Tay; and it seemed only a question of time before the stubborn knots which fought on grimly must be overwhelmed. MacBeth made for Brodie's busy squadron which, somewhat ragged now, still wheeled and hunted and rode down.

"Crinan?" he shouted, to his friend. "What of Crinan? Have you taken him?"

"I know not," Brodie called, panting. "He rode off. Got away. Before we struck. We have slain Fortingall and Dalmarnoch and Cranach. Captured others . . ."

MacBeth cursed, and wheeled his mount round to spur away northwards to where he could see young Mar with his troop assailing a group of half-naked hillmen.

"Martacus," he cried. "That pair you halted? Was one of them Crinan?"

"No. No, Highness. I have never seen him. But these were not old men. They yielded to us. One, they say, is Glentilt. The other I know not who!"

"Damnation! Crinan must not escape — or we have it all to do again! Where in God's name is he . . . ?"

He hurried back. There was no elderly mounted man like Crinan obvious in all that bloody and chaotic scene; but since many of the royal force were still horsed, and there was nothing to distinguish friend from foe in dress, it was by no means certain that he had escaped. MacBeth issued orders that the field should be searched for Crinan's body.

A man was brought to him who declared that he had seen the Mormaor of Atholl riding off southwards towards the Pass, at an early stage in the attack. MacBeth bit back his exclamation of disappointment. He was a fool! He should not, after all, have stood there playing the general, but himself headed Brodie's cavalry wedge and never lost sight of his uncle. Leaving his lieutenants to try to restore some order on the battle-field, and to send men quickly after him to help deal with the rear half of the rebel army beyond the Pass, he himself rode southwards.

The fighting in the Pass had ceased likewise, and he was picking his way amongst the bodies which littered the road and banks, steeling his heart to the misery of many wounded everywhere, when he perceived a group coming towards him, on foot, Neil Nathrach in the forefront.

"So, Son of Life — you won the day, I hear!" his brother called.

"Aye — here and so far. But there will be much to do yet, man. Have you heard how Murdoch does! Is he holding them, yonder?"

"I do not know about holding. But the noise of the fighting gets further ever off. And lessens. I would say that they are in retreat. I have sent for tidings . . ."

"Retreat? The rest of the rebels? Soul of God — that may mean that Crinan has reached them. And is hastening back to Dunsinane. For whatever force remains there."

"Not Crinan, no. That traitor lord lies back there. He will lead no more rebellions, Brother."

209

"You mean . . . dead? Crinan is slain?"

"Most certainly. I slew him myself."

"You . . .!"

Neil Nathrach grinned, grimly. "To be sure. He tried to ride through us. Fleeing. He was dragged from his horse. And brought to me. I soiled my dirk with him, there and then!"

"Neil — you slew him? Captured! Not, not in fight?"

"I did. He had to die, Brother. I feared that *you* would not slay him. Grown too nice! Although I have seen the day when you were otherwise! So long as that man lived you and your throne would be in danger. He was a traitor, and father and grandsire of those who would bring you down. It was the cleanest way. Better than captivity and trials and intrigues. Was it not?"

MacBeth stared at his half-brother, silent.

"Come, then. I will take you to the body . . ."

It was only a few hundred yards. There at the side of the trampled, bloodstained roadway, a little apart from any other dead, lay Crinan mac Duncan, on his back, as noble-seeming in death as he had been in life, features calm, aloof. Someone had crossed his arms on his chest, partly hiding the blood.

MacBeth sank down on one knee beside the body, face wiped clean of expression. "Should I mourn him?" he demanded, of no one in particular. "He was my aunt's husband. Father of my cousins. Primate of Holy Church. One of the lesser Kings of Alba."

"He was a traitor. He rose against the *High* King."

"He never swore allegiance to me. Never acknowledged me as King. I slew his son. Now . . . this!"

"So *I* slew Crinan — lest you would not! He was no uncle of mine! You should have dealt with him long ago. Then so many others need not have died."

MacBeth rose. "Have his body carried back to Dunkeld. To the Lady Bethoc. With care and due dignity. He was a Prince of Scotland. I will go on, see how it fares with Murdoch and the rest . . ."

Well beyond the pass-mouth they found Murdoch of Oykell himself, with most of his original force, Neil's detachment and the reinforcements — and no sign of the enemy save for prisoners and wounded. The rebels were in full retreat, he announced. There had been little real fighting. None seemed to have been in command of the tail of the column, lengthy as it was. They themselves, as ordered, had been content with

210

making a demonstration of strength and preventing the Atholl-men from pressing forward to rejoin the front of their army. But when fleeing men began to come along from the north, they deliberately let them through, or some of them, to carry the tale of disaster. Quickly thereafter the panic spread, and the rebels began to stream away southwards, in small parties and large. Murdoch had a mounted squadron out behind them, keeping them on the run. And to send back word if there was any stand made. But that he judged highly improbable. These leaderless heroes would not halt until they were safely back the dozen miles to Dunsinane.

MacBeth accepted that, but sent forward an additional contingent to assist in the matter. Then he and his lieutenants turned back.

At the battle-field they found at least a semblance of order being established, prisoners being marshalled, the wounded being roughly cared for, the dead laid out in rows, friend and foe, arms and booty being stacked. The captives amounted to many hundreds, more having surrendered than died, although undoubtedly not a few had escaped by swimming the river. There was considerable debate as to what to do with them. They were mainly Athollmen of course, although there were some from other mortuaths. MacBeth had no doubts. Let them go, disarmed, he commanded. They had learned their lesson, and would be loth to rise in rebellion again. They were, to be sure, all his subjects.

Their leaders, however ineffective, were a different matter. Five thanes and half-a-dozen lesser chieftains had been captured alive, but mostly wounded. Of the thanes, three were of Atholl — Glentilt, Dull and Fandowie. The other two were Kinnear, from Fife and Strowan from Strathearn.

The King had them brought before him. He dealt with the three Athollmen first. He looked at them long and hard, frowning.

"Have you anything to say?" he asked, at length.

The youngest, Thane of Fandowie, slight, pale from loss of blood, spoke. "Lord King, the Lord Crinan our Mormaor, commanded it. Ordered that we raise our men and join him. We could do no other."

"I say that you could. Had you refused to rise against your King, he could not have forced you. You, Dull — say you the same?"

"I say only — mercy, Highness."

Glentilt stared ahead of him, unspeaking.

"Very well. Since you are all thanes of Crinan's, obeying his command, even though I could have your lives, as rebels and traitors, I shall be merciful. You will be banished my realm henceforth. During my pleasure. Go where you will, outwith Scotland, from my sight. Take them away."

Neil of Cawdor, nearby, snorted his disapproval.

"Now these other two," the King said. "Cosgreg of Kinnear and Kerald of Strowan. You both I know. You have supped at my table. What have *you* to say?"

"Mercy, lord King," the first faltered.

The Strathearn thane, although twisted with the pain of multiple wounds, glared proudly ahead and scorned to plead.

"You both saw me seated on the Stone of Destiny. Both came thereafter and swore allegiance to me, before God, as your High King. These others did not. They were not present that day. Yet you have risen in arms against me. I say that you are foresworn traitors and should die. Can you deny it?"

Neither found words.

"So be it. I offer you this mercy only. Your own swords. Take them, if you will. And fall on them. Or else hang. Choose you."

There were swift breaths drawn, and gulps, not only on the part of the prisoners. None spoke.

"Neil of Cawdor — this is work for *you*, is it not? Take them. At once. See to it. I have better things to do. And let these lesser men go. Like the others."

Turning abruptly on his heel, MacBeth called for his horse.

17

GUNNAR HOUND TOOTH presented himself at the House of Spynie just as the pitch-pine torches were being lit in the lesser hall, with the fading of the grey early November daylight, and caught up young Cormac, now five years old, in one great hand, and his little sister Eala in the other, to raise them high and shake them at each other, like dolls, to their yells of mirth. He was now in his seventieth year but, if bent a little about the shoulders, still as strong as an ox. Continuing to hold the children up, he

212

made what served him for a bow towards Gruoch — something he could never bring himself to do for MacBeth — and grinned.

"Lady — how is it that you grow younger with each year? Unlike others. And with these two warriors to wear you down? Not to mention those three other sons of yours!"

"Flatterer! You must be wanting something, Gunnar? What could a Viking want of a woman in her middle years — when, if all we hear is true, he lacks not for youngling queans yonder at Torfness! Even at three-score-years and ten!" Gruoch, now thirty-five, indeed grew the more lovely as the years passed, despite her five children, of a serene dark beauty.

"Ach, the best wine is that kept for a while, woman, I say! More taste and body!"

"As well that my husband is not from home, Pirate, or you might sweep me off my unsteady feet! Where have you come from? I thought that you were in Orkney."

"I left the Brough of Birsay yesternoon. And landed at the borg two hours back."

"So-o-o! And you come here thus soon. You must be in haste, then — not just to trade flattery with silly women!"

He set the children down. "There is some call for haste, yes."

"Cormac — go for your father . . ."

"No need." MacBeth appeared in the doorway. "I heard that the *Dorus Neamh* suffered raiders! Greetings, old friend. I did not know that you were back. It is good to see you, always."

"I am just come, King."

"And in haste. He only left Orkney yesterday noon," the Queen said.

"Tidings from Thorfinn?"

"Trouble," the old Viking answered briefly.

"Trouble? It is not like the Raven Feeder to admit trouble. Only to make it! What is this?"

"It is that Rognvald Brusison again. And this new King of Norway, Magnus Olafson. Kings can be as the plague, King!"

"The Earl Rognvald? I thought that all was settled with that young man."

"So thought we all. But Magnus has stirred him up again. Using him against his uncle. To try to win Thorfinn's allegiance to Norway, a curse on him!"

"Come you," Gruoch said to the children. "Men's talk. You will eat with us presently, Gunnar?"

Rognvald Brusison was Thorfinn's nephew. Sigurd the Stout

of Orkney had had three sons by a previous wife before he married Malcolm's daughter Donada, and so produced Thorfinn — Somerled, Brusi and Einar. That was why Malcolm had given his grandson Caithness and Sutherland for an inheritance — since he could not hold them safe himself against the Norse and Orkney raiders. Sigurd, however, had divided Orkney and Zetland amongst the four sons — ensuring endless dispute, with Thorfinn, as he grew older, tending to win more and more. The three elder half-brothers were all dead now, Somerled and Einar leaving no heirs. But Brusi had left a son, this Rognvald, and sent him to Norway for safety. Canute had sought to use the boy's claims to part of Orkney — he was the son of an elder brother, after all — to bring pressure to bear on Thorfinn to acknowledge him as his sovereign lord and pay his due tribute to Norway. With marked lack of success. At Canute's death, however, Thorfinn had voluntarily recognised that his nephew had some rights in the matter and settled some of the less valuable and populous Orkney isles upon him. And Magnus Olafson, attaining the Norse throne, had created him earl. For seven years there had been peace between uncle and nephew, with Rognvald in Norway most of the time. Now, it seemed, Magnus was emulating Canute.

"Thorfinn believes this move to endanger him?" MacBeth wondered, scarcely believingly.

"More than believes! The danger is there. Magnus gave Rognvald a fleet of longships and many men. He sailed northabout, by Iceland, gained more men and ships there from Thorfinn's unfriends, and drove south for the Hebrides. There he has slain the Earl Gillaciaran and defeated in battle the son Somerled. He now holds Colonsay and Islay and Coll and other isles. And is believed to be intending to join with Echmarcach of Dublin and Man, and other Irishry, to bring down Thorfinn himself."

"Saints alive — and I have heard naught of this! But what of Thorfinn himself? He has not sat idle through all this, surely?"

"He was in Galloway when he gained word of the fleet at Iceland. Thorkell Fosterer sent him word that something was amiss and he had better come home. He dared not bring a large force with him — for he has to watch your Cumbrian border, with that Siward, like a hawk. So he came fast and alone, with only a couple of longships. The Fosterer sent for me, with all I could bring from Torfness. Others likewise. The Earl is mustering a great force and fleet. And sends me to you, King."

MacBeth went to throw a log on the fire, frowning. There had been two years of peace since Crinan's death. Siward had not struck in force — although he had nibbled away at Cumbria, and even Teviotdale and the Merse, his feud with Earl Godwin of Wessex continuing to preoccupy him. The last thing that MacBeth wanted was to become involved in war, at this stage, and against the Norse. His realm was prospering, the benefits of peace like a benison on the land, law and order established as never before. Yet — could he turn down his brother's call for aid? Thorfinn had never failed in his help, when needed — even when not needed!

"What does he want of me?" he asked, reluctantly.

"No great deal. The Raven Feeder does not plead aid from any man. He would but have you go to Galloway. With some strength. And let it be known that you go. It is to your own advantage. Lest Siward and that Maldred think that they can strike while Thorfinn is occupied elsewhere. But if you are there, Echmarcach of Dublin will think twice of moving against him. If you gather all the shipping of Galloway. Facing Man. He will not dare go to Rognvald's aid, with the King of Scots and a fleet only twenty-five miles from Man."

MacBeth nodded. "That I can do, at least. Might well do anyway. But — it is late in the season for campaigning. Especially by sea."

"Yet Rognvald *chose* to strike now. Perhaps Magnus could not let him have the men and ships earlier. He arrived at Iceland only three weeks ago."

"And what is he doing now? Since defeating young Somerled?"

"He is taking over the other islands, one by one, in the Hebrides — Mull, Tiree, Jura, Rhum, Eigg. The Outer Isles, likewise. So that he has a firm base from which to threaten Thorfinn. If he can hold the Western Isles, in alliance with the Danes of Ireland and Echmarcach, and with Iceland threatening from the north and Norway from the east, Orkney could be in the claws of a lobster! In especial, if Siward took a hand."

"Very well. I will start for Galloway as soon as I have gathered a force. And leave King Echmarcach in no doubts of my intentions."

"Good. The Raven Feeder will do the rest . . ."

It took only three days to scrape together a token force of men from Moray and Ross, amounting to about one thousand. Most men, like their masters the thanes and chiefs, were indeed glad enough at the prospect. With the last of the harvest long in, the beasts back from the high shielings pastures, there was not a lot of man's work to be done at this time of year. And peace, however satisfactory for women, bairns, churchmen — and the King — began to pall on the active of the male sex. Chopping, carting and sawing logs for the fires, cutting reeds for thatch, digging peats, smoking meat and brewing and drinking ale and spirits — these a man can quickly tire of.

It was a long way to Galloway, nearly 200 miles even as the crow flew; and the highest passes were already under snow. MacBeth chose to march down the Great Glen to the Western Sea at Lochaber, with no really lofty heights to cross. There he engaged Thane Ewan — now much in his debt through having been granted considerable portions of the former Breadalbane territory consequent on the death of its rebel lord — to gather together every available vessel from a lengthy and quite populous sea-board fit to make the voyage to Galloway. Ewan of Lochaber was prepared to do this, but not to provide men for the expedition; for he had ominous tidings from the north and the islands, in especial that the Earl Rognvald had now captured the great and important island of Skye, only fifty miles to the north, and even made raids on the mainland at Ardnamurchan — which was much too close for comfort. The thane required all his manpower for home defence.

MacBeth sought to soothe him by assuring that Rognvald would soon have more to occupy his time.

The King could not afford to wait overlong for this assembly of boats, for nothing was surer than that news of it would reach the islands eventually, and the last thing he desired was for a squadron of Norse longships to descend upon his motley fleet, like wolves amongst sheep.

And it was a motley fleet which, three days later, set out down Loch Linnhe, scores of craft of all shapes and sizes, mainly fishing-boats inevitably, but with some chiefs' galleys amongst them, and some heavy trading ships belonging to the Church, used for transporting hides, wool, grain and the like. Despite their numbers, little more than half of the force could be carried in these for a 150-mile voyage in winter seas. So the rest were sent off, marching southwards by land, around all the sea-lochs, with instructions to pick up more vessels on their way, in Lorn and Cowal and even the Clyde estuary.

At first the straggling, awkward collection of ships kept close to the shore, in the interests of secrecy — for it was not Rognvald whom they wanted to impress with their presence and numbers. At least, not at this stage. Entering the Firth of Lorn, they kept east of Lismore and crossing the mouth of the Sound of Mull, deliberately by night, they slipped down the narrow Sound of Kerrera and so into the welter of islets which flanked the lower firth and then the Sound of Jura on the east, keeping out of sight of Mull. They had to go at the speed of the slowest, of course — and that was very slow. Soon they were strung out for miles, with the galleys hurrying to and fro to act like sheep-dogs for an unruly flock.

The weather was not good; but on the other hand, it might have been a lot worse. It was wet and chilly, with a long oily swell which had most of the passengers seasick, cold and miserable for much of the time. But there were none of the dreaded storms, and nothing to impede the voyage save their own inadequacies.

Down the coast of long Kintyre they could keep reasonably well inshore. But off the perilous Mull thereof they had to take to the open sea, to give good clearance to the tide-races and currents and cross-seas which, at the junction of the Clyde estuary, the Hebridean Sea, the Irish Sea with the Atlantic itself, made this a graveyard for shipping. Now, moreover, they were finished with secrecy, Rognvald's longships being unlikely to be thus far south. MacBeth *wanted* his presence to be noted and relayed to the Lochlanners, the half-Norse, half-Celtic kinglets of the Irish east coast, and to the Isle of Man no great distance now to the south. So, after sheltering the third night in Machrihanish Bay — a death-trap of a place in different weather conditions — the ungainly fleet set off with the dawn seawards, on a dog's-leg course which took them far enough south to be seen plainly from the Ayres coast of Man. With the sun sinking, MacBeth gave the order to turn and run before the south-westerly breeze for the Solway mouth.

Darkness caught them, unhappily, in the wide entrance to Wigtown Bay. The shoals and shallows of that place were far too dangerous to risk night-time navigation. So they had to heave-to and spend a highly uncomfortable twelve hours in the jabbly waters of Solway. Inevitably the vessels became much dispersed in the process, and in the morning much time was spent in getting all rounded up again. A change of wind to the south-east also complicated matters; and they had to wait off Sliddery Point again, for the tide to allow them into the shallow landfall of Cruggleton Bay. It was noon before the demoralised, cold, hungry, seasick Northerners eventually landed, below the towering cliffs of Dun Sliddery of Cruggleton.

Sween Kennedy, Ingebiorg's cousin, was unashamedly relieved to see them, despite the task and cost of catering for such a multitude of visitors. He was an easily-alarmed man, and the rumours circulating in Galloway since Thorfinn's sudden departure were not calculated to let him sleep easy of a night. He believed that both Echmarcach and Siward intended to descend on Galloway, and possibly some of the disaffected South Cumberland lords also, who saw an opportunity to add to their territories. The lack of any strong king in England encouraged all such brigandage. The arrival of the King of Scots himself reassured the man almost pathetically, even though he brought no large army.

In the days that followed, MacBeth was very busy ranging far and wide over Galloway and even across Solway into North Cumberland. His activity was admittedly mainly making a show, for he hoped very much not to have to come to blows with anyone. But if he had to, the preparations he was making so obviously, even spectacularly, could have their practical uses. Harald Cleft Chin, who was still Thorfinn's military deputy in Galloway, had his headquarters at Kirk Cuthbert's Town, forty miles to the east on the Dee estuary. But from the point of view of invasion from Man or Ireland, Cruggleton on Wigtown Bay was more central — if less effective for any assault from Northumbria. So the King set up two almost independent commanderies, the western one under Brodie; while he himself rode the entire territory, day in day out, unkingly as the process might seem, instead of summoning the lords and chieftains and leaders to his side at Cruggleton — there were no thanes in Galloway.

His main concern was with local musters all up and down the land, not trying to form any large central army. That and assembling shipping and even quite small craft at every port, fishing-haven and boat-strand of the long, indented Solway seaboard. He had no least doubt that sufficient word of both these moves would reach Echmarcach who was thought to be on Man at present; and inevitably he would have to think twice about either invading Galloway or sailing north for the Hebrides to the aid of Rognvald. MacBeth judged him not to be a rash man.

The Earl Siward the Dane was altogether a different story. Siward was not unlike Thorfinn, anything but cautious, a vigorous, cunning, ambitious man, certainly the man to take advantage of a situation such as this if he could. Yet Harald Cleft Chin, who maintained quite an army of informers and spies along the Northumbrian border with Cumbria, declared that he had no word of any suspicious moves westwards. Most of Siward's admittedly large manpower was said to be concentrated in Deira, South Yorkshire, in long-sustained skirmishing warfare with the Earl Godwin of Wessex, the late Canute's brother who, ostensibly in the name of his son-in-law Edward the Confessor, was seeking to bring Siward under control — although in fact the enmity was much more personal. Whether Siward could mount a thrust on Cumbria at the same time was debatable.

The remainder of MacBeth's force from the north arrived in groups up to a week later, some having had to ride all the way. A surprise was the appearance of a completely new company of some 600, under Murdoch of Oykell, sent by Neil Nathrach overland, on his own initiative. Most of these were sent to man the Northumbrian border.

On the last day of November, the Feast of Saint Andrew, a single longship swept into Wigtown Bay from the north, its square sail bearing the black raven device. It brought Somerled mac Gillaciaran, with the news that all was over. Thorfinn had met and utterly routed his nephew Rognvald in a great battle, on land and sea at Waternish in Skye. Rognvald was indeed now dead, and most of the Norse and Icelandic ships sunk or captured. He had fled from the defeat, but had been caught at Papa Stronsay in Orkney, and slain by Thorkell Fostri. Thorfinn sent his thanks to the King. He suggested that they celebrate by keeping Yule together, at Torfness.

* * *

Thorfinn arrived in Moray in great style only a week after MacBeth himself got back — who had come via Fortrenn, well aware that he must keep the southern half of his kingdom fully informed and concerned in all that went on, however much he might prefer his own North. His brother brought Ingebiorg and their children Paul, Erland and a three-year-old daughter, a second Ingebiorg; also Thorkell Fosterer and a great train of Viking notables — which made the King of Scots' establishment look modest indeed.

They presented themselves at the House of Spynie *en masse*, on Yule Girth Eve, the eighth day before Christmas, on an afternoon of feathery snow-fall — and one glance at the crew behind the earl and countess, both this side of the causeway and that, promptly changed MacBeth's and Gruoch's minds as to suggesting that the visitors should stay at Spynie instead of Torfness. The *Dorus Neamh* was only a moderately-sized house, no palace, and no suitable establishment for a Viking horde.

Arms wide, Thorfinn came striding up, his costume making no concessions to the weather — although behind him Ingebiorg was like a blonde snow-goddess, largely wrapped in polar-bearskins. He all but felled his brother with the heartiness of his greeting, shouting his joy.

"Son of Life — a sight for saints! Sober as one of your own judges, by God, Yule or none! And sprouting grey hairs, on my soul! An old man before your time, hey? To look at you, who would say that you were the Raven Feeder's saviour!"

As, choking from that drastic embrace, MacBeth sought breath to protest, his brother flung him away and stepped over to pick up Gruoch bodily, raising her high and stamping around with her, bellowing nonsense. Even the Queen's habitual serenity was put to the test, as her children, and many of the Orkneymen, hooted and chortled their glee — although it was the children's turn next to be manhandled.

Ingebiorg kissed MacBeth uninhibitedly, pink cheeks cold but red lips warm. "His foolishness grows with his belly!" she confided. "It is good to see you, after so long. A woman's thanks for what you did for us all."

"I marched across Scotland. Sailed some boats from here to there. It will tax even Thor to make a saga out of that!"

But Thorfinn did not fail to try. He was vociferously grateful, for him, if just slightly mockingly so, over the Galloway expedition; and though he did not equate it with his own activities, he insisted that it was an integral part of the whole notably successful enterprise; moreover MacBeth's cockleshell shoal was both the greatest bluff and the greatest joke since the man Noah sailed his ark. He had a new skald, one Arnor, he announced, who would make a worthy epic out of the entire affair — or hang!

Ingebiorg had changed little with the years, and seemed to thrive on motherhood. The son Paul was now twelve, the same age as Farquhar, but big-boned and loose-limbed where his cousin was compact, neat, contained. The second son, Erland, at ten, was stocky, ruddy, solemn as an owl, unlike his contemporary Luctacus who, although slight and pale, bubbled with high spirits. As for the little girl, young Ingebiorg, who for some reason appeared to be known as Lug, she was like a butter-ball, all fair, plump amiability and dimples. Cormac and Eala took her over there and then amidst elemental mirth.

Even though they resiled from the notion of putting up all Thorfinn's company at Spynie, at least they could provide a repast for the multitude, in the greater hall; and as this was being prepared, and the ale flowed, the visitors' Yuletide gifts were produced and handed out, to much exclamation and excitement — an extraordinary and diverse collection ranging from gold and silver plate and jewellery — little of it Norse in origin and some distinctly ecclesiastical — to skins and garments of seal and wolf and bear and arctic fox, from Muscovy blankets and Eastern rugs to small swords and axes for the boys, and even a live brown bear cub, amiable and cuddlesome, for Cormac and Eala, which Thorfinn declared could be taught to dance — but which Gruoch, unlike her offspring, viewed with misgivings. The Scots offerings were much less dramatic, although a pictorial tapestry with a design of longships and ravens, worked by Gruoch's own hands, probably represented more care and thought than all the rest put together. But the guests, who were clearly better givers than receivers, did not seem to notice any discrepancy, in their hearty enthusiasm for their own contributions.

The meal, understandably, was somewhat delayed in appearing, with raiding of ice-houses and game-larders necessary to provide for so many, Gruoch having to calculate numbers, plan expedients and instruct servants while continuing to play the gracious hostess and grateful present-acceptor — her husband blissfully unaware of any stress or crisis. To help fill the interval and possibly to reduce the noise, MacBeth proposed that Thorfinn should give them some account of the battle with Rognvald, of which they were agog to hear. His brother declared strongly that he did not feed hounds in order to have to bark himself, and called upon Arnor Earl's Skald to earn his bread, amid loud and impolite encouragement.

A husky, hairy young man, far-out kinsman of the Earl, was pushed forward, reluctant — and was seen to be blushing delicately beneath all the hair. He produced from a satchel the tools of his trade, an ornate dagger and a small, simple, three-stringed lyre. With these, he took up his stance before one of the two great log fires of the hall, and waited patiently, or perhaps apprehensively, for the advice and contumely to die down.

"The Raven Feeder and the Three Black Crows," he announced throatily.

The title at least was well received. The raven, in Norse mythology, was a renowned and noble bird, familiar of the gods; whereas the crow was a scavenger, three crows an obscenity.

It took a little while for the rhymer to get into his stride, and at first the twanging of the three notes of his instrument the most positive part of the performance. But eventually, in self-defence, he had to assert himself, and presently he acquired a degree of confidence and fluency. Words began to pour forth, with only rhythmic punctuation from the strings.

It was quickly clear, to MacBeth at least, why his brother had preferred that the skald shōuld tell the story. From the first, the build-up for the Raven Earl, his might, his fame, his courage and his wisdom, was tremendous — and such as a modest man might hardly emphasise himself; and that of the Three Crows, the Earl Rognvald, the Goden Hjalmar of Iceland and King Magnus, correspondingly shameful. He told how the trio of scavengers had cast covetous eyes on the Raven Feeder's territory and banded together with other like slammerkins from other parts to harry and seize and steal. Twing-twang-twong went the strings.

Thorfinn nodded in rapt approval — while his wife made faces at MacBeth.

There was a lot more of picturesque and one-sided flourish before the composer got down to the vital battle — with the King of Scots getting a look in as the noble Raven Feeder's brother and helper, twing-twang. But the armed encounter itself was more authentic. Obviously Arnor had been present himself, and he described aspects of the scene and situation vividly, with a seeing eye and ready tongue. Now the dagger came into play more often than the lyre, as the story unfolded. He told how the Earl Thorfinn had gathered together each hero and each longship from every isle of Orkney and Zetland, even from the far Faroes, and sent the brave Thorkell Fostri across the Pictish Sea to Caithness and Sutherland to muster the outland clans there and march them down through the Westland to Skye. How the great fleet set sail from the Brough of Birsay westwards for the Hebrides; and how the Raven Feeder and his foster-father had met the Three Crows at Waternish in the north of Skye and there fought and won two distinct battles on land and on sea, slaying mightily with axe and mace and sword and spear, burning with fire-arrows, ramming with iron prows, Thorfinn slaying his scores, Thorkell his dozens. How Rognvald sank with his ship, his skull cloven in two, the Icelander Goden fell to Thorkell's mace, and the Norse crow's representative, the Earl Hundi, a hound indeed, yielded, so that his head now adorned a dun's walls at Waternish, with a thousand others. Great work. Twang. MacBeth King of Alba meantime kept the other scavengers at bay, twing. Hail the Victor! Hail the Heroes! Hail the Raven Feeder!

It made stirring telling and went down well, especially with Arnor's employer. The skald was toasted and back-slapped and forced to slake his dry throat with vast quantities of ale.

The servitors marched in with steaming cauldrons and platters, to prolonged cheers.

The serious business of great eating — and drinking — proceeded thereafter for literally hours. This was inevitable, in view of the problems of unexpectedly having to cater for vastly larger numbers than anticipated — over seventy sat down — but also it was intentional, for this was an especial night, and it was as well to prolong the table-sitting until midnight, when further activities were due. Even the children were permitted to remain in their places until the end, for once — and if some of them were apt to be asleep much of the time latterly, so too were not a few of their elders. Whilst they waited for the successive courses, there was entertainment, to be sure, fiddling, singing, dancing, juggling, story-telling. MacBeth himself contributed a tale of the mighty exploits of the Sons of Uisneach for love of Deirdre nic Feidhlim, a stirring and romantic account, semi-factual, semi-legendary, only enhanced by the low-key style of the royal delivery — and accompanied by sundry Viking snores. Arnor Earl's Skald was called upon for another offering, but was found to be too drunk to comply.

At length, noises from without, bagpipe music, singing and shouting, intimated the approach of midnight, and a move was made outdoors by all capable of it. Torches were lit, coats and plaids donned, MacBeth in his newly-acquired wolfskin cloak, Gruoch a vision in white fox. Outside, the scene was striking. The snow had ceased, leaving a thin white covering over all, and now it was freezing, a still night of bright stars. The flickering light of scores of torches made of it a gleaming and sparkling wonderland. Across the loch a large and noisy crowd had assembled, come from the hall-town, neighbouring townships, the fishing-havens and the Keledei cashel and college on Rose

Isle, their torches setting the sky aglow and reflected in the dark water which was beginning to grow a skin of ice, their pipes wailing and shrilling. Cheers greeted the appearance of the royal party.

Waving, MacBeth took Gruoch's arm on one side and Ingebiorg's on the other, and signing for Lulach and his children, and Thorfinn and his, to follow on, led the way down to the waterside jetty, the youngsters delighting to be allowed to carry their own torches. There a large flat-bottomed barge, used for ferrying horses, was waiting, oarsmen ready. Into this they piled, and were rowed out to midway between island and shore, one hundred and fifty yards from each. There they waited.

The slow, sonorous clanging of a great bronze gong from the hall door-way marked the midnight hour, this special midnight, the turning-point of the winter solstice, the Birthday of the Unconquered Sun and Return of the Burning Wheel, of ancient Pictish and pagan worship, as well as the Christian celebration imposed thereon, the first day of Christ's Mass and start of the Haly Days. At the first reverberation the shouting and the piping died away.

The King stepped up on to the raised prow of the scow, and when the last pealing note of the gong had quivered across the loch, raised his hand.

"My people and my friends," he called, deep-voiced, into the hush. "I greet you all this God-given night. I wish you well, and seek your own good will towards myself, the Queen and our family. Aye, and towards the Earl and Countess of Orkney and theirs. And I ask Holy Church's blessing upon us all, and upon this realm and people."

There was a murmur, like the making tide on a long strand, and then a single strong, clear and musical voice was uplifted.

"God Almighty keep you all. Bless, preserve and cherish you, in soul and in body, and on all on whom you seek His love. In the name of the Father and of the Son and of the Holy Spirit, One in Three and Three in One." That was the Keledei abbot from Rose Isle.

Even the Vikings were silent.

Then MacBeth spoke again. "I now declare to you Yule Girth," he called. "Sanctuary, in the name of the Christ who was to be born in seven days. Freedom for all, even the wrong-doers, from imprisonment, from arrest, from man's punishment, from this hour until Up Haly Day, the twentieth day of Christmas. All note and heed. It is my royal command. All man's punishment of his fellows is but lent from God, the true judge. And God was born to die for sinners at this time. This to remind us. I proclaim Yule Girth. Let no man break it — or be given cause to break it." He paused. "I and my wife and family wish you all the peace of this season. You will pleasure us by drinking to our health. And we to yours."

Now the cheers broke out, loud and long, the solemnities over — especially when other torch-lit boats were to be seen coming out from the Hall Isle laden with casks and barrels and baskets. If any had wondered at it, this was why Gruoch had had to take heed to her catering that evening, lest the traditional hospitality for the Yule Girth crowd should be too much encroached upon. A minor miracle or two of wine, loaves and fishes would not have come amiss.

*   *   *

That Yuletide of 1046/47 was certainly one of the least restful that the MacBeth household could remember — although they were celebrating peace on earth in general and in Scotland and Orkney in particular — Thorfinn and his entourage seeing to that. Whether they behaved thus back in their own islands, or whether it was due to the holiday atmosphere away-from-home and the reverberations of victory, was not to be known. But clearly they had come to enjoy themselves, and no opportunity was to be missed nor under-valued. Much of which enjoyment applied likewise to their hosts. But the pace became slightly wearing for non-Vikings.

The traditional ceremonies of the festive season fell to be observed, of course, and they were many; but it is safe to say that never had all been celebrated with such gusto before in Morayland, with extra Norse revelry added to the native Celtic ones. There was the Mistletoe Bough saturnalia, with licence between the sexes scarcely approved by Holy Church — although the Celtic Church was more broad-minded in such matters than the Romish one. There was the Norse Animal Carnival, when the young people dressed up as birds and beasts, wolves, herons, bears, eagles, to go round the townships singing carols and choruses that seemed to have strangely little to do with Bethlehem, to be rewarded with cakes and ale — although perhaps many of the cottagers presented these to the capering Vikings more out of alarm than from piety.

There was something of a clash of traditions on 24th December, when the Log Even's high jinks, concerned with the selecting

225

and dragging and setting alight of the Yule Log competed for favour with the very different Holy Night ceremonial of the Christians. Christmas Day itself, in consequence, proved to be something of a blessed oasis, with attendance at the Nativity Processional and Holy Communion thereafter obligatory on all, providing a most necessary interval for recovery from various kinds of exhaustion. On this occasion, however, the comparative peace did not last the day out, for it was Thorfinn's turn to play host at Torfness for the prescribed Christmas feast.

It proved to be, as could have been anticipated, a whole-hearted not to say extravagant affair, with quantity rather than variety the basic theme, oxen roasted whole, venison by the haunch, salmon by the score and liquor sufficient to float a longship. The Borg hall, huge, bare, gaunt and draughty, was hardly ideal for festivities, but holly, ivy and fir branches in abundance helped to relieve the bald stone walling, and two great square sails from the longships had been brought in to hang side by side, the two black spread-winged ravens facing each other.

The entertainment this time was provided partly by Arnor Earl's Skald and partly by an older man, one of the longship's oarmasters, Njal by name. Arnor had composed a new piece, a skit on Thorkell Fostri, as a mighty warrior who waxed valiant and terrible but always on mistaken targets, with consistently embarrassing results, a comparatively brief comic turn which brought the house down as Thorfinn's ape-like foster-father alternately roared his laughter and gnashed his teeth with rage. But Njal, a grizzled veteran lacking an eye, chose to render an old favourite of countless Yules — although not at first sight particularly applicable to the celebration of Christ's birth. This was the song of Odin, God of War, and the Two Ravens. These renowned birds, Hugin representing Mind and Munnin representing Memory, were appointed by the other gods of Valhalla to sit one on each of Odin's shoulders whilst he conducted his battles, giving good advice and consequent victory. Thor the Thunderer, his son, was jealous of the ravens and sought to borrow them now and again; but Odin would not part with them. So the beautiful Regner Lodbrocksdotter, who was in love with Thor, wove and embroidered in one single night, a splendid double-raven banner for the Thunderer. She could not guarantee quite such miraculous powers to her woven ravens as to the live ones, of course, but assured that when the birds

226

on the banner seemed to stand erect, ready to soar, victory would be Thor's; but when they drooped, his arms were destined to defeat — so it would be wise to avoid battle on such occasions. Since, clearly to all seafarers, it would be the wind which ensured the one or the other, Thor and his Viking successors took due heed of the fair Regner's advice ever after, with suitable results. Hence Thorfinn Sigurdson, in due line of succession, kept his own raven duly fed on flesh. But, Njal added grinning, there being a tradition that it was apt to be only Munnin the Memory, on the left, which occasionally drooped and slept, the wise earl chose to fly only one raven on his sails and banner, Hugin — and so always won! Wild applause greeted this new quirk at the end of an old story, none more delighted with the notion than Thorfinn. The draughts of that vast echoing hall, rippling the painted hanging sails and seeming to make the black ravens nod and flex their outstretched wings, enhanced the story-telling.

The eating over, through lack of further capacity rather than any lack of meats, and the rest of the night dedicated to serious drinking, Thorfinn denied himself in the interests of the few women present and announced to his principal guests that he had a different entertainment in store for them now. At Gruoch's protest that she had partaken so fully that all she was fit for was bed, her brother-in-law assured that that was anticipated and what they were going to do now was designed to cope with full bellies, and would moreover send them off to bed in due course in proper fettle to do justice to the occasion — this with large leers and nudges. However, Ingebiorg was equally and more persuasively insistent, and the royal party rose to leave the hall. Outside, the young people were put in Paul Thorfinnson's charge and sent off on their own — the infants having been left asleep at Spynie — even though Lulach for one looked extremely doubtful. Their elders were conducted across the snow-covered yard of the fort, to a low range of buildings on the west side, part of which almost seemed to be on fire from the amount of smoke issuing therefrom — although some of this proved to be only steam.

"A bath-house!" MacBeth exclaimed. "Do not tell me that we are going bathing? At this hour?"

"What else!" Thorfinn declared. "What better way to end an evening? And to begin a night!" He slapped his brother on the back. "You will be twice the man you are now, in an hour's time, I promise you, Son of Life! And these ladies even more

227

desirable than they are now! We Norsemen know how such things should be arranged. In here with you. Gruoch with Inge."

The two men entered a small torch-lit chamber where a fire burned brightly and where an aged attendant greeted them. Here they undressed. MacBeth had heard often of these Norse steam-baths, but never had occasion to sample one. He was not too sure that he wanted to, even now; but Thorfinn was vehement that it was an essential part of the evening's programme, and something not to be missed — especially in present company.

Naked as the day they were born, the earl led the King through a doorway into the next chamber — and the blast of hot air set MacBeth coughing and choking. Never had he felt such overpowering and encompassing heat. He faced a dense yellowish mist, steam illumined by the firelight and the glow of whale-oil horn-lanterns — for torches could not have survived alight in that moisture-laden atmosphere.

The half-brothers were very differently made, in more than their natures. Thorfinn was, of course, heavily-built as he was tall, massive in every way, notably well-endowed but acquiring a distinct belly. MacBeth was almost slight by comparison but leanly muscular and with no thickening of the middle as yet — he was, to be sure, a year or two the younger. Also he was very much the more hairy in body, furred all over.

Thorfinn eyed him up and down, frankly. "You wear well, Brother," he admitted. "Even though your famed moderation in all things is . . . evident."

"If you mean that I am not a Norse bull of heifers' delight, I shall not contest the matter. But I have heard no complaints from such as might be concerned! And I have sired more lawful offspring than you have. If fewer bastards!" He panted a little in the heat.

The other grinned. "To be sure, Little Brother. Come, sit on this bench. And cross your legs if you would feel happier . . . !"

Thorfinn went to pick up one of a row of wooden buckets of water, and threw its contents over a railed-off area of large flat stones, a sort of paving at one side of the chamber, to produce an explosion of steam in dense clouds — for the slabs were fiercely hot, with oven-like fires beneath, responsible for the smoke outside.

A door opposite their own opened and the women came in, Ingebiorg leading in something of a rush, and giggling like any

228

serving-girl. But that was the only resemblance to any serving-girl. She was as naked as the men, a large, satisfying, substantial and mature woman, with great thrusting breasts, heavy but not gross, a generous belly over a large and darker triangle than might have been expected from her blonde colouring, strong round white buttocks and massive thighs. Had she been less tall and altogether Junoesque, the effect might have been less pleasing, less essentially right, a mother-figure indeed but an undeniably desirable one still, and making basic demands on any full man fortunate enough to see. MacBeth was sufficiently appreciative, not to say stirred — although a little surprised that she kept her head bent and even in that steamy twilight could be seen to be flushing pinkly at face and throat, moreover with hands uncertain as to employment. But head down or not, she could be seen to be eyeing MacBeth intently.

Oddly enough, that man's real surprise was with his own wife. He would have been quite prepared for her to have refused to take part in this performance, this display, traditionally Norse as it was; or if not refusing, to have insisted on wearing some modest covering. But no, she was as unclothed as Ingebiorg, yet otherwise totally different — and not only physically. Gruoch walked in slowly, calmly, head up without being held in any way defiantly, without giggles or evident embarrassment, completely assured it seemed in being herself. As indeed she had reason to be, perhaps, for she was very lovely, of body as of face. She had had five children, yet at thirty-five she showed little sign of it. Slenderly built still, her neck and legs were long and heart-catchingly turned, her breasts shapely, modest compared with Ingebiorg's but firm and with large and dark aureoles, her stomach not flat but smoothly rounded. But it was her bearing as much as anything which impressed, engaged the attention, the proud but unprideful way she held herself, the confident carriage of shoulders, the unhurried, graceful walk. The pride was MacBeth's as he looked at her, a glow of sheer satisfaction and acclaim. Here was a queen indeed.

Thorfinn's swallow was audible, his throat-clearing eloquent. It was not often that that man was at a loss for words. Gruoch glanced over at him briefly, almost enquiringly — but only for a moment, for like Ingebiorg, her regard was concerned with MacBeth.

He rose from his bench. "Mere mortal men were never so privileged," he said quietly, but with a half-smile for each of them to take away histrionics or pomposity from his words.

229

"Do we deserve these, Thor? I think not. You do not, at any rate!"

"Adroitly put, husband!" Gruoch commented. "I wonder that you have the wits for it, or for anything, in this heat."

Ingebiorg raised her head, looking from one man to the other, keeping her hands clasped in front of her now. "My great bear has lost his tongue," she said, her voice gaining its old confidence. "I never thought to see it. You, it must be, Gruoch my dear — for I have never achieved the like! Good-brother — I see that you are well-named, Son of Life."

"*I* have lost nothing!" Thorfinn declared loudly. "As I will demonstrate in due course. And you should have seen this one when he was given that name — a red, squalling brat, like a lobster without claws."

"We develop our claws as time goes on," the King observed. "But I had not thought to come here to be boiled! Can you cool it down, Thor?"

His brother, instead, took the opportunity to throw another bucketful of water on the hot stones, producing still more steam, gesturing towards the bench. Rather thankfully they all sat down, the women in the middle.

It was easier to sit side by side. Soon they were able to converse more or less naturally if less than vigorously while they sweated. The men took it in turn to empty the buckets on the stones.

Presently Thorfinn announced that they had had enough of heat, and that too much would serve them nothing — although his wife suggested that more of it might help to take some of his shameful belly off him. He led the way through another doorway into a much cooler chamber, which was both a relief and sufficient contrast to cause a quick shiver. Here, although there was no steam, were more if smaller buckets of water. MacBeth was interested when his brother picked up one of these — but received a major shock when the water was suddenly tossed over his shrinking person. For, although in fact luke-warm, by contrast to the present heat of his body it seemed as cold as though he had involuntarily plunged into the sea. His gasps were drowned in Thorfinn's laughter, as that man grabbed another pail, to serve Gruoch in the same way. At least she had this warning, although even her poise scarcely stood up to such treatment, as her uncontrollable squeal evidenced. However, Ingebiorg retaliated on her husband, and thereafter there was something of a free-for-all as they sluiced each other down until all the buckets were empty. And after the first douche, and with the leaping about, the impact was much less unpleasant.

If the cold splash had been a shock, what succeeded was as unexpected. Taking down one of a set of bundles of slender birch-twigs, like besoms, from a shelf, Thorfinn began to belabour his wife with it, across shoulders and rump and thighs, chasing her round the apartment uttering ferocious yells — until she in turn grasped one for herself, and still being basted, turned on MacBeth to treat him likewise; whereupon her busy husband switched his attentions to Gruoch. This treatment too, after a swipe or two, proved to produce quite a pleasing and stimulating sensation. The besoms were made out of the very tips of the birch-twigs, feathery and light, and the application was more of a stroking and sweeping than actual beating. The effect was to set the blood racing and tingling, after the induced torpor of the steam, giving a real feeling of well-being and arousal — although perhaps the business of belabouring naked bodies of the opposite sex might have contributed. The two tyros were made quickly aware that this sort of thing, if allowed to go on for long, could have unpredictable results.

Thorfinn had not finished with them yet, for flinging open the outer door of this chamber, he ran out into the night air to hurl himself down in the snow and roll about in it, bawling. But this last the others, even Ingebiorg, drew the line at — more especially as now not only the old attendant but sundry other Vikings were standing there admiring. Leaving the earl to his rolling, they discreetly withdrew to their respective dressing-rooms to resume their clothing. Undeniably they felt much braced and enlivened by the entire exercise. Ingebiorg confided to her sister-in-law that a large proportion of the Orkney population tended to be conceived after just such exercises.

Thorfinn made the same point when he came in for his own clothes, suggesting to his brother that if he felt the miles back to Spynie as productive of too much delay, in the circumstances, he could provide a bed for them here in the Borg with the greatest pleasure. MacBeth acknowledged the thoughtfulness, but gratefully declined. There was something about his own bed, he asserted . . .

That night's varied exertions led, in the morning, to the activities of Saint Stephen's Day, with the pageantry for the first Christian martyr, the retaliatory Stoning of the Devil, carried out at the nearest ancient standing-stone or stone-circle, the procession to church thereafter and finally the distribution of the martyr-cakes, each with its dab of red dye, by the King and principal men — from the legend that the stones hurled at Stephen, when spattered with his blood, fell to the ground as little loaves of bread for the faithful.

Two days later was Childermas, or Holy Innocents' Day, always something of a riot, when the children not only dressed up as their elders and betters but for the day were invested with a certain amount of domestic authority — with predictable results. Young Cormac and Eala became King and Queen for the day, Erland ruled the Vikings, and the youngest Keledei novice reigned as Abbot. Perhaps wisely, it was the tradition that no work was started that day, no undertaking commenced. However, just as a reminder, not only of what it was all about but what conditions would revert to on the morrow, Childermas always started with a whipping for the youngest member of the household.

Hogmanay, of course, infinitely more ancient than Christmas, its origins lost in the pagan rites of sun-worship, with the seeing of the old year out and the new in, was celebrated with unrestrained enthusiasm by the visitors, ably assisted locally, a process which extended itself seemingly indefinitely. So that, by Up Halie Day, or Epiphany Eve, when at last the prolonged marathon of nominally holy festivity finished, a kind of prostration was beginning to assail not only the weaker brethren. But not the Norsemen apparently. Thorfinn throughout had frequently referred to the fact that they would be missing the Up Helly A festival in his native isles, expanding on its excellences. But in default of this, the Burning of the Clavie at the Borg-head of Torfness was the next best thing on Up Halie Night, and this year it must certainly be graced by the royal presence. MacBeth had attended this extraordinary affair before, but Gruoch, Ingebiorg and the young people had not. Somewhat weary of excitements, he agreed. His brother was, after all, celebrating a major victory and delivery.

The proceedings commenced at a hillock at the landward end of the Torfness peninsula on a night of squally winds, sea-spray and sleet-showers, amidst a strong smell of melting tar distilled from pitch-pine. Great crowds were gathered, despite the weather, not only from the Norse town's folk but local people from as far away as Elgin and Forres. This year's distinguished visitors produced an extra large attendance and comparable enthusiasm. The affair was divided into two distinct parts, one major and wholly Norse, one very minor and of Celtic origin.

As to the first, nobody present could inform the newcomers the real reason behind it all — although there were many far-out guesses — save that it all obviously stemmed from the early Scandinavian fire-worship and associated tests of manhood.

First of all, on the hill-top, a small barrel was ceremoniously filled with hot, liquid tar from a smoking cauldron on a large bonfire — quite a hazardous undertaking in itself, from splatters of the boiling stuff and the need to all but stand in the fire to cope with the cauldron. Then, to ringing cheers, the barrel was hoisted on to the top of a sturdy five-foot pole, where an iron crib for it was fixed, and set alight. The pole and flaring Clavie as it was called, heavy and awkward as it was, then was handed over to a young Viking who, surrounded by a shouting group of his fellows, set off at a staggering run down the hill, with it held approximately upright, and on into the town. The crowd streamed after.

Up and down the dark, narrow streets of Torfness this strange procession paraded, egged on by the onlookers. It was most evidently a dire test of the young men's strength, stamina and courage, for the thing was not only unwieldy and a great weight but giving off intense heat, and worse, its jerky progress inevitably showering down burning and melted tar on the bearer and those close by. The youths wore helmets, but even so their hair was often on fire, and the scalding splatters must have burned their skins agonisingly. Bearers ran until they fell exhausted, or in such a burning state as to be incapable of holding the Clavie upright, when it was grabbed by a companion, and the mad, shambling race continued without pause — and no concern or sympathy lavished on the fallen, even it seemed by their nearest and dearest, so caught up in the fierce excitement were all.

After every part of the town had been visited, the still-blazing tar-barrel was carried out to the ships which could be reached in the harbour or drawn up on the boat-strand, fishing-boats, trading-craft and longships all, a still more dangerous proceeding involving climbing the sides of the vessels and leaping from deck to deck, yet keeping the Clavie more or less upright, the burning tar unspilled. Casualties came in rapid succession now, amidst yells and screams, but always more young men were eager for the task, to prove their manhood. They left a trail of small fires, as well as their injured, behind them.

The available ships all visited, the reeking, flaring trophy was carried up to the top of the eminence at the extreme tip of the ness, known as the Doorie, and there set up on a cairn, provided with a socket for the pole. As the exhausted runners, who had been able to finish the course, lay around gasping and writhing, the crowds gathered and cheered and sang and drank. And presently, with seemingly strange nonchalance and entirely changed attitude, at a given signal, the youths seized the still-burning Clavie once more and went to toss it over the cliff-like slope, where it went rolling and bounding down, to fall and shatter in blazing fragments on the tide's-edge rocks below. And now, many of the crowd, men, women and children, went scrambling down the steeps after it to try to grab one of those flaming embers to take home in triumph, cherished trophies, assurers of good luck, specific protection against witchcraft.

At this abrupt end in anti-climax, Gruoch was not alone in demanding, a little breathlessly, what it all signified, especially this last contemptuous finale.

None could adequately enlighten her, although Thorfinn suggested that it represented man's triumph over fire, turning it from master to servant.

There was still the Celtic epilogue, as it were, although comparatively few of the Norsemen waited to see it — which the Queen and Ingebiorg thought was very rude, but Thorfinn advised to wait and see. This new development also involved tar and fire, a much smaller cauldron brought from the main bonfire and a large wickerwork hamper which proved to contain about a score of live pigeons. The birds were ceremoniously taken out, splashed with the tar, set alight by torches, and released. Exclaiming at the cruelty, the visitors were nevertheless enthralled, fascinated, by the picture of the blazing birds flying through the wild dark night, down amongst the shipping and on over the roofs of the town, spreading fire as they went, an evilly beautiful sight.

"Now you will see why our people did not wait to watch this Pictish nonsense start," Thorfinn said. "They are all gone to save their houses and ships, to put out fires in thatched roofs and rigging."

"But . . . but why? What is the sense of it?" the Queen asked. "Why torture the poor birds so? Is it as meaningless as all the rest?"

MacBeth could explain this last, at least. "It is an ancient tradition — although not so old as the Clavie, to be sure. The daughter of one of the Pictish kings was given in marriage to a Norse prince — who brought her here but shamefully ill-used her. The indignant Cruithe had no fleet to challenge him and his, but for revenge for their princess they loosed hundreds of flaming pigeons to fly amongst the longships anchored in this haven and bay, and so destroyed them by fire. Also much of the town. Or so goes the story. Perhaps there is a grain of truth in it somewhere — for this Ness of the Bulls was a sacred place of the Cruithe long before ever a Norse pirate descended on our shores."

"Aye — and it was time that we came, if your Picts had to get pigeons to do their fighting for them!" the earl declared.

Gruoch shivered. "I think that I have had enough," she said. "I am cold. Enough for one night. Enough for one Yuletide!"

Her husband nodded. "Rested and renewed, we baptise the Christ tomorrow — Epiphany!" he said, almost grimly.

"And *we* go home," his brother added. "You can manage that one by yourselves . . . ?"

18

MacBeth paced the floor of Gruoch's pleasant and comfortable sitting-room in the palace of Cairn Beatha, tripping a little, and not for the first time, on one of Thorfinn's handsome white polar-bearskin rugs. He kicked it irritably, a reaction not typical.

"Am I to tell this proud Saxon that I will not accept his proposal, then?" he demanded, of his wife. "If I do, I must give due reason. I cannot find any fervour, even willingness, in our churchmen to do anything for Galloway. They are not interested. They say that it is not, has never been, part of the Columban Church. They say that the people reject any monks and teachers they send, have always rejected them. Even Malduin accepts no responsibility there, as Ard Episcop. So what can I say to this Saxon bishop? On the face of it, what he asks is right and in reason. The Galloway folk should not be condemned almost to heathenry within this Christian realm of mine. And yet . . ."

"Yet if you give way to this Bishop of Durham over Galloway, you open the door to so much more," Gruoch said. "The Merse, Teviotdale, even Lothian itself — all could be claimed to belong to the Saxon faith rather than the Columban — that is, now, to Rome. Could they not? Bishop Malduin and his friends show little interest there either. Let the Saxons gain but a foothold in Galloway, and these will be their next demands."

"I know it. I have told Malduin and Cathail and Ewan. Even Robartach in Iona. But they see it as no concern of theirs. They are here to do God's will, not an earthly king's, they say! Their Church seeks no earthly kingdom, save in the precious souls of men! A plague on them — are they not able to see that the Romish Church thinks otherwise? That it *seeks* domination. And that its domination could weaken my kingdom. And *their* independence. Malduin is my Chancellor. He must see this . . ."

"Oh, he sees it, no doubt. As Chancellor. But as Bishop of St. Andrews he sees it differently. And even if he did see it your way, my dear — what could he do? He is Ard Episcop, yes, senior bishop of our Scottish Church. But he does not rule that Church. He is not Primate. Indeed, since Crinan died, there is *no* Primate is there?"

"That is the curse of it! The Primacy, and the Abbacy of Dunkeld, are hereditary in Crinan's line. So that the Primate now should be Maldred mac Crinan — since Duncan's lawful son Donald Ban is too young. An exile and rebel — and dwelling in this Saxon bishop's land, Northumbria! Aye, and Malcolm his bastard nephew still calling himself Prince of Strathclyde and Cumbria!"

"You believe Maldred is concerned in this? This . . . device?"

"Not himself, I would think. I see Siward's hand in it. If he cannot beat us by invasion of arms, the Dane can use the Church to penetrate my realm. He who is as good as a pagan himself! To prepare the way for his sword, when he shall have finished his wars with Godwin of Wessex."

"If you believe that, then you must reject this bishop. No?"

"Aye — but what do I tell him? What excuse can a Christian monarch give for seeming to deny the proper ministrations of Holy Church to large territories of his kingdom? I cannot just say no to him, and so leave it."

"Siward would! As Malcolm would have done. Duncan, no doubt, also — if he had thought to care."

"But . . . I am different, God helping me! And I am known as a *supporter* of the Church."

"The Columban, the Scottish Church. Not the Roman."

He frowned at her. "Have you no help to offer me in this?"

She smiled. "Should a mere woman raise her silly voice in

the affairs of Holy Church? Is that not anathema? But . . . why not temporise? Say that here is a problem you have already given much thought to. And that you have decided to appoint a bishop there. A Bishop of Galloway. So that this of Candida Casa is unnecessary. Would that not serve, for the moment? Even though you do no more than make such appointment?"

"I cannot appoint bishops to anywhere!" he protested. "That is not the duty of the King. Only the Primate and the High Council of the Church."

"Robartach of Iona and Malduin, with Cathail of Scone and Ewan of Abernethy, all your friends, could do so, surely? If you asked them . . ."

The clatter of hooves on the cobbles outside, and raised voices, interrupted her.

"A plague! They are here." MacBeth stepped over to the open window. "God be good — the man comes in a silken horse-litter! Like some eastern queen! With acolytes and singers. Come, see . . ."

"My heart — we must not be seen to peer out of windows, like cottagers!"

He drew back. "No. Do you wish to receive this Saxon with me?"

"Perhaps I should come later."

MacBeth waited for the visitors in the lesser hall. The two bishops were led in, and bowed. Summoned, Cormac of Glamis and Ewan of Abernethy, came in to flank the King.

"My lord King," Malduin said. "Here is the good Edmund, Bishop of Durham, or Lindisfarne, come to bring greetings from the Archbishop of York, and to speak with you on sundry matters."

Edmund bowed again. He was a large, smooth man, mitred and richly robed as for a cathedral service, jewelled rings and cross sparkling — perhaps the reason for his travel by litter. Beside him Chancellor Malduin in his simple dark and long-skirted habit and leathern girdle looked like some poor mendicant monk. All they seemed to have in common was the bishops' croziers, which each carried, the one man-height and white-painted, with an elaborate gold crook set with rubies, the other less tall, of gnarled ash topped by a smaller bronze head, only a simple half-crescent but most richly chased with intricate Celtic design, battered-seeming as though indeed long used for herding a flock.

"Welcome to my house, Bishop Edmund," MacBeth said

237

carefully. "My friend Malduin will have looked to your comfort whilst in my realm, I have no doubt. Here is the Thane of Glamis, my High Constable. And the Abbot Ewan of Abernethy, High Judex."

"High King," the Saxon prelate said, "our father in Christ, the Lord Archbishop of York, sends you God's blessing."

"A sinner, I need all such," the King acceded. "And I thank him, and you. Although he is scarcely *my* father in Christ! But — he sends more than that, I think?"

Edmund inclined his head slightly. Because of his mitre, his tonsure, in the Romish style on the crown of his head, was not visible, whereas that of Malduin, above the forehead in the Celtic tradition, was very much so, especially in contrast with the longish greying hair which fell almost to the shoulders.

"I bring as gifts this ring and this cross — poor things, but offered in Christian love and esteem, Highness."

MacBeth signed to Abbot Ewan to bring the proffered jewellery to him — for the two bishops stood at a few yards' distance — magnificent pieces both, and clearly the craftsmanship of some far land.

"Too fine by far for this poor realm," the King said, admiringly. "But we shall cherish the kindness. I thank you. We must think of some small token for you to take back to Northumbria — if nothing to match these. But then, there can be little in Scotland which would tempt you, and those who sent you, I think, my friend? Save, perhaps, things less . . . material!"

The other's smooth round features remained expressionless. "I come seeking no gifts, Highness. Only offering the good will of Holy Church. And that we, your Church and mine, may work together in harmony for the good of Christ's reign on earth and holy evangel, and the hurt of all evil-doers."

"Ah. How excellent a purpose! I am sure that Bishop Malduin, and Abbot Ewan here, with others, will rejoice to work with you towards that good end."

"I do not doubt it. But . . ."

"But . . .? That does not suffice you?"

"High King — we need *your* aid in this matter also. Your, h'm, intervention."

"In good will between the Churches, bishop?"

"Not in the good will, perhaps. But in active co-operation. Which is required."

"And this our bishops and abbots cannot provide?"

"It seems not. Not fully. They say that they have not the

authority. Only you, Highness, it seems, in the Columban Church, have the authority. With the Primate exiled . . ."

"The Primate is not exiled, friend, since there is no Primate appointed at present. But the chiefest office in our Church is held by the Abbot of Iona, Columba's successor. And the Bishop of St. Andrews, here, as Ard Episcop, chief of the bishops. It is not your system — but it serves."

The other pursed his lips but remained silent.

"In what way, Bishop Edmund, is the authority of these insufficient for your purpose?"

"King — it is that, there being no true hierarchy here, none of these may pronounce upon a matter outside their own see and sway. Only you can, it seems. As in the matter of the diocese of Whithorn."

"Hah — so now we have it, bishop! But there is no diocese of Whithorn. If you refer to the Whithorn in my province of Galloway? Or Candida Casa. Or is it some other Whithorn? It could be a common name, after all — the White House."

"No, it is Whithorn in Galloway I speak of. And your pardon, High King, but there *is* a diocese of Whithorn or Candida Casa. It was founded in the Year of Our Lord 727, under the Archbishopric of York. Out of the Blessed Ninian's parish, and his place of burial."

"*Was*, bishop — not is! Far be it for a mere monarch to instruct a churchman on Church matters, but the see was abandoned in the year 875, if I recollect aright, and has not been in existence in the two centuries since."

"Not abandoned, King MacBeth, but reserved. No see of the one Holy Catholic and Apostolic Church, created by the Vicar of Christ himself, the Pope in Rome, can ever cease to exist. Whithorn may have been for a time abeyant, but it is still a see of Holy Church. It is one of the four original dioceses of Northumbria, and so under the pastoral jurisdiction of my episcopal charge of Durham."

MacBeth stroked his small pointed beard. "You say that the Pope of Rome created this diocese. But, my friend, we here in Scotland do not recognise the authority of your Pope, outside his own communion. Save as the chief bishop of a large part of the Church. But not *our* part. We respect him for what he is and recognise his great power. But he has no authority here. Our Celtic Church accepts only one Vicar with God — the Lord Christ Himself."

Edmund looked pained. "When the diocese was created,

Highness, Strathclyde and Cumbria was an independent kingdom, not in Alba or Scotland, I would remind you. And Strathclyde recognised the authority of the Supreme Pontiff."

"That, I think, is open to doubt, Bishop. For Strathclyde and Cumbria was a Celtic kingdom also. And although Saint Ninian himself adhered to Rome, there were three centuries of Columban churchmen before your Romish diocese was set up." MacBeth shrugged. "But this, to be sure, is an old story. And, I swear, not what brought you here today."

The other cleared his throat. "In part it is," he said. "It has been long a source of distress to myself, and to the archbishop, that the people of Galloway are insufficiently ministered to, their spiritual needs much neglected. Your Columbite Church is little concerned with them. Bishop Malduin admits that they are not within his authority. I cannot believe that the Abbot of Iona includes them in any responsibility of his. Nor other of your higher clergy. This is a grave matter. Souls are at risk. And we, whose diocese this is, or was, the one Church, Holy and Universal, desire to resume our ministry there."

"You make it to sound, Sir Bishop, as though Galloway was some heathen province! Devoid of religion. I can think of a score of monasteries. That of Saint Cuthbert on the Dee. Saint Machute's of Wigtown. Those of Kirk Medana and Kirk Madrene in the Rhinns. Capel Finnian of Mochrum. Kirk Claugh of Fleet. But enough."

"These there may be. But they lack spiritual oversight and direction, Highness. This is a grievous state of anarchy. It much weighs on our minds and consciences. Since we consider ourselves to be still responsible to the Holy Father and to Almighty God for the souls of these in our abeyant diocese." Edmund took a deep breath. "Therefore we do request that the see of Whithorn or Candida Casa be restored to the oversight and care of Holy Church in the Diocese of Saint Cuthbert of Durham, and in the Archbishopric of York."

MacBeth raised his brows, as though utterly surprised. "Do I hear aright?" he demanded. "Are you indeed asking for Galloway to be handed over to your jurisdiction, bishop?"

"In spiritual matters only, my lord King."

"But this is scarcely to be believed! Part of my realm of Scotland, a whole province, to be given to England? Can you conceive that any King of Scots could so agree?"

"Not that, King MacBeth." Even Edmund of Durham looked a little agitated. "It is not to England that this see would be transferred. But only to Holy Church under the pastoral care of myself and the archbishop. For the benefit of all. To fill a spiritual void . . ."

"None, I think, have discerned this spiritual void save you, bishop! How say you, Malduin?"

That man looked unhappy. "I have not deemed Galloway greatly to lack the ministry of the Gospel," he said.

"And yet you accept no spiritual responsibility for it?" Edmund charged.

"The Bishop of St. Andrews is Ard Episcop of Alba. And Galloway and Strathclyde were never included in Alba." That with an apologetic glance at the King.

"In whose jurisdiction then *is* Galloway and Strathclyde, bishop?"

"Bishop Edmund — I will thank you, in my royal presence, to address *me*. And not to question my ministers in front of me," MacBeth said sternly. "To answer you — unlike your own, our Celtic Church is not divided into dioceses and territorial jurisdictions — as you well know. It is of a monastic order, and each abbey, monastery and cashel rules its own family and territory."

"But . . ."

"Lord King!" Cormac of Glamis burst out. "I say that you are over patient! This is not to be borne. Let me throw this insolent Englishman out of your presence! Who dares to hector the King of Scots in his own house!"

"Silence, Thane of Glamis!" MacBeth commanded, "Is the Bishop of Durham not our guest? We must suffer him . . ."

It was at this juncture that Gruoch chose to enter the hall. No doubt she had been listening behind the hangings of the door, and decided the moment was opportune. All bowed, and the tension lessened perceptibly.

"I greet you all kindly, good lords," she said. "In especial our friend from England, in the succession of the great Saint Cuthbert."

"Bishop Edmund wishes to emulate Saint Cuthbert in winning Galloway, my dear!" MacBeth observed. "Not, I think, for Christ so much as for the Archbishop of York!"

"Galloway? Win Galloway? You jest, husband!"

"Not so. Or our friend does not. He seeks our Galloway as a diocese of the see of Durham. On the grounds that once it was so, and that our Church neglects that province."

"Neglects? How can that be? You will have told him of your

plans? For Galloway. For a new Keledei mission there. Perhaps a new abbey. And a bishop to oversee all."

MacBeth swallowed. "We had scarce got so far, my dear. We have been hearing only Bishop Edmund's claims. He conceives our Celtic Church to have failed there. And thinks to do better. Under Rome."

"And he does not know of this Keledei?"

"I . . . have not spoken of it. Yet," he said, cautiously feeling his way.

All were looking at the Queen with as much conjecture as her husband was seeking not to show.

"It is not for me, a woman, to speak of such matters," Gruoch said modestly. "My foolish prattling tongue! Forgive me, my lord King, if I go too fast. If I may have revealed your intentions out of time. Or perhaps you have decided against it . . .?"

"Er, no. No. It is but that we have not yet reached so far. In our discussion. We have heard the Bishop of Durham's views. Not given him ours, in any fullness. Speak on."

"Even of the MacDuff lands?"

He moistened his lips. "Why not? As well from you as from myself. Or from others. As well as Queen, you are chiefest of all Clan Duff. If MacDuff is concerned in this, who has more right to speak?" That was the best that he could do in his mystification.

"Very well. The Bishop of Durham will know well how MacDuff, Mormaor of Fife, supported our foes and fled Scotland — since he fled to the Bishop's own Northumbria. Where he was notably well received. Perhaps the Bishop himself succoured him? Now, we hear, he has gone further south still, to the Court of King Edward of England."

"Lady — he came to us as a man in need. A fugitive," Edmund said. "We could not turn him away. In Christian charity."

"Your charity does you credit, my lord Bishop. As shown to many another of our realm's unfriends and rebels. It was necessary that the Mormaor MacDuff and his people should learn their lesson. As outlaw, all his lands could have been forfeit. But my lord King is merciful. He took only certain of the Fife lands. As example to others. These lands he has held, but would not seek profit from them for himself or the Crown. So now he thinks to give them to Holy Church. We have spoken of this many times, to decide what is best. Is it not apt, to give them to the Keledei, the Friends of God, to aid them in

242

sending of their number to Galloway? There to establish new churches, possibly a great abbey, and help to pay for the work of a new bishop to oversee God's cause in that province? Apt in that the Mormaor of Fife has fled Alba, and his lands should be used for Christ's work outwith of Alba?"

There were moments of complete silence as she finished, as the men, all of them, gazed at her, all but open-mouthed.

"Dear God!" MacBeth breathed — but *beneath* his breath.

Cormac of Glamis recovered first. "Ha!" he exclaimed, and grinned broadly.

With a quick glance at him, Gruoch added, "I ask you to forgive my halting account. The High King could have told it to much better effect. But since this concerns Clan Duff, and Duff the King was my great-great-grand-sire; and since Lulach my son is Prince of Strathclyde . . ."

"My heart," MacBeth said — and now he strove hard to hide his relief, satisfaction and sheer admiration. "You have put the matter entirely well. Most fully. Even, I venture to assert, Bishop Malduin here could not have explained the position better. How say you, friend?"

"I . . . ah . . . no, Highness. Or, yes. I, I could not have so . . . spoken. I . . ." His voice faded away.

"So now the good Bishop Edmund can return home to Durham, informed and comforted. And assured that the people of Galloway are not to be neglected and their religious requirements well looked to," the King announced, with an air of finality. "And, if perchance, he should encounter the Mormaor MacDuff, he can expound to him the excellent uses his former property is being put to!"

Tight-lipped their visitor bowed stiffly.

"Malduin — see you to our friend's comfort and well-being for so long as he chooses to honour my realm with his presence. Meantime, I shall discover some small token, however inadequate, for him to take back, in humble acknowledgment of these magnificent gifts!" He held up the ring and the crucifix which he had been clutching the while. "Perhaps a Columban reliquary, to remind him of our modest but ancient Church?"

Backing to the door, the two prelates bowed themselves out.

Barely were they gone before MacBeth strode over to his wife, heartily to embrace and kiss her there before the other two.

"My beloved, joy of my heart!" he cried. "Blessed art thou amongst women! The dearest and most cunning, as well as the

243

most beautiful! How you conceived all this I do not know. But I thank you, my love, I thank you."

"You, my good lord, commanded me to come to your aid in this matter," she reminded. "I invented little or nothing. Only put together what was already there. Put in such order and fashion as to seem apt and honest."

"As only a woman could, I swear! It was most shrewd. Working on the man's weakness, his guilt. This of MacDuff. . .!"

"Lady — you smote that priest hip and thigh!" Glamis exclaimed. "*I* would have sent him off in a scurry before ever you came in. But I rejoice now that the King was over-patient. To see you bring the Saxon low. Proud priests I cannot thole — with all respect to the good abbot here."

"I found him little to my own liking," the gravely studious Judex admitted. "And his spiritual pride towards our ancient Church the greater sin. The Queen's Highness is to be congratulated. We are rid of that bishop this time. But we cannot leave it thus, I think. If we do not act on this, in some degree, we shall hear a deal more of it."

MacBeth intervened. "Come, my friends. If we are to consider this, let us do so in more comfort than standing in this hall. If the Queen will have us in her chamber . . .?"

"The Pope?" Gruoch asked presently, when they were sipping wine in her sitting-room. "Could the Pope interfere, Abbot Ewan?"

"If petitioned he could, I think, Highness. Whether he *would*, I know not. But the Roman Church is very jealous for its territories and sway, however long past. As you have just heard. An appeal to the Pope by the Archbishop of York could result in much trouble for us, for Scotland . . ."

"Why?" Glamis broke in. "What has that old German, Leo, in Rome, to do with us? We owe him nothing, no allegiance, no concern. What have we to fear from him? We do not need to heed his anathemas."

"Wait you, Cormac," the King said. "Let us hear Abbot Ewan out. He knows more of such matters than do you or I. If he scents trouble, danger, we must hear of it. Go on, friend."

"Highness, the danger is this. If the archbishop appealed to the Pope — and it could be that he would bring in his colleague of Canterbury also, possibly King Edward of England likewise, by-named the Confessor so strong for the Romish faith is he — then the Pope might have to act, even though he might not be greatly concerned. He could issue a papal declaration that

Whithorn and Galloway was within his spiritual rule. And not only these, but Teviotdale, the Merse and Lothian also."

They stared at him.

"That would give a cherished weapon into the hands of all Scotland's enemies. Unite them, in a holy cause against us. If we rejected the papal decree, they could proceed against us in arms, with the Pontiff's blessing."

Glamis protested, but MacBeth urged Abbot Ewan to proceed.

"At present, only the Earl Siward is our professed foe. And he is engaged in his feud with the Earl Godwin of Wessex, to our comfort. But unite these two — and they are kin — and we could face the whole might of England. Godwin is the true power behind Edward's throne, his daughter Edward's Queen. And be sure, like King Canute, they wish Scotland brought into subjection to England. Here could be opportunity. Bishop Edmund would not have come here lacking Siward's approval, where all power in Northumbria lies. This was *Siward's* move. He would put Duncan's bastard on your throne, Highness, and rule Scotland through him as puppet. He is Canute's cousin. Edward the Confessor is a weakling, although a man of God. With papal blessing he might be persuaded to launch full war. In name to recover these provinces for his Church, but in fact to subdue the Scottish realm. In especial if he had Danish and Norwegian aid."

"Danish! Norwegian! Save us — why these, man?"

"Neither are greatly Christian realms, by our thinking. But in name they belong to the Romish Church also. King Magnus has suffered bitter defeat, at the hands of the Earl of Orkney, assisted by yourself, my lord King. He cannot love you. Siward is a Dane. Godwin half one. Echmarcach of Dublin also smarting under being outwitted, likewise pertains to Rome. The Pope holds the key of more than Saint Peter! A word could bring all these against Scotland."

Even Glamis was impressed now, but he found voice. "All this is only conjecture, Sir Priest. None of it may come to pass, or even be considered."

"Admittedly, my lord. But it *could* happen so. I have long feared some issue which could unite all these against us, and not seen it until today. Perhaps Siward saw it first!"

"Blessed Saints — what have I done, then?" Gruoch wondered.

"You did what *had* to be done, my heart. The question is,

what do *I* do now?" MacBeth asked. "What could cause the Pope to reject such appeal?"

There was silence for a space, as they eyed the Judex.

"I see no very clear road in the matter," he said at length. "But — you might act first, perhaps. Send an envoy to the Pope, yourself, flatter him. Declare your respect for him as chiefest bishop in Christ's Church. But complain. As a Christian prince. Complain that this Bishop of Durham has come making wrongful demands, like to cause disharmony between the Roman and Celtic Churches, to the disservice of Christ's cause. Blame, I would say, only this Edmund, not the Archbishop. The Pope might feel bound to support an archbishop. Request that this bishop be restrained from any further such interference in the affairs of your realm."

"Could the Pope accede to that? Would he not be bound to support his own?"

"If you could offer inducement. Or threat. In especial, if your representation reached him first. To be sure we do not know that the archbishop, or others, will appeal. But I think that they will." Ewan frowned in his concentration. "We must consider the position in Rome. Leo the Ninth has trouble on his hands. His Church is sorely divided. He was not appointed by the electoral college. A German, the Emperor *imposed* him. To do so, the Emperor deposed Benedict the Ninth, appointed when but a boy of twelve years. But *he* still claims to be the lawfully elected Pope. Leo calls him Antipope . . ."

"God Almighty," Glamis exclaimed. "And this is Holy Mother Church!"

The abbot ignored him. "Perhaps, Highness, you could make good use of this situation. Leo will not be looking for further troubles."

"Yes, I can see that. The Romans would do well to set their own house in order before ours! But apart from this of trouble, what have I to offer?"

"Recognition. Recognition from a non-Romish monarch that he is true Pope. And competent to mediate between the Churches. It might be possible to use the Irish Celtic Church also. Certain Irish abbots sent to Clement the Second to seek his answers to questions. Use that, also."

"You have agile wits, my friend — but then I knew that when I named you High Judex. This seems like any battle. Using stratagems where we lack real strength. But . . . it is scarcely firm ground!"

"There might be a further inducement, I think. Orkney, Zetland and the Hebrides."

"Heaven, be good! What do you mean, man?"

"To whom does the Church in Orkney and the Isles adhere? If to any!"

"God only knows that!"

"Almighty God, yes. And the Earl Thorfinn! Our Columban Church has no least hold there. Our Columban missionaries took the Gospel there once, however, from Iona. Then the pagan Norsemen came and burned the churches and slew the saints. In the Orcades and Hebrides. But now, Norway and Denmark pay at least lip-service to Rome. What of the Norse in the Isles?"

"I know not," the King admitted. "My brother is little concerned, I fear."

"So, Highness — if *you* do not know, is Leo in Rome like to know?"

"I see much possibility here," Gruoch said. "Thorfinn might come to your aid, my dear, at little cost. As you went to his, against Rognvald."

Ewan of Abernethy was always cool, detached, scholarly in manner. Now even his careful voice took on a persuasive note.

"Hear me, my lord. The churches and cashels in the Orcades, few as they may be, in fact pay allegiance to none in matters of governance. Certainly they pay none to our Church. Yet, if this Bishop of Durham can claim that Galloway was a mission from Lindisfarne, and the diocese set up three centuries ago a Romish one, then so can we claim that the Orcades were a mission from Iona, and so should remain an extension of the Celtic Church. In truth it is not so — any more than Galloway is Roman. But here you have something to trade with the Pope, have you not?"

"Devil burn me!" Glamis cried. "This is beyond all. Trade! I ever said churchmen were traders at heart! But to trade with no goods and empty pouch."

"It is shrewdly judged, yes," MacBeth acceded. "But I have no authority in Orkney or Zetland. It is not Scots territory."

"But in name the *Hebrides* are Scots, Highness — even if Earl Thorfinn controls most of them. The Earl, therefore is all-important in this. If he would say that his territories might acknowledge Rome rather than the Celtic Church — then you have what you need to trade with the Pope."

"What has he to lose?" Gruoch asked. "The Norse acknowledge the Pope. It would be but a gesture on his part. And greatly aid you."

MacBeth agreed. He would go to Galloway in a day or two, where Thorfinn was presently summering — to see if he would concur, whilst Abbot Ewan proceeded to Rome.

"I? To Rome?" It was the churchman's turn to stare.

"Yes. Who else so able? Who better to persuade the Pope? It has to be a cleric. Is any more apt to the task? You must go, and so soon as you may. Before the English do. You said so, did you not?"

The abbot looked doubtful.

"Meanwhile I shall at once make over these forfeited Fife lands to the Church. So that all, not only the Pope, will perceive my strong support of our Celtic faith."

19

THAT MACBETH AND Thorfinn, with the Abbot Ewan in attendance, should be setting sail from Torfness some nine months later, for Rome via Scandinavia, was a development none of them could have foreseen that previous September day at Cairn Beatha, many circumstances being outwith the control of even monarchs, Viking earls and the like. The Earl Siward of Northumbria and Deira was reliably reported to be seriously ill; King Magnus Olafson of Norway had been brought down by his own people, and was now superseded by a man of very different character, Sven Estridson, Canute's sister's son, who had first grasped the throne of Denmark and now Norway also; and the Abbot Ewan was but recently returned from his visit to Rome, his embassage only partly successful, bringing with him an urgent invitation from the Pope Leo for MacBeth to come to discuss their problems with him in person. The Archbishops of York and Canterbury had indeed appealed to the Vatican over the Galloway situation; and Thorfinn had cheerfully agreed to go through the motions of accepting the Pontiff as spiritual head of the Church in his domains — albeit with hooted asides.

So now, with Siward ill and an appeal in hand to the Pope,

there seemed little likelihood of any invasion of Scotland for the time being, and MacBeth felt that he could risk leaving his country, for undoubtedly the English pressure on Rome required to be countered. Equally certainly, the swiftest means of reaching Italy was by sea, and in a Viking longship. Thorfinn desired to see the new King of Norway, to make sure that he appreciated the especial and independent position of Orkney and Zetland, and to convince Sven if possible that Iceland too could do with a good, strong governor or viceroy — namely himself. He was prepared to sail MacBeth to Rome and there say his piece about the Orkney Church, if his brother would first accompany him to Norway and support him with King Sven. At the speed he proposed to travel, he reckoned that they could do all within six weeks. For purposes of prestige, if not threat, as well as to carry ample spare rowing-crews to maintain maximum pace, he was using no fewer than six of his fastest longships.

Since MacBeth and Gruoch had been crowned jointly and she was a queen-regnant rather than just a queen-consort, it was unnecessary for any council of regency to be appointed during the monarch's absence. Gruoch would rule very well, assisted by Lulach and the high officers of state, Chancellor Malduin, Glamis the Constable and O'Beolain of Applecross the Sennachie, supported by the Council of Mormaors — less Martacus of Mar who, with Farquhar, was travelling with the King. Paul and Erland Thorfinnson were also making the journey, each commanding a longship. So the expedition looked like being a lively one. Ingebiorg had come south to keep Gruoch company at the House of Spynie.

They had an impressive send-off, with what seemed to be a large proportion of the Moray population present, not to mention the Norse garrison of the Borg and all the notabilities, to wish them God-speed. It was the first time in memory or tradition that a King of Scots had left his own realm, save to go into England or on a foray to the Irish coast, and considerable was the excitement, in the bright May sunshine of the Eve of the Ascension.

The Boar Banner of Scotland flying at the high dragon-prow of Thorfinn's flagship — although the Raven flew higher, at the masthead — oars flashing to churn and spray white water, they led the squadron out to sea in spirited style, gongs beating, horns ululating and men bellowing the rowers' chants. They might not be going hosting or to war, but Thorfinn and his people at least were convinced that it was to be a triumph of some sort.

They headed due north-east, and with a fair south-west breeze behind them did not fail to keep up a spanking pace suitable for Thorfinn's reputation. There was really no need for the oars, but the Earl kept up with the rowing as a matter of principle, asserting that rowers were there to row and that idle men on a long voyage grew fat and soft. He aimed to maintain 200 miles a day throughout — that is, from sunrise to sunrise — but if this wind lasted, they should see the Norwegian coast well before nightfall the next day. They were out of sight of Scotland in just over the hour.

It made an exhilarating experience, in the best sailing weather of the year, with the Norse Sea not gentle but less daunting than usual, sun, high cloud and consistent winds. Each ship had two spare oar-crews, so all were fairly crowded; and to pass the time there were races between the vessels — the dragon-ship never actually losing — singing, wrestling bouts on the high stern-platforms where even the rowers could watch and wager, and other activities. The crews were changed every hour. Rowing was halted during the hours of darkness, but these were brief indeed in late May so near the Arctic Circle, and the stars always pale. Men slept where they might, in net hammocks, on decks and platforms, on gangways and rowing-benches, propped against bulwarks, wrapped in cloaks, plaids and skins beneath the great straining raven-painted square sails.

MacBeth had never before made a voyage out-of-sight of land, and found the novel experience much to his taste. There was a remarkable and welcome feeling of suspension of concern and responsibility, a timeless and carefree atmosphere in which he could forget that he was a reigning monarch — and the Vikings certainly did not make a point of reminding him of the fact.

He was, indeed, almost disappointed when, the following afternoon shouts of triumph greeted sightings of land ahead — which could only be the Norwegian coast. Thorfinn, in contrast, was delighted, declaring it the fastest passage even he had ever made, and indicating that his excellent navigation had much to do with it. That would be the point of Stattlandetnes, he declared — almost 500 miles in thirty-two hours. Was there anyone else in Christendom, in all the world, who could rival that? His brother was prepared to allow him his exultation.

They turned considerably more into the north now, along a coast that looked remarkably similar to that of Western Scotland and the Hebrides, mountains and cliffs, islands and skerries, with the yawning mouths of sea-lochs opening frequently. Sundown found them passing between the islands of Hitra and Froya, which masked the mouth of the Trondheim Fiord. Here, in a sheltered bay, the flotilla anchored, Thorfinn announcing that the fiord was long and winding and not to be negotiated in poor light — Nidaros, their destination, chief place of Norway, being some thirty miles up.

Sunrise saw them probing in line astern up the black waters of the shadowy abyss that was the fiord, between soaring rock walls of mountains which were now seen to be very different from the Scottish ones, much more steep and barren, those inland ahead of them still snow-capped, denying the light of the stripling sun to the entire seaboard. Where there was any coastal plain, it was forested with dark pines and the light green stippling of opening birch; but all above was bare rock, mist-wraiths and cascading white water. Of inhabitants there appeared to be few signs, no villages save for a small fishing-haven or two at boat-strands or timber jetties, with scattered farms amongst the foothills.

Nevertheless, presently when the sun had burst over the lofty snowfields ahead, transforming the scene with its level brilliance, it was to be seen that blue smoke columns were ascending into the morning air from headlands and eminences on both sides of the fiord.

"So the sluggards have awakened!" Thorfinn commented. "They warn belatedly the strangers' approach. This Sven Woman's-son can be but an indifferent hero, I say! Had it been I who dwelt here, and six strange longships headed up my coast and into my fiord, I would have had this place blocked long ere this, and a score of ships challenging."

"Perhaps your raven-device is sufficiently known even here, and respected?" his brother suggested.

"Known, no doubt. Respected, perhaps. But scarce welcomed, I swear! Magnus Olafson, I think, would not have welcomed me!"

"They say that this Sven is a very different man . . ."

In a couple of hours of uninterrupted rowing, with still no sign of other shipping in either welcome or opposition, the fiord took a major bend to the south, and widening notably thereafter revealed a distinctly different scene, hitherto hidden by thrusting hill-shoulders. Here there was a great basin before the fiord narrowed again north-eastwards, with the mountains drawing back, green foothill pastures and more gently-rising

251

forests clothing the mountainsides. At the southern edge of the water a town, not large, clustered, where the Nid River joined the fiord, with its jetties, warehouses, curing-sheds and boat-building yards around a narrow-necked but seemingly sizeable harbour.

"Is that the principal town of all Norway?" MacBeth wondered. "Even Torfness is larger."

"The Norse are not folk for living in towns," his brother said. "There are but the three cities in all Norway — Bergen, Oslo and this. As a town Nidaros was founded but fifty years ago by Olaf Tryggvesson. He had his house here. When he took up Christianity, he built a church beside it. But it was the monks and churchmen who made the town, rather than Olaf."

As they drew closer, they could see the masts of considerable shipping in the harbour, behind a sea-wall. But no craft put out to challenge them. Presently they could see also that the harbour area at the river-mouth was fortified strongly, with a fort on a small island dominating the narrow entrance to port and river. Many men could now be descried, and the glint of steel.

Approaching near the fort, Thorfinn himself signalled his orders by clanging loudly on the dragon-ship's gong, and thereafter bellowing the first bars of a song. From all the flotilla the singing broke out, not just the monotonous chant of the rowers but a recognisable melody, somewhat ragged at first but quickly becoming synchronised, and still to the fast beat and rhythm of the oars, the speed increasing notably. Although presumably to indicate peaceful intent, it sounded markedly martial and confident.

They were quite close to the walls of the island fort when a creaking clanking sound penetrated the singing, and a disturbance in the water just ahead heralded the surfacing of a massive chain being raised by winchmen across the harbour entrance. A foot or so above the waves-level it rose, to stretch, hanging green, dripping weed from the sea-floor, and effectively barring all entrance. Even the dragon-ship's fearsome projecting iron ram would avail nothing against those mighty links.

Shouting to his oarsmen to back water, and fast, the Earl raised his hand, clanged the gong again, and the singing died away on all the longships. Rowers all but stood on their thirty-foot oars, four men to a sweep, to reduce speed in time.

"I am Thorfinn Raven Feeder of Orkney," the earl yelled. "Come in peace. To speak with Sven Estridson. Greetings! Lower your chain."

252

There was a distinct pause. Then a hoarse voice answered across the water. "We know who you are, Raven Feeder. And want none of you. The king is not here."

Thorfinn frowned. "Who speaks there?" he demanded.

"Eric Jarl. Of Trondheim. Keeper here."

"Then Eric Jarl, lower your chain. So that we can speak together decently. As jarls should. Not shout like huscarls."

"No!" That was bald.

"A plague on you! We come in peace, I say."

"If in peace, why six longships filled with men? A thousand men!"

"I am Earl of Orkney, and do not sail with less."

"Then you do not enter Nidaros, Earl of Orkney."

"A God's name — why?"

"Because I do not trust you, Raven Feeder. I fought you at Waternish of Skye. And will fight you again, if I must."

"Ha! You were with Magnus. You do well to fear me, then! Where is your King Sven?"

"He is not here."

"Where, then? I have come a long way to see him."

"He has returned to Denmark. These three weeks. He is at his house of Roskilde."

Thorfinn swore.

MacBeth touched his brother's arm. "Tell him that I am here — the King of Scots. Come to see his master also. Say that I promise him and his no harm. He has no reason to fear *me*."

But when this information was shouted across, the Jarl Eric was no more forthcoming. If the King of Scots sailed in bad company, he announced, he must take the consequences. They would not land at Nidaros.

The Abbot Ewan came forward, and asked to be allowed to say something — although he clearly found the shouting difficult. He said that he was an abbot of Holy Church in the King's and earl's company, and could assure all, in Christ's good name, that they came in peace. Nidaros was known as a holy place, sacred to Saint Olaf the King. They respected its sanctity, as a place of pilgrimage.

This plea was likewise bluntly rejected.

"God's Blood, fool — then we will land elsewhere and come and burn you and your miserable town!" Thorfinn raged.

"Try it, Raven Feeder! Your ravens will not feast here — save on your own carcases!"

There was a roar, as the earl raised a pointing hand. "You are

253

a dead man, for that, Eric Jarl! None speaks so to Thorfinn Sigurdson." He turned, to shout to his own people. "Heat the pitch-barrels. Fire-arrows. Prepare fire-arrows . . ."

Again MacBeth spoke, gripping the other's elbow. "Wait, man. Do not be a fool, also. Think. What will fighting here serve? We came to treat with Sven, not to offend him. Leave this Eric and his town. Go see Sven in Denmark, if you will. Complain there . . ."

"Fiend seize him — I do not complain! I act! If you swallow insults, I do not. Even if we do not land here, fire-arrows over yonder sea-wall and ramparts, into the harbour, will burn shipping and sheds . . ."

"And ruin your mission! If it was of sufficient importance for you to come all this way, seeking Sven, it is sufficient to leave this churl to his own ill manners and sail for Denmark. For if you burn and slay here, you must needs go home. Or go on to Rome. For you cannot see King Sven."

Thorfinn drew a great breath. "A curse on you and all white livers!" he burst out. He flung away, and raising a fist, shook it at the unseen speaker in the fort. "I shall deal with you another day, Eric Jarl!" he cried. "Start praying!" Then he turned on his own oar-master. "Row, damn you — row!" He pointed back down the fiord, whence they had come. He flicked a hand at his sail-master to trim the sail, and snatching out his sword, began to slam-slam-slam at the gong furiously.

Pulling round in a tight circle, the dragon-ship beat off westwards again, the other vessels of the squadron getting out of the way quickly.

None spoke for a little. Then, curiously, it was Martacus of Mar who raised voice, at the King's elbow.

"A bad business," he commented, in his hesitant voice. "But, if I had been in this Eric's place, I might have done the same!" He had to repeat that, to make himself heard above the gong's clangour. "That town will not hold 500 men, much less our thousand."

The King nodded.

All but Thorfinn gazed back at Nidaros on its peninsular site within the twisting river-mouth, at the two wide and intersecting streets — wide to lessen the danger of fire, for all the houses were of wood — at the great long-house on its eminence, which was the Kongsgaard or royal palace, and at the multi-roofed and gabled timber church of Saint Clement, with its gleaming gold paint. The sense of anti-climax was strong.

MacBeth quickly turned back to his brother. He recognised well how bitter a draught must have been this snub and mortification for the all-conquering Raven Feeder, more especially in front of his own sons.

"How far to Denmark, Thor?" he called, seeking to keep his voice as casual as he might, when the gonging ceased. "To this Roskilde?"

Thorfinn glanced at him, almost glaring, then shrugged. "Three days sail. Four."

"Further than we have already come?"

"Yes. Roskilde is on Zealand. Down the Kattegat. Far down."

"This Sven, ruling two kindgoms — is Roskilde his true home? As it was his uncle's, Canute's?"

"He is said to winter there. In summer, I was told, he came here. To Norway."

"We shall do better there, I think. Than in this barren land. Denmark is said to be a kinder place."

"Kindness I do not seek. Only a man to face!"

They left it at that.

The ships were rowed down the long fiord, with the westerly breeze in their faces now, and the sails all but furled. Thorfinn looked at the two or three fishing-havens they passed with an assessing eye, as possible targets for his resentment, but managed to restrain himself. His companions kept their distance.

But once the open sea was reached and they turned southwards, the motion of the waves, the handling of the sails, the rowers' chanting and the general demands of seamanship amongst the offshore islets and skerries, restored Thorfinn most of the way to his normal self. Men relaxed noticeably — although not at the oars. Speed appeared to be in greater demand than ever.

They reached Cape Statlandetnes, the most westerly point of Norway, with the sunset staining the sea on their rudder-sides, and the flotilla much strung out, some of the skeids, swift-sailers as their name meant, being hard put to it to keep up with the great dragon-ship, fiercely driven as it was, with its thirty-two rowers' benches against their twenty-four. With darkness falling, however, Thorfinn relented and allowed the oars to be shipped, for with the turn of the coast they now had the wind on their steering or starboard beam, and the sails could carry them adequately. Beneath the lypting, the stern-platform, that night, Thorfinn got roaring drunk; and all who knew him congratulated themselves that he would be his normally cheerful and hearty self in the morning.

The weather changed next day, and rain-storms and bright intervals succeeded each other regularly, with a gusty veering wind which raised the seas. But since all the gusts were from points westerly, and they were now heading ever more into the south-east, parallel with the South Norway coast, making for the Skagerak, their pace was little affected. Despite the heaving decks and driving rain-squalls, the wrestling-matches, shield-fights and similar contests were resumed.

They sighted the Danish coast fine on the starboard bow as the sun rose on the third morning, Thorfinn declaring it to be the Skagen Horn itself, the most northerly tip of Jutland, entirely pleased with himself — although Biorn, who was really shipmaster, muttered that he reckoned it to be Hirtshalsnes, twenty-five miles to the south-west. Perhaps fortunately for them all, the earl proved to be right, as presently they were able to identify the long narrow peninsula of Skagen itself and the coast falling away southwards, and congratulations were called for — and well received.

But MacBeth's assumptions that they would reach their destination by that evening were negatived by his brother, who declared that they had 120 miles of the Kattegat to cover before they reached the great Isefiord, off which the Roskilde Fiord branched, and then thirty miles of that, it being almost as long as that of Trondheim, with Roskilde town at the very tip. Indeed another eight or so miles and it would have cut Zealand in two. They would lie up overnight in the mouth of it, as they had done at Trondheim, and make their approach up the narrows in daylight.

Evening saw them entering the great, almost land-locked bay-like expanse of the Isefiord, between two headlands only a mile apart. It made a very different landfall to the Norse one, with no mountains nor even hills, no islands and few reefs or skerries and cliffs, but long sandy shores, low promontories, green soft slopes and much broad-leafed woodland. Villages could be seen on either side of the rapidly widening fiord, which was really a large salt-water lake. There was much coastal shipping evident. Thorfinn declared that the Danes would not need to light signal fires here to inform of their approach.

With no islands to shelter behind, they sailed in at the mouth of the Ise, more like a firth than a fiord, and after a mile or two, avoiding villages and signs of population, found a quiet shallow bay on the west side, where they dropped anchor. The cattle and sheep grazing nearby were a strong temptation for Vikings who had had to live on dried meat and smoked fish, rancid butter and hard bread, for the last five days; but Thorfinn forbade all shore-going. There was much coming and going between the ships, and the ale at least was still plentiful.

The next morning's first light revealed a surprise, as the mists lifted. A line of vessels, longships, and skutas and galleys, was stretched across the mouth of their bay, motionless, waiting, fully a score of them.

Thorfinn stared, and then slapped his thigh and laughed loudly. "Here is the kinder reception!" he cried. "They wait on us, whoever they are." He grinned. "So, then — let them wait! Let *us* eat in comfort, break our fast, then we shall see to them."

MacBeth stroked his little beard. "If they wait on us, Thor, then let us show an equal civility. They must have sailed through the night. They also will be hungered. Send one boat, with greetings, to their leader. Declare who we are, and request his company to break fast with us, whoever he is."

The earl punched his brother on the shoulder. "Well said, Son of Life! To be sure. That is good. Young Paul shall go." He bellowed across to his son's skeid, anchored close by. "Paul, boy — stir yourself. Get out your oars. Row out to yonder ships. Seek out the chiefest. Tell them that Thorfinn Raven Feeder of Orkney and MacBeth King of Scots come visiting Sven Estridson. Thank the leader for his escort. And say that we would have him greet the day by eating with us, he and some of his. You have it? Then off with you."

It took a little time for Paul's ship to up anchor and row the half-mile out to that waiting fleet. But thereafter things moved promptly enough; indeed movement became general. A central longship came forward alongside Paul's, to row back with him; another, a skuta of fifteen benches, turned and set off swiftly, purposefully, in the opposite direction, up-fiord; and the rest of the line of ships stirred and moved forward slowly into the bay some way, in a gesture eloquent enough of strength and warning.

"They send to inform Roskilde as to who is come," MacBeth interpreted. "And while accepting our invitation, seek to show us who is master here. This man knows what he is at."

The leading longship was also flying a raven banner, but three ravens on red, signifying presumably the three kingdoms

257

of Denmark, Norway and Sweden — although of the last, Scania alone was still under Danish rule. Its sail, like those of most of the fleet, was striped red and white vertically. The men on its high lypting were all armed and armoured, wearing bulls' horned helmets.

"Come aboard, friends," Thorfinn hailed, as they drew near. "I am the Earl of Orkney, of whom you will have heard. And this is King MacBeth of Scotland, my brother. Are you of King Sven's people?"

"I am the Jarl Einar — Einar Einarson," a voice came back. "Sent by King Sven to welcome whoso visits his realm, for good or ill. If indeed you be the King of Scotland and the Earl of Orkney, we are the more honoured."

"Come then, Einar Jarl, and see for yourself. Our provision we would share with you. It is modest shipmen's fare — but come eat with us."

The newcomers drew alongside, and a tall, good-looking young man, hair so fair as to be almost white, led a group of others in jumping aboard the dragon-ship. Well-built as he was, however, he still had to gaze up at Thorfinn, as had his companions, and his bulls' horns, however fierce, looked less so beside the other's mighty winged helm. Amongst them all, MacBeth in his simple saffron kilt and leather jerkin was scarcely to be noticed. Save perhaps for something about his carriage.

The Jarl Einar nevertheless, after a quick glance from one brother to the other, bowed to MacBeth. "Lord King," he said, "your fame is known to us. Thorfinn Jarl, you also. The Raven Feeder's is a name none takes lightly." That upturned gaze was wary, assessing.

"Save that Eric of Trondheim!" the big man growled. "We put in to Nidaros, seeking Sven. But that oaf would not so much as have us land."

"No? That was uncivil. But perhaps he feared you, Raven Feeder? Some men, I think, might do so. Was Eric Jarl not with Magnus Olafson in that of the Hebrides, three years back?"

"Those unhappy days are past, Jarl Einar," MacBeth said. "Now we seek only peace and goodwill. And much thank you for coming to meet us. Here is the Abbot Ewan, of Holy Church . . ."

"Though you knew not who we were!" Thorfinn interrupted, less affably. "Who did you expect to find here?"

"We did not know. But . . . there are many raiders. Wends.

258

Goths. Svears. We have our own pirates in these seas, King MacBeth. As, I understand, have you." The young man's glance flickered towards Thorfinn. "Not all bringing peace and good will!"

"Come, eat," the earl said shortly.

So presently, escorted by the large Danish flotilla, the Orkney ships were conducted across the Iscfiord to a narrow, almost hidden opening on the other, eastern, side, only a few hundred yards in width, which proved to be the entrance to the Roskilde Fiord, its two headlands, strongly fortified, reminding MacBeth of his own Sutors guarding the Cromarty Firth. In a mile or two, the fiord opened out somewhat and took a major bend southwards. Thereafter it was like sailing up a wide lowland river through a fairly populous countryside of marshland, pasture, farms and woods, a soft-seeming land to have produced the warlike Danes.

They had a score of miles to go, the central third of it through narrows where the tide-races taxed the oarsmen and strung out the entire convoy to a great length. But once this was past, with the group of low islets at its southern end, they were into a wide and placid lake, ringed by villages and homesteads, and at the far south tip the smoke of what was obviously a large town.

But it was not the town, its size and spread, which impressed the visitors as they drew near, so much as the amount of shipping anchored there in the basin or drawn up at quays and jetties. There were hundreds of vessels, of all sorts and sizes, lying there, by no means the majority trading or fishing craft. Even Thorfinn fell silent as he counted the longships, skeids, snekkja and skuta, warships all. He might be the terror of the northern seas, but here was a concourse of naval power such as he had never before seen assembled. His counting failed him and he turned to the Jarl Einar, who had remained with them in the dragon-ship.

"Is Sven Estridson mustering for some great project?" he wondered. "A war, or invasion? So many ships . . .?"

"No," he was told. "Half of the Danish fleet lies here, at Roskilde."

"Half . . .!"

"Half, yes. The rest lies at other havens. In Jutland, Slesvig, Funen, Langeland and Laaland. And Norway, to be sure. But here is the King's house, so half is here."

"I had scarce thought so many ships existed!" MacBeth admitted — even though his brother would not. "How many?"

"Not sufficient, I say," Einar declared. "Denmark and

Norway have a great length of seaboard to protect. Many thousands of miles. Sven has perhaps 500 ships of war. But Canute his uncle had 1200. And even Harald Blue Tooth had 700."

MacBeth looked at Thorfinn — who for once had no comment to make.

Threading their way through the anchored shipping, with most of their escort now left behind, they were brought into the extensive harbour area itself, where berths had been cleared for the six Orkney vessels at one of the central jetties. Here a large company was awaiting them, much of it richly clad. A mighty blowing of horns marked the dragon-ship's touching of the wharf's timbers.

The Jarl Einar tapped MacBeth's arm, and gestured towards the gangway which was being pushed across.

A boyish-looking young man in his mid-twenties came striding up the planking, his curling blond hair all but hiding a gold circlet of much the same colour around his brows. He had an open, freckled face, scarcely handsome, bright blue eyes and an engaging smile. He glanced quickly from MacBeth to Thorfinn and then back again, noting Einar's guiding hand.

"I am Sven Estridson," he announced. "I welcome you to my kingdoms. Do I greet the famed King of Scotland?"

"I am MacBeth mac Finlay, yes, lord King. We use the term King of Scots, not of Scotland, for sufficient reason. I rejoice to meet the King of Denmark, Norway and the Swedes, Great Bracelet-Giver and Lord of the Inner and Outer Seas." He understood that this was the correct style. "And esteem your coming to welcome us as kind indeed."

They grasped arms, Viking fashion.

Thorfinn, at his brother's shoulder, cleared his throat strongly, frowning slightly.

"And this, King Sven, is my brother of Orkney, the Earl Thorfinn, Mormaor of Caithness and Sutherland."

Sven's cheerful smile faded just a little, and looking up, he nodded, but did not extend his arm. "Ah, so," he said. "It could be none other than the Raven Feeder! Greetings, Thorfinn Jarl, since you come in peace."

"Would I have come otherwise?" the big man asked bluntly.

"Who knows? The Raven Feeder has done so much. Lesser men are wise to be ... cautious!" Sven turned back to MacBeth. "You also, Highness, we have heard much of. And to your good."

"You are kind. Most men remember that I slew my predecessor, King Duncan!"

"He who poisoned the Danes? Or so my mother tells me. Should I disfavour you for that?"

"Your lady mother is well informed, King Sven."

"She is, and had to be. She was Knut Svenson's sister! But, come — we shall go see her. She awaits you in my house . . ."

Greetings for the others over, they landed and set off in a procession through crowded streets, to continuous horn-blowing — although it was noticeable that the crowds did not cheer or seem particularly welcoming. Roskilde, like most others in Scandinavia where towns were a comparatively new conception, was little more than half-a-century old, although the royal residence had been there earlier, placed at one of the few localities on the long sheltered fiord where there was a sufficient depth of water for shipping to berth conveniently; also there was a famous mineral spring here, sacred to the old gods, and duly taken over by the Christian missionaries and made a holy well for healing of body and mind, for which that newly-converted and zealous tyrant Harald Blue Tooth had built a large timber church. The other buildings of the town were of wood also, many gaily-painted, which gave an atmosphere markedly different from the stone-and-thatch towns and villages at home — more lightsome but less permanent and settled-seeming.

The Kongsheim palace, successor of the old long-house of Leire of the Gods, was not set apart from the rest, but formed one side of an entire street, not so much one as a series of houses, with nothing of the fortress about it. Clearly the Danish monarchs looked on their position in a different light to that of most kings of Christendom, closer to the people, at least to the freemen thereof — but then, of course, the throne had been established for little over two centuries, whereas the Scots and Picts, for instance, traced their royal line back for over one thousand years, if somewhat imaginatively.

Sven led his principal visitors into the palace, which proved to be more extensive than appeared from the street, across a central space or courtyard and into a succession of inter-communicating halls beyond, which opened on to gardens and orchards, the town not encroaching or even visible at this side. In one of the halls, a group of men awaited them. These the King introduced as the remainder of his Hird, or Court, known as the House-carls of the King. They raised hands in greeting.

They appeared to be some sort of company of privileged friends of the monarch, rather than a collection of jarls, chieftains or officers — something not known in Scotland.

Doors were open to the garden, on this day of early June, and the sound of music could be heard in the occasional lull in the talking. Presently men fell silent as a group of women appeared from under the trees, some carrying flowers and greenery, and led by one of striking looks, not beautiful but strong-featured, of middle years, carrying herself with a proud dignity although of slight build. She paused in the doorway, to consider them all, calmly assured.

Sven stepped forward. "Mother," he said, "I have brought our guests. The King of Scots — who will not be called King of Scotland. His son the Prince Farquhar — do I say it aright? His bishop, the Abbot Ewan. And his half-brother the Jarl Thorfinn of Orkney. You will, I think, perceive which is which!" He smiled. "The Lady Estrid Svensdotter."

The newcomers bowed, Thorfinn only marginally.

The lady did not smile, like her son, but considered them almost thoughtfully. MacBeth, beneath her calm scrutiny, felt almost like a boy again, as he had not done for long. Clearly her son felt similarly. It was not that she was daunting or severe, merely that she carried a cool and unquestionable authority with her. He did not realise that he bore a not dissimilar air of his own. Also, at first, he had the impression that they had met before, then realised that it was her resemblance to her brother Canute.

"MacBeth Finlayson, is it?" she said, very much taking her time. "You are younger than I had thought of you."

"I would say the same, lady, if I may," he answered. "I admired your brother. And now, your son. We rejoice to be welcomed to this realm." He turned towards Sven. This was a little difficult, with regard to the formalities, for however formidable, and a King's daughter, the woman was not Queen, her late husband Ulfdarl only a jarl. Although the unmarried Sven clearly treated her as though she was a queen. "This is my brother, Princess — Thorfinn of Orkney."

"Could any doubt it?" she asked, level-voiced. "A brave man indeed — to venture into Denmark. To which he has denied due tribute and allegiance for so long!"

Thorfinn's indrawn breath was audible to all present. "I pay tribute to none on this earth, Estrid Svensdotter!" he gave back strongly. "Nor offer allegiance. Magnus Olafson discovered

262

that — who was less wise than your brother Knut, lady. Friendship, now — that is different. I come offering *that* to King Sven, here."

"Friendship? At a price, no doubt?" She turned back to MacBeth. "Does this pirate jarl yield you no allegiance or tribute either, Highness?"

"I fear not, Princess. But his friendship, apart from our blood-tie, I have reason to value above all others. I commend that assurance to King Sven!"

"Ah! I see that my brother was right. He said, I recollect, that MacBeth Finlayson wore iron beneath the simple linen he affected!"

"I am flattered that King Canute remembered me, lady. But I have brought no iron beneath my *leine croch* here, I promise you. Only good will, admiration, and some support for my brother."

"Support for what, my lord King?" Sven asked.

"Thorfinn Sigurdson has a suggestion to make to you, Highness — a representation. Of worth, I think. But — I leave that to himself, and a more private occasion. Here is the Abbot Ewan, my High Judex, chief judge of my realm, Princess . . ."

"The good abbot is welcome. And which of these is the prince, your son?"

"This is Farquhar of Moray. And these are Paul and Erland, sons to Thorfinn . . ."

Further discussion was postponed meantime, as the visitors were conducted to their quarters in the Kongsheim, Sven personally taking MacBeth to his room. There was mead and refreshment provided, with information that they would eat presently, an hour after noon.

Long before that, Thorfinn found his way to his brother's chamber, and in no affable mood.

"See you, I have had my bellyful of this!" he exclaimed. "I will not be treated like some housecarl of yours! Or what that sister-of-a-dog calls a pirate jarl! I do not bide here to be insulted. If this is to be the way of it, we sail again this very day!"

"That would be folly, Thor. We have come a long way. None invited us. You have a cause to plead. Or, at least, to make. Be patient . . ."

"Am I an ox? To stand patient under the lash? They treat me as of little account. Not only that woman, but all these Danes. It is not to be borne! You they bow to and smile on —

263

King MacBeth this, Highness that! Me they ignore. Or decry. Yet, who wields the power, brother — you or me?" That was fierce.

"There you have it, Thor. Do you not see? You they see as a danger, myself none. Did you not fight and defeat Sven's predecessor, King Magnus? And slay many of his men. He claimed that you were his vassal, for Orkney. This Sven may do likewise. So you could be considered his rebel . . ."

"Would I have come here, offering friendship, offering to treat? If I was some sort of mere rebel — the Raven Feeder!"

"Why *did* you come, then, Thor? I have never been entirely sure. This trouble of Iceland seems scarcely enough to bring you so far."

"I told you. The Icelanders stabbed at my back, when I had done them no hurt. They must not do so again. They have grown over-proud, above themselves. *There* are rebels, if you like! Against these Danes. They need to be taught a lesson."

"You do not usually seek another's permission before you teach your lessons!"

"Permission, nothing! But if I deal with these Icelanders, I want no Danish or Norwegian fleet attacking my rear. Or Orkney. So I treat with this Sven first."

"But . . . what have you to treat with? Iceland is as independent a land as you have made of Orkney. It is not part of the Danish realm. Nor the Norse. What can you offer Sven there?"

"I can offer him what he could not have otherwise. To be lord of Iceland — in name. Always since the franklins and freeholders fled from Norway and the oppressions of Harald Haarfager near two centuries ago, the Kings here have wished to control them. As they have wished to control Orkney. To make the new land their territory. Some even in Iceland would have it so, I am told. Now, I can offer Sven the name of King in Iceland, at least. If he will name me his governor or viceroy. So my rear is safe. I go there with the King's authority. And never again will the Icelanders assail the Raven Feeder when his back is turned!"

"And would this be just a hosting? A punitive raid you wish to make? Or more than that? Are you seeking to *take* Iceland? For yourself?"

"We shall see, Son of Life!"

"You would add Iceland to all the rest? To Orkney and Zetland, the Hebrides and Galloway. I think that you have your eyes on Man, likewise? Is it an empire you are seeking to carve out, Thor? Would you be another Canute?"

"Not me, no. But Sven might think to be! See, I but seek to ensure that never again shall I have Icelanders creeping upon me. Or Danes either. Man I may take, yes. So that Galloway is secure. That Echmarcach needs his lesson, likewise! You should thank me. You will aid me in this? With Sven?"

"I do not see what I can do. Or why I should . . ."

"You wish to go to Rome, do you not? And have *me* aid you there?"

"To be sure. But . . . I have nothing to support you with, here."

"Have you not? In *fact*, no, you have nothing. But in words not a little, brother. Play the King, I say! Kings are ever strong on words, names, titles! Tell Sven that you are willing to resign all your claims to overlordship of both Iceland and Man. To him. If he names me governor."

"Claims? Me? I have no claims to either, man. As to Iceland, how could I have . . .?"

"As good a claim as Sven — in name. The Norse were not the first in Iceland. When they came there, who were there? Picts, Celtic folk from Orkney and Zetland and Scotland. Ruled by priests. Keledei. From Scotland and Ireland. There are still people of that blood there."

"That old tale! That is for bairns . . .!"

"If the Pope, and the English, can claim Galloway and Whithorn after three centuries. And Canute could claim half Christendom! Or use such tales to justify his wars. Can you not do the same for Iceland? And Man? Man is part of the Sudreys, the south part of the Hebrides. And you claim the Hebrides as part of Scotland, do you not? So Man also should be part of your realm, no?"

"We have never said so . . ."

"Then do so now, when it may serve some good. As I say, play the King. This is how kings play their games, brother. But offer to yield your rights in this matter to Sven. Out of love — and if he appoints me governor."

"He would laugh at me! Unless he is a fool . . ."

"Would he? Or that mother of his? They are not to know the full truth. He is new to kingship. And he is Canute's nephew, and now, in part, successor. The Emperor of the Angles, Saxons and Scandinavians, was it not? With that woman behind him. She is the power, I swear. Aye, and I swear too that he will not laugh."

MacBeth shook his head. "I do not know. I must think more on this. It all seems folly, swording with shadows. But . . . we shall see. And you will require to summon all your patience . . ."

At the repast which followed, MacBeth was placed between Sven and his mother, Thorfinn on the other side of the Lady Estrid, and Farquhar on the King's left. So there was no opportunity for Thorfinn's discussion, since he and the lady scarcely exchanged a word. But afterwards the earl forced the pace. He declared bluntly that they had a long voyage ahead of them, to win to Rome, and it behoved them to deal with the issue, which had brought them to Denmark, forthwith. Sven's suggestion, that it could wait for the morrow, and that surely, after days being shipbound the visitors would wish to ride abroad, hunt, hawk or see the land, fell on deaf ears. At length their host acceded to at least a preliminary discussion at once.

They went to sit outdoors beneath the apple-trees, Sven and his mother, with two or three of his councillors, and Thorfinn, MacBeth and Abbot Ewan. Uncaring for royal usage or protocol, Thorfinn made the running from the first. Nor did he beat about the bush. He declared, without preamble, that the Icelanders were a danger to the peace of the northern seas, threatened his islands, the Orcades and the Hebrides, and must be controlled.

"Iceland?" Sven said, with a wondering glance at his mother. "No doubt but you are right, Thorfinn Jarl. But how does this concern me? The Icelanders are a law unto themselves. Many hundreds of miles from my shores. And a stubborn folk. Why come to me? Should they heed me?"

"They do not heed the King of Scots."

Sven's brows rose, as he looked from one to the other. "Why should they do so? Do they trouble *you*, Highness?"

"No," MacBeth admitted. "Not . . . as yet."

"Then I do not see . . ."

"They trouble *me*," Thorfinn interrupted. "And they are some man's men, are they not? My brother's, or yours—which?"

"I do not understand you," Sven said, frowning. "I have not considered the Icelanders to be any responsibility of mine. And I cannot see how they can be that of King MacBeth."

"Orkneymen, Zetlanders, Scots, were settled in Iceland before our Norsemen came. It was ruled by the Keledei — the people of the abbot, here. My brother could claim Iceland as rightfully his."

"And do you . . . ?"

266

"That would be foolishness!" the Lady Estrid put in. "I cannot think that the Lord MacBeth would be so . . . unwise. My brother claimed Iceland as his. As did my nephews Harald and Hardicanute. So did Magnus Olafson. Where comes Scotland into this?"

"Canute claimed Man also, lady. As did the others. But Man is in the Sudreys, the Southern Hebrides. Part of the Kingdom of Scotland. Is that not so, Brother?"

MacBeth smoothed his beard. "I might make fair claim to Man," he said carefully.

"But — what *is* this, Thorfinn Jarl?" Sven demanded. "What do you seek? I cannot accept that Iceland belongs to the King of Scots. If it belongs to any, it belongs to me. Of Man, I care not. What are you asking of me?"

"Asking nothing, Sven Ulfdarlson. Offering! I offer you Iceland. Just as I offer MacBeth mac Finlay Man. If you will appoint me governor there. Your viceroy."

"Soul of God!"

There was silence for a little, under the apple-trees, as they considered the implications of that. Thorfinn, who was standing now, folded his arms and actually turned to stare away from them all.

MacBeth spoke, slowly. "My brother puts it bluntly, Highness. But there could be sense in this, I think. If you lay claim to Iceland. Do you?"

Again the King's swift glance at his mother.

"He cannot do other than assert his right to Iceland," that lady said. "As King of Norway, Norsemen dwell there. This of the Scots being there first is nonsense."

"I would be prepared to resign any claim," MacBeth mentioned, flatly.

"Why do you wish to be *my* governor, Thorfinn Jarl?" Sven asked. "The Raven Feeder sails under his own banner, does he not?"

"If it *is* your territory, better that I descend upon it in your name than as your invader. Is it not?"

"And you are decided upon at attack on Iceland?"

"I am decided that they shall not attack *me* again. I but seek my own people's safety. But it could be to your advantage."

"You must convince me of that, I think."

"It is simple. At present, Iceland is beyond your grasp. Even though you may claim it. If I go there in your name, with my longships, they will have to accept me. And so accept you also, as overlord. You have gained a right and authority, in name, without having to lift a hand. Is it not so?"

"And you gain . . .?"

"I gain only what I fight for?"

"We shall have to consider this," Estrid said, and rose, to show clearly that she at least had had enough for the moment. The others stood up likewise.

"To be sure," Thorfinn nodded. "But — we sail tomorrow." He paused. "With the King of Scots' assent!" He bowed mockingly to his brother, and turned to stroll off.

Estrid Svensdotter looked from her son to MacBeth. "My brother did not trust him," she said. "Should we?"

"None may force him, or cozen him," MacBeth answered, after a moment. "But all may trust him at least in this — to do as he says!"

They left it at that meantime.

There was entertainment and much drinking of mead that evening — which had to be interrupted so that Thorfinn and his lieutenants could hurry out into the town and try to bring some order to the streets where his longships' crews were showing the Danes what real Vikings were like, and cracked heads and bloody noses were the order of the night. This exercise seemed greatly to improve the earl's spirits, and by the time he was ready to seek his couch, he was amiability itself, very drunk and making rude suggestions even to the Lady Estrid, before finally making off with a plump serving-wench and singing hugely.

MacBeth reassured their hosts — but warned that this did not mean that his potent brother would be any easier to deal with in the morning. When he himself retired, Sven and his mother were in earnest conference with the Danish Kanzler, Drost, Marsk, Jarl Einar and other high officers.

MacBeth was talking with Farquhar, who had a small room next to his own, before settling to sleep, when the Abbot Ewan came knocking at the door. He had been approached, he said, by his opposite number, the Drost, or High Bailiff. It seemed that King Sven — or his mother, more likely — was inclined to accept Thorfinn's proposition, provided that they could be assured that the earl did not intend any trickery or deception. The King could scarcely ask another monarch directly for assurances that his own brother was honest in this matter — so he, Ewan, was being used as go-between.

MacBeth nodded. "Tell the Drost that I am not my brother's keeper," he said. "Say also that I have already told them that

Thorfinn may always be trusted to do what he says — although often somewhat more than that! But you can say that I can see no hurt to King Sven and his interests in this — and that is the truth. Meantime he has no least hold on Iceland. Whatever claims his predecessors may have made. Whatever gain Thorfinn may win out of it all, it cannot be at Sven's cost. And he will certainly much increase his claims to sovereignty there if Thorfinn acts in his name, as governor. And, to be sure, if he esteems Thorfinn to be at fault at any time, to be acting against Denmark's interests, he can always withdraw his royal authority and proclaim it so. Tell him that I can see what he may gain, but not what he could lose."

"My own view, lord King — although I fear not for King Sven but for the Icelanders!"

"Yes. But they are a strong and independent people. Thorfinn may find them harder to herd than he thinks. He may well have to come to terms with them. But that is his business . . ."

In the morning, Thorfinn was formally informed by the Kanzler, or Chancellor, Karl Alvarson, that King Sven was prepared to give him a charter appointing him temporarily as governor and commander of his province of Iceland and the Faeroes, withdrawable at the King's pleasure. And to King MacBeth an assurance that Denmark yielded all claims to the Island of Man.

Having gained what he wanted, Thorfinn became affability itself, a prince of visitors, dispensing largesse and even going so far as to bestow a handsome golden serpent-bracelet on the Great Bracelet-Giver himself, however doubtful the propriety of this — or the origins of the bracelet. He also declared that he might put off his departure for another day, as a gesture of esteem — and although the Danes looked somewhat doubtful about this, after the previous night's riot in the town, they could scarcely urge otherwise.

Possibly it was as much as anything to try to get the Orkneymen away from Roskilde's streets, ale-houses and brothels, that Sven proposed an excursion to Jellinge, some miles round the fiord on the east side, where there was a sacred grove to the pagan gods, with runic stones, where traditionally the Danish monarchy was supposed to have originated, and where Harald Blue Tooth had set up a monument in memory of his father Gorm the Old and his mother Tyra Danmarksbod who built the great wall known as the Danevirke. Clearly Sven was very proud of this place. But all the many hundreds of Thorfinn's men could hardly accompany their betters on this trip. so Paul and Erland, with Farquhar, were left behind to organise boat-races, rowing contests and other diversions out in the fiord, well away from the town — MacBeth for one not entirely sanguine as to results.

Jellinge proved to be interesting, with its standing-stones and runic inscriptions — although most of the alleged earlier links with the royal house were patently imaginary. Even Thorfinn however forbore to point this out to Sven, who as High Priest as well as monarch was cheerfully enthusiastic about it all.

On their return journey, long before they reached Roskilde all could hear the noise. The sports and races were evidently over and the Orkneymen back in town, and celebrating, presumably victorious. If the night before had been wild, this was doubly so, with smoke already rising from some of the fiord-side warehouses and what amounted to almost set battles going on in the streets.

Thorfinn did not seem greatly perturbed, but Sven and his people did.

MacBeth drew his brother aside. "Thor," he said urgently, "if you wish to keep that governor's commission in your pocket, I would counsel you to get your men out of the town and back to their ships forthwith. Aye, and sail thereafter! This is too much."

"It is but high spirits, man. This mead they make here is heady stuff."

"I will tell Sven so — that they are not used to it. But go you — or our journey here will have been wasted . . ."

So a vigorous hour or so followed, blowing horns, breaking up fights, clearing ale-houses, haranguing, threatening direst consequences, and herding tipsy Vikings back to the jetties. Also, on MacBeth's part, apologising to their hosts; and on Thorfinn's, unfairly berating his sons, who had proved quite incapable of controlling the crews.

For once his brother took MacBeth's advice and sailing orders were broadcast — although it meant lying up in the fiord over-night somewhere, for few ships' companies were in a state to put to sea. Farewells therefore, with Sven and his mother, were somewhat abrupt and hurried — but it was noticeable that their hosts made little attempt to restrain them.

In the early June evening, then, the flotilla was heading raggedly northwards into the fiord, this time lacking all escort. Tuneless if vehement and unco-ordinated singing, so different from the rhythmic rowing chants, echoed across the calm waters from the longships — but none from the shore.

"The Danes will not soon forget the visit of Thorfinn Raven Feeder — even though they will scarce remember the King of Scots, I think!" MacBeth observed grimly to Abbot Ewan as they looked back. "Sven will be considering anew whether he has been wise in this of the governorship."

"Perhaps," that grave man acceded. "But I think not. I judge him rather to be well enough pleased with himself. Over all."

"How that?"

"Because while the Earl Thorfinn considers that he has won the day in this matter, got what he wanted — so does King Sven. For now Thorfinn of Orkney has admitted Sven to be his king, himself only a governor under him, a vassal. He may not see it so, but Sven does. So now he can claim not only Iceland as his, in name, but Orkney also. Something even Canute could not do!"

"So-o-o! Yes. Yes, I see it. Save us — you could be right!"

"So who wins, my lord King?"

"I do not know. But . . . we will not mention this to my brother meantime, I think, friend Ewan!"

They lay overnight at the far end of the fiord narrows, and sailed heavily for the open sea at first light. As they passed out between the twin horns of the Isefiord's mouth into the Kattegat, looking back they saw the Jarl Einar's fleet lined up far astern. No cheers crossed the water, to send them on their way.

20

THE VOYAGE TO Rome took thirteen days. Although it was usual for shipping to follow the coastline where possible, at a safe distance, there was nothing like that about Thorfinn, and he headed straight out across the Norse Sea, south-westwards. Indeed, after the low Jutland coast faded behind them at the Ness of Hirtshals, they did not see land again until the equally low-lying Friesian Islands were sighted two days later, after much rowing to sweat the ale and mead out of the Viking pores, for now they were fairly consistently heading into the prevailing winds, light as these were at this season.

Thereafter they skirted the Flanders, Normandy and Breton coasts until, turning almost due southwards between Cap de St. Mathieu and the Isle of Ushant, they could leave all land again for a further two days, across the Sea of Gascogny, noted for its storms. But the summery weather held, the light westerly airs on their quarter now, aiding the rowers, and they sighted the Galician mountains of the Kingdom of Leon sooner than Thorfinn had expected.

After Cap Ortegal, heading ever more directly southwards, they went no less expeditiously but rather more warily. Hitherto Thorfinn had been supremely confident that none would be so unwise as to challenge or seek close contact with any flotilla displaying the dreaded emblem of the Raven Feeder. Now however they were nearing the Moorish lands, and after Leon they would be skirting the great Caliphate of Cordoba and the Emirate of Granada for three or four days, and these fierce Islamic infidels might not know what was good for them, the Berbers in especial. But although they saw much shipping, their tight group of longships was not assailed nor even approached.

By the time that they turned eastwards at last, beyond Cap de St. Vicente, it was their eighth day at sea, and the men were much in need of a spell ashore. But Thorfinn was for once concerned that his high-spirited crews should not cause any disturbance to the local people in these Moslem territories, as they were so apt to do, which could result in a fleet of Barbary galleys descending upon them. So they followed round the great Gulf of the Kadis until they found a chain of small islands off the Algarve shore, only scantily inhabited by sardine fishermen, and here they landed for half a day and a night. Unheard of, they paid for all they received — or at least Thorfinn and MacBeth did — however much it went against the grain for the Vikings. MacBeth was interested to find that the folk were of the Celtic race, relics of the older people before the Iberians and the Moors.

They sailed again next day, leaving no animosity and with no call for reprisals.

Now they approached the famed narrows of the Jebel Tarik, where Iberia came to within nine miles of Africa, and a mighty rock dominated the Straits of Hercules. The passage of this was, of course, the key to the entire Middle Sea, for entry could be closed at will by the Moorish Caliph and his Kadis, or the

Berber pirates — hence Thorfinn's unlikely caution hitherto. A close-knit and strong squadron such as theirs was unlikely to be assailed or even forced to pay toll, unless the local authorities on either side had been alerted previously and gathered sufficient strength to challenge them.

In the event, they passed the straits without incident, quite close under the towering 1500-feet rock with its powerful Moorish castle, although two or three feluccas and other strange-looking craft came near enough to inspect them carefully. But the fierce aspect of the longships, their bristling barriers of shields, gleaming armour and large numbers of men in evidence, perhaps even the confident singing, kept them all at a discreet distance.

Now they had a direct sail of almost one thousand miles north-eastwards to their destination. With the breeze fairly consistently westerly, sail was the operative word and rowing not usually necessary — which was a welcome relief, for now it was warm, with a heat few there had ever before experienced. So the men were often able to laze through the sun-filled days — shorter days however than in their own northern summers, for here the sun sank earlier and rose later — as they drove through the intensely blue waters, out of sight of land almost wholly, save when they passed sundry islands, large and small. Oddly, they made their greatest speed during the evenings and mornings, for when the sun sank and before it rose to any height, it was surprisingly cold, and the men were glad to row. Despite the lazing, a sharp look-out was kept, all the time, for the Barbary coast was none so far to the south, haunt of more corsairs and pirates than the rest of the world put together; and these could unite to form major fleets. But though they saw much shipping, and not a few craft which less formidable groups would have been well advised to steer clear of, nothing sought to interfere with the longships. Possibly the fame of the Vikings had reached even the Middle Sea.

The fourth day beyond Jebel Tarik they sighted lofty mountains ahead which Thorfinn claimed to be the heights of Corsica or Cyrnos. Entirely confident as to his own navigation, he declared that there were in fact two great islands here, separated by a narrow strait, the southern one, called Sardinia, somewhat less high, although larger. He aimed to sail between them. As they drew nearer, many even of his most trusting companions began to express the opinion that they were off course, that there were no islands ahead but a major land stretching in a vast barrier of mountains as far as eye could see north and south blocking their way. But the earl had infinite faith in himself and sure enough presently what had seemed to be a vast bay narrowed into what was practically a funnel between two land-masses — the Strait of Bonifacio. With the sun setting behind them they passed through into the Tyrrhenian Sea, Thorfinn almost beside himself with satisfaction. Rome, he assured, was now directly ahead about 150 miles. They would be there this hour next day. Had any of them ever heard of so able a navigator?

Actually pride had something of a fall, for next afternoon when they did make their final landfall, in unsuitably hazy weather, they came upon a most flat and dull coastline with no major features to guide them. Rome was supposed to be built on seven hills, but nothing like a hill could be seen up or down that level seaboard. There should also be a great river estuary, the Tiber, Thorfinn complained; but although they beat up and down the coast for some hours, they could see nothing of the sort, not even a discoloration of the water. At length, behind a low headland, they put in at a fishing-haven of small white houses, beached boats and drying nets. The folk were distinctly alarmed at the descent of the tall, fair-haired strangers, and either backed away into the vineyards clothing the slightly rising ground behind, or shut themselves into their houses. But one old crone in black, drawing water at a well, seemed fearless, indeed cackled at them derisively when Thorfinn spoke to her, asking where they were in very bad Latin. MacBeth tried, with no better result. But Martacus of Mar managed to get the word Roma across to her, and this produced hoots of scorn at their ignorance but a gnarled finger pointing definitely southwards. When they tried to discover how far south they had to go, however, they achieved nothing. Thorfinn declared that the tidal flow in this Tyrrhenian Sea must have set them grievously northwards.

They sailed on down what was presumably the Latium seaboard, now amidst much coastal shipping.

It certainly seemed no inspiring approach to the capital of the western world, a flat coastal plain of extensive marshes lifting only very gradually to the most modest of hills, scores of miles of it. To men used to the dramatic shores of Scotland and the Orkneys, of mountains and cliffs and skerries and sea-lochs, it was all a grievous disappointment. It was only after two hours of rowing that the setting sun's levelling rays lit up

274

for them what appeared to be the mouth or mouths of a greater river than any they had seen hitherto; and since many fishing-boats and other small craft were homing into this, the chances were that it was the Tiber, Rome's famed river. Certainly the ground rose to rather more recognisable heights some miles inland here. There was no real bay.

As they steered in, and the other shipping drew heedfully aside to give the formidable strangers passage, they could see two squat stone towers or beacons set on headlands, no doubt marking the entrance to the main channel.

A mile or so up, on the south side, they passed the vestiges of the abandoned harbour and town of Portus, which had succeeded the greater Ostia, as the port of Rome when the river silted up and the sea receded. Now both were only ruins. The sluggish river wound and twisted through the extensive marsh-lands, its waters foul, its banks black mud. In creeks opening off were drab little communities crouching amidst the towering but crumbling masonry of great buildings, now only wooden shacks on piles and stilts, presumably fishing-hamlets. A sort of miasma hung over all in this high summer season. Presently another arm of the river, almost as wide as their own, joined on the north. Evidently the Tiber had two mouths.

"They say that the Roman legionaries hailed our Tay as a second Tiber!" MacBeth commented. "They must have lost their wits, or been pining for home out of all understanding. Although perhaps it improves higher."

Darkness overtook them, and with navigation uncertain, they pulled into a shallow creek to anchor. The consensus was that they would be asking for death of fever if they sought to go ashore. If this was the heart of the Holy Roman Empire, they said, then the emperors, the popes or for that matter the caliphs and infidels, were welcome to it.

In the morning however, in clearer light, they began to see further and better, with a modest range of hills on the eastern horizon and great ruins multiplying everywhere. Along the riverside and stretching as far inland as eye could see the ruins proliferated, the wrecks of mighty structures such as none of the newcomers had ever seen, pillars and columns, tombs and colonnades, towers, temples, plinths, statues, bridges, canals, aqueducts, stretches of stone-paved highways, all broken, shattered, some in complete isolation, many even rising out of the reedy marshland where cattle wallowed. So this plain had once been very different, reclaimed and drained, splendidly

275

engineered and built upon, but now left abandoned and reverted to its original state. More than mere abandonment, of course, for such havoc in such mighty structures must have been the work of deliberate and furious destroyers, presumably the Vandals, Suevi and Visigoths of whom the story-tellers told. Impressed despite themselves, the Vikings, with their own reputation as destroyers, became less critical, indeed often fell silent in sheer wonder.

Gradually, after some dozen miles from the river-mouth, the ruins as well as growing ever denser began to be neighboured by buildings and structures and houses which were not broken and abandoned, but used and occupied. These displayed a notable variety, from proud palaces and tall churches of stone and what looked at a distance like marble, to huts and hovels of timber and clay and mud, squalor and magnificence seemingly side by side. There were people now, the smokes of fires and many small boats plying the filthy waters.

The longships aroused much interest, even excitement. Probably ships of their size were but seldom seen thus far upstream, their shallow draught unusual. Soon they were rowing into the centre of the city proper, although even here mighty ruins were almost as prevalent as modern buildings.

When they could go no further by reason of a great many-piered bridge spanning the river, below which their masts could not pass, they pulled into stone-lined banks, now much gapped and weed-hung. There were the remains of quays here, broken-down warehouses and a general air of decay. Also an over-powering smell and stifling heat. Although many idlers watched their arrival, children screamed at them and dogs barked, it appeared to be nobody's business to receive them or enquire their business. The visitors looked in vain for the famous seven hills also. There appeared to be a few eminences about the place, covered in buildings, but nothing which could be called a hill, even by Orkney standards, nothing higher than some of the masonry columns and church domes and towers which rose on every hand.

What to do now was not obvious. Clearly Rome was an enormous city, far larger than any community the northerners had ever seen or visualised. They might be nowhere near the Pope's house. Moreover, they were not entirely sure as to who actually ruled the city. The Pope was Bishop of Rome and ruled the Church, yes; but Rome was in theory also the capital of the Empire; and although the Emperor Henry the Third was a

German and lived at Aachen, Charlemagne's city, he might have a governor here. Moreover there were the so-called Papal States, with Rome the principal, semi-independent of the rest of the Empire; but whether the Pope ruled them directly was doubtful. MacBeth had heard of a magnate called the Count of Tusculum who was reputed to be the major secular force here. Just what his position might be was equally uncertain.

Uncertainty was utterly foreign to Thorfinn's nature, to be sure. He declared that they would leave half of their force at the ships, meantime and with the other half march strongly through the streets, and whenever they came across anyone in authority demand to be conducted to the Pope's house, this Lateran or whatever it was called. His brother, who had made up his mind that here in Rome *he* must take the lead, and keep it, if his mission was to be successful, had to concede that at this stage he could think of no better procedure. So leaving Biorn Bow Legs in charge — Thorfinn was not risking his young sons in command again — with strict instructions that even such miserable creatures as these locals were not to be interfered with or aroused meantime, the leaders and some 500 Vikings set off on their march.

It made a strange progress through the most famous city in the world, the stranger for it seeming to be quite oblivious as to their presence. People stared at them, of course, even pointed, hooted and jeered at their odd appearance, ungainly size and fair hair; and they gathered a following of children and dogs. But as far as the Roman authorities were concerned, it seemed that they might not have existed — a new and unflattering experience for the Vikings.

MacBeth was indeed afraid that his brother, in consequence, might make his presence felt by behaviour of a nature certain to attract the attention of the civic powers. Fortunately the appearance of the city itself helped to preoccupy them all. The amazing size of it all, the mixture of grandeur and decay, spendthrift magnificence, shabby and wretched building and sheer grinding poverty and degradation, was everywhere present. The stench was stomach-heaving, the heat all but prostrating for the northerners. Wonderfully paved streets and avenues were deep in refuse, in which ragged children played and pigs and poultry rooted and scratched. The effects of disease and starvation were evident on all hands, in deformed bodies, blindness and hideous sores. Beggars were unnumbered — and indeed the only folk who actually approached the newcomers, with

277

clutching hands and incessant appeals for alms. It was from these, to whom he distributed some small part of the money he had brought with him for the Pope, that MacBeth continually asked, in his stiff Latin, the way to the Lateran Palace. There was little understanding of his speech, or their replies; but the word Lateran clearly was generally understood, and fingers pointed in an easterly direction.

Presently the bemused marchers found themselves on a notably wide and imposing thoroughfare which ran approximately east and west, lined with palace-like buildings, churches, colonnades, more ruins, triumphal arches and statues, but also with the booths and stalls of traders and craftsmen under ragged awnings against the fierce sun. Here were many people of the better-dressed sort, soldiers and innumerable richly-clad clerics. From one of these who understood MacBeth's Latin, they gathered that the Lateran Palace was not far ahead, on what sounded like the Caelian Hill — presumably where, on their right front, the buildings seemed somewhat higher.

Martacus of Mar announced that he had now counted his hundredth church of stone, some obviously converted from earlier heathen temples. The citizens of this Rome must be notably pious. They rounded the vast circular bulk of the Colosseum, unmistakable to all.

It was the presence of armed men in fairly large numbers, in the vicinity of a particularly large and handsome church, which gave them intimation that they had reached their destination. The steps and pillared front of this vast building were being used as some sort of a market, with vendors selling many goods, including candles and oil, fruit and vegetables, and poultry and pigeons in baskets, while the soldiers or men-at-arms lounged or sat around gaming, arguing, or sleeping. There was much coming and going in and out of the wide-open doors of the church itself, with little aspect of worshipful intent.

At sight of the regiment of Vikings, there was at last stir and reaction, with the men-at-arms starting up in some alarm, and a few of the tradesmen actually gathering up their goods and disappearing into the church itself. An officer appeared, in tawdry splendour, to demand their business, in the usual bastard Italianate tongue with the dregs of many other languages than Latin in it. MacBeth's and the others' scholars' Latin explanations were just as incomprehensible to this individual; but a richly vestmented priest was brought out, and communication of a sort was established. This was Saint John Lateran, the mother-church of all Christendom, he told them haughtily. If they had come for penance, atonement and possible absolution, matters might be arranged, at a price.

MacBeth explained that they had come to see the Pope.

The cleric stared. Then turning, he apparently translated this to the officer, who guffawed his mirth.

"His Holiness is not the keeper of some wayside shrine, to be seen of all wayfarers!" they were told sternly.

"That we recognise," MacBeth acknowledged, a hand pressing on his brother's arm warningly. "But, humble followers of Christ as we are, we may not necessarily be esteemed as wayfarers, friend. Or, only of a sort. I am the King of Scots. This is the Earl of Orkney. And here is the Abbot of Abernethy, of the Celtic Church of Scotland."

The other looked surprised, but scarcely impressed. "Has His Holiness been apprised of your coming?" he asked.

"Not by us. How could he be? We have travelled far and fast."

"The Holy Father requires to be apprised before any may have audience."

"Then, Sir Priest, tell us where he is to be found. And we shall go apprise him."

Looking almost amused, in a pained fashion, the cleric pointed to the east, across an open square or paved court, with a fountain and statuary, to what appeared to be the wing of a palatial building.

"That clerk requires schooling!" Thorfinn commented grimly, as they moved across the courtyard.

But now guards and soldiers came hurrying from all directions, as the large numbers of the Viking company descended upon the Lateran Palace and became evident, presumably alerted by the officer who had brought the priest. A group, with other officers, came to bar their way, hands on sword-hilts. Thorfinn's own hand sank to his weapon, as did those of many of his people. MacBeth, on the contrary, raised his high.

"Greetings," he called. "I am the King of Scots come to visit Pope Leo. In peace and friendship. I ask that you conduct us to him."

General incomprehension was apparent. It had never occurred to MacBeth that the Romans would not understand Latin, or at least his sort of Latin, learned from a monkish teacher. Since Thorfinn's was a deal less orthodox, he turned to Abbot Ewan and Martacus. They were proving little more successful when a tall, martial figure came pushing through the throng of

279

excited men-at-arms, an individual in gleaming chain-mail under a white linen surcoat emblazoned on the breast with a black cross surmounted by an ecclesiastical crown, and wearing a small steel helmet with down-pointing nose-guard. This person, clearly authoritative, eyeing the Vikings, gestured to the scowling officers to be silent, and spoke in Norn, the said Vikings' own tongue.

"I am Sir Roger Despard, Captain of the Day in the Papal Guard," he said. "To whom have I the honour of speaking?"

"Thank the good God for a man who can speak a Christian language!" the earl exclaimed. "I am Thorfinn Raven Feeder of Orkney. And this is the King of Scots, my brother."

The newcomer, evidently a Norman — MacBeth recollected now that the new Pope, a German, distrusting Italians, had appointed Norman knights to be his bodyguard — gazed as though he could not believe his ears.

"King . . .?" he said. "King of Scotland? King MacBeth? And, and the Raven Feeder? The Earl? Earl of Orkney?"

"The same. Thankful to discover one here other than a fool or a scoundrel!"

"I am MacBeth, yes, Sir Knight. We have come far to visit Pope Leo. Can you conduct us to him?"

"Lord King — your servant. Does His Holiness know of your coming?"

"He has not been . . . apprised!" MacBeth admitted wryly. He spoke the Norn almost as well as he spoke his own Gaelic. "We would have outsailed any courier."

"Yes. To be sure, Highness. I will conduct you to the Papal Chamberlain of the day. I cannot bring you into the Pope's presence, in person. All audiences must be through the Chamberlains. If you will come with me." He looked at the Viking regiment. "These, I say, should go to the barracks of the Guard." He pointed southwards, to the rear of the vast palace area, and jerked a command to the officers. "They will receive refreshment. Highness, will you and the earl follow me?"

The Norman, a well-built youngish man apparently, though his features were hard to distinguish behind the helmet and nose-piece, led them round to the east front of the Lateran, where something of its enormous size became apparent. Never had any of them conceived of so large a building. It stretched before them seemingly endlessly, more like the side of a lengthy avenue than any single edifice, with its arches, pillars, pediments, architraves, tympana and sculpturings, its glazed windows by the hundred, its fronting of terracing, fountains, balustrades and statuary.

"Is all this, this construction, the Pope's house?" Thorfinn demanded. "What is it for? Who can occupy all this?"

"There are said to be over five hundred chambers in the Lateran," their guide informed. "I believe it — although I have not seen a tenth of them.

"When I was in Rome before, I saw the Pope with a deal less trouble," Ewan said. "It was not here, but at the Castle of Sant'Angelo. A mighty building, but less large than this. I cannot see what a man of God requires with so many and great houses."

"His present Holiness occupies only a few modest rooms in one corner of the Lateran," Sir Roger said. "He is a man of simple tastes."

His hearers looked disbelieving.

They passed a number of fine and ornate entrances, all guarded by armed sentries, until they came to the greatest portico of all, with a flight of wide but shallow steps leading up to it, flanked by statuary. Curiously, nearby, standing isolated, was another stone staircase under a sort of pillared canopy, with well-worn treads leading up to nowhere.

"That is the Scala Sacra, the steps of Pilate's palace. Brought from Jerusalem," Despard mentioned. "Up those our Saviour climbed to judgment."

The visitors gazed, silent. Ewan had not been brought to see this before.

The Norman led them up to the portico and into a huge and lofty vestibule, its domed ceiling gloriously painted with saints and angels, its walls marble, its floor tessalated in black-and-white. This magnificent place seemed to be used as little more than a passageway for clerks, functionaries and servitors, although it was larger and more splendid than any hall the northerners had ever seen. Here, after ordering wine to be brought to them, Sir Roger left, to go inform higher authority of their presence.

They had a lengthy wait, which set Thorfinn fretting — although wine and cakes did arrive for their refreshment. But in time Despard came back with a tall stalking crane of a man, attended by a secretary and two acolytes, a sour-faced cadaverous individual in a long robe, richly jewelled and a tiny skull-cap, who eyed them critically. The Norman introduced him as the Cardinal Deacon Giovanni Faranelli, Chamberlain of the

Day, and referred to him respectfully as illustrissimo. After due inspection, this prelate thrust out a beringed hand towards them, at face level. When there was no reaction from the visitors, Sir Roger murmured, in Norn, that it was the custom to kiss the Cardinal's ring.

Thorfinn snorted. "Not where we come from!" he said. "We reserve our kissing for the women!"

His brother inclined his head, but made no other move. Frowning, the Cardinal withdrew his hand. He said something in the Roman tongue.

"We speak only Church Latin, Illustrissimo," MacBeth said. "I am the King. We have come far to speak with the Pope. Will you inform him of our arrival? He has already seen Abbot Ewan, here. Some months ago. He sent us invitation to come."

The other coughed. "What is your present business with the Holy Father?" he asked flatly.

"That is between himself and us. But *he* knows, in part. It is important. And concerned with Holy Church."

"It is necessary to say more than that. Many say His Holiness has invited them. He does not grant private audience save in especial circumstances and at his own command." The Cardinal Deacon had a rasping voice.

MacBeth's own voice rasped a little. "Does His Holiness ignore the visits of monarchs from other lands?"

"Monarchs are as humble as other men in the sight of Almighty God," the prelate reminded sternly.

"Ah — is that the way of it? But Pope Leo is a man himself, is he not? And therefore equally humble. As are even you, sir — although you call yourself illustrious! And it is not Almighty God we seek in audience!"

Sir Roger bit his lip, looking unhappy. Catching MacBeth's eye, he shook his head slightly.

Thorfinn addressed the Norman. "Tell this old crow that we have not come thus far to stand chaffering with nobodies! I have a thousand men with me, and am named the Raven Feeder. Remind him. Perhaps he will understand *that* language!"

Despard cleared his throat. "That would be unwise, my lord earl. Here, all is done according to strict rule, custom."

Thorfinn grinned wolfishly. "I shall tell that to my heroes!" he promised. "And we shall see!"

In agitation the young knight turned and spoke quickly to the cardinal, in his own tongue, at some length.

The older man did not alter his sour expression. But after a pause he spoke, in Latin. "I shall inform His Holiness of your presence." And turning about, he stalked stiffly off. After a moment's hesitation, Despard hurried after him.

"These miserable churchmen require to be taught manners!" Thorfinn declared loudly. "Perhaps we should offer them some small demonstration! Their soldiery are not fit to sweep out cow-sheds! We could have this city in our hands in an hour or two!"

"Perhaps — and find yourself excommunicated an hour after!" MacBeth reminded. "That is their power, their sanction. It need not greatly concern me, since I am not of their Church. But you are, Thor — after a fashion. Would it suit you to be excommunicate, Brother?"

"Tcha! Words! Mummery! I would trouble more over a sore tooth!"

"It would relieve all men, all of this religion, of their duties, agreements and commitments towards you, man. All be debarred from dealing with you. On pain of excommunication for themselves. As Sven Estridson! The Icelanders would rejoice in that I think."

His brother eyed him blankly, and fell silent.

They had another prolonged wait. Their impatience mounted. It was Abbot Ewan who suggested that they might go outside and inspect the Pilate steps while they waited. There were other relics here at the Lateran, too, he had heard, when he was in Rome before. There was reputedly a fragment of the True Cross. And somewhere what were alleged to be the skulls of Saint Peter and Saint Paul. In the Church, probably . . .

Since anything was better than this standing waiting like mendicants, they trooped out into the blinding sunlight. And it was on the worn steps that their Saviour had once trod that, humbled and in awe for the moment at least, they were found by Cardinal Faranelli and Sir Roger, presently.

"Despite inconvenience, I have informed His Holiness," the prelate said, thin-lipped. "He is prepared, of his clemency, to grant you audience. In two days time. At the hour of noon."

"Two days . . .!" MacBeth exclaimed.

"In two days, yes. And you are much favoured."

"Does he say two days?" Thorfinn shouted. "God's Wounds — do I hear aright? This, this German clerk will keep us waiting for two more days! This is not to be borne! He will see us now, I say, or he will learn the price he pays for insolent delay . . .!"

"That is impossible, my lord earl!" Despard interjected, in

major alarm. "The Holy Father is at his devotions. He cannot be disturbed further. Each day he prays long. For Christendom, all Christendom, for Holy Church, for all men. And he has many duties, meetings, councils, other audiences . . ."

"Not with the Raven Feeder and the King of Scots, I tell you!"

"His Holiness has made the decision, my lord. We cannot go back to him. In debate. It is impossible. None may constrain the Pope . . ."

"As to that, we shall see!"

"Lord King." Despard turned to MacBeth. "Do you not see? To make trouble now will not serve your cause. For whatever you have come to see him. If it is important enough to bring you here, surely better to wait a day or two than to ruin all?"

The Abbot Ewan spoke briefly. "He speaks sense."

"Yes, Thor — they are right," MacBeth said. "We gain nothing by losing patience now. Two days will pass. We would wish to see this Rome and its wonders. We shall see it first, instead of after. I would not throw away my kingdom's weal for two days."

Seeing his opportunity, Sir Roger went on urgently. "His Holiness sends you greetings. And meantime, he puts the Clemente Palace at your disposal. Near the Colosseum. You are his guests. It is large. He knows that you have many men. All will be provided for. He has commanded me to remain with you. To see to your comfort and entertainment. It will be my pleasure . . ."

Slightly mollified, the visitors were preparing to accept the situation with better grace when the cardinal, who had been standing by with disapproving expression, spoke again, in Latin.

"Gifts," he said. "Gifts for His Holiness should be presented *before* audience. That is the custom."

"Gifts . . . ?"

"It is the custom for suppliants and visitors to bring gifts for the Holy Father." The prelate raised two fingers over them in a sketchy gesture which might have meant anything, and left them to re-enter the palace.

"Fiend sieze him — sieze all of them!" Thorfinn had gathered sufficient of that to understand. They had indeed broughts presents for the Pope. MacBeth had brought a gold loving-cup and a handsome enamelled mazer, also a chestful of coin, for he had been told that at Rome a fair supply of money might gain more, and more swiftly, than many fair words; and his brother had brought a white bear-cub — which, however fetching, had been a considerable nuisance throughout the voyage, requiring an inordinate amount of fish. They had scarcely expected their offerings to be solicited so openly and peremptorily, however.

Despard again sought to explain. The exchange of gifts was traditional, he pointed out, arising from the early Christians' offerings to their priests, and to help pay for the Elements of the Mass. But of later years advantage had sometimes been taken of the custom to insinuate gifts of a different sort, with intent to insult or injure the Pontiff, even items treated with poison. So now inspection had to be made beforehand. More-over, the young man added with a smile, it had in fact become customary to bring along also a gift for the introducing official, the Chamberlain of the Day!

Sending for the Viking bodyguard from the barracks, they assembled in the courtyard between the mounted statue of Marcus Aurelius and the tall Egyptian obelisk of Thotnes — which Sir Roger said was the highest in the world, brought from Thebes. Then they marched off back whence they had come for some way, along the broad avenue between the Capitoline, Caelian and Aventine Hills which, they learned, was called the Via Sacra, or Sacred Way. Before they reached the Colosseum again, with the great triumphal arches of Trajan and Constantine, another square opened, here called a forum or piazza, and off this was another fine church, St. Clemente's, erected apparently over an ancient Mithraic temple. Behind this were the quarters assigned to them, a long rambling range of buildings, part magnificent, part shabby and indeed semi-ruinous. It was certainly sufficiently commodious for their great numbers, and the Norsemen took it over with the cheerful expertise of hardened campaigners, with neither respect nor complaint — but already on the look-out for women. Roger Despard said that the Normans' own quarters and barracks were nearby, and that he would have provender, cooks, blankets and the like sent along at once.

Thorfinn despatched a party to bring most of the remainder of his company from the Tiber-side, leaving only a small guard on the ships.

So, although they were somewhat reluctant at first to admit it, commenced an enjoyable interlude for the travellers, a holiday indeed — which, truth to tell, when the two days'

285

interval was up, none were so eager to see ended. There was so much to see and experience in this, the greatest city of the world, awe-inspiring even for those not easily overawed or particularly interested in history and antiquities. Despard made an attentive and knowledgeable guide, and the leaders of the northern party grew quite attached to him as a likeable young man. He brought some of his Norman colleagues to aid in conducting them round the city — for sightseeing could scarcely be done by the thousand — and these proved friendly also, and informative. Of course these knights were themselves of Norse extraction, as their name indicated, descendants of the Vikings who had settled in northern Gaul, even though their blood was now much mixed with that of the Franks.

MacBeth was more interested in the sightseeing than was his brother, and most of the Vikings, and with Farquhar, Martacus and Abbot Ewan was happy to visit so much that he had heard of and more that was unknown to him. They saw the circular papal castle of Sant'Angelo, fortress of Rome, formerly the Tomb of Hadrian, on the Tiber; the most splendid church of all Rome's 300, Saint Maria Maggiore; the Campus Martius, or Field of Mars; the Mamertine Prison at the foot of the Capitoline, really a deep vaulted well, where Saint Peter traditionally had been incarcerated; the famed Catacombs, also underground; the Colosseum itself, with its breathtaking magnitude, with stone seats for 50,000; and scores of other features too numerous almost to absorb and memorise. The great engineering works, aqueducts, sewers, fortifications, bridges and walls, much interested them and were an eye-opener as to what could be done with stone, to visitors from a notably stone-rich country.

But it was not all sightseeing, in hot and trying conditions. MacBeth especially had long discussions with Despard and the Normans, and learned a lot that was valuable to know, and not only about Rome and the Popes. As a soldier and a ruler he was especially concerned with the military skills and theories of these Norman knights, whose expertise in the arts of war was renowned — and which accounted for their employment here as the papal bodyguard. Their cavalry tactics particularly interested Macbeth, for he had always been very much aware that mobility in warfare could frequently be the deciding factor, and he recognised the effect on morale of horsed fighter over foot, something little considered by either the Norsemen or the English. Indeed, so thoroughly did he question them on this subject, that the Normans offered to provide a demonstration of cavalry and knightly skills and tactics, in the cool of the second evening, on one of the many grassy open spaces of the Caelian Hill. This proved to be an exciting and valuable occasion, something of a tournament, with mass and individual displays of combat, horsemanship, manoeuvres and weapon-handling, by the steel-clad knights and their practised and armoured mounts. MacBeth there and then decided that he must introduce trained cavalry into his army, somehow.

He sought more information, too, about Pope Leo himself — whom clearly Despard admired. He was a German of Alsace, named Bruno of Egisheim, and had been Bishop of Toul when the Emperor Henry the Third selected him for the papal throne after forcibly deposing three Popes. The papacy had, of course, been in a scandalous state of decadence for long, especially in the 1030s and 1040s, election obtained by bribery, intrigue, violence, even murder. In less than one hundred years twenty-eight Popes had died by poison, strangulation or cold steel. Popes had been paraded on asses through the streets with their noses and tongues cut off. One, Formosus, had managed to die in his bed but months later was dug up, made a mock of by his successor, and his corpse thrown into the Tiber. Benedict the Ninth had been only twelve years old when elected. And at one time there were three Popes in Rome. The Holy Roman Emperor, Henry, had at length been forced to act, and in 1048 the tough and ascetic Bruno had been installed as Bishop of Rome under the name of Leo the Ninth, charged with the enormous task of cleaning up the Holy See and restoring its authority. In the two years he had achieved much; even though there was still more to be done. Bribery was now practised only secretly by senior churchmen, corruption was greatly reduced, immorality no longer countenanced and open, and a measure of austerity introduced into the huge papal establishment. Moreover the city itself had benefited, there was less tyranny and oppression, and the poor aided and cherished in some degree. Leo was apparently much concerned over the poor, for he came of humble stock, and the surest way to his heart was through charity to the downtrodden, Despard declared.

MacBeth was interested in this. He said that he had been advised that he must be prepared to hand over money, much money, to obtain satisfaction from any Pope; but this sounded otherwise? The Norman agreed that money was always useful in Rome, as elsewhere; but that if he distributed some part of his treasure to the poor, first, the Holy Father would quickly get to hear of it, and it might well be better spent than in greasing the palms of greedy intermediaries.

So, in their movements about the city, MacBeth made a point of distributing his largesse and, since he had only a day or two to do it in, in princely fashion — which produced its own inconveniences and Thorfinn's scorn. Moray was the richest mortuath in Scotland, and he had considerable wealth, apart from the national treasury, which was usually empty. He had, in fact, made little differentiation between the realm's gold and his own — to the benefit of the former.

So it was in a distinctly different frame of mind that the three of them, MacBeth, Thorfinn and Ewan, presented themselves at the Lateran Palace again a few minutes before midday on the Eve of Saint John the Baptist, Sir Roger again in attendance. This time another cardinal, one Guido Scelba, was waiting to receive them, and they were conducted, without delay, along what appeared to be miles of statued corridors, through marble halls and ornate painted reception-rooms, to the audience-chamber. Here, between ranks of cardinals, bishops and other clerics, they were led by their Chamberlain of the Day towards the papal throne at the far end of the noble apartment, on its three-stepped plinth, where a burly figure sat, a plainly-clad friar at one shoulder and a line of Norman knights behind.

Leo, the only man sitting in all that company, was unremarkable in face as in person, a thick-set, red-faced individual with a fringe of greying beard, blunt peasant features but small shrewd eyes. He wore a gorgeous cope stiff with gold and precious stones, and a mitre much taller than the Celtic type, round the base of which was a jewelled tiara. The man at his shoulder was very different, a lean and sallow ascetic with burning eyes, dressed in a simple hooded dark robe of wool, with a leather girdle, no doubt the Cluniac monk Hildebrand of Tuscany whom Ewan had told them was the Pope's right hand and whom he had brought with him from Germany, a zealot for reform and strict discipline, largely the power-behind-the-throne indeed.

Some distance off Cardinal Scelba halted and announced them. "Pilgrims to kneel before the Throne of Grace," he intoned, in Latin. "The King of Scotland, by name MacBeth. The Count of Orcady, by name Thorfinn. And the Abbot of the Erse Communion, by name Owen. They prostrate themselves before Your Holiness."

The three visitors remained notably upright, bowing in differing degrees, Thorfinn scarcely at all.

"Welcome to the Holy See, my sons," the Pontiff said. He had a slow, deep voice, almost guttural.

They moved closer to the foot of the three steps, and so stood, flanked by their escort. Despard whispered again.

"It is customary to kiss His Holiness's toe."

MacBeth remained unmoving, expressionless; but his brother growled, in the Norn, "Customary for mice, perhaps — not men!"

The Pope spoke — and, to their surprise, in the same Norse tongue. "None would mistake you for mice, my northern friends! Bears perhaps, but not mice!" He smiled faintly. "The Celtic Church abbot I remember."

Thorfinn looked a little taken aback. MacBeth bowed again.

"Your Holiness, we greet you," he said. "And rejoice that you can speak our tongue. We have come far to see you. On your own invitation. Brought by the Abbot Ewan, here. We have waited these two days, patiently. Enjoying your hospitality. We are now glad to see your face."

"Then I hope, King MacBeth, that I do not gravely disappoint. I am but a poor simple man, and unworthy. But my office is otherwise. The kissings and trappings are not for myself, but for the Lord Christ's Vicar on earth."

MacBeth inclined his head but did not comment on that.

"Your faith does not accept my office, I am told, my son? Yet you come to visit me. And have brought notable gifts, which I gratefully accept — for Holy Church. The little bear I have called Peter — who was also interested in fish!" The flicker of a smile again. He still spoke in Norn. It was not dissimilar to some of the North German dialects, of course. Apart from Hildebrand presumably, who although an Italian had long lived in Germany, and the Normans, none other there would be likely to understand what was being said.

"We accept Your Holiness as Bishop of Rome. Which is the greatest see in Christendom. And acknowledge your great power in many matters," MacBeth answered carefully.

"I understand. And it is that power which you wish to invoke, I think?"

MacBeth paused, and then nodded. "You speak plainly, Holiness. As well as in our northern tongue."

"I am a plain man, Sir King. As I recollect my conversation

289

with your good abbot, you wish me to support you, as against my own bishops?"

MacBeth looked around him. He had hardly expected to have to enter into any exposition of the historical and ecclesiastical situation between Galloway and Northumbria before a hallful of prelatical watchers, even if most would not know a word that he was saying. He shrugged.

"To remind you, then. I am concerned with peace between my realm and England, between the Celtic Church and yours of Rome. I have maintained that peace for the ten years of my reign. But now the Bishop of Durham and the Archbishop of York are laying claim to the spiritual rule of my province of Galloway. Saying that it was once a bishopric of their Church."

"And it was, my son?"

"It was, yes. But that bishopric died out 300 years ago. The former small kingdom of Galloway has long been part of the Scots realm, and the Roman Church has had no presence there."

"Once a diocese of Christ's Church, always so, my son. It can sleep without dying. So I told this abbot."

"If that is so, equally so is the Celtic Church still the Church of Orkney and Zetland, Holiness. Since its missionaries converted those islands, and long ruled there."

"Ah." The Pope looked thoughtfully from MacBeth to Thorfinn, then up at the monk Hildebrand — who stooped and murmured. Leo listened and nodded, then went on. "I see that you come to bargain, my son. Holy Church, I fear, cannot deal as in the market-place. As to the facts of this matter I shall have to investigate, take advice and consider. But, if you have proposals to make perhaps I should hear them now."

MacBeth nodded. "I propose, Holiness, that when you have considered the matter, you consider this also. That if reason does not prevail over Galloway and the so-called See of Whithorn, I shall be forced to draw the sword to ensure that my realm remains inviolate. And, to be sure, seek my brother the earl's aid — for he governs Galloway for me. We are come here directly from the Court of King Sven of Denmark and Norway, with whom the earl has entered into treaty. England is riven with dissensions between Saxon and Dane, as you will know. I cannot believe that Your Holiness would wish to see the northern kingdoms plunged into war and at each other's throats, over so small a matter. Most of them of the Romish faith."

There was silence.

It was the monk Hildebrand who spoke. "Do you threaten, Sir King?"

"No, I do not. I am a man of peace, as I say. I have not drawn the sword, save against my own rebels, in my ten years as King. If I sought to gain by threatening war, I could do it from Scotland, I would not be here. I have come because I believe that the issues between Christian nations should be settled by reason and honest interchange, not by the sword. And I think that the Bishop of Rome must believe the same."

The Pope stroked his fringe of beard. "I perceive the distinction, my son," he said slowly. "Yes, you have given us much to consider. I shall do so, make enquiry, and communicate with you again. That will be best."

"I thank Your Holiness. But may I remind you that I have a realm to rule? A long distance off. That I have been away from it for too long already. As has the Earl Thorfinn from his islands and Galloway. I fear that we cannot linger for much longer."

"I understand. Although I also have other matters to engage my attention. But I shall not delay unduly. Now — go in peace."

The Pontiff raised two fingers to sketch the Sign of the Cross, and the audience was over.

They were led out by a disapproving cardinal and a wondering Norman.

*　　　*　　　*

In the end, Pope Leo surprised his visitors by the speed with which he acted. Perhaps he was not unaware of the problems involved in having a thousand Vikings loose in his city. That very evening the monk Hildebrand appeared at the Clemente Palace to talk with MacBeth and his colleagues, and came surprisingly well-informed considering the remoteness from Rome of the subject matter and personalities concerned. He proved not an easy man to deal with, being abrupt, assertive and challenging; but on the other hand he was highly intelligent, swift to take a point, and with a clear mind for essentials and for ultimate advantage. Thorfinn he more or less ignored; but clearly he found the Abbot Ewan more to his taste — to whom, in consequence, MacBeth left much of the debating.

They talked well into the night — although Thorfinn soon left them to it — with the Tuscan acutely questioning every contention, making swift acceptances or curt dismissals, demanding, probing, evaluating. MacBeth could not like the man, but he was impressed, almost admiring. When he left them he gave no indication as to what his advice to his master would be; but at least they had gone over the entire scene and situation, and Hildebrand was in no doubts as to what was at stake.

The very next afternoon a messenger from Leo announced that the Pope would grant them private audience that same evening, after the Angelus.

This time Sir Roger conducted the trio not by the great central entrance to the Lateran Palace but round to a small side-door in a wing, and across a quiet courtyard to a small library, fine enough but modest compared with the great apartments they had seen previously. Here a clerk awaited them, and presently they were joined by Leo and Hildebrand only, Despard taking his leave. The Pope had dispensed with cope and mitre and wore only a simple monkish robe and purple skullcap. He greeted them, quietly genial, and they sat around a table, with a flagon of wine.

"My sons," Leo said, "my good friend and counsellor Hildebrand had informed me of your discussion last night and of all that is at issue in this of Galloway and Candida Casa. He has given me his valued guidance in the matter, and we have debated it with care. I have, accordingly, reached certain conclusions. These, I recognise, may not altogether satisfy you, King MacBeth, nor you, Earl Thorfinn. But at least they should go some way towards meeting your problems and wishes."

"We have much confidence in Your Holiness's wisdom," MacBeth said.

"Have you, my friend? I would wish that *I* had! But perhaps between us we can come to the reason you spoke of yesterday. For also I am a man of peace — even though I too will fight for the right, if need be."

They waited.

"You will understand that I have to concern myself also for the needs and honest aspirations of Holy Church in the realm of England, and the rights and mission of my brothers of York and Durham, who look to me for support and wise guidance in Christ. I have not heard their representations in the matter. And they may have intimations which could affect my judgment. But meantime I feel that in the interests of peace between the northern realms, and between your faith and mine, the archiepiscopal see of York should not seek any resumption of the diocese of Whithorn or Candida Casa, notable as are the traditions there. I shall write to my brother of York to that effect."

Leo paused, and raised a finger when MacBeth was about to speak.

"On the other hand," he went on, "I cannot accept that Orkney and Zetland and the other northern isles are not now and for ever part of the Holy, Catholic and Apostolic Church which it is my humble privilege to cherish and sustain. Under no circumstances can I accede that the communion of saints there, part of the archiepiscopal see of Nidaros in Norway, was ever a recognised limb of the Celtic Church of Scotland, or or Ireland. Nor that it could ever be used as part of an unseemly bargain or chaffering. That, my friends, is certain. As the successor of the blessed Saint Peter I will not trade away any single portion of his heritage, in faith or in territory. I see the Galloway situation as different, in that the first bishops in Candida Casa or Whithorn were sent from Lindisfarne, which was an outpost of the Celtic Church."

MacBeth exchanged glances with his friends, seeking to keep his elation from showing too plainly. It was all that they had come to Rome to seek, the Orkney business merely a gesture. Thorfinn was grinning, but Ewan kept a sober face.

"I understand Your Holiness's decision and recognise the reason behind it," MacBeth said, maintaining a level voice. "Since reason, not force, is what we both seek, I see reason here. But, should the Bishop of Durham, of his own decision or because he is constrained by the Earl Siward, seek to take what is wanted, despite your papal injunction — for I believe that Siward the Dane is behind it all — what then? Must we then draw the sword, after all?"

"My son, any man who disobeys a specific papal injunction, be he bishop or beggar, king or even emperor, is liable to the dire penalty of excommunication. Where the peace of Christ's Church is concerned, I should not hesitate to impose such excommunication. Our friends in England will have no doubts on the matter."

Satisfied, MacBeth nodded. "I thank Your Holiness. Also Brother Hildebrand for his good offices. For our part, I see this as a good day for northern Christendom, for understanding between Scotland and the Holy See, for the Celtic and Roman Churches."

"May it be as you say, King MacBeth."

Hildebrand smiled — the first they had seen from that man.

When they rose to take their leave, Leo spoke, in a different voice.

"You are not of our faith — although this Orkney bear is said to be! But will you accept an old man's blessing? You who remembered the poor?"

Unspeaking, MacBeth sank down, then Ewan, then even Thorfinn, however awkwardly. They were all on their knees, at last.

The Pontiff raised his hand over them. "Benedicat . . ."

They sailed for home the next day, before the Vikings got really out of hand. Sir Roger Despard and other Normans were at the riverside to see them off, bringing handsome gifts from the Pope. They parted good friends. MacBeth declared that if he, or others of their kind, ever sought a change of employment, there would be a warm welcome for them in Scotland.

21

DESPITE THE VARIOUS delays, Thorfinn's ..ssessment of six weeks for their journey proved to be only just over a week out, and the travellers arrived back at Torfness on the Eve of the Magdaline in late July. They found all well at Spynie, with no serious problems having arisen, in Scotland at least, in their absence. The Mormaor of Strathearn had died suddenly, but he had never been a potent or very reliable character and his nephew and successor was actually an improvement. Lulach, Prince of Strathclyde, had become involved in what was amounting to a feud with Lachlan of Buchan — and this would have to be stopped. But otherwise all was well. Gruoch was happy to have her husband and son home, but seemed to have thrived on responsibility. Ingebiorg said that they could have stayed away for at least as long again, as she was enjoying herself very well and in no hurry to return to Orkney. Actually, sending home the bulk of his men, Thorfinn stayed on in Moray for another week before departing northwards.

Two days after Thorfinn and Ingebiorg departed, MacBeth and Gruoch set off southwards for Fortrenn, Alclyde and a leisurely tour of the kingdom, before harvest, to let all see that the King was home. They took Lulach with them, advisedly.

They wintered that year at Dunsinane. There had been no overt move by Bishop Edmund of Durham.

It was in March that they heard from Gunnar Hound Tooth that Thorfinn had been ill. He had just returned from Galloway, apparently, and was feasting in his own hall, when he had fallen back off his bench unconscious, blue in the face. He had made a good recovery, with the Countess watching over him like a hen with one chick, and was well again now. Indeed, he was reputed to be dismissing it all as a nonsense, a mere mistake, not true sickness — he who had never known a day's illness in his life. Something he had eaten, undoubtedly. He would have to hang his cook.

MacBeth was inclined to agree with that verdict; but Gruoch, womanlike, was less confident.

An interesting and unexpected echo of the Rome visit reached MacBeth in the spring, in the person of a wandering Cluniac friar, one Odo, a Norman, seeking the King of Scots at Dunsinane. He came, he said, from England, from Peterborough, where the sainted King Edward the Confessor presently held his Court. He had come to Scotland at the behest, not of the King but of a fellow-countryman of his own, Sir Osbert Pentecost, Captain of the King's Norman bodyguard, whom he had brought to England with him after his long exile by Canute in Normandy. Now all Normans were finding life very difficult in England, for the Earl Godwin of Wessex, the King's father-in-law who really ruled the country, like most Saxons had a hatred of them and was seeking to drive them all from the land. Pentecost and the others, indeed, were under notice to leave the King's service, and England, the Norman guard being dissolved, unhappy as was the King-Confessor over it all. Sir Osbert had heard that King MacBeth was friendly towards his compatriots, and interested in Norman military skills and prowess, and now wondered whether he would be prepared to employ some of Edward's former bodyguard? Friars could travel at will, hence Odo's mission.

MacBeth agreed that he was indeed interested — but equally so in learning how such information had reached the Court of the King of England?

Friar Odo explained. One of Sir Osbert's lieutenants was Sir Hugo Despard, whose brother had spoken with King MacBeth in Rome. Sir Hugo had sent a letter to his brother relating the present sorry state of the Norman knights in England and asking whether there might be suitable employment for them in Rome. The answer mentioned the King of Scots.

MacBeth accepted that. He would be happy to welcome Sir Osbert and a number of his colleagues to Scotland. Not as a bodyguard — for which he felt no need — but to teach the Scots useful skills in the art of war. The Normans might come as soon as they wished.

The friar had to point out a difficulty, however. His compatriots were watched all the time, by the Saxons. Earl Godwin was a suspicious man, and he was more or less at permanent feud with Earl Siward the Dane. He desired the Normans to be sent back to their own country, not to go over to his enemies. He would never permit them to travel northwards openly, to or beyond Siward's territories. So, their coming would have to be secret, contrived.

It did not take MacBeth long to decide that the escape must be achieved by sea. The Normans must be picked up on some lonely stretch of coast. It had better be on the Mercian shore, rather than the Anglian. Earl Leofric of Mercia hated his rival Godwin, and, if he came to know of it, would be unlikely to prevent the Normans from sailing, if it was to spite Godwin. A small, fast Scots flotilla would collect them, with Odo acting as go-between.

In the end MacBeth put Farquhar and Martacus in charge of the venture, as good experience for them of independent command — Lulach he could scarcely rely upon, unfortunately. In four galleys they left the Tay a few days later, taking Friar Odo with them. They would drop him by night as near to Peterborough as they could win, then retire northwards some way, to lie off the Mercia coast at an agreed point, out of sight of land by day but moving in at night, watching for signals — say two beacon fires some distance apart — to indicate when the refugee Normans were in position. It was hoped that the business could be arranged and carried out in two or three days. But if anything went wrong and the Normans were unable to make their escape, an alternative signal, perhaps *three* fires, would be given, and the ships would turn and make home for Scotland. A heavy responsibility would rest with the friar, but he seemed to be prepared to accept that.

Gruoch was in a nervous state for the next ten days, imagining all kinds of disaster to befall their sixteen-year-old son's first real responsibility of any importance. But in the event all went according to plan, and the flotilla arrived back in the Tay only a day or two later than anticipated owing to a longer wait off Mercia than they bargained for, to pick up a second group of Normans who had to come from London, in addition to those from Peterborough.

No fewer than eighteen knights had elected to come to Scotland, with their esquires and body-servants. They made an impressive party, although some had had to leave hurriedly without their fine armour, colourful heraldic insignia and panoply of war. Also, of course, their powerful chargers, which could not have been transported in the galleys anyway — so that remounting them would be a problem. Sir Osbert Pentecost, their leader, was a striking figure of a man in his mid-forties who in full armour undoubtedly would require a mighty horse to carry him. Despite present misfortunes he appeared to be of a cheerful disposition. Sir Hugo Despard had come with him, a younger man bearing a striking resemblance to his brother in Rome, but lacking one eye from some wounding. Their companions all gave the impression of being effective, capable and disciplined men, of the sort that were very much to be preferred as friends than foes. Young Farquhar already seemed to be under the spell of their single-minded military dedication. MacBeth imagined that these were men that England could ill afford to lose, and recognised that he should be grateful for the Saxon-Norman enmity.

He feasted them at Dunsinane and installed them meantime in the old fortress-palace on the hilltop there.

The provision of suitable horses for the newcomers was now a preoccupation and priority. Fortunately the problem was eased by the fact that although such animals were not to be found in Scotland, the Normans had their own sources of supply, in Flanders especially, where they bred these great destriers capable of carrying heavily-armoured men, and protective armour for themselves; and the Scots had close trading and shipping links with the Low Countries. It was decided to send a purchasing mission, under Sir Hugo, to Flanders, in the first convenient trading-vessel from the Diseart of Saint Serf in Fife. It would all cost MacBeth a deal of money; but his finances were in fair shape and he looked on the Normans as something in the nature of an investment for the future. One day the Earl Godwin, an old man getting, was going to die, and Harold his heir was of a very different character. Siward then was going to be freed of his danger in the rear, and being the man he was, would almost certainly turn his fierce attention to Scotland. A corps of trained cavalry would then be an invaluable weapon of defence.

Meantime, with neither the King nor Pentecost in favour of idleness, a training area was marked out, near Dunsinane Hill, for the practice and tuition of cavalry tactics, manoeuvres and tourneys — for competition in arms was as good a training method as any. They had to make do with light Scots garrons and dismounted exercises for the time being. To these were summoned many of the younger generation amongst the nobility, chiefs and landed men. Although he took a keen interest himself, MacBeth wished to put Lulach, as tanist and heir-apparent, in nominal command of this development, as a means of bringing him out and into more national prominence. But that moody and withdrawn young man showed little interest and less aptitude, and his half-brother Farquhar was substituted. Pentecost, of course, was really in charge; but the young Scots nobles were not to be expected to take orders from a mercenary Norman knight.

Lulach and his future were tending to become one of the very few points of disharmony between the King and Queen. He was now approaching his twenty-first year, and his coming-of-age would have to be celebrated in some suitable fashion. He had grown into a rather good-looking young man, in a fine-featured way, who looked delicate but was not. But the guarded, wary look of his childhood had never quite left him, although it was now largely hidden beneath an almost permanent air of abstraction, as though he was really hardly with the company he was in. This, needless to say, had caused considerable comment and criticism for the Prince of Strathclyde; and indeed the forthright and impulsive Farquhar had already been involved in an unsuitable fight with a contemporary who had referred to his half-brother as Lulach the Fatuous. The prince was in fact far from fatuous; but he appeared to live in a world of his own, and evidently scarcely a happy one. Nor did he seem to make any effort to make himself more acceptable. His popularity therefore was minimal. It was all a source of considerable distress and worry for his mother; and of anxiety of a different sort for his step-father. For if MacBeth was to die or to be slain, what sort of a king would Lulach make for Scotland?

One day in the autumn of that year, after delivery had been taken of the first batch of Flanders horses procured by Sir Hugo, with a number of suits of armour also acquired, and a trial of the new animals and equipment made on the tourney-

298

ground, the matter of Lulach came to something of a head. The prince had not attended the exercise but, returning to the palace afterwards, a group of the young nobles had met him coming with his falconer from a hawking — he was keenly interested in falcony, more in the birds themselves than in the actual sport. Lachlan of Buchan had made some derogatory remark, Lulach had ignored him, and the new Mormaor of Strathearn, Malpender, had suggested that falconry would not be of much service in defending the kingdom if and when Siward the Dane struck. Lulach had said something brief and dismissive about playing at soldiers, and uproar had followed with both Buchan and Strathearn challenging the prince to armed combat, in the Norman style, to see who did the playing; and young Farquhar had stepped in, as before, to take up the challenge on his brother's behalf. When Buchan had declared that men did not fight with boys, he had been slapped across the face. So next day Farquhar was to fight Buchan, horsed, with lance and sword, in the lists. Friendly bouts were to be encouraged, of course; but there was bad blood here, and Lachlan of Buchan was a difficult man of uncertain temper, and being married to the Princess Cathula, Duncan's sister, was no friend of the present royal family.

MacBeth, when told, was angry, declaring that he would not have the future leaders of his army fighting together in hot blood and childish temper. That was not why he had brought the Normans and their expensive horses and armour to Scotland. He ordered Farquhar to apologise to Buchan for striking him, and told Buchan that there would be no contest and to guard his tongue towards the princes in future.

But this did not solve the basic problem of Lulach the misfit, and that night in their own bedchamber MacBeth and Gruoch debated the matter, and less amicably than was their usual.

"What am I to do with that young man?" he demanded. "This cannot go on."

"Are you called upon to do anything, my dear?" his wife asked, with just sufficient emphasis on the word *you* to make clear her protective mother's role. "He is not of your warrior's mind. But why should he be? He is not your son."

"*I* am no warrior — as well you know. But I have a realm to protect. And I require the heir to my throne to aid not to hinder me."

"The heir to *our* throne," she reminded.

He shrugged. "Does that make any difference? When it is his

299

turn to reign, he will not manage it with falcons! Nor by offending his mormaors."

"He is young yet . . ."

"He comes of age in two months. A grown man. And we shall have to signal that event in some way. God knows what would serve, in these circumstances!"

"I am but two paces from you, my heart! There is no need to raise your voice."

"I . . . I am sorry." MacBeth turned to pace the floor. "It is customary to give a young man some added title and authority, on such occasions. To arrange a marriage, if he is not yet wed or betrothed. But Lulach shows no more interest in women than he does in command or rule or the will to lead . . ."

"He saw sufficient of the will to rule and lead as a child!" she interrupted tensely. "When he watched his father burn that Duncan might rule."

"M'mm. He was only two years. That cannot be the cause on this . . ."

"It has affected his whole life. He dreamed of it for years — he still may do so. So terrible a thing . . . !"

"Yes. To be sure. But — that is done and cannot be undone, my love. What are we to do with him? Now. Or *for* him? He is Prince of Strathclyde and Cumbria already. I cannot make him more than that. I had hoped that I might have given him some command in Galloway, under Thorfinn. In especial now that Thor is less well in health. But — can you see it? Can you see either of them working together? Anyway, Lulach would not thank me."

"No, that is not for him." She shook her head. "Not soldiering, not commanding armed hosts. But, see you — some other sort of responsibility, authority, might serve better. I have thought often of this. Being Prince of Strathclyde is merely a style, a title as heir to the throne. It carries no real duties, no lands or wealth. If he was a mormaor, now, with a mortuath to rule? Farquhar is Mormaor of Moray, Luctacus of Ross . . ."

"I cannot make mortuaths out of nothing. And to seek to create a new mortuath anywhere would demand a strong hand indeed to make it other than a mere name. Or, would you have me take Ross away from Luctacus and give it to Lulach?"

"No. Not that. But there is another . . ."

"Atholl? Lulach could never control a hostile Atholl. The Athollmen would crucify him! I have left Atholl in Bethoc's youngest son's keeping, Malmore, since Crinan's death. Whilst his mother, my aunt, lives. He is harmless. His brother should be mormaor now, Maldred . . ."

"Not Atholl either. Lulach would have no right there. But there is another — Fife. MacDuff has abandoned it, and is forfeit, a traitor. I am heiress of Clan Duff, and Lulach my son. He *should* be Mormaor of Fife. Make him so. It might well be what he needs. A territory of his own, for which he is responsible."

MacBeth frowned, and chewed his lip. "See you, my dear — I am *Ard Righ*, High King, yes. But that does not mean that I can make or unmake the lesser kings, at will, like some tyrant emperor. MacDuff is Mormaor of Fife. He may be my enemy, fled the country — traitor, if you like. But he is lawful mormaor. More so than is Maldred mac Crinan, who has never been installed as such by his thanes and chiefs. It is not for me, *Ard Righ*, to topple the order on which our Scots realm is built — but to protect it. Fife is being administered by a council of thanes. I cannot make Lulach their mormaor."

"Or will not?"

"I have managed to work with the Fife thanes. As is necessary. It is a rich and powerful province. To do as you say would much offend them. You know that. We have ruled this kingdom for a dozen years now. You, of all, know how it has to be done."

She was silent.

He eyed her consideringly. "What I might do, what might be possible . . . is to put Lulach in *charge* of Fife. Meantime. Not mormaor but perhaps as a governor. Since none of the thanes is higher than the others, it could be said that Fife requires a master, lacking MacDuff. In the interests of the realm, and the mortuath itself. Indeed that is true. The thanes probably would prefer to have the Prince of Strathclyde placed over them than one of their own number. And one who is heir to Clan Duff. I might make Lulach Governor of Fife?"

"Yes. Yes — that would serve, I think. It would give him responsibility, opportunity to make his mark. To consider the needs of other than himself. There is nothing wrong with his wits. Or his will . . ."

"We could try him. If he shows no interest, there is little harm done. I can revoke the governorship. But he *could* do much there. The churchmen at St. Andrews are showing the way, developing trade and shipping, panning for salt, setting up smoke-houses to cure fish and so increase the trade of fishing. Building boats also. It has been my desire to increase peaceful

301

crafts, and the wealth and well-being of the realm. It must not all be left to the churchmen and merchants. Perhaps Lulach, who mislikes soldiering, would find this more to his taste?"

"Oh, I pray so! I will talk with him, show him how much he could achieve." She paused. "And there is something else, my dear. I have thought of this many a day. Of marriage. A young woman might be what Lulach needs. But he has shown no interest, although I have sought to put more than one in his way. It seems that if he is to wed, *we* shall have to choose his bride. And, with this of Fife, there is one suitable indeed. Malvina nic Gillachrist MacDuff, sister to the Abbot Ewan. She is a pleasing girl and comely enough, daughter of the Thane of Lindores and kin to MacDuff. Such marriage would aid in this matter."

"M'mmm. She is a bonny quean enough, yes. And I would think, good-natured. It might please the Fife thanes. But — have you considered that whosoever Lulach weds will one day be Queen of this realm? Queen-Consort, though not Queen-Regnant. Would this Malvina be suitable for that? Of the stature? Or the rank? There are mormaors with daughters who might look askance at but a thane's daughter."

"She is kin to a mormaor. And a MacDuff. Indeed she is kin to myself, although far out. Can you think of other? More apt?"

He shrugged. "I have not considered it. If only Thor's daughter, young Ingebiorg, was older . . ."

"She is but eleven years! No, one day my love, you may be *forced* to find a new mormaor for Fife. This union would greatly help you."

"And what of Lulach himself? Think you he will find Malvina nic Gillachrist to his taste? If he has *any* taste in the matter!"

"Leave Lulach to me . . ." she said.

22

THE TRAVELLERS EYED the towering cliffs of Hoy, ahead, with mixed feelings. This was not how they had ever anticipated visiting Orkney. They had talked often of coming, but somehow they had never achieved it, for one reason or another, with so much else to be done and a kingdom to rule. And now they had next to left it too late, by all accounts. Thorfinn had been ill again, and although he was now somewhat recovered once more, it was clear that he was no longer the man that he had been, and was liable to take more of these attacks — and who could tell which might possibly be the last? Ingebiorg had sent word that Thor wanted to see his brother and that if they wanted to see *him* again in anything resembling his old self, MacBeth and Gruoch should come soon. That ominous message was not to be ignored.

So here they were approaching the Orcades, in a galley escorted by two of Gunnar's longships, sailing the summer seas in gentle airs, even the Pentland Firth glassy — yet scarcely in holiday mood. Apart from anxiety about Thorfinn, MacBeth was uneasy at leaving his kingdom this summer of 1053 — even though he could return to it in a day's fast sailing. For the Earl Godwin of Wessex had died, leaving a void in the power structure in England, such as Edward the Confessor was not the man to fill; and Siward, after years, could feel free, if so he chose, to turn his fierce face northwards at last, the new Earl Harold and his brothers constituting no threat to his rear. It could be, of course, that Siward would choose rather to seek to fill Godwin's place, and dominate southern England, forgetting Scotland in this new situation. But the Scots certainly could not rely on that. There had been no word of musterings or major movement of armed men from Northumbria to be sure — or MacBeth would never have left Fortrenn. And the summer was more than half over, so that it might seem probable that there would be no attack this campaigning season. But there was no certainty, and MacBeth remained anxious. That Lulach was left in nominal command, in the interim, was scant reassurance — even though, in fact, Glamis, Bishop Malduin and Abbot Ewan were in effective control. But, now of full age, the heir to the throne had to be given his due place and authority. And, to be sure, he had improved, in his step-father's eyes, in the past year. He had married — or rather, acquiesced in marriage to — Malvina of Lindores, at an elaborate wedding ceremony, and the unenthusiastic pair had settled down in apparently mutual toleration in the old palace of Forteviot across Tay, amidst scores of hawks and falcons. There had been no real opposition, on his own part or on that of the Fife thanes, to his becoming governor of that fair province, and he was indeed taking some interest in the great mortuath and its development and problems, although great results were not yet visible. But at least it was all some betterment — and, what was important, Gruoch was enheartened. The rest of the family, Farquhar, Luctacus, Cormac and Eala, all of whom doted on their Uncle Thor, were with their parents on this visit. Lulach had never found the Raven Feeder to his taste.

Their destination was the Brough of Birsay, on the west coast of the Orkneys' largest of sixty-seven islands. Hoy, further south, was the second-largest and much the highest. It was coming up now on their starboard quarter. They were surprised at the dimensions of it. They had thought of the Orkneys as low, flattish islands, rather dull compared with the picturesque and mountainous Hebrides of the west. But this Hoy had quite high, heather-covered hills, and stupendous cliffs that soared to 1000 feet above the sea, precipices of a strange red and golden stone which seemed to glow with its own fire in the sunlight. Stacks and pinnacles rose dramatically from the waves, some slender as the obelisks of Rome, and great caves yawned darkly. Today, although the sea was so calm, the mighty Atlantic swell broke whitely in surging power all along the cliff-girt seaboard. And it was long indeed, so much longer than they had envisaged: and seaboard rather than shore, for on it all they could discern only the one small stretch of beach, the rest all this fearsome palisade of rock, crag and stack. This island, Hoy, MacBeth reckoned, must be all of fifteen miles long. Clearly they would have to revise their notions as to the size of Thorfinn's island earldom. The galley's master told them that the Orkneys, in fact, covered an area of some fifty miles by fifty; and added, with some of the most difficult and dangerous waters for navigation in all Christendom.

They gained some indication of this as they crossed the narrows of the Sound of Hoy separating that island from the south-westerly end of Hrossey, as the Orkney mainland was called. The small isle of Graemsay sat in the middle of this sound, forcing the tide into two still narrower channels. At the height of the rising or ebbing, forced through these funnels, the Atlantic swell could reach as much as twelve knots; and this flow was complicated by the very different levels of the sea-floor between the various islands and the fact that there was an especially deep area at the other side of Graemsay into Scapa Flow, known as the Bring Deep. The result was a roaring turmoil of waters, called here a roost, a mixture of tide-race and overfalls, which quickly had the three vessels tossing and heaving wildly, twisting off course and causing the rowers to labour mightily and exert themselves to extraordinary manoeuvres. If it could be like this in such calm conditions, the travellers were left in little doubt as to what it would be like in rough weather. They were assured that there were hundreds of such roosts in the Orcades.

The succeeding coastline of Hrossey was very different, reefs and skerries and low rocky headlands and bays mile after mile, rising inland by green braes to very modest heights, scattered with groups of what seemed to be tiny farms, a great many of these, their cattle and ponies dotting the land as far as eye could see. This was a populous terrain, then, more so than most parts of Scotland, it appeared — as it must be, of course, to produce the Raven Feeder's thousands of armed Vikings. Not much tilled land was visible, however; these people were herders and fishers and warriors, not tillers of the soil.

For almost two hours they beat up this rockbound coast. Small circular forts crowned almost every headland, strange stone towers, round as bee-hives but tall, windowless, ending apparently in parapets, which the shipmaster called brochs — a name evidently compounded of the Norse borg and the Anglo-Saxon burgh, but clearly duns of a sort. At length they reached a much larger bay than any they had yet seen, more than a mile across, with low ground behind forming a wide gap between the green braes and rolling moorlands. The bay was rock-ribbed like the rest of the coast, and unprotected from the westerly winds and Atlantic seas, although a river entered at its centre. But its northern horn was remarkable for an abrupt rocky islet, really no more than a squat, broad, almost circular table, detached from the mainland by only a narrow belt, rising to perhaps 150 feet, with a flattish top, a most peculiar formation that dominated the whole bay and coast. On its summit was another fort, but not a broch, much larger, with ramparts of earth and stone, clearly an early Pictish strength, within which were many buildings of timber and clay, almost a village.

"The Brough of Birsay," the shipman said.

As the others exclaimed at its dramatic style and position, MacBeth looked puzzled.

"But — where is the anchorage? The haven?" he demanded. "This is as dangerous a landfall as I have seen. Look at those reefs and breakers. In any weather less calm than this, that bay will be a death-trap. And there is no vessel to be seen."

"Wait, you," the skipper advised.

They sailed on, close under the towering rock; but not too close, for it was guarded by its own screen of jagged reefs and skerries, over which the tide boiled whitely. It could be seen that there were the deep black mouths of caves opening into the rock, into which the seas surged. Beyond the stack, northwards, they found only the open sea, for the coast here turned away eastwards at right angles, this Brough Head being in fact the westerly tip of Hrossey.

Now their longship escorts were pulling tightly round to starboard, to head into another and much smaller bay, north-facing, round this side of the detached rock, and entering it through a gap in the savage line of skerries. The galley followed, and then as the escorts continued to row ever further round to starboard, until they were actually facing south-eastwards instead of north, a small hidden inner bay opened, directly under the east side of the stack, protected from every wind that blew, with even a brief shingle strand at its head. This was notably full of craft, longships, birlinns, drawn up in marshalled ranks; and further over to the east, really on another bay of the mainland, they could see a fishing-haven, with more boats, backed by a wide scatter of cabins and cot-houses. Also to be noted, as they entered the Brough bay, were the two ends of a great chain, its centre submerged, plus the winding-gear therefor, on the flanking rocks. The Jarl Eric of Trondheim was not the only one to recognise the advantages of a bolt to his door.

As they drew in to the short stone jetty — carefully, for there was not a lot of room in that tight-packed haven — they could see that a group was waiting to receive them. There had been plenty of time, of course, for they must have been in view for the best part of an hour. None would be apt to creep up on the Brough of Birsay unawares. MacBeth's heart lifted to see there a massive figure towering head and shoulders above all others. Somehow he had been prepared to find his brother if not bed-bound, at least house-bound.

With the galley warped in and the gangway run out, however, Thorfinn did not come striding aboard but waited there on the jetty for his visitors. MacBeth hurried down, and the other called out, "Son of Life — you have been long in coming! Were you hoping that I would save you the trouble?" That was a stout effort, and the grin that went with it almost as of old. But the voice was certainly not, breathless, throaty, lacking body, sufficiently so to slow down MacBeth's pace involuntarily.

"Thor!" he said. And again, "Thor!" And could find nothing else to say at that moment.

The change in his brother was extraordinary, not so much as it were in quantity as in quality. He was as big and massive as ever, indeed almost more so, although perhaps the term bulky would now replace massive. But it was as though the framework within all that bulk had somehow softened, its essential force evaporated. The man was still a giant, still a dominant presence; but the dominance now was by a conscious effort of will, the stature a facade. Nevertheless, if the features had a fleshy look to them, the jowls noticeable, the colouring purplish, the eyes at least were the same, hot, glittering, intensely blue.

Ingebiorg, at her husband's side, came hastening forward to throw herself into MacBeth's arms. "Oh, my dear, my dear!" she said, half-sobbed. That was all.

"Yes lass, yes," he told her, soothingly, stroking her still-yellow hair, and holding her tightly for a moment. "Inge, the strong one!" He released her, and went on to his brother. "So you are on your feet, Raven Feeder? I need not have hurried!"

"Hurried? You!" They grasped each other's upper arms, and their eyes met and held. "But — I am glad to see you, Brother."

Ingebiorg brought Gruoch to him, to be embraced.

"Oh, it is good to see you, Thor," she said. "We have thought of you always, wishing you well. We have plagued the good God on your behalf. You should not have come down to meet us."

"He comes down the hill so that he may travel up again on his new toy — the great bairn!" the countess said, but her voice held a quiver.

The young people, at least, laughed heartily when they perceived the mighty Thorfinn's transport arrangements. A sort of sledge to which a heavy chair was attached, waited at the foot of the steep zigzag track up to the fort, with two sturdy Icelandic ponies harnessed; and to this the earl was led, set-faced. There, Arnor Earl's Skald got him seated, amidst a sudden silence from the watchers, and went to the ponies' heads. Gruoch broke the hush.

"*I* would like to go up in that too, Thor. May I? Can your horses take me also? I grow old, I think."

"Come," he said, almost eagerly. "There is but the one seat. But my knees are not so feeble that they will not support the Queen of Scots!"

So, with his arms round the woman whom once he had

brought fugitive to his half-brother, complaining that she would not wed him, the Raven Feeder was dragged up the stiff incline to his own house. Sundry Vikings looked on, expressionless.

Ingebiorg, on MacBeth's arm, indulged in a few hoarded tears.

On the summit of the Brough, the visitors found a large and comprehensive establishment within the Pictish ramparts, almost a self-contained community, in the Norse style, rather than any conventional castle or palace, centring admittedly around a vast longhouse, but with barracks, stables, kitchens, bakehouses, blacksmith's forge and armoury, brewhouse, horse-mill and warehouses, even a wood-carver's yard. All in stone, clay-covered — for timber was scarce in the islands — with turf roofs. One building which perplexed the visitors, and which MacBeth took to be some sort of covered well-head, proved in fact to be the housing for a deep and wide shaft cut down through the living rock to one of the great caves beneath, where meat and fish was kept stored in the cold. It was provided with winding-gear and a hoist large enough to take men — for the caves had other uses besides storing food. There was also a large underground reservoir, cut out of the rock as at Torfness, for maintaining a water supply should the well be inadequate — another relic of the Picts, who had been not inconsiderable engineers. Over all flew a huge raven banner on a tall staff — to rouse mixed feelings in the viewers.

Everything about that sea-king's eyrie seemed to emphasise to the newcomers, as they settled in, the hopelessly unsuitable and helpless state of its lord. For all here was geared to the active life, to voyaging and hosting and fighting, to hunting and fishing, seal-catching and whaling, boating, herding, cliff-scaling for eggs and the like — none of which Thorfinn the Mighty would ever do again, most evidently. The least exercise exhausted him and left him breathless. He lay most of his time, in fact, on a sort of massive couch with handles, which could be carried here and there about the Brough by four men and, in this summer weather, Ingebiorg explained carefully, spent the days out on the very edge of the cliff, amongst the wheeling seabirds, staring out to sea, ever staring, especially northwards towards Iceland, the sheer longing in his eyes a pain to behold. Sometimes, she confessed, she feared that he might indeed hurl himself over the edge, in his utter and terrible frustration.

It was apparent now, to his guests, how greatly the earl had taxed himself to come down to meet them at the jetty.

That evening, after they had eaten — with Thorfinn only

toying with his food — the brothers talked long into the night, in the famed Orkney summer-dim half-light, with the others retired to bed. The earl had much difficulty in winning to sleep, he confessed. Alone, they need not maintain the attempts at normal converse and superficial bonhomie; but however he felt, Thorfinn at first sought not to allow any sorry-for-himself attitude to show. He was particularly eager to hear about the position in England, especially as regards Siward, whom he still managed to curse with a fair semblance of fervour. The sorrow that Almighty God had not smitten that oafish barbarian as He had seen to smite himself, he asserted — the first real indication of his fought-back bitterness.

"They say that Satan looks after his own sort, Thor!" MacBeth said. "Some have named *you* Satan, in your day. Take it as a good omen if that one has deserted you!"

"What you are saying, man, is that I deserved this? If I did, I could name others, as well as Siward, who deserved it as much and more, yet go free." He had to pant as he said it.

"Perhaps. I do not say it is a judgment, Thor — God knows, *I* dare not, I who slew the King of Scots!"

"That rat! Do you still blame yourself for that? You well served both God and man that day!" His brother mustered a smile. "No, Son of Life — my judgment I brought upon myself. For bending the knee to that German Leo, in Rome! I knew that I would pay for that weakly act!"

"For a Romish churchman of a sort, that is heresy, is it not? At least, His Holiness kept his compact with us. There has been no more from Bishop Edmund, no trouble against Galloway."

"Now that Godwin is dead, Siward will strike — nothing surer, man. He is the strongest man in England now. And nothing the Pope can do or say can stop him."

"Perhaps, being the strongest man in England, he will turn his eyes southwards instead of north? Take Godwin's place, and over-rule Edward the Confessor? The new Earl Harold of Wessex will not stop him."

"He might do that. But if he does, God help *you* afterwards! For then he would be stronger than ever. But he will come for you, sooner or later, brother — be assured of that. When he married his sister to Duncan, he made that certain. He has an old bone to pick with you — and a long memory."

"It may be so. I am doing what I can. I have had all the mormaors to increase and train their forces, to practise swift mustering and movement of men. I have brought a score of

Norman knights from England, to teach my people how to fight on horseback, and other modes of war. We now have a cavalry force led by these, three squadrons of one hundred men, well horsed. Also mounted archers. I keep a close watch on all my borders. This shadow has hung over me for long, Thor. I never forget Siward."

His brother clenched a great fist and beat on his knee. "And I lie helpless here! It is damnable! But you can still rely on my aid, see you. My sons will bring my longships, at your call. Thorkell Fostri is old now, too old for hosting. But he can still see that the ships are ready, supplied, men trained. Harald Cleft Chin, in Galloway, is sound. I plan to send Erland there, soon, in my place. And there is Kalf Arnison, Ingebiorg's uncle, a fine fighter . . ."

"Always I have known that I could rely on you, Thor — and I thank you. Although I have tried to build up a fleet of fighting-ships of my own. Old Gunnar, at Torfness, has been aiding me in this. There are more *Scots* ships than Orkney in Torfness haven today. Although building ships is slow work, for folk little used to it. But—these fine sons of yours? They must be a joy and consolation to you? They are in Iceland now, I understand. How is it with Iceland?"

The earl shook his head. "I could wish that land sunk under the sea!" he said hotly. "Always it has been a plague and a burden to me. Sitting there to the north. Waiting until my back is turned, to raid and harry. Zetland is never safe from them, in especial. And then, when at last I was ready to deal with them as they deserved — this! Governor of Iceland — only once have I set foot on that accursed land since I gained Sven's commission — and even then I was unwell."

"Is it so important? To fret over? For long you scarce thought of Iceland. Before that of Rognvald and Magnus Olafson . . ."

"They stabbed at my back. None does that and fails to pay. Or . . . did! They have grown above themselves of late, those franklins and goden. Up-jumped peasants!"

"They are Norsemen, the same as your own folk. Vikings of a sort . . ."

"That they are not! They are peasants, I say — diggers in the earth, herdsmen, keepers of hens! There is not a jarl amongst them. They fled Norway to escape Harald Fair Hair's taxation. Instead of fighting the tax-gatherers. As we in Orkney did . . ." Thorfinn was gulping and gasping in his indignation.

"That is an old story, Thor. Nothing to concern you now.

310

And your sons will teach them who is governor there now, I have no doubt . . ."

"I do doubt it, man. They are weak, soft! Good lads enough, but lacking spirit, fire. Their mother has spoiled them! *They* will never tame the Icelanders."

MacBeth forbore to point out that his brother had just named the Icelanders as tame peasants, not true Vikings. He was concerned that the other was working himself up into an anger and resentment which could only be damaging to his condition. He sought to change the subject.

"Have you had any further dealings with Sven Estridson?" he wondered.

"Dealings! With that bitch's whelp! No — nor shall I. The creeping snake!"

"Save us — I esteem him better than that, Thor!"

"Then you are a fool! As was I, at that Roskilde. To trust him. He sends messengers to me — to *me*, Thorfinn! For tribute. Tribute for *Orkney*! To the Norse crown . . ."

"That again? But that, too, is an old story."

"The wretch claims that because I am his governor for Iceland, I am his jarl and he my liege lord! Here in Orkney, as well as in Iceland. Have you ever heard such folly?"

"M'mmm. There was, I suppose, always the risk of that, Thor. But so long as he only *asks* . . ."

"I think he may not ask again! He said that I might choose my own tribute, so long as I acknowledged him as overlord. So, the second time, I sent him back my choice of tribute — the head of his messenger! One of these housecarls of his Hird. Wrapped in a raven banner . . ."

"Oh! I . . . ah . . . you did?" It seemed time to change the subject once more. "See you — you have heard that Lulach is wed? To Ewan mac Gillachrist's sister, Malvina. A MacDuff."

Thorfinn was not interested in Lulach. "My heart bleeds for her!" he said flatly. "This of Sven. It is his mother, to be sure, who has put him up to it. She is an interfering vixen, that Estrid. I always said so. God save us from masterful women . . ."

MacBeth came to the conclusion that he was doing his brother no good by staying up and talking with him, in this mood, only getting him the more roused, the more frustrated, the more breathless. He pled weariness, at the next pause, and sought his bed.

The royal family's stay at Birsay was not to be a catalogue of woe, depression and resentments, however. Presumably Thorfinn had worked off his pent-up feelings and anxieties that first night, for thereafter he was on the whole extraordinarily cheerful, and though hardly reconciled to his lot, sought to spare his guests. Indeed, in the week that followed, he organised so full a programme for their entertainment as to all but wear them out. They were taken sight-seeing, visiting other islands and townships, hunting and hawking — for the name Birsay was only a corruption of the Norse *Birgisherad*, meaning hunting-ground — fishing both at sea and in the innumerable lochs, cliff-climbing, cave exploring, even walrus-harpooning. They investigated great stone-circles, the crumbling settlements of ancient peoples, rock-carvings, giants' graves and tumuli, brochs and forts. Clearly there had been age-old settlement here, long before the Norse era; and MacBeth began to wonder if the trumped-up claims for a Scots-Pictish hegemony were less specious than he had assumed. The islands had been heavily populated by an active and far from backward people.

The young folk rejoiced in it all, and even MacBeth, at forty-seven, to some extent found himself renewing his youth. Gruoch stayed more often at the Brough, with Ingeborg, and in consequence saw more of Thorfinn than did the others — but with her he was still male enough to attempt to be the hearty, sex-conscious Viking — which, in fact, wrung her heart more than if he had let his disability run full rein.

The long evenings — for it was never really dark — were a succession of feastings, story-telling, singing, dancing, contests of strength and skill and stamina, almost as taxing as the days' programmes. Viking hospitality was nothing if not thorough.

All but exhausted, as though after a strenuous campaign, MacBeth sat with his brother and their two ladies on the last night of their visit, watching the waves break whitely on the rocks and reefs far below, in the soft silver-gilt memory of the sunset which glowed over all the wrinkled sea.

"What think you of Orkney, then, Son of Life?" the Earl asked, out of a long silence. "You may not see it again. Nor myself, I think."

"Who knows what any of us may see again, or not see, Thor? Even tomorrow's dawn — if you have dawns in these strange parts! But I find your islands much to my taste. I can well see why you love them, you and all Orkneymen. Aye, I could dwell here, myself, pleasantly enough. Perhaps I might yet *have* to — if my enemies could drive me off my throne!"

Gruoch stirred. "Do not speak so," she requested, low-voiced.

"That I do not see, ever," Thorfinn asserted. "You, Brother, will only be *carried* off that throne of yours, I vow. Never leave it. That Stone of Destiny means too much to you, lump of rock as it is."

MacBeth said nothing.

Ingebiorg spoke quickly. "In winter, here, it is very different. Sometimes we cannot win out of the house for days. Cross the threshold. For the wind. Spray covers us, even this high, hiding all prospects. Seas pour over us, shake the rock, thunder in the caves beneath. Seaweed, fish, lobsters, even rocks bigger than a man can lift, fall on us. We cannot hear ourselves speak, at times. There is little snow and frost, but the storms are terrible. And the days only a few hours long."

"They used to make our beds but the snugger," her husband said. "And a woman's body the kinder."

They heard Ingebiorg swallow.

"Bears always sleep all winter, I have heard," MacBeth said, with an attempt at lightness. "But you wake for your Yuletide festival, do you not? Your Up Helly Aa."

"It is not all gales," Thorfinn said. "I have seen winter days so calm that we have heard carls laughing as they herded beasts on the Knowe of Marwick yonder, more than two miles off, across the bay. But I like the storms — man's weather. I . . . still do. I am waiting for a truly mighty storm. To go."

MacBeth opened his mouth to speak, but closed it again.

"It will have to be a terrible one indeed, Thor," Gruoch declared, finding a smile. "To dislodge the Raven Feeder! Or even to flutter the bird that sits on his wide shoulder. Hugin, is it not?"

"Ha! You remember, woman? I thank you."

"It is getting cold," Ingebiorg said. "It is nearly midnight."

"What matters the hour, lass? When we have eternity ahead of us!"

But the women rose.

They sailed in the morning — and Thorfinn was down at the jetty again, to see them off, having left the house on his own, unannounced, earlier. The parting was a strained one.

"You believe what the churchmen say, Son of Life?" he asked, at the end as they gripped arms. "You always have, have you not? The fortunate one!"

"Not *all* they say, Thor. In much I am a doubter, I fear. But where my reason and my inner heart tell me the same as they teach, and more, I believe, yes."

"So — we shall see each other again, Young Brother? One day?"

"I have no doubts of that. And you will be the you that you have made of yourself, here. And I, me — God forgiving us!"

"Aye. So be it. Off with you, then. It is enough. I shall look for you . . . when Birnam Wood comes to Dunsinane . . . !"

23

To THE SURPRISE of many and the joy of the Queen at least, the Princess Malvina of Strathclyde was brought to bed of a son in the late June of next year, 1054. They named the child Malsnechtan. Nechtan was a favourite name for the former Pictish kings — and, in the providence of God, one day this infant might well be King of Scots.

If the actual birth was quietly received, MacBeth made much of the christening celebrations some weeks later, with the dynasty to think of — even if a part of him could have wished that Lulach's line would not have perpetuated itself, so that one of his own blood, Farquhar or other, would eventually succeed. Infant baptism was not essential in the Celtic Church, but on this occasion it was deemed advisable, and the ceremony took place at Scone Abbey, Cathail, now an old man, officiating, and a large proportion of the realm's nobility attending.

The brief service over, they were making for the celebratory feast in the abbey's eating hall, when a weary, travel-stained messenger from Galloway changed all abruptly. Siward had struck, he announced, invading Galloway from both Northumbria and South Cumbria. Paul Thorfinnson, Harald Cleft Chin and Sween Kennedy were doing their best to hold up the attacks; but having to split their force into two left them weakened. They required immediate help.

MacBeth did not hesitate. He had, after all, lived in expectation of something of the sort for years, and had only to put his planning into operation. It was fortunate that so many of his chiefs and leaders happened to be assembled there at Scone when the alarm came, saving much time. Ordering an immediate full-scale muster, and leaving Gruoch, Lulach and the womenfolk to wind things up at the abbey, with Farquhar and Luctacus, he hurried the three miles to Cairn Beth, to change from their finery into armoured tunics and helmets. He ordered Sir Osbert Pentecost to have as many of the Norman-trained cavalry as was possible to assemble at short notice waiting for him at Dunsinane, ready to ride for Galloway forthwith. Glamis assured that he would have 500 men mounted and ready within three hours, three times that number by the morrow, 3000 in a couple of days.

Early that same evening MacBeth and the two princes rode south-westwards for Stirling, through Strathearn and Strathallan, with about 700 men, of whom 200 were the trained cavalry, leaving Glamis in charge of the mustering, to send on the main force as and when he could.

All night they rode through the July half-light, to cross the Forth at Stirling and then over the Kilsyth Hills in the misty dawn and down into Strathkelvin. Then the long weary lift up to the Lanark moors and into Clydesdale. But hard as they went, for the King it was a frustrating progress. It quickly became apparent that however excellent the great Flanders cavalry horses might be for tactical fighting, they were slow, slow for this cross-country travelling, lumbering, heavy brutes which held back the garron-mounted remainder grievously. After a brief rest at the Kelvin, MacBeth decided that he must leave them behind, to come on at their own pace.

Thereafter the 500 made better speed, despite growing weariness, the sturdy, shaggy garrons once again proving their worth. By the Clyde they rested, but only for three hours. Then over the hills between Douglasdale and Tintock, the Hill of Fire, to the Clyde again, having cut off a great bend. Then up the Potrail Water through the Lowthers and down the Pass of Dalveen to the Nith. There, many almost asleep in their saddle they had to halt again, for longer, over one hundred miles covered in thirty-four hours, day and night immaterial.

A mere four hours and they were on again, climbing once more, all against the grain of the land, up into empty uplands and heather moors of Glencairn and Lochurr and the Glenkens. Another two dozen miles of this and they came down to the Water of Ken, and Saint John's Town of Dalry, where one of the new Keledei monasteries from Loch Leven had been established as part of the campaign to keep Galloway Scottish. Now there were only a score of miles, down Ken and Tarff, to the Dee and Kirk Cuthbert's Town on that estuary, capital of

Galloway. Fifty hours after leaving Fortrenn they straggled into Harald Cleft Chin's headquarters, all but exhausted, man and beast.

They found only Sween Kennedy there. His young cousin Paul, with about 1000 men, was in the mid-Nithsdale area, seeking to hold that line, with Harald himself and the main Galloway strength holding the coastal plain where the Nith reached Solway. The word was that they had held the two-pronged enemy assault along the Nith. He, Sween, was collecting and despatching onwards more men.

MacBeth was thankful at least that the invaders had got no further, and that the main mass of Galloway was as yet not over-run. It was fear of this that had spurred him on so urgently these last days and nights. The Nith line was about thirty miles east of this point. Until his main forces reached him from the north, he could offer only moral support to Harald and Paul. Sween was singularly vague as to which might require aid most urgently, or indeed as to what stage hostilities had reached; presumably the actual fighting-men did not feel that he was worth keeping fully informed. He was sending on companies of reinforcements more or less equally to the two fronts as they became available.

It was not in the King's nature to wait idly by, however weary. He felt certain that the veteran Harald would have chosen to put himself in the position of most significance, if he could, and sent the youthful Paul to deal with the less vital assault — if he knew which was which. After one good night's rest, then, leaving his 500 to recover, MacBeth was off again, with his two sons and only a small escort, heading east by north and skirting the Solway's many shallow indentations, for the Nith estuary.

Cleft Chin was not hard to find. Some score of miles along the coast from the Dee the great isolated hill mass of Criffel, the Split Fell, rose abruptly from the lowland, stretching inland, northwards for some eight miles, although its greatest and steepest height towered above the southern shoreline, over-looking the Nith estuary. Here it left only a very narrow strip of carseland between tide and hill, easily defendable. But only a small proportion of Harald's force was here, a company strengthening the naturally strong position by digging defensive ditches, building barriers of felled trees, and, on the higher ground, gathering rocks to hurl down. This was for the main strength to fall back upon and hold, if the river-line broke.

316

They found Harald, grey-haired now but more villainous-looking than ever, some four miles further north and east, at Saint Conal's Kirk, another newly-established Keledei establishment just above the marshy flats where the Nith changed from estuary to river, his men deployed to stretch northwards as far as eye could see. Half-a-mile to the east, across the water and more marshland, the enemy army was in clear view, occupying a similar position, They too were drawn up in seemingly endless ranks up-river. No fighting appeared to be taking place at the moment.

The Viking was much relieved to see MacBeth. Not so much because he was plainly outnumbered by the host opposite but because he was unhappy and somewhat mystified over the strategic situation. The enemy had sat over there, idle, for three whole days, he declared. They did not seem to be gaining any additions of strength. Why should they wait for that anyway, when all too clearly they were at least four times his own numbers? There had been the preliminary skirmishes at that side of the river, but no major attempt to cross after he had done so, only one or two probes here and there, not sustained. The same situation prevailed further up, facing young Paul, who was holding the river-line east of the Troqueer and Terregles Hills, outliers of Criffel, ten miles or so northwards, opposing a somewhat smaller force that was equally inactive. Obviously Siward was waiting for something. What?

MacBeth could not answer that. It made him uneasy likewise. It could be that a sea-borne invasion was planned for their rear — Echmarcach of Dublin again perhaps. But it was not like the fierce and bold Siward the Strong to be so careful when he was in strength himself, to be waiting upon another. It could be, of course, that it was Siward himself whom the enemy was waiting for, that the earl had not yet come up, delayed somewhere. But that again was not Siward's style, to launch this long-delayed invasion before he himself was ready to join it.

Harald was not to be blamed for his doubts and forebodings. Puzzled, the King left him to ride on up the riverside. Harald's people lined the low-lying and swampy banks all the way, fairly thinly strung-out inevitably; but since only in a few places was the river shallow enough to ford, and to launch a sufficient crossing by boats would give time for concentration of defenders from elsewhere, this was not too serious. Opposite the quite large township of Dunphreas, which clustered round its former Pictish fort, and where the river *was* fordable,

Harald's and Paul's forces joined. All the way, on the other side, the enemy was as evident, waiting. It was a crazy but ominous situation.

When eventually he reached his nephew, in the Terregles area, Paul however exhibited a quite different attitude and found little wrong with the state of affairs. The wretched English were afraid, that was all, he averred — cowards. They had double his numbers, but dared not attack across this river. He was considering whether he ought to attack, himself. Cross over and show them how to fight. He, Paul Thorfinnson, was getting tired of waiting here.

His uncle commended his spirit, but suggested patience. Reinforcements were on their way. They might as well do all properly.

Almost scornful, the youth hinted that the King was as bad as old Cleft Chin — the creeping caution of old age, he implied. Farquhar and Luctacus tended to agree with him. Evidently, despite his father's earlier strictures, Paul had a good deal of the Raven Feeder in him. He pointed out that these English opposite were poor creatures anyway. Not true warriors, not even real soldiers. They were no more than an unruly horde of peasants and soil-turners, scarcely an armoured and helmeted man amongst them.

This observation, at least, registered with his royal uncle. The Nith was narrower here, and consequently the enemy not so far away. And staring across the King did gain the impression that this was less than a disciplined and well-equipped force facing them, strong in numbers but having little appearance of quality, scarcely the sort of army that Siward would be likely to use as spearhead for his invasion, however many flags and banners flew amongst them. Moreover, they gave the appearance of being encamped over there, rather than drawn up in any line of battle.

More thoughtful than ever, and commanding Paul to make no move meantime unless attacked, MacBeth rode back to Harald's Saint Conal's Kirk.

He spent the night there. And although sentries patrolled every yard of the riverside throughout, there were no developments. Nor did the morning show greater activity. Leaving a perturbed Viking to watch and wait, he returned to the Dee and Kirk Cuthbert's Town.

The first instalment of his main force from Fortrenn had arrived just before him, under Colin of the Mearns, tired but

318

thankful not to have missed anything, another 800 men, horsed. They announced that they had passed Pentecost and the heavy cavalry some ten miles or so back, coming down Tarff Water. They should arrive shortly.

In fact, next to appear were not the Normans but two dishevelled couriers from Glamis, the Constable, so way-worn as barely to be able to speak. Incoherently they gasped out their tidings. Siward had crossed into Scotland on the east in major strength, over Tweed from Northumberland and was marching on Fortrenn with many thousands. A great host, and reported as under Scotland's own Boar standard, they had already crossed the Merse into Lammermuir and Lothian.

Set-faced MacBeth stared at the messengers. So — this was the answer to their Nithside questions! He had been outwitted. This Galloway thrust was a mere feint, to draw him and the main Scottish strength away across the width of the country to this remote corner, so that Siward could strike directly at the heartland and with only secondary opposition. No doubt these English facing Harald and Paul were indeed no more than the scourings of Siward's manpower, mere numbers to counterfeit an invasion. And, like a fool he, MacBeth, had fallen into the trap.

At least, there were no doubts now as to what to do. He had to turn all his weary travellers round and send them back whence they had come — and faster, if humanly possible, however much they might protest. Every day, every hour, would count. Others on the way must be turned back. It was the only action now, however desperate. One gleam of hope there was only — Siward the Dane, like the Saxons also, had no tradition of the large-scale use of horses in warfare. So, save for a few leaders, his army would almost certainly be marching on foot, comparatively slow-moving however hard they might push.

Sir Osbert Pentecost's and his Normans' faces were a sight to see when they arrived, to be informed that they must turn their brutes round and retrace their steps forthwith.

It was late afternoon, but the King never so much as considered waiting until morning. All must start back right away, whatever their state of fatigue, making the best speed they could. Two moves he set in hand before he himself started off northwards again. He instructed Pentecost to acquire a couple of hundred Galloway ponies, a local type of garron, short-legged but barrel-chested, in plentiful supply in this green-pasture country, and to use these to ride back on, leading the heavy chargers unburdened save to carry the armour. This ought to improve their pace considerably. The second instruction went to Harald Cleft Chin, informing him of the situation and commanding him to send as strong a detachment of his men as he could spare — since he was unlikely now to have to do any major battling with these people facing him — eastwards, by the dales of Annan, Dryfe, Esk and Teviot, to the Merse, to threaten the English rear and seek to cut Siward's links with Northumberland. It was a gesture which might possibly have valuable results.

Thereafter it was just hard and endless riding for Scotland's monarch.

*　　　*　　　*

That was a nightmarish journey across the backbone of the land, of unremitting effort, gnawing anxiety and major discomfort as well as near prostration, for the weather broke down to rain driven by unseasonable winds. MacBeth made no attempt to keep any large force with him, but pressed determinedly ahead, all but killing his horses, leaving others to make the best pace they might. He halted and turned back one force of some 600, still on its way to Galloway; and twelve appalling hours later caught up with another and still larger company, under Lachlan of Buchan, who had had one of Glamis's messengers and had turned back on his own initiative. This was in mid-Clydesdale. Taking command himself, the King speeded this force considerably on its way, treating all grumblers harshly.

Two nights and a day after leaving Kirk Cuthbert's, he was back at the Kelvin, in mid-Scotland, with some 1200 red-eyed men — the rest of his forces trailing behind, scattered across the spine of the land. His aim was to cross the Kilsyth Hills into the Forth valley and turn eastwards, hoping to reach Stirling and that vital river-crossing before the enemy did, there to try to hold up Siward as his grandfather had held Canute. But in Strathkelvin the King and his dead-weary followers were brought up short by further messengers from Cormac of Glamis. A large English galley-fleet had sailed up the Tay, Siward himself with it. This in addition to the army marching from Tweed. Fortunately the Scots fleet summoned from Torfness, with the Moraymen under Neil Nathrach and a Viking contingent under Gunnar, had reached Tay just the day previously, and had been able to halt the English ships before they got into the river itself, blocking the channel. But Siward was landing men by the thousand on the Fife shore of the estuary, and more ships were arriving. Neil's force had joined Glamis's own reserves to line the Carse of Gowrie shore opposite Fife, to repel any crossing if they could, to protect the realm's base area of Scone and Dunsinane.

MacBeth, almost too tired to think straight, nearly wept in his chagrin and disheartenment. He, who had been forewarned and prepared for this for so long, had failed in the end, failed Scotland and all that he held dear. Siward had out-thought him and out-manoeuvred him at every turn, made a fool of him. What could he do now? What in God's name could he do?

Flogging his reeling wits to practical, purposive thought, he sought to banish all regrets and irrelevances. Desperately as he needed men for this side of the Tay, he nevertheless decided to split his present numbers and send the larger part, under Lachlan of Buchan, to try to hold the Forth crossing at Stirling, as intended. Even detaching two-thirds, 800 was a ridiculously small number for the task, but he dared not spare more. The army advancing through Lothian must be halted, if at all possible — and Stirling, with its bridge and causeway, was the place to do it. There would be some local men, of the Lennox, whom Lachlan could enlist. If he had time. So this contingent was sent off direct for Stirling, to hold Forth to the end. MacBeth despatched couriers back to hasten the oncoming companies and stragglers, especially the Normans, who were to follow *him* northwards for the Tay. Then, with only 400 now, he also headed over the hills for the Forth valley, but west of the others' line. The great Flanders Moss, twenty miles long by five wide stretched as a vast barrier before them there, waterlogged, impassable. But a few miles west of Stirling there was a little-known way across at the Fords of Frew, a Clan Alpine cattle route, which Lennox had shown him once. This could cut off miles.

As the reduced force pushed on thereafter across the low hills of east Lennox and into Strathearn, the King racked his brains for a strategy to meet this desperate situation. Somehow he had to use surprise, and the land itself, to fight for him since of men he had so few available. Siward would not *expect* to see the King of Scots on his flank, at this stage. If Glamis and Neil managed to hold the north shore of Tay against major landings — and the Carse of Gowrie had a shallow, marshy, muddy coast, difficult to land on for many miles — then Siward's shipped army would be held up on the north-west Fife shore, presumably as

321

high up-estuary as he could get. The chances were that he would be concentrated in the Lindores-Rhind area, for immediately above that the Tay narrowed abruptly to river instead of estuary, and it would be strange indeed if the Torfness fleet was not packed tightly in there, denying further access. If that was all so, there was one major feature which might be used against the enemy — the mouth of the River Earn, which here joined Tay amongst marshy tidelands. There were tactical possibilities in that. And MacBeth could think of no other, in his present state of mind.

So, reaching the wide Earn valley in the Tullibardine vicinity, they crossed the Kinkell ford and turned eastwards along the north bank — country the King knew well, for his palace of Forteviot, Lulach's new home, lay just across the river here. It was late evening, and although the weather had improved, the Earn was running high for summer — which might well prove to be in their favour. He was pushing on towards Moncrieffe Hill, a long, isolated escarpment reaching to some 700 feet above the flats, which thrust out to within a mile or so of the Earn's mouth, on this north side.

Despite the rain stopping, it was still cloudy and the light was much poorer than usual for late July by the time they reached the west end of Moncrieffe Hill. Leaving his exhausted people in woodland there, MacBeth pressed on, with only Farquhar as companion, for another two miles, to near the steep eastern point of the scarp. And considerably before they reached their viewpoint, he knew the answer to at least one of his questions — the ruddy glow in the slate-grey sky ahead told eloquently of the large numbers of camp-fires of a great host. Siward's army was indeed still south of Tay.

At the extreme tip of the hill's edge, the leaden-eyed King and his yawning son drew rein, gazing out into the dim half-light eastwards, seawards. Details were impossible to distinguish but the pin-points of red, which were the fires, were sufficiently clear and numerous to establish the situation. The great mass of them were concentrated on the south side, most of all in the middle distance, possibly as much as four miles off, presumably around Lindores — the cashel and abbey of which no doubt Siward had appropriated as his headquarters. But there were fires along the north shore also, a thin but very long line of them, stretching away along the Carse; clearly the Scots defenders still holding their ground, however attenuated. There were no fires immediately below, this side of the Earn's mouth.

Satisfied he returned to his own camp. They could sleep now. But before MacBeth permitted himself that indulgence, he sent off two very reluctant messengers; one to cross Tay by the Elcho ford to find Neil Nathrach and Glamis and tell them of his whereabouts and the manpower situation; the other to make for Malpender of Strathearn's house at Auchterarder, commanding the mormaor to send every man fit to bear arms to Moncrieffe Hill at the earliest possible moment.

The morning saw them rejoined by Colin of the Mearns and some 300 men. The total 700 was all too few to risk in confrontation with Siward's thousands, even across a river, but MacBeth could not afford to wait. He could not hide these numbers, either, and the enemy was bound to learn of their presence quickly. The entire advantage of the Earn-mouth situation would be lost if Siward came across at them before they were in position to hold it. So the Scots moved off early, eastwards, along the slopes of the hill.

They had not gone a couple of miles before their scouts ahead hurried back with news that transformed the situation meantime. A force of the enemy was already across Earn, apparently foraging, in the low ground of Kinmonth and Rhynd. Cursing, MacBeth spurred ahead, in the cover of the scrub woodland, to investigate.

From a viewpoint he surveyed the scene — and was relieved at what he saw. It was not a large party, 200 or 300 only apparently, driving rounded-up cattle back towards the river-mouth. Awaiting them at the Earn was a collection of small boats. No doubt they had crossed in these, purloined from Tayside fishermen, and had not used the ford of Rhynd, a couple of miles higher. They would be going to swim the cattle across the hundred-yard-wide stream. But, in fact, it was not this immediate foreground situation which held the King's attention so much as the middle-distance and background. In daylight, the great enemy host could be seen in all its might, and clearly forming up in distinct divisions at four different points along the south shore of Tay, each perhaps half-a-mile apart. And at these points the English galleys, scores of them, were being marshalled side-by-side across the narrowing estuary, to form floating bridges. The Tay hereabouts was about one-third of a mile wide, but there were major sandbanks, almost islands, in the centre, which were being utilised much to narrow the span. At low tide men would be able to pour across these pontoon-bridges to the north shore.

It was time that the King of Scots demonstrated his presence, however inadequate his strength.

Back at his people he divided the force. About a third of the total was to ride down, and with all speed, across the low ground to the riverside, under Mormaor Colin, then to turn along it to get between these cattle-stealers and their boats. They would be seen, but so long as they reached the boats first this would not matter. The remainder would advance along the escarpment to its end and then throw themselves down upon the foragers, who would be caught between the two and much outnumbered. It should be the simplest of attacks.

So it proved indeed. Colin's men, although they must have come in sight of the main enemy army across Earn fairly early in their dash, remained screened from the forage-party until they were practically at the boats. When they were observed, there was uproar and hasty reforming, which changed to complete chaos when the King's larger company, hidden by trees and the curve of the hill, hurled themselves down the steep against them. There was no real fighting, although individual Northumbrians struggled bravely enough before being cut down. It was mere slaughter, swift and complete. In a few minutes the enemy was wiped out almost to a man, no prisoners being wanted — although a few fugitives, more nimble than the rest, may have managed to reach the river and tried to swim across. The alarmed cattle streamed away westwards again, free.

MacBeth now sent a party to sink the boats, while he marshalled his force in such a way as to perhaps make it look larger than it was from a distance, spread out, groups hurrying hither and thither, to give the impression of much activity. There was reaction across the Earn, of course, with presently quite large numbers being sent to the river, to face across to the Scots.

The King made much play with his royal standard and other banners; but nothing would disguise the fact that there were no very large numbers with him.

After some time an impressive leadership group came riding to the river, mounted on presumably stolen Fife horses — although, gazing across, heedfully just out of bowshot, MacBeth recognised the thick-set and bull-necked figure of MacDuff of Fife himself. The King had never actually seen Siward the Strong, but the huge gaunt personage, bull's-horn-helmeted and grey-bearded, beside MacDuff, could surely be none other. A young man on the other side of the elderly giant, even at this distance could be seen to have a notably large head for his body and shoulders — Malcolm mac Duncan Canmore undoubtedly, grown to man's estate.

Fortunately, at this rather inactive and awkward juncture, a small but hard-riding group arrived from the west, and proved to be Neil Nathrach himself, with Martacus of Mar, come from Saint John's Town of Perth.

"Praises be, Son of Life!" Neil panted, coming to embrace his brother. "God be thanked that you are come! But — where is all your host?"

"Coming straggling across Scotland, man. What do you think? It is 150 grievous miles from Galloway. And Lachlan of Buchan has some at Stirling, seeking to hold the Forth."

"Yes. Yes — but will these others be here soon? What of the Normans?"

"They are on their way. God knows when they will arrive. Their animals are worn out with marching. Siward yonder has been cunning, More clever than I."

"Aye, I see him. Damn him to deepest hell! And the traitors I see with him!"

"It had to come one day, brother. But you? And you, Martacus lad? What is *your* state?"

"None so good. We have some 5000 men, all told, yes. But we are stretched thin as any rope! With all the Tay to line. From Saint John's Town to Clashbenny in the Carse. Ten miles at least."

"You can leave that reach of Tay. Either Siward will cross by his bridges of galleys yonder — in which case Glamis will require all *your* strength to meet them there. Or he will choose to assail me here, across Earn. Or both. He cannot attack higher up Tay until he has conquered here, whilst your ships block the upper river."

"What, then? Shall I move my people to join you here? Or join Glamis?"

"It is difficult to know what Siward will do. He may decide to go for *me*. Think that if he can bring down the King of Scots, the rest will fall to him anyway. If I was Siward, I would choose to attack here. The Earn a lesser barrier than the Tay . . ."

He paused as Siward and his group of leaders was seen to make a move — not back to his main force but south-westwards along Earn-side, at a fast trot. Inevitably he had to keep some way back from its soft, mud-lined and creek-eaten bank.

"Aye — there he goes to view the scene for possible crossings.

325

He will find nothing until the Rhynd ford, two miles up. I have hawked geese and heron here. There is no way across, save by boats."

"How wide? The ford. Could he put over many men at once?"

"Wide, yes. He could cross in fair strength there. But, see you, the Earn makes a great loop there, forming a narrow tongue of land between. This side. So once he is across, he is still awkwardly placed."

"And other fords higher? I do not know this country."

"Not another for a further mile. Less good. There is a small sandbank in mid-river, below Kinmonth. The Earn shoals there, and can be crossed."

"Then if the English attack here, they must use these two crossings. One or both. At the Rhind ford, or at Kinmonth. A mile apart. With level cornland between . . ."

"Yes. On which we could use my cavalry — if they come! It is the best that I can do, I think."

"Aye, brother. I will go back, then. Set my people moving. Here. And hope that you have judged aright! It will take some time . . ."

"Hasten, Neil. And leave a small company to guard the main Moncrieffe ford back there. In case . . ."

MacBeth himself rode off to inspect the tongue of land he had spoken of, where the Earn made its long U-shaped loop, in especial the neck thereof, barely a quarter-mile across, where the farm-toun of Wester Rhynd nestled in a strong defensive situation. The farm folk were less than glad to see their King, in the circumstances; but when they looked across and observed the English leaders surveying the position, from the Fargmouth, only half-a-mile off, they recognised realities. MacBeth satisfied himself that he could use this position to good effect, and watched Siward ride on further westwards, to look at the Kinmonth ford. With MacDuff to guide him, he would be well informed as to the terrain. It was all MacDuff territory that side of the river.

That afternoon parties of the Galloway force kept dribbling in. Malpender of Strathearn arrived with some 800 of his people, locals, an untrained, ill-assorted crowd of doubtful fighting value however willing. In the early evening Neil of Cawdor and Martacus of Mar came back with most of their host, Moray and Mar men, from the positions they had held around Saint John's Town of Perth, Scone and Kinfauns. And as the sun set, at last the Normans limped into the Moncrieffe camp, to loud welcome, a mixture of cheers and jeers.

MacBeth now had some 4500 men assembled here, of very mixed fighting qualities, and most very weary. But before he allowed himself an hour or so of sleep that night, the King had another decision to make. A courier arrived from Lachlan of Buchan urgently requesting reinforcement. He was holding the Forth causeway so far, but how long he could continue to do so was very doubtful. He was hopelessly outnumbered and his men dropping with fatigue. Doubtfully, reluctantly, MacBeth gave orders for a precious 500 men to march off southwards.

*   *   *

It seemed only moments after he eventually closed his eyes before he was awakened to be told that sentries along the Earn bank were reporting activity on the other side. Boats were being assembled again opposite, near the mouth, brought in from the Tay. It seemed that Siward did intend a major assault over the Earn. And not just at the fords.

MacBeth divided his yawning forces into four groups of roughly one thousand each. Neil to take one westwards to the Kinmonth ford area; Colin of the Mearns to the east, to face the boat threat at the river-mouth; Martacus and Malpender to hold the reserve here on the higher ground; and himself to take the fourth down to the central Rhynd ford and tongue of land within the loop of the river, where he anticipated the main enemy thrust. They moved off, with still a couple of hours till sunrise. The King took Farquhar and Luctacus with him. Most men were dismounted, at this stage, the garrons held in long horse-lines behind.

It was a strange business waiting there in the half-dark, hundred upon hundreds of men, silent, above the swirling, gurgling river, waiting, listening — and hearing only the sad wheepling of curlew, the quack-quack of mallard and the chatter of redshank and oyster-catcher. Most men slept on their feet, leaning on sword, spear or battle-axe.

MacBeth had just become aware of a lightening of the eastern sky and an increase of activity amongst the wildfowl, when the noise suddenly broke out, to the north-east, shouting and the clash of arms, faint on the easterly breeze. That could only be at the boats, over a mile away. So the attack had started there. Yet that was the least hopeful sector from the enemy's standpoint. There was no sign nor sound of movement opposite here, at

Rhynd and Culfargie, as yet. To start the attack back there thus early, before daylight, must be for good reason. That reason must be linked with the darkness. Something to hide. Siward was as cunning an adversary as could be met; and he was fond of feints. The probability was, then, that this attack with the boats was to distract attention from elsewhere, to give the impression that it was the major thrust, to draw the defensive forces thither.

Although his every instinct was to be up and doing, to hurry men to the scene of conflict, the King forced himself and his followers to wait where they were, inactive. Colin had a thousand men to repel this gesture, and could send to the reserves for aid if essential.

The sound of battle went on and on, and all the time the light strengthened and visibility improved. Mists still lingered over the area, but they were patchy and thinning. No runner came from Colin of the Mearns.

Then, at last, it was sufficiently light to see quite distant movement — and to see it not eastwards, where MacBeth had looked for it, but due southwards, half-a-mile away around Aberargie, where the riverside flats rose through scrub woodland to the Ochil foothills. As they stared, they saw that there was much movement. Siward, then, had made a great southwards detour into the Abernethy area, in the darkness, where he could be unseen and unheard, and was now advancing towards the Earn parallel with the Farg Water, in strength. No doubt a similar host would be approaching the Kinmonth ford from the same general direction. MacBeth sent a runner to warn Neil.

This time the Dane's ruse had failed. But he had more than ruses at his disposal.

So, doubts and questions past, the Scots awaited conclusions.

If Siward was disappointed to see his enemy still in position behind the Rhynd ford, MacBeth was anything but elated at what *he* saw. As the English drew near he assessed their numbers at 3000 at least, a disciplined, heavily-armed host advancing deliberately in its might. Presently it could be seen that Siward himself was in command. Also it was revealed that his shrewd generalship was not confined to feints and detours. His men were carrying with them much timber, slender birch-trunks and poles, and other objects which they decided were hurdles woven of willow-boughs and alder boughs. Also ropes of twisted bracken and straw. MacBeth's heart sank at the sight.

Siward went about his business with unhurried efficiency.

328

Lining his host along the riverside in companies, he set men to tying up the birch-logs into large rafts, many rafts. At the same time he pushed forward his hurdles to the very water's edge, scores of them, and set them up on props as screens and barricades against arrows.

Siward seemed in no hurry to make a start, prepared to wait while the rafts were constructed. No doubt too, now that surprise was lost, he all the time was hoping for his southern army to come on the scene. MacBeth felt notably helpless, watching him; but apart from shooting arrows, of which the Scots had only a limited supply, there was nothing that he could do meantime.

Noise from the boats area still continued; but no messengers came to tell of victory or disaster.

At length, the wailing of bulls' horns up and down the enemy line signalled the actual assault. With loud cheering the English front hurled itself forward in a furious wave, the main mass in the centre to plunge into the river at the shallows of the ford, seventy or eighty yards in width, those on the flanks to drag the rafts into the water and launch out, as many as could on top, others clinging to the sides with one hand and swimming with the other, so propelling the heavy, clumsy contrivances forward.

Now the Scots surged down to meet the foe, their own archers busy for so long as was possible. Little less than halfway across the Earn the two sides met in bloody hand-to-hand conflict. The water here rose little above men's middles, and the bottom, being mainly silt and pebbles, made fair footing.

MacBeth himself held back, as did Siward. There was just not space for more than a small proportion of the two forces to operate. The leaders waited to throw in larger numbers where they might do most good. The King was more anxious about his flanks, at this stage. He thought possibly they might control the ford crossing meantime; but these rafts, scores of them, stretching upstream and down, were a major distraction and demanding too much of his manpower to deal with. They were very slow, of course, and tended to slew and swing downstream with the current.

It made a chaotic, yelling, splashing and stumbling clash, there on the ford, with both sides hurling in extra men as the struggle ebbed and flowed. Soon the water was running red and many bodies were being carried away down towards the Tay. Then a curious situation developed, which presumably Siward had not foreseen. The current was stronger than anticipated, and carried those rafts immediately above the ford slantwise down on to the struggling mass of men in the shallows, with disastrous results. The heavy laden timbers were not to be halted, and bowled men over, the people aboard them unable to do anything about it. With four of the rafts nudging and swirling through the press of fighters, utter confusion prevailed and the attack faltered and broke up. Siward's horns sounded a retiral as other rafts bore down to add to the confusion, and those of his men who could staggered back to the south bank.

Farther down one or two of the rafts had won across, but the enemy thereon were quickly rounded up and despatched.

The Scots cheered.

Gratified as he was, MacBeth recognised that this was only a breathing-space. Not one quarter of the English strength had been engaged as yet. And the Scots casualties had not been negligible. Siward would not make that mistake again.

While the enemy reorganised, the King sent Luctacus and a group back to bring horses, garrons, in sufficient numbers to mount a troop. There was no room for any large-scale horsed operations here, but he thought that there was a part mounted men might play.

Siward changed his tactics, and used his larger numbers greatly to widen his attack, and thus disperse the defence. He spread his rafts far along the riverside, left and right. Inevitably MacBeth had to send increasing numbers to rebuff them, weakening his centre grievously. But the English retained about a dozen rafts at the ford, and these they formed up side-by-side into a long line, with the massed waders drawn up behind. The flank attacks had already started when, at a signal, those at the ford, in the front ranks, started to push the rafts, empty, before them, as a sort of floating ram.

The Scots found this difficult to deal with. Their archers admittedly achieved some initial success; but then, as before, they were masked by their own men. Hand-to-hand fighting was all but impossible. At one stage it developed into quite a ridiculous stalemate, with defenders and attackers facing each other across the width of the rafts, pushing with all their might and all but stationary.

MacBeth sent Farquhar and some of the mounted men to the downstream end of the raft-line. He judged that there was space for them in the shallows. If the enemy had used a few more rafts, he could not have done this. But the floating barrier did not extend for the entire width of the ford. So there was room for the horsemen to get round the end, there to tug and haul the first raft away, while their colleagues hacked and speared at the English pushing it. The current assisted, of course, and the raft swung loose and drifted off. They started on the next.

Siward reacted swiftly, throwing in more men at this down-stream end of the ford. MacBeth retaliated with further horse-men. Soon a second and third raft were gone, and in the resultant space, the horsemen could prove their advantage of height and reach, with their weapons, the garrons themselves aiding with sheer trampling weight and brute force.

The attack wavered.

The King had only part of his attention on this central sector. He was concerned about his flanks. The situation upstream was not good, with some of the rafts across and quite a number of the enemy on the north bank. He sent the remainder of his horsemen to aid the defence there to drive these back into the river.

Fortunately the central assault broke up at this stage, with the raft front shattered and the English assailed front and side. The confusion was so great that Siward ordered his men back, and to bring their rafts with them. When this became evident to the flanking forces, they tended to lose heart — since it would be no man's choice to be left isolated on the wrong side of Earn. Most who had got across elected to return, either on their own rafts or swimming.

The second attempt had failed.

MacBeth sent for more garrons. Although his sons and some of the other Scots leaders, were elated, he knew only too well that, with his overwhelming numbers, time was apt to be on Siward's side. He would keep trying, wearing the defence down. Now he was in process of tying the rafts together, and more of them, having recognised his previous miscalculation. The next attempt would span the entire width of the ford shallows.

It was at this stage that a horsed messenger arrived from the west in panting agitation. The Thane of Cawdor required immediate aid. The English had won across the Kinmonth ford in major strength, and he could not hold them. They were fighting well back from the river now. The Scots rear would be overwhelmed if the King did not do something, and quickly.

MacBeth beat his fist on his saddle-bow, his mind going blank for a moment. He forced himself to think, methodically. Presumably Neil had already sent for the reserves under Martacus and Malpender, so the situation must be very black.

There had been no word from Colin of the Mearns. This three-point battle, with miles between each sector, was the worst possible for an outnumbered defence. But he dared not allow his rear to be over-run and taken, Siward in front or no Siward. When that man heard that the Kinmonth ford had fallen, he would switch large numbers of his force there, to cross.

MacBeth made his desperate decision. He personally must go, to try to save the rear. He would leave Brodie in command here, with Farquhar. He believed that the boat-attack at the Earn-mouth was little more than a feint. He sent a rider to Colin to tell him to leave only a small covering force there, and to come back westwards with most of his people, to join him, picking up their horses as they came. He sent another courier to find Sir Osbert Pentecost and the Normans, to bring them to him. Then, leaving the royal standard flying, to try to disguise the fact that he was gone, he and Luctacus slipped away as inconspicuously as possible, two more messengers, to ride up the tongue of land behind. At the Wester Rhynd farmery they turned westwards, riding hard.

The battle a mile ahead was very visible, but it was difficult to see what went on, all appearing to be no more than a vast, incoherent mass of struggling humanity amongst the corn-rigs. But as he galloped closer, the King could see tall horses tower-ing above the heaving press. So the Normans were involved already. One more hope gone.

Martacus of Mar came hurrying up, the hesitation in his speech more pronounced than ever in his excitement and anxiety. All the reserves were thrown in, he announced. The Normans also. But they were still outnumbered two-to-one. The English were under Siward's own son, Osbern, Earl of Deira. Neil of Cawdor was wounded, but still leading the fight. Malpender was fallen.

"The Normans!" MacBeth cried. "What are they doing in there? They ought to be outside it. Cutting up this battle. That is what they are for. God in His heaven — what folly is this?"

"Your brother, lord King. Neil has not learned to fight with mounted chivalry. Up in Moray. Wounded, he ordered the Normans to come and form a secure ring round him. As centre of the battle. A bodyguard . . ."

"Saints have mercy! The waste — the damnable waste! We must get them out. The horse-lines. Quickly . . .!"

They reached the ranked garrons just as Colin of the Mearns and the first of his people came up. The mormaor began to tell him of the situation at the Earn-mouth, but the King cut him short, ordering him to get his party mounted and lined up into a spearhead formation with all speed, those who had learned some cavalry tactics at front and flanks, others in the centre. Placing himself at the apex of this group of about seventy, with Luctacus, Martacus and Colin, MacBeth barely allowed time for them to form up before he spurred off.

His headlong assault was not just a blind dash. He swung round to the north side of the battle area before wheeling his company and plunging directly into the mêlée where it was thinnest, immediately behind the leadership stance in the centre, signing and yelling to his followers to close up more tightly in formation. Thus they thundered down upon the struggling mass of men.

Their own folk, of course, were first to be hit and ridden down by that arrowhead charge, inevitably. MacBeth, sword pointed directly ahead of him, could by no means help that, and steeled his heart. Furiously, without pause, they drove a bloody wedge through the press, mainly Strathearn men here, ears closed to the yells of rage, resentment and fear. Then they were into a detached group of the enemy, fighting *behind* Neil's beleaguered position. Now the King and his foremost and outermost colleagues slashed and hacked as they cantered; the majority could not do so, from their inside position, where they contributed only essential weight to the charge. Surprised, overwhelmed, the English went down before them, under them, and they were through, unscathed — to find themselves facing a ring of steel-clad Norman cavalry on their tall armoured horses.

Pulling up his garron rearing on its hind legs, MacBeth was all but flung right into that stern barrier by the impetus behind. "Fools!" he shouted. "What do you here — idle?" He saw Pentecost's massive figure in gleaming steel and great plumed helmet, behind the tight ranks. "Aside! Let me through — through, I say!" Waving back his followers, he plunged on into and through the Norman ring.

He found Sir Osbert actually supporting Neil Nathrach in his saddle, under the Moray banner, his brother bloody and grey-featured but still controlling the battle insofar as he could.

"Neil, man — enough!" he cried. "You are sore hurt. Off with you. Get back. Back with you, I say. Colin mac Conquhare will command here. You!" He swung on the Thane of Belhelvie. "Take my brother back. See him safely disposed." He turned

333

back to Pentecost. "Sir Osbert — what folly is this? Did I bring you to Scotland to stand sentry?"

"Sire — I but obey orders. My lord Thane of Cawdor commanded here. I told him this was not our role. But he insisted. Your brother . . ."

"Aye — enough! Enough! Take your Normans, now, and do what you can. What you are here for. Two companies. Cut up this English array. Cut. Split. Divide. Harry. Go, man — go!"

So a new stage in the battle was commenced, with the cavalry tactics, in which MacBeth put so much faith, given a chance to operate in wedges or columns, boring into selected parts of the enemy mass, and endeavouring to cut through them and detach them from the main body; and when this was achieved, to turn on them and ride them down piecemeal, crushing them with the weight of horseflesh. This was the warfare of mobility, something little known north of Normandy, and it put the enemy at major disadvantage.

Nevertheless, the horsemen suffered casualties, a continuous steady drain, even the Normans, mounts as well as riders. Spears accounted for some, hamstrung garrons for more. The Norman horses, being themselves part-covered by armour, fared better; but agile men could dart in, slip below their bellies for a moment and rip these open with a single upward slash of a dirk. Many knights fell thus.

But the English advance was held. Had the enemy not been constantly reinforced across the Kinmonth ford from Siward's main host, they might even have been driven back.

MacBeth debated off and on within himself as he led sally after sally, with two garrons killed under him, whether in fact he ought to be doing this, acting the captain again rather than the general? Whether he should not rather be standing back, supervising all, considering the whole field. He recognised that he might be failing in some major strategy by being too closely involved in the immediate tactics. Always at the back of his mind was the position of Brodie and Farquhar, facing Siward back there. Clearly the Dane and his full force had not transferred here to Kinmonth, so the Rhynd ford must still be threatened. If only he knew what was going on . . .

He had decided that he must resign this spearheading role to another and go back to Rhynd after this present sally, when he perceived a sort of eddy in the battle scene opening before them, a less dense corridor, at the far end of which flapped the banner of Deira itself, carried high. That must be Siward's son. It was too good an opportunity to miss, a chance to bring down the enemy leadership here. Shouting his changed commands, the King wheeled his weary formation round once more, and plunged into the fray in the new direction.

The so-called Earl of Deira saw them coming, endeavoured to interpose more of his people between — which could have been wise leadership rather than any cowardice. But MacBeth, in this savage mood, was not to be baulked. On through all inter-vening press of smiting, cringing and trampled bodies he drove, ably supported right and left and pushed onwards by the impetus at his back. The last screen of men flung themselves aside before him, as well they might, and there was the slender, yellow-haired young man, in fine silver scale-armoured tunic, richly accoutred, mouth open, blue eyes wide, battle-axe raised. Even as the royal sword crashed down, its wielder knew a pain at his heart and the refrain in his mind saying so young, so young. Then on over the red ruin of Siward's heir he was swept. The rider on his right hand grasped at the reeling Deira banner, to carry it off in their onward rush.

The wedge beat its way round in a wide scything arc, to smash through to open ground again.

There, momentarily drained of emotion, the King was seeking to still a strange trembling of his limbs, when a single rider came pounding up, shouting his news. Siward was across. He had broken through. The English were streaming up the neck of land to Wester Rhynd. Brodie was down. The Prince Farquhar was trying to hold them, but it was hopeless . . .

Desperately MacBeth pulled himself together, flogging his battered wits. It was too much, all too much. He was tired beyond belief. Farquhar. Brodie fallen. What to do — in God's name, what to do?

He sent urgent messages to the two Norman units, now notably smaller, to Martacus and Luctacus, ordering them to leave all and hurry eastwards after him. And to Colin, telling him of this latest threat. He must switch part of his present force eastwards. Then he pointed his sword wordlessly in the same direction, to his own battered group, now less than fifty strong, and urged his sweat-soaked beast into renewed action.

He was too late to seek to hold the neck of the peninsula at Wester Rhynd, as he had hoped. Already the enemy had over-run that. But the farmery buildings occupied a position some 300 yards in from the actual root of the isthmus, before it opened out into the carseland; and here the remainder of the defenders' force were still making a stand, to prevent the English from flooding out into the wide levels. But clearly they were not going to withstand the pressure for much longer.

Pounding up, MacBeth was relieved at least to see Farquhar still apparently unhurt, and trying to rally and direct his weary people, a sorry shadow of the original thousand. The King's arrival, with shortly afterwards Martacus and a few score more mounted men, put some new heart into the wavering remnant admittedly; but nothing was more evident than that they could not hold Siward here, in any barrier of flesh and blood. Besides, this was not the best way to use his mounted men — on this MacBeth's reeling mind was clear at least. The fact that he had cavalry, however few and tired, and Siward had none, was the Scots' only remaining advantage.

So he began to organise a phased withdrawal, groups to fall back alternately whilst others protected them, never more than one-third moving at a time. This was the intention, at least, although inevitably in the clash of battle it was only partially successful. Then, with the arrival of the Normans and some more garron-mounted men under Luctacus, the King withdrew Farquhar from the defensive command to his own side, and put Formartine, one of the Mar thanes, in charge of the foot, ordering all mounted groups to detach themselves and ride back some way, clear.

It looked like desertion of the foot, of course — and not a few undoubtedly saw it as such, and sullenly yielded ground in consequence. But with only minimum delay thereafter, the impact of the cavalry tactics was amply demonstrated to all, the King himself, with Farquhar, leading his spearhead first into the enemy west flank. Soon five horsed wedges were assailing and seeking to cut up Siward's crowded host as it emerged into the open plain, and the Scots took heart again, at the enemy's preoccupation with his flanks.

So commenced another and most desperate phase of that interminable and complicated battle, which had now continued for what seemed untold hours, with noon well past. None would claim that the cavalry charges were as effective as they ought to have been, any more than the infantry defence, with men and beasts exhausted and numbers ever dwindling. But the enemy were tired also, their casualties heavy and their hopes continually dashed. Fairly quickly the cornlands of Rhynd and Kinmonth became one vast bloodstained chaos of struggling, stumbling, wounded and dying men, with no recognisable fronts, no coherent centres, no sure victories or defeats. In and through, to and fro, round and about in it all rode the horsed wedges, growing more ragged, smaller and smaller, slower and slower, less and less efficient. Presently there were only the three of them, and these at much reduced strength, many of the men continuing to ride wounded, the King himself dazed, with an arm limp, and Farquhar with a speared thigh. One of the Norman groups had disappeared entirely, Sir Osbert Pentecost with it, although Sir Hugh Despard still led the other gallantly.

The Battle of the Earn was, in fact, in process of grinding to a halt in sheer prostration.

Then, extraordinarily, in mid-afternoon a new factor came to affect that ghastly and terrible situation, and to have an impact utterly unexpected by all concerned. It was the arrival on the scene, from the south, of the fleeing Scots force from Stirling, under Lachlan of Buchan, or part thereof. Overwhelmed, at last, at the Forth crossing, they had taken to the hills as the best way of eluding the pursuing English host, and streaming through the Ochil valleys, emerged down Glen Farg on to the Earn plain near Aberargie. There was not one thousand of them, and they were strung out and largely demoralised. But that was not evident from a distance, and Lachlan had kept his leadership group tight under his Buchan banners. Siward and his people, seeing it, misconstrued, imagined it to be Scots reinforcements in major strength, and lost all heart for further fight. No doubt the deaths of Siward's son, and many others of the English leadership, contributed. At any rate, the English decided that enough was enough, and a retiral movement was started. It was an orderly withdrawal, of course, and no panic retreat, with the Scots in little state to exploit it. Siward fell back on the Rhynd ford and the remnants of his son's force did the same at Kinmonth.

MacBeth and his people harried the crossings, but only in token fashion, so desperately weakened and weary were they. They did not pursue across the water. For them also, enough was enough — especially as they saw that Siward was not pausing and regrouping on the south shore, but pushing on eastwards towards his ships on the Tay.

Now would be the time for Glamis to make some cross-Tay gesture.

When Lachlan mac Caerill came up, he was surprised indeed

to find himself greeted almost as hero and saviour for, brash man as he was, he had seen himself as a failure. The Forth battle, he reported, had been desperate, hopeless, with the English using boats to cross below bridge and causeway, and some damnable traitor, probably of MacDuff's faction, revealing to them the hidden Fords of Frew crossing further up. He just had not sufficient men to fight on three fronts, or even two, and so they had been outflanked. He had lost some hundreds of men, and would have lost all had he not retired when he did. But at least he had personally slain the enemy leader, another Siward, a sister's son. The enemy had not dared follow him through the narrow Ochils valleys in force. But they were coming northwards by the normal main route, by Allan and Ruthven Waters to the Earn. They should be here before darkness.

"How many?" the King demanded.

"Four thousand, at least."

MacBeth groaned.

But dazed and in pain as he was, he had to do better than that. He sent messengers to Glamis, in the Carse, ordering him to detach at least half of his force and send them here, across the Elcho fords of Tay, and swiftly. Siward was unlikely, at this stage, to mount any cross-estuary assault. Then he set about marshalling his battered, scattered forces, tending to the wounded and collecting and laying out the dead. Rest was not yet.

The tally of casualties proved to be dire indeed. All in all something in the region of 2500 were dead, Malpender, Mormaor of Strathearn and the heirs of Lennox and Angus amongst them; also Brodie, Oykell and half-a-dozen other thanes. Also Pentecost and fully half the Normans. Adding the 500 or so Lachlan said that he had lost — although some of these might still survive — Scotland had lost nearly 3000 men slain, the greatest slaughter on Scottish soil for a century at least. And the number of wounded was legion, almost more injured than there were unscathed. It was scant consolation that they counted 1500 English dead left behind on the field, including Siward's only son and nephew. Malcolm Canmore was not there, nor was Duncan MacDuff. None could give news of these.

In the midst of this grim tidying, watchers pointed out black smoke columns rising in the late afternoon air to eastwards, approximately where Siward's ships were assembled. Look-outs sent to higher ground reported presently that it was some of the English ships on fire. So Glamis had not been idle. And shortly

afterwards, the same look-outs sent the blessed word —
Siward's army was embarking, some of his vessels already
moving off eastwards for the open sea. It was too far to see
details, but Glamis's force appeared to be assailing the embarkation from small boats.

The King sent Martacus, unwounded, back to set the Moray
fleet in motion, where it was blocking the Tay at Kinfauns, to
further harass the English shipping, however denuded they were
of crews.

Farquhar had lost a lot of blood from his thigh wound, and
the King was seeing to him being sent off behind Luctacus to
Cairn Beth, when a rider arrived from the south, from Malpender's hall-house of Auchterarder. The enemy army from the
Forth had almost reached there, and then halted and was now
turned back. They were in full retreat.

Clearly Siward had sent them orders to retire, confirmation
that his own departure was in process.

The Battle of the Earn was over, then, and the King of Scots
left holding the field. But at what a cost! In terms of losses, he
told himself, it was a defeat not any sort of victory.

All but dropping on his feet, he dragged himself up on to a
blood-spattered garron, to ride for Cairn Beth and Gruoch's
comfort.

24

THE PASSAGE OF time proved that hard-fought struggle by the
Earn to have been more defeat than victory for the Scots. For
although Siward's armies retired, they only went as far as the
Lothian shore of Forth and the Scottish Sea. The Dane himself,
slightly wounded evidently, put his fleet into the firth, dropped
Malcolm Canmore mac Duncan and MacDuff of Fife at
Stirling, to command the retiring army of his dead nephew and
to hold Lothian and the South with a force of about 5000, and
then sailed for his headquarters at Bamburgh in Northumberland.
So now the vital Forth crossing was held *against* the Scots. And
to all intents MacBeth had lost Lothian, the Merse and Teviotdale, with much of Strathclyde seriously endangered and
Galloway isolated. It was a grievous price to pay for survival.

For the realm was in no state to mount a sufficiently major campaign to oust the invaders. Lothian could be reinforced quickly from Northumberland by land and sea — and by sea also could come further flanking attacks to the Scots rear, should they march southwards. MacBeth was learning now how much he had owed to Thorfinn's former mastery of the seas. Siward would never have dared to make that sally to the Tay had Thorfinn been other than a house-bound wreck. So, in effect, MacBeth's kingdom had shrunk to Alba again, Scotland north of the Forth and Clyde, with Galloway an appanage and weakness in present circumstances, rather than any flanking strength — for nothing was surer than that Siward would not be long in seeking to grasp for Galloway again.

Within weeks of the battle the enemy's further strategy was made evident. Malcolm Big Head declared himself *de facto* King of Strathclyde, Cumbria and Lothian, and *de jure* King of Scots, clearly with Siward's backing, a puppet but a dangerous one. Various inferences could be drawn from this. A permanent occupation of Lothian and the South must be intended; and a further attack on Alba, the North, sooner or later.

MacBeth found his internal position sadly weakened. As well as the heavy loss of manpower, he had lost some renown and credibility inevitably, his people's faith in his invincibility shaken. He felt that it was not so much the fact that he had been defeated — if defeat it was adjudged — but that he had been outwitted, outmanoeuvred. Perhaps this failure was more in his own mind than in his people's — so Gruoch assured him — but he felt it strongly. Moreover, the Scots monarchy depended greatly, by its very nature, on the lesser kings, the mormaors. And MacBeth was now totally weak in this respect. Fife was an outright enemy. Atholl was without a mormaor. Strathearn was dead, leaving only an infant son. Lennox was now old, his slain heir leaving only a daughter. Angus was sickly and weak, *his* heir also slain. Which left only the group of North-East mormaors, Colin of the Mearns, Martacus of Mar and Lachlan of Buchan — since Moray was Farquhar's inheritance, Ross Luctacus's, and Caithness and Sutherland Thorfinn's. And Thorfinn's only reported activity these days was the building of a fine stone church or minster at Birsay, of all things, to be called Christ's Church and to be the earl's burial place. This news spreading all over Alba, was seen by many as the writing-on-the-wall indeed. So the centre of gravity of the Scots kingdom suffered a distinct and definite shift to the North-East, towards the old kingdom of the Northern Picts in fact, with unavoidable weakening of Fortrenn and the South.

All this did not leave MacBeth inactive or spiritless, to be sure, however ominously he looked on the future. Indeed he led one military counter-stroke, modest in scale but important and successful. Malcolm Canmore, based in Stirling, had put a small force *north* of the strategic Forth crossing, to hold the causewayhead there, below Craig Kenneth, so that any Scots assault would have to run the gauntlet of the narrow crossing, instead of *vice versa*. Making a sudden surprise attack on this from the Allan Water front, really a feint, the King slipped a larger force down behind, to the east, through the Ochil passes, by night, to take the causewayhead from the rear and then to turn and trap the enemy between his two companies, wiping them out. So now the Scots held and manned the causeway again, and the King slept somewhat easier in his bed of nights.

But that easier sleep was only comparative. It was a grievous state of affairs to have the English permanently established only some twenty-five miles, as the crow flew, from Cairn Beth, Dunsinane and Scone. Until he could manage to mount a full-scale attack over Forth on Lothian, and eventually on North-umbria, it was not practical politics to maintain his seat of government in so exposed a position. So, with mixed feelings indeed, he transferred his Court and administration north to Moray, and Gruoch and the family to the House of Spynie. He himself felt bound to spend a considerable part of his time in Fortrenn still, although he shut up Cairn Beth and occupied spartan quarters in the old palace of Dunsinane, with what remained of his Normans. Here he maintained a small but alert and highly-trained standing army, ready for immediate action, under Glamis the Constable, who though now an oldish man, remained vigorous and the best soldier in the land.

Word from Galloway was not immediately alarming. Young Paul Thorfinnson was now permanently there, as his father's deputy, although Harald Cleft Chin, who had married a Galloway woman, remained in effective control, and Sween Kennedy called himself Lord of Galloway again. The invading force there had indeed been only a sham, to distract, and having served its purpose was withdrawn. MacBeth appointed his nephew Paul Governor of Galloway in his father's place, which regularised the situation and might help to keep the Orkney forces, and especially sea-power, active in the Scots interest. Although with Thorfinn's strong hand removed from the steering-oar, how long that power would mean much, was doubtful.

So passed the remainder of 1054 and early 1055, with Scotland as it were partitioned but with no major hostilities. There were cross-Forth and Scottish Sea raids, on both sides, some revolts in Lothian against the invaders, enemy armed excursions into Strathclyde and the like, but no real warfare. Malcolm Canmore, MacBeth learned, although nominally in charge of Lothian and the Merse, still spent most of his time in Northumberland, as did MacDuff, leaving control of the occupying forces to professional soldiers.

Then, the following spring, Siward died suddenly, transforming the situation. Apparently he had never been quite the same man since returning from Scotland. He had been slightly wounded, but it was in the spirit that he had been more gravely hurt; for if MacBeth saw it as a defeat, so did Siward; and the loss of his only son was a dire blow. The old warrior suffered a stroke, made but a poor recovery, and then was felled by another.

With his nephew also slain at the Earn, the only heir he left was his younger sister Queen Sybil's son, Donald Ban mac Duncan — whom he had always scorned and mistreated. In this situation, King Edward the Confessor saw his opportunity to remove a danger and divisive factor in his realm, and appointed Tostig, his brother-in-law, the late Earl Godwin's third son, as Earl of Northumbria and Deira.

MacBeth knew a considerable relief, for Tostig's interests were all towards the South of England and he was unlikely to inherit Siward's fondness for Malcolm Big Head. There was the danger, of course, that this could cut both ways, and that Malcolm, no longer in favour at Bamburgh, might be the more urgent and active about his Scottish ambitions.

The King decided to try to take a hand in this power-game. He made proclamation that in the new circumstances he was prepared to overlook past inimical acts of his subjects. Donald Ban mac Duncan in especial had taken no part in the recent shameful invasion of Scotland; and as eldest legitimate grandson of the late Crinan, was true heir to his mortuath. He therefore appointed him Mormaor of Atholl, and would welcome him back to Scotland, to take oath of fealty to him as Ard Righ. Also his lady-mother, the former Queen Sybil, if she cared to come. But not the illegitimate Malcolm Canmore, who had taken arms against his lawful sovereign, named himself King, and now by force occupied part of his monarch's domains. Likewise Duncan MacDuff, formerly of Fife.

MacBeth's hope was to drive a wedge between these half-brothers, and possibly Maldred also, and so break up something of the threat from the house of Crinan, under the new dispensation in Northumbria. He did not know where Donald Ban might be, but it was just possible that this might fetch him.

*　　*　　*

MacBeth reached his fiftieth birthday that year, and the fifteenth anniversary of his coronation. Gruoch insisted that they celebrate, although her husband was scarcely enthusiastic. Games were arranged for a great gathering at Forres, contests of skill and strength and arms, the King himself taking active part despite his newly-discerned venerability, and both Farquhar — fully recovered from his wound — and Luctacus distinguishing themselves. There was a Norman-style tournament organised by Sir Hugo. Because Gruoch found all this rather too evidently military, reflecting present preoccupations and forebodings, different sorts of activities were added, competitions and displays of piping, fiddling, dancing, metal-working, design, even stone-carving, a Pictish art which still flourished richly. And in the quiet September evening of the Exaltation of the Cross a great open-air feasting for hundreds, on the shore of Spynie Loch, the royal family in the midst.

It was towards the end of the repast, with most of the eating done and the drinking scarcely started, that two young men came pushing through the throng towards the royal table, dressed richly but clearly for the road rather than for feasting, tired-looking and indeed peat-spattered. Gruoch grasped her husband's arm.

"Lulach!" she murmured. "He has not failed you, after all."

Lulach had been invited to the celebrations, of course, but had not said that he would come — and MacBeth for one had scarcely expected to see him.

The King rose to welcome his step-son, as did all at the table — for this was, to be sure, the heir to the throne, however detached and unpopular. Gruoch probably was the only person there who had any real regard for him, although his half-brothers and sister tried their best.

"I rejoice to see you, son," MacBeth said, less than truthfully, as the other made his sketchy obeisance. "You have come from

343

Mamore? A long and rough road. You have not brought Malvina?"

"She is with child again," the younger man said expressionlessly, and went to kiss his mother. He turned back in his abrupt way. "I have brought another. Whom you have not seen. The Prince Donald mac Duncan."

Astonished, MacBeth turned to the other young man. He was stocky, notably fair-haired to account for his by-name of Ban, with undistinguished open, indeed freckled, features — but with a distinctly wary look not dissimilar to Lulach's own, although otherwise they had little in common. Save perhaps their destiny. He was about the same age as Farquhar, twenty years.

"Greetings, cousin," the King said, holding out his hand. "Your grandmother and my mother were sisters. Yet we have never met."

The other dropped on one knee to kiss the outstretched hand. "Your servant, lord King," he said thickly. "Our paths have been laid down . . . apart."

"True. Where, then, have your paths taken you these past years? Not in my realm?"

"But yes, Highness. I have been dwelling in the islands. Of the West. The Hebrides. In a monastery on the Long Isle, called Rowadill, Harris. But — I fear that I am not made for a monkish life."

"Save us — in the Isles! And I knew not of it. For years? Yet none told me — Thorfinn, Gillaciaran, Somerled, Abbot Robartach . . ."

"None knew, Highness. It was kept close."

"But why? And why there?"

"It was feared . . . what you might do. My Uncle Maldred persuaded my mother to send me. From Bamburgh, five years ago. The Earl Siward did not love me. My uncle was kind. He said that perhaps I should be a priest. After all, I am grandson and heir of Crinan, the Primate. One day I might be Abbot of Dunkeld, he said . . ."

"Or King of Scots!" MacBeth murmured softly.

"No, lord. That, they said, was reserved for my brother Malcolm. The Earl Siward was hot on that. The Abbot of Rowadill was kin to us, so I was sent there, secretly. It is a remote place. But . . . I have discovered that I am no priest, Highness."

Introductions over, they sat the young man down between

344

the King and Gruoch, Lulach at his mother's other side, and plied them with food whilst the entertainment proceeded. Donald seemed to be a straightforward and uncomplicated individual, with little of the attitude which might have been anticipated towards the man who had slain his father — whom, of course, he had scarcely known.

When the edge was off the visitors' hunger, MacBeth went on, after having congratulated Lulach on his further proof of virility.

"What made you flee the monastery, cousin? After five years."

"A bishop from Iona visited us. He knew who I was and told me that you, Highness, had proclaimed me Mormaer of Atholl and offered me place in Scotland again. At first I thought it but a ruse, to get me into your power, to use me, perhaps, as hostage, against my brother Malcolm. But Bishop Colbain said that was not your way, that you were an honest prince, fair, that I should trust you."

"The bishop spoke truth in that, at least."

"I had long felt confined on Harris. I recognised that I would never be of the stuff of monks and priests. This, this seemed opportunity to get away. I could say to Abbot Drostan that it was a royal command. He had to let me go. And I had heard that the Prince Lulach was, was . . . that he lived apart from your Court. Remote in the Drumalbyn mountains beyond Lochaber. I thought that he would tell me honestly if it was safe to come to you. So . . ."

"I am glad that I am esteemed honest! Even by Lulach!" the King said. "You will assume your Mortuath of Atholl, then? Take your rightful place as a mormaor of this realm? In allegiance to myself?"

"Yes. If you will have me."

"And your half-brother Malcolm? What will he say to this?"

"I care not. We have never been close. He is . . . not as I am."

"And Lulach? He has brought you here. But how does he see this?" MacBeth had lowered his voice.

"He would have me to do it. He understands my position. We could be friends, I think."

"That would be . . . interesting. Yet you could be a danger to him. One day."

"How so, Highness?"

"When I am gone, he will be King of Scots. You are the

lawful son of the last King. You might choose to claim the throne."

"No. I have no such desire. That is Malcolm's wish, not mine."

"Malcolm is a bastard, with no claim to be King. Your father, who doted on him, made him Prince of Strathclyde and heir to his throne. But that does not make him legitimate, or give him any right in the succession. Any such right could only lie with *you*. Whatever your own wishes, some might choose to set you up against Lulach — who is not every man's friend. I should require your sworn word that you would not be so used, and would rather *support* Lulach. Even against your own brother."

"You have it. But, Highness, you are not so very old. God willing, you will reign for many years yet. This of Prince Lulach is for many years to come. When all may be changed . . ."

"Perhaps, lad. But a king must ever take thought for the succession. And remember that he is mortal! I, now, am left in no doubts as to that last! But enough of this. I will establish you as mormaor. And one day, who knows, perhaps support your claim to the primacy? And you will support me. And thereafter, Lulach. Is it a compact?"

"It is, yes. And I thank you . . ."

25

THE FOLLOWING MAY, MacBeth returned from a visit to Gallo-way, to organise more celebrations — this time the coming-of-age of Farquhar — and found Gruoch ill at the House of Spynie, and with no mere ephemeral or passing ailment. He had been away for three weeks, and the very day after he had left Moray she had been afflicted with severe abdominal pains and cramps. These had continued. But despite her young people's urgings, she had refused to allow them to send to inform their father and suggest his return. When he did get back, he was shocked by the change in her, in so short a time. Although she endeavoured to maintain a cheerful front, she was drawn and pale, great-eyed, and had lost grievously in weight already. She had always been slenderly built, but never thin. Now, in these few weeks, her bone-structure had become evident.

"My dear, my dear!" he cried, in distress, a distress amplified as he embraced her and felt something like brittleness in her person. "What in God's name is this? What has happened to you? You are sick? So thin. What is wrong, Gruoch my heart?"

"It is just some silly woman's ailment," she assured, but a little breathlessly. "Nothing to concern yourself over. It will pass, as these pains do . . ."

"You have never been one for pains and sicknesses," he protested, almost accused. "Never the feeble sort."

"How do you know, lord and master?" she asked, with an attempt at lightness. "Can a woman not have her little aches and pains without always running to complain to her husband?"

He stared, chewing his lip. "But . . . you have grown thin. In this short time. And you are weakened — I can tell it. We must get Abbot Dungal." Dungal was the Keledei Abbot at the Rose Isle of Spynie, skilled in healing. "At once."

"I have seen the good abbot," Gruoch said. "He has given me brews, most unpleasant. Bled me also. Ordered me to eat this and not to eat that. I do not think that he is very knowledge-able about women's ailings — although he tries his best."

"Then we must find someone who does know. A woman. Some wise-woman who understands these things. My mother would have known what to do. She had healing hands and ancient lore . . ."

"Perhaps. But we shall not seek to raise the Princess Donada's ghost to treat my petty sickness! Fear nothing, my love — I shall soon be myself again. Now — tell me of Galloway . . ."

"No! That is of no importance beside this. Nothing is. We must find someone. I will scour the kingdom if need be, search out physicians and healers . . ."

"You will do no such thing, heart of my heart. You have a realm to rule and guard, soldiers to train, pleas to judge, councils to hold. And, have you forgotten, Farquhar's reaching of man's estate to celebrate? There is only two weeks, with much to be arranged . . ."

"Farquhar's celebration be damned! With you ill, that is the last thing to be thought of."

"Not so. It is important. And not only to our son. The entire kingdom expects it. Moray in especial, for he is their mormaor. To abandon the celebrations now, even to postpone them,

347

would be unwise. Bad for the realm. It would be seen as though you feared the future, feared this Malcolm Canmore. There were great doings for Lulach. Here, in Moray where Farquhar is well loved, he must have his day. I shall be there, and well enough, I promise you."

He shook his head helplessly.

That very evening, on pretext that he had to see old Gunnar at Torfness over Harald Cleft Chin's requirements in Galloway, MacBeth rode along the loch-shore, to call in at the Keledei cashel on Rose Isle on the way. There he confronted, almost challenged, the unhappy abbot.

"What is wrong with the Queen, Dungal?" he demanded. "She is sick, wasting. You have been giving her your brews and remedies. To no effect. What is wrong, man?"

"Who can say, Highness? I am sorry, deeply sorry. I have done all that I can. But clearly it is not enough . . ."

"You do not have to tell me that! You — you have the gift of healing, have you not? Can you not heal your own Queen?"

"Almighty God has given me only a very small talent in this respect, my lord King. Sufficient perhaps for common complaints, lesser sicknesses. But this, this is . . . otherwise. Beyond me, I fear. She, the Queen, is in God's own good hands in this . . ."

MacBeth clenched his fists, as though to prevent him from reaching out to shake the abbot. "What is it then, man? Do not prate to me of God — but tell me, of a mercy. What is wrong with her?"

"I fear, I greatly fear, that you said it yourself, Highness. It is my belief that she has the wasting sickness. That this is no matter for herbs and potions? But something only for the Maker of us all."

"Lord Christ!" The King stood for a moment or two, and then turned about without another word, and walked away, treading carefully.

He did not afterwards recollect crossing the loch back to where his horse waited, or indeed where he went thereafter, until, some unspecified time later he found himself in rising woodlands, amongst fallen pines and opening bracken, still afoot, and had some little difficulty in making his way back to his garron. He forced himself then to ride on, to Torfness, and to make a level and expressionless report to Gunnar Hound Tooth, and to arrange for a relief fleet to be sent to Galloway.

That night as he lay beside Gruoch, he did not close his eyes before cock-crow, still as she forced herself to lie in seeming sleep.

The next two weeks were a trial indeed, for both of them, for Gruoch in that she did not reveal, or at least make too evident, her pain and growing weakness; for MacBeth in that *he* did not reveal that he was aware of the dire seriousness of her malady, while the planning and preparing for the festivities went on. He did send far and near for persons renowned in the arts of healing, to be sure — for he had said that he was going to do this, anyway — but he could not submit the Queen to an endless succession of physicians, leeches, hospitallers, even spae-wives. So he had to interview these folk himself, secretly, and try to pick out from the many who came, or were sent by well-wishers, a few whom he hoped might be the most effective, using Abbot Dungal himself as adviser in the selection. Gruoch patiently put up with the examinations and ministrations of the chosen — with neither she nor her husband, in fact, having any expectation of betterment, and lacking perhaps the faith for faith-healing. At any rate, no improvement developed. And time and again it came to the man that this was far from being how this woeful interval should be spent; that it might be better for them both to try to accept realities and seek to comfort each other as best they might, without the pretence. But somehow, that did not seem possible, and this grievous make-believe had to go on — and partly for the young people's sake.

Gruoch fulfilled her promise, and represented herself as able and anxious to play her full part in the activities of Farquhar's birthday, the Eve of the Blessed Augustine. What it cost her, only she knew. It was a day of high-sailing cloud galleons, darting swallows, sun and shadow. It had been their endeavour not just to make it all a repetition of the recent celebrations, with more emphasis on youthful doings and predilections — although care had to be taken not to seem to emphasise this, for young men reaching majority seldom wish anything like immaturity to be emphasised. But it all did add up to a fairly active day, with much moving around, music, high spirits and noise — a trial indeed for one in pain and weakness. MacBeth, of course, watched his wife like a hawk throughout, and frequently sought to stop her from taking part, moderate as such participation had to be, to spare her from anything which he thought might over-tax what remained of her strength.

Inevitably that first day's programme ended with the usual feast and entertainment. Only toying with her food, Gruoch had sat through most of it, until MacBeth noticed that she was swaying back and forth in her chair, her eyes fixed ahead of her but not on the entertainers. She had made him promise to stop asking her how she was feeling, if she wished to retire and the like, but he had once again begun to do just that when, at one of her sways, she pitched forward over the table-top on to her uneaten viands and so lay sprawled.

Starting up with a groan, the King raised her head, to find her unconscious. He picked her up bodily in his arms, and she was light indeed. Farquhar materialised at his shoulder, then their other children and Neil Nathrach. Harshly MacBeth dismissed them, telling them that their duty was to see to their guests' cheer. He would look after his own. With all the company rising to their feet, he strode with his burden from the hall.

They were in the old palace at Forres, the House of Spynie being inconvenient for such large gatherings. The place was crowded with the visitors, of course, but MacBeth took Gruoch to one of the bedchambers, which was strewn with other folk's clothing, laid her on the bed, and ordered the guards to admit no one. He went back to her side, took her limp hand in his own, and so sat watching, a man in torment.

Farquhar was the first to come — Lulach was not attending the festivities — and entered despite the guard. His father scarcely saw him. Eala and Cormac came next, anxious-eyed; then Luctacus, slightly drunk, tearful. The King, at last, said that he would send for them if there was any change, anything that they might do. To suggestions that they send for Abbot Dungal or other physician, he gave a curt negative.

The night dragged on.

He dozed over towards morning, chin sunk on chest, and woke with the sunrise to find Gruoch's eyes open. Her lips moved when she saw that he was awake, but no sound came. He leaned forward to kiss those trembling lips, to whisper not to try to talk, but to rest, to harbour her strength. She managed to nod slightly, and he felt the hand still within his own tighten a little. She did not close her eyes however.

Despite himself he dozed again.

When next he came to himself, she was watching him, with such a depth of love and affection in her dark eyes as to bring a lump to his throat. Her lips moved again, and this time there was a faint murmur. Leaning close, he heard her.

"Poor . . . my heart! So long . . . a night. This no . . . employ for the . . . Son of Life!"

He shook his head, his turn to be wordless.

It took some time for her to summon strength to speak again. "Where?" she whispered. "Where are we?"

"Still at Forres. In someone's room. Are you in great pain, my dear?"

Her fingers gripped his. "Did I spoil . . . Farquhar's, Farquhar's . . .?"

"No. Not so. You became over-tired, that is all. I brought you here. To rest. The feasting went on. He came to see you, later. Farquhar. And the others. But you slept . . ."

Presently she asked him, "Take me home. The *Dorus Neamh*. The best place . . . that I know. I would . . . make my end there. In my own bed. *Our* bed."

He swallowed. "Do not say that, Gruochie — never that. We shall get you well again. I will take you home, yes. But not yet. I do not think that you are strong enough. For the journey. Ten miles. Presently we will go . . ."

"Please! Now. I would . . . be there. I do not think . . . that I have much time. Better to be going there, at least . . . than, than . . ." She gasped for breath. "On my way."

Biting his lip, he gazed at her as she pleaded this of him. He nodded.

Leaving her, he arranged for a litter to be contrived, slung between two staid old garrons. Wrapped in plaids and furs, the Queen was gently carried out to this, and escorted by her family, they set out at a walking pace. To ensure that this pace was not exceeded and that there was the minimum of swaying and jolting, MacBeth himself walked between the horses' heads, while Farquhar and Luctacus walked behind, to steady the litter.

The journey took almost three hours, Gruoch only half-conscious much of the time.

At last she was installed in her own bed in the House of Spynie — and was sufficiently aware of it to whisper that now she was content, before slipping away into something like sleep.

For three days and nights she lay, and in that time MacBeth was never far from her side. She would eat nothing — and when once, he insisted that she tried, and with great difficulty got a mouthful of gruel and milk down her throat, the resultant convulsions were so desperate that the man feared that he had killed her, as he held her frail, racked body in his arms. All she could take were sips of watered wine, and that infrequently.

On the fourth day she seemed to rally somewhat, although she had moaned a lot during the night, something she had not done hitherto. Faintly she chided him. He was a king, was he not? With a realm to rule. Not a nurse or foster-woman. He must be off, about the realm's affairs, not waiting about a weakly woman's bedside. There was much to do, always much to do. And he had sworn on the Stone to cherish his kingdom, *their* kingdom, as a father. He must go do his duty, or she would not know any peace of mind. Never fear, she would be awaiting him on his return. It took her a long time to get all that said.

It was true, of course. Matters, problems, decisions which only he could take, were piling up. Neil did what he could, but he was not the same man since Earn-side, something vital gone out of him. Since Gruoch did seem slightly stronger — she could not have spoken thus, otherwise — he allowed himself to be persuaded. He rode to Forres, sending out summons to a council, at short notice.

In late afternoon Luctacus arrived at the palace in panting haste, bursting in on the conclave. His mother had been siezed in a most dire attack. They had feared that she would not survive it. Still she might not, although it had eased a little when he had left. She was not conscious latterly . . .

Without a word MacBeth rose from the table and hurried out.

The Queen was still in a coma when he reached their bed-chamber, her breathing weak and erratic. Again he sat at her side, hour after hour, food and drink brought to him there by their young people. Eventually, in the middle of the night, without her having regained consciousness, he laid himself down beside her, and slept.

He was awakened some unspecified time later by a voice, Gruoch's voice, quite clear, even louder than of late.

"Hold me, beloved. Hold me close. I need . . . your strength. For a little. It will not be long now."

"Dear heart!" Gripping her, he choked, and could say no more.

"Never fear, my dear. I only leave you . . . for a time. I am not frightened. It is but . . . another journey. A good journey, I think. And your love will accompany me, all the way. So I shall not be alone. Until you join me, your own self. That is sure. Do not fear. For me. Or for yourself."

He shook his head against her dark, damp hair.

She was quiet for moments, her breathing a labour. When she spoke again, her voice was much less strong, less sure.

"It is only Lulach I fear for. The others are well enough.

Strong. Like you. But Lulach — he has never known true happiness. Look after Lulach, my heart, I pray. For our love's sake. It is not his fault."

"Yes."

"I thank you. I do not know, but I think, I think . . . oh, hold me, hold me, Son of Life!"

Wordless he clutched her twitching, twisting person, so slight, kissing her hair, her brow, her neck. Presently the spasm faded.

He murmured in her ear, but she did not answer now. He spoke brokenly, incoherently, telling her of his abiding love.

After a little she suddenly found words again, distinct, with a kind of certainty.

"Your hand, my dear. I shall look for you . . . when Birnam Wood comes to Dunsinane."

She heaved twice within his arms, and breathed no more.

He continued to hold her until the sun rose.

26

MacBeth took Gruoch to Iona for burial. The Church forbade men and women to be interred together; but at least they would lie in the same small and lovely isle when his time came, a time he now looked forward to without apprehension. But he rejected any elaborate funeral obsequies, such as undoubtedly she was entitled to as Queen of Scots, but which she, no more than he, would have wanted. Only the family stood round the grave on Tor Abb that June morning, and when the monks' chanting died away they heard only the sigh of the waves and the cuckoos calling from the twisted island thorn-trees and the oyster-catchers wheepling on the white cockle-sand shore. The King was dry-eyed now. He would not weep again, ever. Lulach wept, almost the first time he had been seen to show emotion since early childhood.

MacBeth thereafter took up the burden of his kingship again with a sort of stern energy. He went down to Fortrenn, visited his forces facing occupied Lothian at the Forth, made a progress to whip up support and morale in nervous Strathclyde right to the edge of Galloway, where he summoned Paul

Thorfinnson and Harald to meet him, to discuss strategy. He called three conferences at Dunsinane; one with Glamis and all his military leaders, including Gunnar from Torfness who was no subject of his; one with the Abbot Ewan and the other officers of state, to appoint a new Chancellor — for old Bishop Malduin had died suddenly, full of years; and one of Church leaders, to appoint a new Bishop of Saint Andrews and Ard Episcop. All matters which had been too long delayed. From these councils a more aggressive military plan against the Northumbrian invaders of Lothian and the Merse was drawn up; Abbot Ewan became the new Chancellor; and one of the Iona bishops, Tuthald by name, became Ard Episcop and Bishop of Saint Andrews.

So passed a busy two months of that summer, with MacBeth driving himself, and all others, hard — partly in duty, to compensate for what some might see as his recent neglect of the realm's pressing problems, partly to drug his personal desolation with work and physical weariness.

It was not until the beginning of August that he found time to do anything definite about starting to redeem his promise to Gruoch on the subject of Lulach. Back at Spynie, he sent for his step-son. Lulach came, reluctantly it might be inferred, from his mountains fastness in Mamore, and again brought Donald Ban with him, these two lonely young princes seeming to have become close friends, a strange development.

The King spoke to Lulach alone, pacing the *Dorus Neamh* orchard in the golden evening light, the older man little more eager than the younger.

"See you, lad," he said, more abruptly than he knew or intended. "You cannot continue in this way. Hiding yourself in your mountains, living like some eremite who has rejected the world of men. You are the heir to the throne, and you should be taking your part in the rule of the realm."

"It was never any wish of mine to be heir, sir," he was told flatly.

"Nevertheless it is your destiny. You were born to it. As I was *not*. You have to face the facts of it."

Lulach took him up quickly. "If you were not born to it, and yet are lawful and accepted King, why not another? Make Farquhar your heir. Your own son. He would king it well enough. A deal better than would I."

"Farquhar might rule, yes. But that is scarcely the point. Some men call me usurper, because I slew Duncan and became

King in his stead. Some fight against me, because of that. I will not have my son so named also, because he reigned when another had more right. You are your mother's eldest son and the right comes through her. Always this has been recognised."

"That was so, once. But now there is Donald Ban. Is he not as much lawful heir as am I? If you will not give Farquhar the succession, give it to Donald — eldest son of Duncan. And thereby heal the breach between the two royal lines. If you named Donald as heir to your throne now, would not all this warfare and struggle fade away? Those who supported Duncan would no longer have any quarrel with you, and you would unite the realm again."

MacBeth paused in his pacing, to stare at his step-son. "You . . . and Donald! Is this what you have been hatching? Donald seeks the throne, after all? I wondered why he clung so close to you!"

"No! It was my notion, not his. But I have thought much on it . . ."

"You have not thought enough, nevertheless! Have you forgotten Malcolm Big Head? He, bastard though he is, claims the crown, as against his legitimate younger brother. Already he is calling himself King of Scots."

"If you made Donald heir, Prince of Strathclyde, those supporting Malcolm must needs think again. MacDuff and the others."

"You deceive yourself. Donald is mild, almost gentle. Malcolm is hard, strong, ambitious. Men who wish to overturn a regime will always support Malcolm's kind against Donald's. Even King Edward of England, saint as he is called, is now so doing, I am told. Calling Malcolm King and telling Tostig to aid him with men and ships. No, lad — we shall not save my throne by calling Donald heir. We shall have to fight for it, I fear."

The other was silent.

"Which brings me to what I would say to you," MacBeth went on. "I know that you are no warrior, nor wish to be — although, God knows, when you are King you will have to use the sword as well as the sceptre. But now you could aid the realm, if you will, in this pass. As Prince of Strathclyde you could call upon many of the chiefs and thanes and landed men of upper Strathclyde and Dalar, your own Highland area, where I have not had time to visit. Call in my name. Seek to have them raise their men, many men. To send to me, for the defence of

355

Strathclyde. They leave all to me. Seem scarce to consider it their concern . . ."

"Perhaps they may favour the house of Crinan? Dalar flanks Atholl."

"It could be so. Although they did not support Crinan in his revolt. But . . ." He paused. ". . . take your friend Donald with you, then! If they see that he has made his peace with me and mine, Duncan's lawful son, they might be the more willing."

The younger man looked less than enthusiastic. "How can I do that . . . ?"

"You have *some* duties towards this realm, have you not? Your mother's realm. Think you that all *I* have to do is to my taste?"

They left it at that.

The very next morning, however, the situation became suddenly more urgent. Gunnar arrived from Torfness with a messenger from Ingebiorg in Orkney. Thorfinn Raven Feeder was dead.

MacBeth grieved for his brother, of course. But numbed already as he was by the death of Gruoch, the sense of loss and pain was dulled. Also, it was no real surprise; indeed the wonder was that Thor had lingered on, like some felled tree-trunk, for so long. MacBeth's true acceptance of his brother's death had been when he said goodbye to him at Birsay that day three years before. Both had known then that they would never see each other again this side of the grave. And the Raven Feeder was probably better dead than lying useless.

But grieving apart, the tidings created all sorts of new demands. Ingebiorg's message assumed that MacBeth would attend the obsequies. Thorfinn of course, must be given the typical and elaborate Viking burial, beneath his own beached and upturned longship, with fires and wild music and saga-telling, even feasting, for the greatest Viking of them all. Much as he would have wished to be present however, the King just dared not go, not at this stage in his threatened realm's affairs. Nothing was more sure than that the news would swiftly be carried to his enemies' ears — and Scotland would immediately become more vulnerable than she had been since Siward's invasion. For so many of her friends would be flocking to Orkney, undoubtedly. Thorfinn's hosts would gather from far and near; anything else was unthinkable, for the sending of a mighty Viking on his way to Valhalla, Christianity or none, was a tremendous occasion, taking days and nights to accomplish properly. So for those days and nights the command of the seas would be in abeyance, and Tostig's Northumbrian fleet need fear no interference. Gunnar himself would be going, with most of the Torfness garrison. Assuredly Paul, now Earl of Orkney, must go, and almost certainly Harald Cleft Chin with him, leaving only Sween Kennedy to command in Galloway. Earl Somerled mac Gillciaran would be there, along with the other Hebridean chiefs. For days at least, Scotland's flanks would be wide open to any determined invader. And Edward of England's recent orders to Tostig and declared support of Malcolm Canmore as King of Scots, was significant.

MacBeth would send Farquhar to represent him — since Lulach would be like a fish out of water at a Viking burial. He might even let Cormac and Eala go too, to their uncle's funeral. Luctacus, who would drink too much, or at least be affected too greatly by what he drank — and yet was becoming an excellent soldier — he would take South with him, since South he must go.

It would all have to be done at once, for the burial could not be over-long delayed at this warm time of the year, and was arranged to start only two days hence.

By afternoon that very day, leaving Neil Nathrach to complete the mustering and bringing on of the Moray and Ross army, and seeing his three Orkney-bound offspring on to a longship at Torfness, MacBeth with his second son and a small, fast escort, turned to ride with all speed for the Mounth passes, heading for Glamis first and then Dunsinane. He would drop off couriers on the way, to Buchan and Mar, the Mearns and Angus, the mormaors and thanes to order musters and to come on immediately themselves.

27

AT THE HURRIEDLY-CALLED council-of-war at Dunsinane, MacBeth stared grimly down the long table at his lords and leaders — or at such of them as he had been able to assemble at short notice.

"So we are faced, my friends, with the same problem and

situation as we were three years ago," he said, heavily. "Having to divide our forces against a possible three-pronged assault. But this time without the aid from the sea, longships. Or few of them. We cannot fight adequately on all three fronts — Forth, Tay and Galloway. And there could be a fourth — up the Clyde firth, to attack our rear from Alclyde. In a week, ten days, we might muster sufficient men to face all, perhaps. But I fear that we will not be given such time. If *I* was Malcolm, or Tostig, I would not wait until the Orkney funeral was over, but would strike now, whatever state I was in. So how do we best divide and dispose our strength?"

"Lord King," Lachlan of Buchan, just arrived from the North with Martacus of Mar, declared, "This, of three fronts, or four, is but guess-work. It may be so — but it may not. After all, this sudden death of the Earl of Orkney will be as much a surprise to our enemies as to ourselves. They will not all be ready mustered, either. So it may take time for any sea-borne force to move against us, up Tay or up Clyde. We know that there are movements in Lothian, yes, with the insufferable Malcolm the Bastard. But the rest is only fears and doubts. I say that we should throw our whole strength at Lothian. At once. Or so soon as our people reach us from the North. Attack across Forth, and seek to defeat Malcolm with one swift stroke. Before any of your feared ship-borne hosts can arrive. Let us be done with defence, always defence, of waiting for others to assail us. Attack, I say!"

There was a fairly strong murmur of agreement from down the table. Because Lothian was now occupied territory, well-wishers there kept the King very fully informed of what went on, and at present they knew of major troop concentrations and movements, indicative of a renewed campaign. The general reaction was clearly that this should be crushed before it got under way.

"I commend your spirit, my lord," MacBeth said. "And if I could be assured that our rear was secure, I might choose to do as you advise. But *I* have the abiding safety of my realm to consider. We might win in Lothian, yet find the heart of Scotland lost behind us. I dare not risk that."

Martacus spoke, his manner so much more hesitant than Lachlan's. "We have some few ships, Highness. Send them out to the mouth of Tay. To the mouth of the Scottish Sea also, perhaps. Not to fight, since we have not sufficient to challenge any English fleet. But to form a screen. If the enemy appears in large numbers, these to skirmish and beat about, to hold up the English for a little while fast vessels bring you the news. So that we are not caught unprepared. As to the Clyde, I cannot say."

"If I am engaged in battle with Malcolm deep in Lothian, that would serve little," the King said. "We must not again waste our strength in hurrying from one side of the land to the other, exhausting our people so that they do not fight at their best."

"I agree," Glamis said. "I say that the King must remain here. At the centre. With the Normans and heavy cavalry. But my lord of Buchan has the rights of it also. We should not wait to be assailed, but attack first. That can only be across Forth. Let him lead our main strength south into Lothian. Leaving the Forth crossing well guarded behind him. Seek out and destroy Malcolm, if he can. But be ready to retire quickly behind Forth again if need be — for he could be outflanked by a landing from ships on the shores of Fife."

"Aye — that is best," Lachlan declared. "And what of you, my lord Constable? What will you be doing?"

"If His Highness is here, at Dunsinane, to marshal and direct the men from north and west as they come in, there is no need for me. I can take a smaller horsed force into the middle of Fife. To be prepared to strike at the north shore or the south, should there be a sea-borne landing. Or both."

"So we are split into three again," MacBeth commented. It went against the grain for him to be allotted a waiting role, at the centre, like a spider in its web, whilst others took the active parts. Yet he saw the sense of such disposition. "This of Fife is well thought of. But *I* will head that force. We may have to move fast and far. You, old friend, will remain here at Dunsinane, to deal with the incoming troops and hold the centre."

"As you will . . ."

"Now — as to Lachlan's strategy, with the main host." It was important that the headstrong Mormaor of Buchan be given fairly definite instructions, as a royal command, lest he overstretch himself, for he was an excellent captain but unproven as a general. "Once across Forth at Stirling — if you achieve that — what do you propose?"

"They say that Malcolm sits at Linlithgow on the Avon. When he hears of our crossing, he will march north. I would plan that we should seek to meet him at Ecclesbreac, where the great Tor Wood comes close and would hide us. Yet there is a good killing-ground for horse in the plain below."

"The Tor Wood is good, yes. But further north than Ecclesbreac there is the mouth of the Carron Water, where it enters the Forth amongst marshes and mud-flats. If you were to use that, with the eastern skirts of the wood, you would protect your flank in case you had to make hasty retiral on Stirling Bridge again."

"It is not my intention to have to make hasty retiral, Highness! On this occasion."

"More experienced commanders than you have had to do so, my lord. You must be prepared to do so, always. Or I must find another to command this host."

The other was silent, jaw out-thrust.

"You may not be defeated, yet require to withdraw nevertheless. Or I may send for you in *my* haste and need. Is it understood?"

So the details were thrashed out, deputy commanders chosen and preparations to move made. Lachlan, with Martacus and Colin of Mearns, would march for the Forth valley with the majority of the troops assembled at Dunsinane, just as soon as their own hosts from Mar and Buchan arrived and were briefly rested. MacBeth would send part of the Moray and Ross contingents after them, and the remainder he would take to Fife. Such shipping as was available in the Tay would sail at once. And Glamis would organise this base at Dunsinane, hold a small reserve and despatch oncoming troops where most required.

It was the Eve of Saint Lawrence the Martyr, 1057.

*   *   *

MacBeth chose a position on the high summit ridge of the East Lomond Hill, directly above Falkland in Central Fife — or Fothrif, as this western half of Fife was called. There he established his look-outs, while encamping his mobile force of some 600 light horsemen in a more sheltered hollow behind the crest. They were considerably nearer to the Forth, or Scottish Sea, here, than to the Tay, of which, high as they were, they could see only glimpses; but the King judged that there was more likelihood of a sea-borne attack at this side, to aid any move by Malcolm. He did plant another look-out post on Dunbog Hill however, about eight miles to the north, across the Howe, which overlooked the Firth of Tay, and from which smoke-signals would inform him of any activity there.

The view from the Lomond ridge was extensive, magnificent.

Southwards, across the gleaming firth, all Lothian lay spread, green and fertile, to the serried ranges of the Pentland, Moorfoot and Lammermuir Hills. Westwards, beyond Fothrif, the Ochils seemed to merge into the mighty Highland peaks of Lennox and Strathearn. And eastward, the estuary widened until it was lost in the illimitable plain of the Norse Sea, island-strewn near its mouth and fringed by golden beaches of sand on both sides. It was all too distant to be able to observe troop movements in Lothian, but any approach by sea would be entirely obvious.

It was pleasant to laze up there in the warm August sunshine, with the bees loud amongst the burgeoning bell-heather, the larks shouting and war and invasion seemingly but evil dreams. But on the second morning dark smoke-clouds billowing up from the north-western parts of Lothian indicated men at their grim work and battle joined in some stage between Lachlan's forces and Malcolm's. It brought the watchers back to reality, if this was needed.

In the event, the northern outpost on Dunbog Hill was not required, for soon after mid-day a great fleet of sail was beginning to be evident at the mouth of the Scottish Sea, coming from the south. And presently this vast concourse of ships could be seen to be splitting up, half turning westwards into the firth, half continuing northwards on the open ocean. So MacBeth's fears and assessments were confirmed. The land thrust was to be aided by landings from both firths. He sent riders to warn Lachlan, whoever was holding the Stirling crossing, and Cormac of Glamis.

The question now was one of priorities. 600 men was too small a force to divide effectively. At this stage the Forth landing was probably the most dangerous, since it could cut off Lachlan's army. Moreover the northern fleet would take some hours longer to reach the Tay, twenty-five miles further, and then to sail another twenty-five miles up its estuary to where landings would be most effective. So the first priority was to try to deal with the southern landing, and then, hopefully, to race north to aid Glamis cope with the other.

The King's tactics, of course, were founded on the temporary vulnerability of armies landing from shipping on enemy territory. If he could allow such landing to start and then descend upon it unheralded, a major defeat might be inflicted. So his next priority was secrecy of approach.

Unfortunately he could not be sure that the landing would be on the north or Fife shore. If it proved to be on the south, he could do nothing about it. But while a southern landing might be effective enough in getting behind Lachlan and cutting him off, it would still leave the enemy on the wrong side of the vital Stirling crossing. Moreover, this fleet could scarcely know of Lachlan's present sally into Lothian; it would have left Northumbria before any such news could have reached there. The King was fairly confident, therefore, that the landing would be made on the north shore, to outflank the defenders of Stirling's bridge and causeway, and then to link up with the Tay invasion. And he reckoned that it would be made as far up-river as was practical without being obvious to the Stirling defenders.

With the enemy ships crossing the widest part of the Scottish Sea, between Largo Bay on the north and Aberlady Bay on the south, MacBeth led his mounted forces westwards, still on the Lomond high ground but hidden from the coastal plain by the ridge, until they could safely turn southwards, down to the Kinglassie area of the Leven valley. But he left scouts on the summit ridge, to watch the fleet's progress. At the Leven, one of these brought word that the English were still sailing up-firth, and nearer to the north shore than the south. He had counted between thirty and forty ships. The other scouts were still following the enemy progress, along the high ground above the coast.

The 600 now sped south-westwards. MacBeth was heading for Clach Mannan, on the western verge of Fothrif, where there was the viewpoint allied to cover which he needed. They rode between Lochs Leven and Ore, keeping to the south of the Cleish Hills and so into the wide valley of the Black Devon, via the Saline Water, all this well inland. As the Black Devon turned southwards, towards its junction with the Forth, it so happened that the latter's north shores sank away to the wide flats and marshlands of Kennet, providing no cover from view for a mounted force. But out of these flats rose the hog's-back ridge of Mannan, named from an early Christian saint from Ireland; who had made his cell there. It was not a high ridge, but it offered a mile-long barrier and vantage-point. Keeping close to the Black Devon bank, the riders could reach this unseen from the estuary, and approach behind the ridge to only a mile or so from salt water.

Past the little cashel of Saint Mannan and the village which had grown up round it, with its black *clach* or Stone of Mannan, they mounted the escarpment, MacBeth praying that, with all this long riding, they were not too late.

Dismounting, the King crept up to the summit, to peer over,

and caught his breath at what he saw. There, little more than a mile away, was the enemy, a long column of ships of all sorts, strung out along the narrow channel, covering a couple of miles perhaps. They were still moving upstream, but slowly now. And looking towards the head of the line, MacBeth grunted. Westwards, beyond the mouth of the Black Devon, the estuary changed character notably, becoming a river indeed, taking a great loop southwards and its course becoming part-filled with large sand-islands. At the neck of the loop was the little township of Alueth, a fishing community connected with the Saint Mannan monastery. Here the leading English ships were clearly moving in, to land.

It was, to be sure, a well-chosen spot. It was only four miles east of Stirling, yet was hidden therefrom by the great bend of the Forth as well as by the rising ground of Tullibody. The banks here were of shelving sand and not mud, as now prevailed elsewhere. And the great loop of the river would enable many ships to unload at one time, close together, not stretched far down the estuary.

Someone in the occupying forces in Lothian, perhaps Malcolm himself, had been using his wits.

MacBeth, nodding to himself, switched his gaze to the hinterland, searching its features and tactical possibilities closely, eagerly. He decided that if the English could use Alueth, so could he.

Hurrying back to his men, the King remounted and led them off westwards again, behind the ridge. They forded the Black Devon before it reached the mud-flats, and cantered across the mile or so of sloping grassland pastures, still hidden from the Forth, to the woodland behind Alueth.

Selecting a viewpoint just within the trees, MacBeth, Luctacus and other lieutenants, surveyed the scene. The landing was in progress all round the U-shaped loop, although some of the ships still waited, unable to find a space, others double-berthed and their soldiers crossing the intervening vessels to the shore. It was not possible accurately to gauge numbers, but they reckoned that there must be 2000 men there, at least. The land enclosed by the loop was only some 300 yards wide but over half-a-mile long, and it was rapidly filling up with men, arms, armour and the stores being unloaded.

It was obvious that there was little time to be lost. Tactics would be elementary, could be nothing else. They would form two wedges of 250 each, under father and son, and charge down the narrow tongue of land as nearly side-by-side as was possible, at the tip to swing right and left to turn back and beat up the two shores. The remaining hundred would come along behind, not as a wedge but forming a broad front across the tongue, to prevent any break-out, moving more slowly, mopping up, killing. No elaborate instructions were necessary.

Dividing his people into these three companies, MacBeth drew his sword and slashed it down and forward over his garron's head, as he had done so often before. With a sudden great shout the Scots surged forward.

It was a complete surprise, a complete rout, a massacre, nothing more nor less, with a little chivalry, no quarter, no respite. The Northumbrians were not yet organised into any sort of formation, their leaders still superintending the dis-embarkation, arms still stacked, armoured tunics largely un-donned on account of the heat. Worst of all for them, there was no room for defensive manoeuvre, or much movement of any sort, the crush too dense to see signals or to hear commands, all penned in that narrow space between the river-banks. Not all were landed yet, and there was utter confusion, with some pushing out from the ships and others pushing back aboard for safety. The entire pack of distracted humanity was helpless before the charging, trampling horses and the flailing swords and battle-axes.

All was over in an incredibly short time, with no need for the Scots to re-form and repeat their charges. It seemed scarcely possible that thousands of men could die so quickly. Not all died, of course. Many managed to get back to their vessels, many leapt into the water and some of these reached the ships. Some few may have escaped as fugitives inland, many wounded would feign dead and so survive. But all who remained trapped on that spit of land between the river-banks fell and remained fallen.

There was chaos, too, amongst the shipping, with no evident over-all command surviving. As the disaster overtaking the landed force became obvious, most vessels pulled out into the already congested waters of the river, the resultant disorder indescribable. Those which were unable, because of the crush, to draw away, were quickly boarded and captured by the Scots.

Despite the speed of their victory, MacBeth permitted no delay, no lingering. He was preoccupied now with the thought of the Tay section of this fleet and what it might be achieving. The Firth of Tay was shorter than that of the Scottish Sea and the Forth estuary. Time was of the essence. Ordering the captured ships to be set on fire, and leaving only a small party to see to the wounded, he sent off messengers to inform the guardians of the Stirling crossing, and Lachlan of Buchan, of the situation, and forming up his now jaded company, led it off north by east at such speed as he could impose.

They had the long barrier of the green, rounded Ochil Hills between them and Strathearn. They headed for the Devon valley — not the Black Devon by which they had come but its northerly sister — following this up through the foothills by Dolair and into Glen Devon. This narrow valley threaded the main massif for five miles, and then a little pass carried them over into the north-opening Glen of the Church, past the little cashel of Saint Mungo and so down into wide Strathearn near Auchterarder. Thereafter it was just hard riding for the seventeen miles to the River Tay at Saint John's Town of Perth.

The news at that alarmed township was that an English fleet had come up the Tay as far as Kinfauns, where the Constable had blocked the suddenly-narrowing river with a barrier of sunken boats. There the enemy had disembarked, in their thousands, but so far had made no advance up-river. Whether they had marched instead up through the Sidlaws pass of Balthayock towards Dunsinane, none knew; but there was still a large encampment of them at Kinfauns, near their shipping, as could be seen from the heights of Kinnoull.

It was now early evening and the King, slightly relieved, pressed on with his weary horsemen the couple of miles more to the Scone ford and across to the abbey. Old Abbot Cathail, who was in constant touch with Glamis, said that so far as he knew all was still well at Dunsinane.

They rode on the remaining seven miles, in the long shadows of the sunset, thankful to proceed now at only a modest trot.

Glamis the Constable was much relieved to see them, and to hear of the destruction of the Forth invasion force. He had only some 1500 men all told, including the Norman heavy cavalry under Sir Hugo Despard, and the information he had was that the English landed at Kinfauns numbered around 3000. He believed that they were under the command of MacDuff — at least they flew the Fife banner. They had pushed an advance force of about 1000 through the Balthayock pass to the northern flanks of the Sidlaws at the Dalreich area only four miles away, and there halted. Glamis had a small screening force between them, holding the line of a swampy burn between Bandirran and

Melginch, and another some miles to the east, at Buttergask, to discourage any attack up Strathmore. But he had insufficient men to make either effective. He was glad to resign responsibility into the King's hands.

MacBeth wearily accepted that as his portion. He weighed choices and gave orders as he ate. Sleep was not yet, if at all — for the enemy might stage a night attack.

On fresh horses at least he and Luctacus rode off again, through the half-dark, two miles southwards, to inspect the forward force under the Thane of Cowie, and found them dispersed along the line of the quite large Melginch Burn, in a marshy area with scattered, twisted old thorn trees. Cowie reported all quiet, with the enemy on slightly higher ground just over a mile away on Dalreichmoor. Scouts out ahead relayed no signs of any immediate advance.

Satisfied for the moment, MacBeth left Luctacus there to support Cowie, and returned to Dunsinane, to snatch a few hours of sleep. But only a few, for he must be ready for action before first light.

*   *   *

MacDuff's attack was unaccountably delayed. The following forenoon passed without major incident, although the Northumbrian force facing Cowie was much reinforced, and another enemy grouping came up through the Sidlaws further to the north-east, by the Kinnaird pass to the Abernyte area, constituting a threat to Cowie's flank. The King ordered some adjustment of line, moving Glamis's eastern outpost somewhat, and waited.

Happily a contingent of 400 Angusmen arrived from Blair in Gowrie and Glen Isla, moreover saying that a still larger reinforcement was on its way from the Mearns. Glamis expected others, likewise, from elsewhere.

It was soon after mid-day that the attack at length developed, with a simultaneous advance on both fronts, some three miles apart with the hilly and rougher terrain of Pitmeudle between, the main thrust being that to the west, at Dalreich, against Cowie. At this stage the King himself remained at Dunsinane, the old fort's 1000-feet-high hill-top site making an excellent vantage-point. The enemy's delaying worried him. It looked as though they had been waiting for something. Something presumably to their advantage. It could be, of course, that they had been looking for the arrival of the destroyed Forth army, had not been informed of its defeat. Or perhaps they assumed Malcolm's victory south of Stirling, and delayed until a junction could be made. But if so, why had they now started the attack? It could be mere uncertain generalship. But MacBeth was uneasy. So he sent forward as many men as he could afford, to reinforce the two fronts, but kept a tactical reserve of about 500, mainly his own light cavalry but including the Normans, with him at Dunsinane.

The fighting took place roughly a couple of miles to the south-east and south-west, the Pitmeudle high ground and escarpments preventing any joining of the fronts, although the watchers on Dunsinane could see both. From there the impression gained was of only moderately enthusiastic assault, less than desperate fighting. It could be that MacDuff, if he it was who was personally in command, was just not a vigorous commander. Or perhaps, having now heard of the defeat at Alueth, he was going warily until he could be reinforced by Malcolm. Somehow, however, the sense was still of some sort of waiting game being played. MacBeth kept raising his gaze from the middle distance where the fighting was, to scan the entire background southwards — which meant in fact the entire range of the Sidlaw Hills from east-south-east to west-south-west — for any hint of new developments. Admittedly it was towards the south-east that he looked most often, for surely if there were any major enemy move in the south-west or Saint John's Town and Scone area, Abbot Cathail would send word. He was in fact afraid of further sea-borne forces arriving in the Tay estuary. There was no reason to assume that *all* Tostig's shipping had been committed in that initial invasion fleet. More might be on the way. And Lothian itself, with its many fishing-ports, could provide many vessels of various sorts. Malcolm could reinforce MacDuff by sea.

Nevertheless, all that as it might be, the battle was real enough over in the Bandirran-Melginch moorland and marsh-land, and no doubt more than sufficiently bloody for those taking part. The Scots were outnumbered, even when some 600 Mersemen arrived under Colin's young brother, and were almost immediately sent forward to stiffen both fronts.

MacBeth fretted at his present idle role of over-all supervision — but knew without old Cormac of Glamis's reiteration that it was wise.

In mid-afternoon there was an enemy breakthrough on the extreme west, where a section of MacDuff's force managed to work round Cowie's right flank and threaten his rear. This had to be countered, and at once. MacBeth, eager for some action himself, led 300 of his light cavalry down, in a swift encircling sweep to south and west, at the same time ordering Sir Hugo and his Normans to advance directly on the breakthrough front. The result was sufficiently effective, the light horse herding the Northumbrians towards the heavy chivalry rather like a flock of sheep, and great was the slaughter — although MacBeth lost some men and beasts through archery.

The threat to Cowie's rear removed, the King ordered a return to Dunsinane. MacDuff was unlikely to risk that again.

But back at the hill-top palace an exhausted courier awaited MacBeth, with evil tidings. He came from the Mormaor Lachlan. The Scots army had suffered defeat in Lothian. On the flats of the Avon-mouth, near to Kinneil . . .

"Kinneil! Avon-mouth! What were you doing there?" the King cried. "I said the Carron, not the Avon. To seek fight between Carron-mouth and the Tor Wood."

"The English made no stand against us there, Highness. My lord of Buchan pressed on towards this Lithgow, on the Avon, to bring them to battle. But we were trapped between two channels of the river . . ."

"God's curse on the man! I should never have given him the command. So all is lost?"

"The army is broken and dispersed. How many slain, I know not . . ."

"And the fallen? Lachlan. Colin of Mearns?"

"He is well — the mormaor. And my lord Martacus of Mar. The leaders, in the main, escaped. Swam the river on their horses. They have returned to Stirling."

"And the crossing? The bridge and causeway at Stirling?"

"Still held, my lord King. The mormaor says that he will hold it, to the last."

"The saints be praised for that, at least! Pray that he does not fail us there!"

"Did Malcolm Big Head command the English in person?" Glamis asked.

"I do not know, my lord. We saw little of the enemy leaders."

"Aye. That I believe!"

"How many men has Lachlan now? Remaining?" the King demanded.

"I know not, Highness. All was confusion . . ."

"Some notion, man? Hundreds? Thousands?"

"Some hundreds, perhaps. More were coming in, all the time. At Stirling. At the bridge . . ."

MacBeth turned away, to pace the ramparts of the old fort, sick at heart. Apart from the loss, the waste, friends and subjects fallen, this could change all. Sooner or later the victorious Malcolm would surmount the hurdle of the Forth. If not at the Stirling crossing, then by boats across the estuary. Lachlan would certainly not have sufficient men to make any pretence at defending the entire lengthy Fife shore-line. And *he* was in no position to send help, meantime. *Meantime* — that was the marrow of it all. Time was all-important now. As so often it was. But now . . .

He turned back to Glamis. "Cormac — we must attack. Change to the attack. Seek to defeat MacDuff, not just hold him off. Outnumbered as we are. Now — before Malcolm can cross Forth. If *both* his sea-borne forces are defeated, he will think twice of pushing on northwards. That will give us time. Time to recover our strength. To build up new commands."

"Aye — but what do we attack with?"

"These — the cavalry. Do what we have just done. But win behind them. I will take my light horse, in a wide sweep to the west. As far as Balgray. To turn their flank. Sir Hugo to make a shorter sweep. To Melginch. They lie open to the west, weak."

"You have scarcely 500, all told."

"Enough to menace their rear. With cavalry. Force them to turn round. Then Cowie to advance. We *must* turn them back, defeat them quickly. Or all is lost. I will lead. You remain here . . ."

Despite the Constable's doubts, MacBeth gave the Normans their orders and rode off south-westwards with all his light horse.

Their going was not secret, nor designed to be. By the time that the King's 400 were crossing the Melginch Burn near Balgray and Balbeggie, the enemy was becoming distinctly restive and beginning to change his dispositions to meet a threat from the flank. And when the Scots light horse were seen to continue on south by east into the foothills behind Dalreich, and the heavy Norman chivalry moved out more slowly in support, the ding-dong battle began to change its entire character. Cowie's hard-pressed fighters obtained something of a breathing-space, to reform preparatory to attempting an advance across the bloodstained burn.

MacBeth, nearly three miles to the south of Dunsinane,

amongst the green valleys and thorn-scrub braes, had made his first contact with the MacDuff rear, causing wild confusion, when a single rider came pounding up behind, an Angus thane's son.

"Highness!" he shouted. "My lord Constable says to come back. At once. To Dunsinane. There is a new danger. You must return."

"Plague on you, man! I cannot go now — any fool can see that! Is Glamis out of his mind?"

"He says you *must*, Highness. It is important. A great new threat. Another army approaching . . ."

"God of Mercy!" The King raised a clenched fist around the hilt of his sword, and shook it in sheerest frustration. Then he called to a thane to take over the command and to continue their present attempt at disrupting the enemy rear but to be ready for a swift recall. He detached a troop of about fifty, and reined round to race back for Dunsinane Hill.

When he reached the summit ramparts, MacBeth was already peering eastwards, down Strathmore — and seeing nothing that he had not seen previously. Then Glamis came hurrying, his grim and grizzled visage grimmer than the King had ever known.

"Not there," he panted. "Not Strathmore. Come. Round here. See — yonder." He pointed, north-westwards.

The King stared. This was no direction to look for trouble, from the Highlands.

"I see nothing," he said. "Are you losing your wits, man? To bring me back . . ."

"Would to God I was! Look. Look well."

The land sloped gently north and west from the foot of Dunsinane Hill, about six miles to the winding Tay, mainly open pasture with patches of woodland, small whinny knolls and cultivated rigs, all wide to view, with nothing of threat to be seen. Beyond the Tay's trough it rose again, as gently at first, but rougher ground now, rising to the Muir of Thorn, by heath and scrub and rocky scarps. The Muir of Thorn stretched back for another five miles or so, and then the land soared up in the dark and forested slopes of Birnam Hill, the first bastion of the Highlands.

"What, man! I see nothing."

"Then I need not blame my old eyes too hardly!" the other said. "Look, Highness — look! Both sides of Tay. Watch the woods. They *move!* There — see it? This side of Cargill."

"Christ . . . God!" MacBeth breathed.

"And there, beyond the Abbey Road. And right back, behind Tay. The Muir of Thorn is now full of trees! Right back . . . right back . . . to Birnam Wood!" The older man's voice broke strangely as he pronounced those last two words.

The King turned to gaze at him, speechless — and seldom could a man's whole appearance have changed so comprehensively, direly, in a moment, at the name of a stretch of woodland. The colour had left features which had aged abruptly. MacBeth's whole person seemed to have shrunk and sagged. He moistened his lips but no words came.

"Trees," Glamis said hoarsely. "Men carrying birch boughs. By the thousand. From Birnam Wood. Moving slowly. A group at a time. None all at once. They have been crossing yonder moor for hours — and we have not seen them. We never looked in that airt. Or if any did, saw nothing to catch their eyes. There is a great host there, descending upon us — and we knew nothing of it."

MacBeth raised a hand that trembled, to point. He found speech of a sort. "So — it has come! At last. Birnam Wood comes to Dunsinane, indeed! This, then, is the end, my friend!"

The other eyed his monarch and comrade with anxiety and compassion mixed, and shook his grey head. "Not the end, no — never the end. Do not say it. A clever move, yes — Satan's own cleverness! But not the end, Son of Life."

"All my life I have awaited this," the King said, quietly now. "Scarce believing that it would ever come. Seeing not *how* it could happen. And now — this! My destiny has caught up with me, I think."

"No! No, I say! It is not destiny — only shrewd wits, cunning, trickery. All Scotland knows the saying about Birnam Wood. The enemy have but made use of this. Play-acting. That and clever fieldcraft. This disguise of birch boughs . . ."

A couple of scouts came running up the hill to them. Glamis had sent a number out, north-westwards, whenever he had realised what the moving woodland meant, at the same time as he had sent for the King. Now this pair gasped their findings. Cargill Wood was full of the enemy. All the Tayside woodland also. Their nearest advance parties were less than four miles away, at Kinnochtry, only a mile beyond the King's palace of Carn Beth. And the flag which flew just within the trees of Cargill Wood was the royal banner of Scotland, the Black Boar on silver.

371

"Ha — the accursed Malcolm mac Duncan himself!" Glamis cried. "We might have known. He has been reared on hate — and will have heard the Birnam-Dunsinane portent from childhood. But — how has he got there?"

"From the Clyde," the King said, flatly, heavily. "By ship to Alclyde. I had forgotten the Clyde. Marched up from Alclyde through West Lennox, by Loch Lomond, to Glen Dochart. Then east by Loch Tay and Atholl. His secret safe in Crinan's country! Clever — aye, clever. He has come to avenge his father's and his grandsire's blood!"

"Come — but he has not done it yet, by God!" the Constable exclaimed. "Highness — enough of this! Be of good heart. Be your own self. Play the King. The Son of Life is not beaten yet!"

"My old friend — stout to the end! There are some roads, see you, which reach a finish, some pitchers which will not mend. But — you are right in this. We shall not skulk. We shall die fighting, at least. Not tamely await our fate. Yes — enough of talk. But . . . what to do? What in God's good name to do now? Between two hosts?"

"There is but one course left to us. Break off the fight to the south. Recall all, here to Dunsinane. Make a stand, up on this hill-top. It is a strong position. They will not easily drag us down. Fight here. And hope!"

"Hope for what, Cormac?"

"Hope for aid. There are still many lords and chiefs in Scotland, with many men. Who could, and should, come to their king's aid. These invaders will seek a quick victory. Deny them that, and we may yet win out of this pass."

MacBeth shook his head and said nothing.

They sent out urgent messengers to Cowie, to the force at Buttergask, to the Normans and to the light horse, to break off all fighting whatsoever, and to return to Dunsinane with all speed and without any delay.

It was, of course, a race against time, with the King's forces wide and scattered. The light cavalry could be as much as four miles away by now, the Normans over two, the main foot hosts likewise — and the new enemy army, although much strung-out as yet, had its advance companies no further off. So much would depend on Malcolm's leadership — and so far he had shown himself to be a shrewd strategist, whatever else. If he did not wait for his full strength to come up, but perceived the retiral movement on Dunsinane and recognised his opportunity to intervene, he could possibly cut off some proportion of the returning Scots.

It was an agonising business to stand there, waiting and watching. Absolutely no sign of reaction from their own forces was evident for long — and all the time the enemy were drawing closer. The messengers themselves of course, had a long way to go. And breaking off hostilities was not necessarily something that could be achieved swiftly. Glamis and some of the others strode to and fro in their impatience; but the King, unlike his usual, stood unmoving, set-faced. His companions eyed him somewhat askance. This was a different man to the one they had known.

At length they could see movement from Cowie's force, a coalescing and the beginnings of retiral. Soon after, there were signs of the Buttergask contingent also, hitherto somewhat detached and out-of-touch. Unfortunately Malcolm would be able to see something of both these movements likewise, and would have no doubts as to the intention. At least the foot was on the way back. But what of the cavalry?

The Normans should have been reached and be returning by now; but there was no hint of them. Sir Hugo must have pressed on into the foothills further than intended. In that closer country, the courier might even have difficulty in finding them.

The enemy to the north and west were now abandoning their birch boughs and massing openly in menacing array in the Kinrossie-Cairn Beth area. Even as the watchers gazed, they saw a substantial proportion of the host begin to march south by east. Horsemen appeared at the head, to lead.

Glamis groaned aloud. "They are seeking to join MacDuff. And to cut off our people as they do so. Saints in heaven — where is the cavalry?"

MacBeth made no answer.

The race now was between the retiring Scots and the advancing Northumbrian front which could get between them and Dunsinane Hill. It looked as though the Buttergask force would make it without much difficulty; but it would be touch-and-go for Cowie's people.

Then a shout intimated the sighting of the Normans, still only on the braeside behind Balgray. At the lumbering pace of their heavy destriers, they would never reach Dunsinane before the enemy front intervened. Almost at the same time the first of the light horse appeared, more than a mile to the east, from behind

Pitmeudle Hill. There was just a chance that *they* might be in time to clear Malcolm's advance.

As they watched, however, they saw the eastern group change direction. Instead of heading straight down and across the low ground for Dunsinane, the light cavalry column suddenly swung away almost due westwards. Clearly they had seen the Normans and their predicament and were going to join them.

"Fools!" Glamis cried. "Now we shall lose them all!"

But the King seemed otherwise affected. He drew himself up from his heavy, slumped stance, as though with a return of decision. Turning, he called for his horse. Also for a dozen horsemen to accompany him.

"Highness — what is this? What do you intend?" the Constable demanded. "You are not . . . you are not . . .?"

"I am going, yes. God forgive me, it required these others to show me my duty! I may be able to save them. Or some of them. Instead of skulking here."

"This is folly! What can you do that they cannot do without you? You are the King, not some captain of horse . . ."

"*Because* I am the King, I go, man. You can do all that is needed here, Cormac. I must show that Scotland is still in the fight. I have a son out there, with Cowie. Would you have him see his father hiding here while his friends die? I brought these Normans to Scotland. Half of them have already died for me." He turned. "Now — my royal banner. The Boar. All must know that it is the King."

"I say that you will throw all away. You will be slain, with those others. To none effect . . ."

"If I am to die, friend — as I think I am — I choose to die fighting. Enough. If I fall, Lulach is King of Scots. If you can, and live to do so, aid him, Cormac. For he will need much aid. Even to rule only the Northern kingdom perhaps. But, never fear: I will bring yonder cavalry back, if I can."

He mounted, beside an unknown young man who proudly held aloft the Boar flag. There were nearer thirty than a dozen volunteers to ride with him — and would undoubtedly have been more had there been horses for them there on that hilltop.

Glamis stepped forward, to reach up and grasp his monarch's forearm tightly, features working strongly, but wordless. For moments they eyed each other. Then MacBeth kicked his beast's sides and rode off downhill, the banner close behind, his party following.

374

Directly for the Normans they dashed. It meant cutting right across the enemy line of advance towards Cowie's retiring force; but it seemed probable that they would just manage it. Malcolm had no cavalry, as such, although some of the leaders were mounted, no doubt on garrons stolen *en route*, since coming by sea to the Clyde it would not have been practicable to bring horses. It looked as though the King would reach the Normans at just about the same time as would the light cavalry from Pitmeudle.

Spurring hard, they passed diagonally across the front of Cowie's force, no more than half-a-mile off — and a little group of the mounted leadership detached itself and came racing to join them, the slender figure leading undoubtedly Luctacus. MacBeth did not know whether to weep or to rejoice. But quickly his attention was involved elsewhere. At this point they were much nearer to the enemy front than to Cowie's, and a ragged but continuing shower of arrows came at them, from the English archers. It was at extreme range and no damage was done. But it was a grim omen for later.

Presently the King found Luctacus at his side. They reached out hands to touch, for a moment, and rode on without slackening pace.

The other cavalry reached the heavily-trotting Normans just before the royal party. All cheered the King as he rode up.

It was no time for cheering, any more than for talk and explanation.

"Three wedges," MacBeth called out, without preamble. "Two hundred each. To support each other. Myself, Prince Luctacus and Sir Hugo command. One hundred light horse to ride with the Normans. Quickly!"

There was some inevitable delay and confusion. But the King could not, would not, wait.

"Son," he cried, to Luctacus. "Your wedge and mine. Side by side. Despard slower, behind. To back us, aid and exploit."

"Aid what?" Luctacus shouted back. "Do we not ride for Dunsinane?"

"Not yet!" his father said grimly. He pointed with his sword over to the north-west. "Yonder the bastard Malcolm flies my royal banner. I want it. And him."

As what was being commanded dawned upon the hearers, there was a moment's hush. Then the cheering broke out again, hoarse, savage. The King nodded, expressionless.

"Arrows," he said. "Many archers. The danger. Your shields.

375

Ride down the archers first. Ride as for Dunsinane. Then, at my sign, wheel round and at them. You have it? Come!"

That first charge achieved complete surprise at least, the three horsed companies, two and one, seeming to be doing the obvious and spurring for the security of the hill-top fort. When, ahead of the first ranks of the Northumbrians, they suddenly swung at right angles and hurled themselves directly upon the enemy, the latter were quite unprepared. With only some 400 yards to go there was little time for any defensive regrouping. With the range rapidly shortening, the archers admittedly were offered an easy target, and some of the Scots and their horses fell. But bowmen unprotected themselves made notoriously vulnerable and unhappy targets for charging cavalry, and those thus imperilled broke and bolted. The two wedges were able to drive a deep salient into the enemy front therefore, before their impetus failed and they had to swing away left and right — whereafter the third and slower wedge moved heavily in to prevent the English from quickly reforming. Nevertheless, the penetration was not nearly deep enough to win anywhere in the vicinity of the other Boar banner, which remained prudently towards the centre of the host.

Circling back, MacBeth and his son met again, with their formations, approximately where they had commenced their charge, and hastily reforming, drove in again without delay, this time diverging as they advanced, to pass on either side of the still-battling group under Sir Hugo. Again they were successful in probing deeper into the enemy mass and causing major havoc and casualties. But inevitably they themselves lost a few more men and garrons. Sir Hugo's unit, being less swift and making better targets, lost more, at least amongst the one hundred or so light horse attached, for the Normans themselves were heavily armoured and better protected.

Perceiving this, the King, in his second retiral, sent orders for these attachments to leave the Normans and return to his own and Luctacus's formations.

So that was the pattern of the battle for three more charges. But the enemy, recovering from their surprise, adopted alternative and more mobile tactics, widening their front, fanning out to north and south to send horns to outflank the killing-ground the Scots were establishing. Also they gave their bowmen protective screens of spearmen, and in consequence much increased their effectiveness. The Scots casualties rose.

The nearest that MacBeth penetrated towards the usurpers'

standard was about a hundred yards. So far the King had escaped injury at the apex of his wedge, save for a spear-thrust scrape on his thigh.

Then, on the frustrated return from that sally, he perceived the threat, such as had been at the back of his mind all along, taking actual shape. MacDuff's force had rallied, regrouped, and was now bearing down upon their rear. And, fortunately or otherwise, Cowie's people had managed to reach the safety of Dunsinane Hill, so they were no longer in any position to help.

Hastily he made his decision. Waving to Luctacus and pointing, he signalled him to continue with his sweeps, in conjunction with the Normans, meantime. He himself led his now much depleted squadron directly south-eastward against the oncoming MacDuff.

At least he made a real impact on that man's array before the charge lost its momentum and he had to pull round and out again, scattering the enemy for the moment and halting the advance. But again with loss, so that as he disengaged and cantered back, a swift count showed him that he had only about seventy of his augmented 200 remaining. The horses undoubtedly had suffered the most heavily.

But concern at this was swiftly superseded by a more urgent anxiety. Malcolm had pushed forward his left or north wing, so that now it constituted a barrier between the Scots cavalry and Dunsinane, narrow as yet but growing. If that barrier was not quickly breached, MacBeth could never win back to his base. Moreover, he saw that Luctacus and Despard now, like himself with but shadows of their former numbers, appeared to have become bogged down, lacking the third wedge. He had to go to their rescue. But clearly this warfare could not continue. He had shot his bolt, he recognised all too clearly, and losses, weariness, overwhelming odds, would end all before long.

It took time to extricate his friends — which did not include Sir Hugo, who was nowhere to be seen. And by the time that the sorry remnant of 600 had won clear for the moment, that cordon between them and Dunsinane Hill was considerably stronger. MacBeth eyed it, and shook his head. His tired, weakened survivors would never break through that. The only possibility was to hurry off, round to the north and east, through the gap which still remained between MacDuff and Malcolm's barrier, and hope to get behind, to Dunsinane that way.

377

Even as he summed up the chances of this, he saw two horsemen making exactly that semi-circular journey but in the reverse direction. Flogging their garrons unmercifully for maximum speed, these bore down on the King's battle-worn group. Not to waste any precious moments, MacBeth headed his people towards them.

One proved to be none other than the Mearnsman Thane of Cowie.

"Highness!" he shouted. "A message from my lord Constable. He says that you will never win through to Dunsinane now. He says not to try it. He says to ride. Escape. He pleads with you, lord King. To ride off, down Strathmore. While you still can. Ride for the North-East. For Moray and Mar. Assemble the North. Then come back to aid Dunsinane. He will seek to hold out there."

It was, of course, sound advice. To do just that had been one of the first things that had occurred to MacBeth after he had recovered from the shock of Birnam Wood. But it would have meant deserting Glamis and these others. Now, if he could not get back to the hill top fort anyway, that no longer held. But it still went against the grain.

"*Can* they hold out? For so long?" he demanded hoarsely.

"He says they will try. It is a strong position. There is plenty of food, and good wells."

"Aye. But . . ." The King drew a deep breath. This was no time for debate or indecision. He had to think of this faithful cavalry remnant. Not just Glamis and those others. Aye, and to think of Luctacus too, his son. He owed the lad his young life, did he not? And the Normans? *They* could not flee to Moray. But they could still ride fast enough to escape pursuing foot.

He made up his mind, without further delay. "So be it," he said. "Form up. Round the Normans. We leave, my friends — we leave. We have done our best. God be with Glamis — and with us also!" He pointed north-eastwards, for the gap of half a mile which still existed between the enemy fronts, down Strathmore. "Come. You also, Cowie. As fast as our Norman friends can ride.

The crowned King of Scots left the field of Dunsinane to the usurper — and only just in time.

AT BLAIR IN GOWRIE the King said goodbye to his Normans, or
what remained of them. Where he was going, and at the pace
he must ride, was not for them and their lumbering mounts. He
left with them, as guides and guards, the least mobile of the
other survivors, the wounded, the oldest, those with the poorest
horses, indeed the majority of the company. These would head
directly northwards into the hills, by the narrow twisting glen
of the Ericht, under the son of the old Thane of Rattray, past
Cally and into the remote strath of Ardle, to lie low in its
fastnesses meantime. With a mere forty or so companions
MacBeth rode on eastwards down Strathmore. Behind them,
some three miles off, near the levels of Stormounth Loch, they
could see mounted pursuit, in no large numbers meantime but
sufficient to keep their flight under observation and to constitute a continuing threat. The King did not think that these
would digress, to follow the slower party up the Ericht, but
would rather pursue him down the main open strath, where they
could keep him in sight. To try to ensure that they did, he kept
his royal banner unfurled, at his side. They would not see it, of
course, at that range, but no doubt would question local folk
to learn which way the King had gone. It was the least that he
could do for those he was leaving.

After that, it was only hard and steady riding.

Men and beasts were desperately weary, once again, of
course; but so, they hoped, would be their pursuers. It was early
evening, and if they could keep ahead until darkness, they would
hope to find somewhere secret to lie up and rest.

It was never pitch-dark of an August night; but after midnight, in the Brechin vicinity, the fugitives were so exhausted
that a halt had to be made. In woodland country where their
move would be unseen, they turned off northwards into the
lonely foothills of Menmuir, and in the quiet hidden valley of
the Water of Cruik, where there was pasture' for the garrons,
more or less collapsed with fatigue. They were unlikely to be
found before daybreak.

Tired as the others, MacBeth did not sleep. His grazed thigh
hurt him, but that was not the cause of his wakefulness. He
believed that he would have plenty of time for sleeping hereafter.

He said he would act sentry for the first spell, over-ruling all half-hearted protests.

As he sat amongst his snoring, groaning, twitching companions, he had, at last, time to think, long and sombre thoughts. Why was he thus flogging himself on, he asked? What was he fleeing from? Destiny and fate were not to be outrun, outwitted, eluded. He was going to die, and soon, he had little doubt. He would indeed, he thought, welcome death at the last. Hopefully to be with Gruoch again, dear Gruoch. And with Thorfinn. And others. If God had mercy on a man whose hands were stained with blood as his were. Why then was he straining thus, against the inexorable tide of fate? Why had he not just flung himself into the heart of the battle, back there at Dunsinane, and ended it all, quickly, cleanly — he who was not afraid of death? What strong urge still drove him on? The mere habit of fighting to the end? Of survival?

It was more than that, he decided. He was the King, and he still had his responsibilities. To his realm, his people, his family. So long as he breathed. It was that, he decided, that forced him on northwards. For Moray. Would Farquhar be back from Orkney yet? He had lost track of days. And Cormac and Eala. He had to try to get young Luctacus home. And muster all Moray and Ross and the North. Lulach too — he could not love him, but he was Gruoch's son and the next monarch. He had to do what he still could, for Lulach's heritage. Although how that young man could ever withstand this Malcolm, even in the Northern kingdom, was not to be known. Farquhar and Luctacus would help him — if they were given the chance. It was *his* duty to provide that chance. And there was Glamis and his beleaguered force to rescue, back there. There was no lack of responsibility, then. Reasons in plenty for him to hang on to his life to the last. Fate might not be cheated, but it might possibly be used. He would, as it were, make a bargain with fate . . .

Still he did not sleep, but somehow easier in his mind, he sank into a dreamlike state, eyes open, one part of his mind still on the alert for any alarm, the rest of it if not at peace at least accepting. He did not wake any relief watch.

They were on their way by dawn, stiff and hungry but somewhat rested.

Instead of following the direct route for the North, MacBeth had decided that since they had this hidden start in Menmuir, he would take the more remote and little-used route up through the mountains, by Glen Esk and the Fir Mounth. It was by no means the shortest or quickest road, indeed the most difficult, but it might well confuse the pursuit. It meant however that Cowie and a few others, from Angus and the Mearns, would be turning away from their home areas. So they parted company there in the misty dawn, and with a mere thirty or so companions, the King set off across the foothill country for Edzell and the mouth of Glen Esk, while the others rode due eastwards. At this stage numbers were of no advantage to MacBeth; indeed, the fewer mouths to feed the better.

The North Esk's glen was wild and fifteen miles long. They rode up it, gaining what food they could at lonely farmeries and summer shielings. They saw no sign of any pursuit as the morning progressed. By mid-day they were at the glen-head, at Loch Lee. Here they had to turn off up the Water of Mark, almost due northwards, heading for the mighty bulk of Mount Keen which towered ahead filling all the prospect. Glen Mark was even rougher than Glen Esk, empty, desolate, steep-sided, vast cliffs overhanging, the drove-road sketchy indeed, often waterlogged, sometimes washed away. Progress became very slow. After a few miles they were thankful to turn off it and climb out of the narrow trough, to keep due northwards and to start their 1600-feet climb that was to take them, in only three miles, up over the lofty shoulder of Mount Keen itself. This was the famed Fir Mounth track, the highest pass in the eastern Highlands, impassable for most months of the year. MacBeth had chosen it for that very reason, that the pursuit would be unlikely to think that it would be used. They had to walk their horses much of the way up that grim ascent.

Within 600 feet of the summit of Mount Keen they halted to rest, on the very roof of Scotland, amongst the racing cloud-shadows and the drifting deer-herds, the grouse rising from the brilliant purple of the heather on every hand, the prospects breathtaking. War and battle and the petty ambitions of men seemed utterly remote and irrelevant up here, and the younger members of the party for a little threw off anxiety and pre-occupation with the precarious future. If the King did not, he was scarcely to be blamed.

A couple of miles of the high plateau and they began to drop down into the north-facing glen of the Tanar Water, and quickly descended to the vast pine-forests of Deeside, lovely wilderness of ancient and mighty Caledonian firs growing wide-scattered out of tall heather and blaeberries, alive with deer and game. The sense of security engendered by these far-flung forests was comforting — and dangerous.

They spent the night there amongst the pines of Glen Tanar, having covered over thirty of the roughest miles in the land. MacBeth was well aware of the insidious dangers produced by the feelings of remoteness and present safety. The enemy would guess that he would be making for Moray, his home and patrimony, where he could raise fresh armies. And to reach Moray, they would know well that he had to cross the great east-west divide of the Dee valley somewhere, whichever mounth route he took. He had chosen the most difficult, to shake off pursuit, and had succeeded in so doing. But other of the routes could have been more speedy. If whoever was in command of the pursuers knew the land well — MacDuff for instance, or any of his traitorous colleagues — he could conceivably, by taking the Cairn o' Mounth route or even the Slugan, have reached the Dee ahead of them. Then, by sending teams to watch the mouths of the various passes, where they opened into the great strath, they might pick up the fugitives once more. Deeside was miles across, fairly open especially on the north side, populous and cultivated land much of it, part of Martacus's mortuath of Mar. It would not be easy to cross unobserved.

There was little pasture for the garrons in the forest, so the beasts would be less strong the next day.

They moved off again through the shadowy glades well before dawn, to reach the low ground at Craigendinnie, ford the Tanar there and within a mile cross the Dee itself at one of the few fords available, below the isolated hill of Craig Ferrar on the north side where there were a couple of small islets of shingle and a major shallowing. The practicable crossings could all be watched — so the King was anxious to cross before daylight. The nearest alternative ford to the west was at Dinnet, three miles, and to the east at Aboyne, the same distance. In the event although they perceived no picket or any living soul, they might well have been seen by hidden watchers and word sent to their enemies. MacBeth's companions, even Luctacus, tended to be scornful of such fears; but the King remained wary. He knew what *he* would have done had the situation been reversed.

Once across, they were in Cromar, with a dozen miles of this South Mar territory ahead of them until the next great hurdle of the Don. If only Martacus had been there, the situation could have been transformed. But Martacus and his armed men were far away in the South, seeking to hold the line of the Forth — if they had not already been overwhelmed. The quickest route to the Don from this ford was due northwards by Braeroddach Loch to Tarland, then through the Leochel Hills; but this was too open and exposed for fugitives fearing discovery. Instead MacBeth swung away north-eastwards, avoiding the cashel of Saint Machar, to reach the wooded valley of the Tarland Burn in the Coull area, with its precious cover.

The dazzle of the rising sun in their eyes was their undoing. While still on the high ground of Balnagowan Hill, they were trotting along a narrow deer-path in single file through the heather, when Luctacus suddenly shouted, pointing. Down on the lower ground, barely a mile away, was a troop of horsemen heading in their direction, the early sunlight glinting on their armour. They must have been in view for some time, but even now the fugitives had to screw up their eyes to see them.

They were not necessarily enemies admittedly, but it had to be assumed that they were, as they were coming from the east. Possibly they had been informed of the crossing at Craig Ferrar ford. There was not much choice of action. The newcomers were in a position where they could cut off the King's party before it could reach the shelter of the Coull woodlands. To avoid them, all MacBeth could do was to turn at right angles and ride northwards over the crest of this Balnagowan Hill, on, on beyond, where for a little they would be out of sight. But it was still open country and they would not be hidden for long.

This they did, cursing. But as they pounded down the fairly gentle slope beyond, MacBeth saw nothing to give him hope of escape. The land sank ahead, bare.

He panted to Luctacus, "How many of them? Did you see?"

His son shook his head. "I did not count them. More than we are, I think. Forty or fifty, perhaps."

"We have fought worse odds! They will not expect that we turn back. See — round the base of this hill we have just crossed. They will come that way, to head us off. We would be hidden until they were almost on us. A surprise. Then fight through them, to reach the woodlands below."

"Good!" Luctacus drew sword and raised it high, pointing back, as clear sign to the others.

So they swung away right-handed, down and round the skirts of Balnagowan Hill, hooves drumming. And presently, turning a sort of spur of it, they found themselves not exactly face-to-face with the other group but only a few hundred yards higher. Down on them they charged, yelling.

It was a very brief encounter. Unprepared, most of the enemy riders sought to pull aside — and it *was* the enemy, for Mac-Duff's burly figure was prominent in front. MacBeth tried to reach and strike that man down, but he became screened behind other men and horses. Outnumbered by more than two-to-one, it was no occasion for a prolonged fight. The King's aim was merely to smash through, disorganise and discourage. This they achieved, and they plunged on downhill. But at a cost, even in so short an affray. Three men fell, four were wounded, two horses were lost. The riderless men were pulled up behind others. MacBeth could scarcely rate the sally as a success — especially as Luctacus was one of those injured. But it did give them a little time, time to reach the Tarland Burn, splash across and enter the large woodlands of the Hill of Coull.

Deep within the cover of the trees, the King took urgent stock of the situation. Luctacus was reeling in his saddle, one shoulder slumped, features white. One of the other wounded had a lance-thrust through the rib-cage and was coughing blood. The others were less serious. Had he made a grave mistake with that charge? It was too late for any regrets. The wounded could not now continue with sustained flight. And two garrons were carrying double burdens. The enemy would rally soon enough, and follow — and catch up, inevitably. They desperately needed a refuge, if only temporarily. Aboyne was not far away, to the east, and Martacus had a dun there, an ancient fort of his family. If they could hole up there, meantime, they might hold out until help was forthcoming. This was Cromar, after all, part of the loyal mortuath of Mar. Once the folk learned that their King was being assailed by a comparatively small band of invaders, would they not come to his rescue? He decided to make for Aboyne.

This meant turning south-eastwards again, following the contours of the Hill of Coull, within the trees. So far there was no sign of MacDuff's people, but they could see for no distance. Presently the woodland thinned in front of them, and there was open pastureland sloping down to the two lochs of Aboyne, with the fort strongly placed in a bend of the Tarland Burn less than a mile away. But, as well as seeing this, they saw more. On the low ground between them and the fort was an encampment of men and horses. And even at half-a-mile's distance, they could distinguish the large flag which fluttered there to blazon a black boar on silver.

"Malcolm!" MacBeth exclaimed. "God in His heaven — Malcolm himself!"

They could not reach Aboyne's dun now. They would be seen and cut off long before they could get to it. Indeed they might well have been observed already. Looking at his strained-faced and almost swooning son, the King groaned aloud, and ordered an about-turn.

They dared not ride directly back, or they would be apt to run into MacDuff again. So he swung north-eastwards, up the hill, a spur of Coull. This kept them in cover for almost a mile, difficult and steep as it was, with fallen tree-trunks everywhere to be negotiated. But at the summit the trees thinned and there, after only a brief dip, rose the much higher hill of Mortlich, craggy and bare.

As he stared, someone shouted and pointed downhill, half-left. Down there was movement, horsemen.

He made his decision. "Leave the horses," he cried. "We must climb yonder." He pointed to the escarpment rearing ahead, steep, rock-strewn. "Horses cannot climb that — ours or theirs."

It went against the grain to abandon their garrons, but none argued. There was no alternative if they were to avoid fighting, this time with no chance of surprise and hopeless from the start. They rode the beasts as near to the foot of the scarp as they could, then dismounted and started to climb. MacBeth, with his stiff leg, supported Luctacus on one side, his former young standard-bearer on the other. The remaining wounded were aided likewise, but quickly the speared man threw up a flood of scarlet blood and fell unconscious. They had no option but to leave him there.

Clambering amongst the rock-falls, screes and ledges, they dragged themselves up. There was some 300 feet of this steep escarpment. MacBeth's fear now was that there might be mounted archers amongst MacDuff's company, and they would make easy targets so long as they remained within range. But although the enemy arrived below and stared upwards, no arrows came. Nor did any dismount to follow them up, on foot. They watched, for a while, then split up, some to ride off left about round the flank of the hill, some right-about, leaving only two or three to keep watch at the foot. Clearly they would be awaiting the King's party at the other side of Mortlich Hill.

What to attempt now? All but at his wit's end, MacBeth

deferred decision, concentrating on getting his wounded son and the others up to the top of the hill, no easy task. Eventually they made it, and collapsed, panting, on the crest.

The land was laid out around them like a map, for this was the highest hill in the vicinity. Unfortunately, all to north and east was bare, open country, a pleasant land basking in the smile of the sun, right to the Corse Hills of Mar proper, to the north. Nowhere in all that spread was there more than a scattering of thorn, scrub and whins as cover, for miles around. They could be seen from great distances in it, and picked up. Yet they could not remain up here, for these eastern slopes of Mortlich were more gentle, and horsemen could ride up them easily enough.

Once again desperate decision had to be made. The only possibility that the King could see was the extensive boggy ground of the Muir of Auchenhove below, to the north-east. All the bottom-land down there looked wet, with the tell-tale emerald green and black of mire and peat-bog. Men on foot would do better than men mounted therein. And a stream led down from this hill into it, in a reasonably deep burn-channel, the source of much of the waterlogging indeed. It might take them down into the bog, unseen.

So they made for the apron of damp ground which represented the genesis of the burn, and went ploutering down into its channel. Soon it was deep enough to hide them from distant view, and they descended in its cover. But slowly now, all weary and the injured much distressed. Luctacus voiced no single complaint, but he was obviously in a bad way.

They reached the bog at the foot, and almost at once perceived their enemies. There were three distinct groups of horsemen to be seen, one to the north-west almost a couple of miles away, another to the south, as far — MacDuff's split company presumably; and a third party, the nearest, strung along the road itself which ran up the farther side of this wide valley. These were less than a mile off — and with the banner at their head.

The Muir of Auchenhove was at least sufficiently wet, and no place for horses, with quaking moss and tussocks, peat-pools, reeds and even small lochans. There were islands of firm ground, of course. It made difficult and unpleasant going, but by jumping and wading and circuiting, men on foot could progress through it, however slowly. Horsemen could not — and clearly those trotting along the road behind the flag, on the east, did not intend to try. The valley ran north and south between the Mortlich and Torphins Hills, to lose itself eventually in the outliers of the Corse Hills above Lumphanan. The bog petered out there, so the enemy had only to ride, watch and wait.

MacBeth and his companions were now merely living from minute to minute. They could do no other. There was another and well-known dun at Lumphanan, rising dramatically on a tall, man-made mound amongst the wetlands, which served it as moat. This was the King's last hope — to gain this refuge and try to hold out behind its ramparts and stout walling. If that failed . . .

It was a desperate progress, apart altogether from the need for haste, floundering, splashing, falling, seldom able to pursue a straight course for a dozen yards at a time, frequently having to back-track where conditions became quite impossible. The wounded were almost having to be carried, and MacBeth's own lameness was now hampering him grievously. They had almost a mile of the bog to cover, before they reached the dun.

The enemy had their problems also, to be sure, at least as far as the Dun of Lumphanan was concerned. And it would be obvious that the fugitives would make for that. Set as it was in the marshlands, it could only be reached, on horseback, by the one route, from the north, along a twisting causeway. To attain this, the eastern party had to make quite a wide circuit of the surrounding foothill skirts, to avoid an extension of the swamp. The northern part of MacDuff's split company had an even wider approach to make, although over rather better ground. The southern section was, for the moment, out of the action.

The last half-mile of their ordeal was covered in a state bordering on semi-consciousness as far as the King was concerned — and no doubt his son and many of the others also. Mercifully, perhaps, they scarcely knew what they did, how often they fell, barely where they went. Keeping going was the one reality, that steep, symmetrical mound of the dun their beckoning goal.

It was strange, but when at least they had somehow managed to thread that waterlogged slough and were faced with the dun's refuge rising only a couple of hundred yards further ahead, neither MacBeth nor any of his companions had any idea as to how to reach it, across 150 yards or so of open water. Their every effort and faculty had been so fiercely concentrated on getting thus far that no real thought had been taken for overcoming the final hurdle. Almost in tears of frustration, they gazed across from the reedy edge, and saw that they could go no further.

With an enormous effort the King forced his reeling mind to consider the situation coherently. The way across would be by the usual underwater causeway, stones set a foot or two below the surface, in a zigzag course to confound those who did not know the pattern. And this, of course, would be an extension of the raised approach causeway across the marshland. Unhappily the eastern company under the banner were already on that causeway. They would most certainly reach the end of the crossing before they themselves could get there. In the other, north-westwards direction, MacDuff's group was further off, almost half a mile, still but making directly for them. Over at the dun itself they could see men watching from the stone-and-turf ramparts at the top of the mound. These no doubt had a boat, and could use it to save them — indeed some of the King's party were already yelling and waving and pleading for them to do just that. But with no response. Maddening as this was, how were the men up there to know, to guess who it was that needed their help? A score of tattered, mud-covered ruffians fleeing from companies of disciplined, armoured horse, one flying the royal Boar of Scotland. Why should they intervene?

Dazed as MacBeth was, one thing was evident to him. They could not remain where they were, and to turn right-handed, eastwards, would be to throw themselves into the arms of Malcolm — if Malcolm was indeed under that banner. They could not swim the moat, any of them, in their present state. Which left only a north-westwards move, towards MacDuff — and somehow, in the King's mind, MacDuff seemed to represent an easier foe, less of menace, than Malcolm Big Head.

So they turned left-handed and struggled on, north by west.

Soon they saw ahead of them MacDuff's men dismounting. Obviously they had reached the end of ground firm enough for their horses and were coming on on foot. There were about thirty of them.

Wordless, the King pointed half-left. There, about a hundred yards ahead, was a slight heightening of the ground, with a few whin-bushes, amongst which rose a single standing-stone, all that remained of a stone-circle. Evidently this land had not always been a swamp and in the far-off days of druidical sun-worship this had been a sacred place, forerunner of the Christian cashel of Saint Finan — which gave the area a corruption of its name, Lumphanan — and which was now situated on firmer terrain some way to the north. More by instinct than with any hope, they staggered on towards this little eminence and standing-stone. At least, as they made their last stand, they would have their feet on firm and once holy ground.

Actually, their eminence provided them with more than that, for not far from the monolith they stumbled on a well, a clear spring of ice-cold water pouring into a mossy stone-slab trough, no doubt used originally for the lustration ceremonies of the Druids. Thankfully they refreshed themselves, the wounded in especial.

But MacDuff's men were approaching and there was no time to linger. MacBeth limped to the summit of the eminence — only a slight swelling in the ground-level, in fact — and formed his people in a tight circle around the standing-stone, the wounded in the centre. Swords drawn, he addressed them hoarsely.

"See you, my good friends — here is a fight which we cannot win. You have supported me on a long, sore road, and I thank you with all my heart. But now, now is the end of that road. For me, the King. But it may not be, *need* not be, for all of you. I say to you — those who would, should leave me now. Go stand apart, arms thrown down, and yield you. They may accept your surrender, and give you your lives. Myself, I yield to no man, but only to God. But for you it is different. Stand apart now, who will. But quickly."

No man spoke or moved.

"Friends," the King said again, unevenly. "Some of you are young, very young. Lives before you. We have only moments now. Quickly, then. Do not think it to tarnish your honour. You have already proved that honour and courage. Go if you would live. Or *might* live, for I cannot promise that they will spare you. And if you go, take my son here with you. And these other wounded . . ."

"No!" That was strong, however much of a croak, from Luctacus behind him. "No, I stay!"

The growl from the others held its own eloquence, although no words were spoken. All remained in their places.

"So be it," MacBeth said, with a sigh. "I can do no more. But — when I have fallen, yield you. Your duty done. And now — God be with you all. And with me also. Here they come . . ."

The dismounted men reached the eminence in ones and twos, and halted, panting, well clear of the determined group around the stone — as well they might. For these made a notably tight defensive circle, shoulder to shoulder, swords bristling in right hands, dirks in left, a hedgehog of steel. From horses they could have been ridden down and over-reached; lances could have frustrated their defence. But the horses had been left behind, and the lances with them, for what man having to negotiate a bog wishes to be burdened with a nine-foot lance? So they held back, unsure.

Duncan MacDuff himself, heavy, anything but nimble, was one of the last to come up. And he too paused, staring and breathing heavily.

"Traitor!" MacBeth called to him. "I have long awaited this day. Come you, and receive your just deserts — you, who placed the crown on my brow and took your vows to support me!"

The other moistened his lips but said nothing. Perhaps he still lacked breath. He gazed over to the east, to where Malcolm's men, at the causeway-end, were now dismounting.

"Coward, I see, as well as traitor!" the King taunted. "Come, man, and put your hatred to the test. You can only die. Are you so fearful of death? *I* am not. Nor are these with me. Come you."

MacDuff muttered something, but to his men, and two of them broke off, to hurry away eastwards towards Malcolm's company. They looked thankful to go.

"Wait, MacBeth," MacDuff said, at length. "Savour a few more minutes of life, you who talk of death. For you will savour *it*, never fear."

"But not at MacDuff's hand, it seems! You are but the jackal. The wolf is yonder!"

It seemed that some of MacDuff's following were less discreet than he was. One man, dressed as a knight, stepped out, sword raised, shouting something in the Norman tongue. Another took up the cry, and a number of the ordinary swordsmen rallied to them. MacDuff said neither yea nor nay. With a yell, about half of the party surged forward behind this pair.

It was at the King that the assault was aimed primarily. But he could not be isolated from his supporters, close-knit as they were. Moreover, since there were less than a score of them on the outer rim, it made a comparatively small circle. So the attack had to disperse itself and work round the group. This left the assailants much less tight-packed than the defenders and consequently more vulnerable to sword-play — even though some more of MacDuff's people joined in. For their part, the

men around the King found this close mutual support heart-
ening but a little cramping for their cut-and-thrust work,
although they tended to stand with sword-arm shoulders
outwards.

That first assault was short and sharp, and a disaster for the
attackers. When, effect and impulse spent and little impression
made, the attempt petered out and the enemy fell back, they left
six fallen and as many wounded, some having to be supported
or dragged. MacBeth himself had a shallow flesh-wound on his
forearm, and two of his devoted band were pushed back to join
the other injured around the stone, the circle now slightly
smaller.

But, although there were cries of triumph from his friends,
the King did not join in. Not on account of his arm, which he
barely felt, but because of what his eyes told him — for he was
facing due eastwards and when he raised his eyes he saw
sufficient to quench any satisfaction. Malcolm's men were now
coming on, on foot, only slowly admittedly — but that was
largely because they were burdened by carrying their long lances
and spears. That was what MacDuff's two messengers had been
sent to ensure.

As the others perceived it, silence fell on the defenders. None
needed to have it spelt out to them. Those lances could do what
swords could not, thrust well beyond arm's length. Now the
end could not be long delayed.

Fixedly they watched the newcomers arrive around MacDuff.
One of the last to come up, although not carrying a lance, was
a stocky and burly man in his late twenties, with an inordinately
large head and a shock of unruly and curling dark hair, beard
forked in the Danish fashion — Malcolm mac Duncan, whom
MacBeth had last seen as a five-year-old in the rath of Dunkeld.

King and prince stared over at each other for long moments,
both expressionless.

Malcolm was in no hurry. He had no need to be; he had all
that he needed for his purposes, his quarry could not escape,
and no force was likely to come to his rescue. He drew up his
men in four ranks, about eighty in all, and formed them into a
square surrounding the King's circle, lances and spears forward.
After conferring with MacDuff and one or two of the knights,
he walked slowly round the front ranks of waiting men,
instructing them with a calm, almost scornful authority. Then,
as though superintending some game or contest, he stepped
back and raised his hand for action.

Without haste, deliberately, his men moved forwards, inwards, spears extended.

MacBeth spoke. "Those shafts are wood. Steel cuts wood!" he said. And a snarl rose from his people.

The strange silent advance halted only about seven or eight feet from the waiting defenders, so that men on each side were looking tensely into each other's eyes, aware of each other's deep breathing. There was a cold-blooded precision and formalism about it all, inevitable as death itself.

Then Malcolm shouted a single word of command, and the four ranks moved. Only a pace or two, so that the men still remained out of reach of the Scots' swords, but sufficient for their lances, spears and pikes to drive home. Down the swords slashed. Some steel lance-tips were sliced off, some were deflected, some jerked right out of the wielders' grasps. But, by their very numbers involved, most were not, and the screams of those transfixed and gouged shattered the grim hush.

Another shout from the rear penetrated the agonised cries, to remind the attackers of their instructions. Swiftly if less than deftly, they obeyed, disengaging their weapons, stepping back, and then, without pause, immediately lunging forward again. It was a more ragged thrusting than the first time, but so quickly was it executed that most of the defenders' swords could not be raised high in time for adequate chopping and parrying. Everywhere points drove in, deep into flesh, metal-scaled leather tunics being ineffective to stop close-quarters lance-thrusts. All around the King men fell or staggered or sank to their knees.

Now all silence was of the past, with men yelling, shouting, shrieking, on both sides. Discipline on the attackers' part was abandoned also, with each man thrusting and retiring and lunging again at his own timing and blood-lust, often at figures already squirming on the ground and, as the outer ring disintegrated, at the wounded revealed within. Now the remaining defenders who could, pathetically few, forsook the failed defensive circle and hurled themselves out at their enemies, to at least kill before they died. Malcolm's knights awaited them, swords ready.

In that so brief but terrible carnage it had taken some little while to dawn on MacBeth that he was being spared, deliberately spared rather than remaining miraculously untouched. No single lance struck the royal person, although he cut through two or three himself, and all around him his companions went down. He realised that he was being isolated, the enemy presumably ordered not to slay him. This recognition came to him at the same moment as, jerked aside and spun round by a toppling comrade, his glance went down — and saw Luctacus lying spread-eagled at his feet, a lance through his throat, eyes glazing.

With a strangled cry, limping, left arm hanging but sword-arm raised in savage fury and pain, he leapt away and forward. Eluding the lance which swiped sideways to fend him off, he slashed down the man immediately in front of him, flung himself upon the next, knocking him aside and so ran on. Twenty yards from him stood Malcolm Canmore and Duncan MacDuff, with two or three knights, watching.

"Come!" he shouted. "In God's name, come!"

Malcolm took a pace forward, and then paused. He turned back to MacDuff, and gestured. Nothing could have been more clear. The crowned King of Scots' person had been saved from common men's steel, saved for their betters. Now Malcolm, who claimed that crown, left the *coup-de-grace* to the other, his supporter.

MacDuff, sword in hand, stood still, frowning. It all took place in mere seconds. MacBeth was running at him, however lamely. He licked his lips, shook his bull-like head, swung on the knight at his side, and pointed, vehemently. It was the same big Norman who had led that first abortive attack on the circle, before the lances arrived. Surprised but nothing loth, the Norman leapt forward. MacBeth, only a few feet away now, saw that MacDuff was not prepared to meet him.

"Coward! Traitor! Felon to the end!" he cried, and with what strength remained to him, hurled his bloody sword from him, like a javelin, at his one-time Mormaor of Fife, one of the lesser kings of the Ard Righ. To the Norman he gasped, "*Lurdan!*" the Gaelic word for knâve, with his last breath, and sought to sweep him out of his way.

The knight brought down his own sword on MacBeth's now defenceless head cleaving the skull. The High King of Scots pitched forward, dead before he struck the grass, anguished spirit released at last to go seek his Gruoch.

MacDuff, a clumsy man always, jumped heavily aside, barely in time. The King's sword struck his arm, scoring his leather jerkin, before clattering to the ground.

"A usurper and a miscreant — but he died well," Malcolm Big Head observed judicially.

HISTORICAL POSTSCRIPT

MacBeth's body, with that of Luctacus, was taken up the hill behind Lumphanan village and temporarily interred in a large Pictish burial-cairn there — still named MacBeth's Cairn — later to be transferred to its final resting-place at Iona. Lulach was proclaimed King of Scots, in Moray and the North. Malcolm assumed the kingship in the South, and seven months later led an army northwards again, which sought out and slew Lulach at Essie in Strathbogie. His body also was taken to Iona, the last King of Scots to be buried on the sacred isle. Thereafter Malcolm the Third reigned undisputed as High King until his death in battle in 1093, when Donald Ban, his legitimate half-brother, gained the throne for a year before Malcolm's son Duncan displaced him. Duncan himself was slain after six months, by his own half-brother Edmond, the first of the Margaretsons. Lulach's son Maelsnechtan survived but never claimed the throne. Farquhar also, whose son and grandson feature in Moray's records.

Malcolm, oddly enough, married Ingebiorg Thorfinnsdotter, in an attempt to gain some control over Orkney and the Hebrides from Thorfinn's rather weak sons Paul and Erland, no happy union. By her he had the aforementioned Duncan and also Donald. Then, in 1070 Malcolm got rid of her, to wed Margaret Atheling, the Saxon princess dispossessed by William the Conqueror, the Saint Margaret of the history books; and through her influence began the pulling down of the Celtic Church and the substitution of that of Rome.

But that is another story.

NIGEL TRANTER

THE WALLACE

Scotland at the end of the thirteenth century was a blood-torn country under the harsh domination of a tyrant usurper, the hated Plantagenet, Edward Longshanks. During the appalling violence of those unsettled days one man rose as leader of the Scots. That man was William Wallace. Motivated first by revenge for his father's slaughter, Wallace then vowed to cleanse his country of the English and set the rightful king, Robert the Bruce, upon the Scottish throne. Though Wallace was a heroic figure, he was but a man—and his chosen path led him through grievous danger and personal tragedy before the final outcome . . .

CORONET BOOKS

NIGEL TRANTER

MONTROSE: THE CAPTAIN GENERAL

The Marquis of Montrose — mainstay of the Stewart cause.

Montrose was the most loyal servant any king had ever had. In the darkest days of the Civil War he risked all in the fight to save his king. His only reward was royal betrayal. Unwavering in his loyalty, he returned from dreary exile to fight for another king, only to experience the final betrayal of the hangman's noose.

The second of two magnificent novels about THE MARQUIS OF MONTROSE.

CORONET BOOKS

MARY STEWART

THE LAST ENCHANTMENT

Mary Stewart's third magnificent and haunting novel of Dark Age Britain finds Arthur King by right of drawing the sword Caliburn from the stone. Merlin, the King's adviser and known as the 'enchanter', is once again the narrator of this powerful, exciting and richly woven story.

'An absorbing and haunting novel'

Daily Mail

'A fascinating novel, a richly woven tapestry presented with a vividness that brings the characters from myth to real life'

Evening News

'Mary Stewart, enchantress . . . an ability to evoke a situation, a mood or a season with a few phrases of prose that are almost verse'

Daily Telegraph

'Magic . . . this is a book which I will cherish for ever'
Newsagent and Bookshop

CORONET BOOKS

ALSO AVAILABLE FROM CORONET

NIGEL TRANTER

☐ 37186 2	The Bruce Trilogy	£7.99
☐ 36836 5	Lord Of The Isles	£3.99
☐ 26545 0	Margaret The Queen	£3.99
☐ 21237 3	The Wallace	£4.50

MARY STEWART

☐ 15133 1	The Crystal Cave	£3.99
☐ 18611 9	The Hollow Hills	£3.99
☐ 25829 2	The Last Enchantment	£4.50